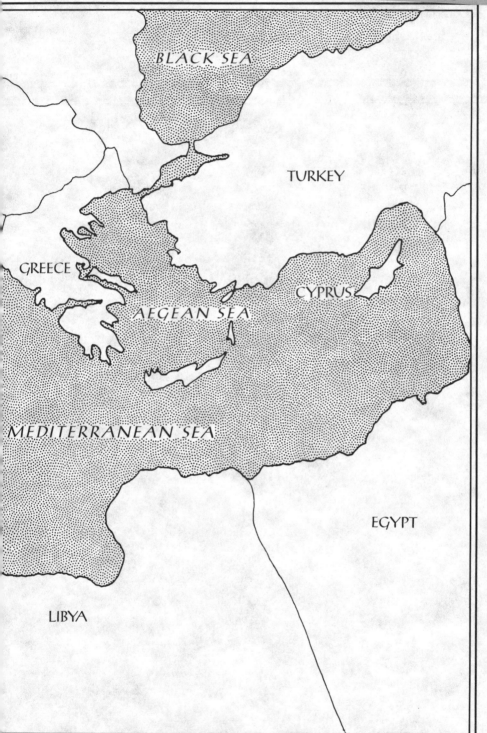

BLACK SEA

TURKEY

GREECE

CYPRUS

AEGEAN SEA

MEDITERRANEAN SEA

EGYPT

LIBYA

FINAL FLIGHT

Also by Stephen Coonts

Flight of the Intruder

STEPHEN COONTS

FINAL FLIGHT

Doubleday

NEW YORK   LONDON   TORONTO   SYDNEY   AUCKLAND

Published by Doubleday, a division of Bantam Doubleday Dell Publishing Group, Inc. 666 Fifth Avenue, New York, New York 10103

Doubleday and the portrayal of an anchor with a dolphin are trademarks of Doubleday, a division of Bantam Doubleday Dell Publishing Group, Inc.

Epigram from *A Book of Five Rings* by Musashi Miyamoto, translated by Victor Harris, published by the Overlook Press.

Lyrics from "The Captain of Her Heart" by Kurt Maloo and Phelix Haug Copyright 1985 Z-MUSIC (SUISA). All rights administered by Almo M Music Corporation in the USA, Canada, Australia, New Zealand. International Copyright secured. Made in the USA. All rights reserved.

Library of Congress Cataloging-in-Publication Data
Coonts, Stephen, 1946–
Final flight / Stephen Coonts. — 1st ed.
p. cm.
I. Title.
PS3553.05796F45 1988
813'.54—dc19 88-12001
CIP

ISBN 0-385-24555-6
Copyright © 1988 by Stephen Coonts
All Rights Reserved
Printed in the United States of America
October 1988
First Edition
BG

4   6   8   9   7   5

ACKNOWLEDGMENTS

FOR THEIR KINDNESS in offering technical advice to improve this novel, the author wishes to thank Lieutenant Commander James Boma; Commander R. E. "Smoke" Davis; Commander Al Diel; Captain Stu Fitrell; Captain Steve Ganyard, USMC; Lieutenant Commander Robert S. Riche; Robert L. Shaw; Barrett Tillman; and Commander Bruce Wood. For reasons that should be obvious, the ship described in this novel differs in several significant ways from *Nimitz*-class carriers.

Confront the enemy with the tip of your sword against his face.

—Miyamoto Musashi

FINAL FLIGHT

THE PILOTS OF the two F-14D Tomcats on the catapults
shoved the throttles of their engines to full military power at the
same time. Up on Vulture's Row, high on the carrier's island
superstructure, the off-duty observers pushed their fingers even
deeper into their ears as the roar of four mighty engines at full
power became an unendurable, soul-numbing crescendo.

The bow catapult officer, seated facing aft at his control console
between the catapults, returned the salute of the pilot of the
fighter on Catapult One, glanced at the signal light on the island
—still yellow—and looked over his shoulder, down the catapult
toward the bow. The bow safety observer had his left hand up, his
thumb in the air. The cat officer again scanned the fighter. Still
okay.

In the waist catapult control console, the cat officer there
looked across the nose of the fighter on Catapult Three at the
signal light on the island superstructure. He, too, checked again
to ensure the deck was clear.

The light on the island turned from yellow to green.

Simultaneously both launching officers scanned the length of their cats, looked again at the planes at full power, and pushed the fire buttons on their catapults.

Down below deck, the giant launching valves opened and steam slammed into the back of the catapult pistons.

Three seconds later the wheels of the two fighters ran off the deck and the wings bit the air.

In the plane off the bow catapult, the pilot, Captain Jake Grafton, slapped the gear handle up with his left hand. He allowed the nose to rise to eight degrees nose-up and held it there as he trimmed and the machine accelerated. At 200 knots he raised the flap handle. With the flaps up, he lowered the nose of the accelerating fighter and leveled at five hundred feet below the slate gray overcast.

Now he glanced back and left. His wingman, who had launched from Cat Three, was several hundred feet away in a loose formation. Jake eased the throttles aft a percent or two to give the other pilot a power advantage, then scanned his instruments. EGT, RPM, fuel flow, oil pressure, hydraulics, all okay. No warning lights.

"You okay back there?" he asked the Radar Intercept Officer, the RIO, in the seat behind him.

"Sure, CAG. No sweat." The RIO was Lieutenant Toad Tarkington. He and Grafton had only flown together three times before today, since Jake, the air wing commander, divided his flying between the two F-14D squadrons, the two F/A-18 squadrons, and the squadron flying the A-6E.

The Tomcat accelerated quickly, its wings sweeping aft automatically as it accelerated through .7 Mach. At 500 knots indicated, with his wingman tucked in on the left wing, Jake Grafton pulled the stick back and pointed the fighter into the overcast.

Not a word had been said on the radio. The radar altimeter and TACAN had not been turned on. And the radars of both fighters were not transmitting.

Aboard the carrier from which the fighters had just launched, the USS *United States,* America's newest *Nimitz*-class ship, total electronic silence was also being observed, as it was aboard the eight surface combatants arranged loosely in the miles of ocean around the carrier. No radars swept the skies. No radio signals were being broadcast. Yet down in the Combat Information Centers aboard every ship the sailors sat and listened for electronic signals from Soviet ships and planes.

Russian planes were aloft this afternoon over the North Atlantic searching for the *United States.* They had been searching for three days now and still hadn't found her out here in these millions of square miles of ocean. The Americans were making the search as difficult as possible. The *United States* had been sailing east under a thick frontal system for five days, hidden from the cameras of reconnaissance satellites ever since she left Chesapeake Bay. Laden with moisture, the extensive cloud system covered a lot of ocean. The task group dashed from squall to squall; the rain would help mask the ships' radar signature from Soviet satellites.

The exit into the North Atlantic had been aided by two nuclear-powered attack submarines. They had sailed from Norfolk the day before the carrier and located the Soviet snooper submarine that routinely lurked at the mouth of the bay. The American boats dashed back and forth at high speed to screen the noise of the departing task group, which slipped away to the southeast while the Russian vainly tried to sort out the screw noises of the warships from the cacophony made by the American subs and the dozen or so merchantmen entering and leaving the bay.

Part of the problem for the Soviets was that the American task group was not now where it should be, on the main sea lane from the Chesapeake to the Strait of Gibraltar. It was almost two hundred fifty miles south of it. So the Russians were still searching the huge, empty ocean, looking for a silent needle that moved erratically and relentlessly.

At present, the nearest Soviet ship was a trawler outfitted with an array of sensitive antennae two hundred miles to the northeast. The trawler's crew would tattle to long-range naval bombers if they heard anything.

The search and evasion were games, of course, for the Soviets and the Americans. Each side was training its combat crews. Each side was letting the other see its capability. Each side sought to intimidate the other in order to prevent the final war that the citizens of neither country wanted.

In the cockpit of his F-14 Tomcat, Jake Grafton listened to the Electronic Counter-Measures equipment, the ECM. This gear could detect the transmissions of Soviet radars while the fighter was still so far away from the emitting radar that the signal would not return in a usable form—in other words, while the F-14 was still out of detection range. This afternoon Jake listened in vain. No radars yet. He watched the altimeter record their progress upward, and occasionally checked his wingman visually.

The two planes emerged from the clouds at 20,000 feet into clear air. To the west the sun was still twenty degrees above the horizon, but it was blurred and indistinct above a thin cirrus layer at about 40,000 feet. The light here was soft, diffused, and the visibility excellent. Jake leveled the flight at thirty thousand feet at .8 Mach, 300 knots indicated.

"Okay, CAG," Toad said over the intercom, the ICS. "I'm receiving the E-2's data link. Our targets are about a hundred and eighty miles away, bearing zero two zero."

Jake came right to that heading and adjusted the brightness and gain on the Horizontal Situation Display on the instrument panel in front of his knees. On this scope he could see a copy of the picture the RIO had on the Tactical Information Display in the rear cockpit. Sure enough: there was the threat display.

Even though the American fighters and ships were not emitting, they could see the Russians. The *United States* was keeping an E-2 Hawkeye radar plane airborne around the clock. This twin-engine turboprop had waited until it was over a hundred miles from the ship before it turned on its radar, and then it data-linked everything it saw back to the ships and to any fighters aloft. The Hawkeye was an eye in the sky. It had located two Tupolev Tu-142 Bear bombers approaching from the north, still scanning the sea with their radars, searching. And aboard the *United States,* Jake, as the air wing commander, had decided to intercept the Bears.

Now the ECM warning light on the right window frame directly in front of Jake began to flash. "We're receiving radar signals from Ivan," Toad said. The main ECM panel was in his cockpit, since in combat the pilot would be too busy to check it.

"I don't want these guys to know we're coming until we're on their tails," Jake told his RIO. "What's their heading?"

"They're going two eight zero at about four hundred knots, sir. You may want to come right another twenty degrees—then when we pass behind their port beam, we'll turn left and accelerate and come in on their stern quarter."

"Gotcha," Jake said, and turned right. He pumped his fist at his wingman and received a nod in reply. The other pilot dipped his nose and crossed under Jake, surfacing on the right wing. From this position he could ease further out and turn in behind the second bomber while Jake took the one on the left.

Jake scanned the instrument panel once again. It was still new to him. He had flown the A-6 Intruder attack plane throughout most of his career and had been checked out in the F-14 only after he had received orders to command this air wing. He still had less than sixty hours in the airplane, yet he enjoyed flying it immensely. It was high-performance luxury compared to the A-6, which was subsonic and designed in the late fifties as an all-weather bomber. The "D" version of this supersonic fighter-interceptor was affectionately known as the "Super-Tomcat" and was equipped with more powerful, more fuel-efficient engines than those which powered the F-14A, engines less prone to compressor stalls and capable of being jam-accelerated in high angle-of-attack, high G-load dogfights. Fast, agile, and stuffed with the latest in air-to-air electronic wizardry, the F-14D was also going to sea for the first time aboard the *United States*.

The view from the cockpit took some getting used to, Jake mused. One large rounded piece of plexiglas covering both the front and rear cockpits, and broken only by a lone canopy bow between the cockpits, constituted the canopy. The seats were mounted high so the pilot and RIO would have the maximum field of view when the aircraft was maneuvering against an enemy. Jake was sitting high and forward on a large projectile shaped like an arrow head. One felt naked, but the view in all directions was spectacular. It was almost as if you were riding through the sky in a chair without the benefit of an aircraft.

As he learned to fly this airplane, Jake found it difficult to keep his right thumb off the trim button on the stick. With a computer automatically adjusting the horizontal stabilizers to compensate for flap changes, speed brakes, wing sweep, and speed changes, an F-14 pilot didn't spend much time trimming. The other trait of the aircraft he found difficult to master was the sluggish pitch response and slow power response when the aircraft was in the landing configuration. To ease the pilot workload, Grumman had installed a thumb-operated switch on the stick that allowed the pilot to raise and lower wing spoilers to control descent on the glide slope instead of adjusting the throttles.

It was the swing wings that made this plane such a sweetheart. The Air Data Computer automatically moved the wings forward or aft for maximum maneuvering efficiency. As the aircraft accelerated through .75 Mach, the wings left their medium-speed position, twenty-two degrees of sweep, and progressed aft, until at 1.2 Mach they were fully swept, at sixty-eight degrees, and the machine had become a delta-winged projectile. To optimize maneuverability, a computer automatically adjusted the flaps and slats when the machine was maneuvering in the subsonic and transonic speed ranges. All this aerodynamic aid allowed the pilot to squeeze more performance from the airplane than Jake had ever dreamed possible.

Jake waggled the stick slightly. The stick had a self-centering bungee installed in the artificial feel system and resisted displacement from center. This control heaviness had bothered him when he first flew the aircraft, but he rarely noticed it anymore.

He scanned the sky. It was great to be flying again, off the ship and out here in the great blue empty. Under his oxygen mask Jake Grafton grinned broadly.

Sixty miles from the bombers Toad turned on the television camera system, the TCS, in the nose of the Tomcat. This camera had a powerful telephoto lens which would enable the crew to see the bombers while they were still too far away for the human eye to acquire them. Toad slewed the camera, searching. The camera automatically pointed at the target being tracked by the Tomcat's radar, but since the radar was silent, the camera was aimed in the direction that the computer calculated was appropriate. So now Toad had to fine-tune the camera.

"I got 'em. Or one of them, anyway. I think they're a couple thousand feet above us."

Jake checked the picture on the Horizontal Situation Display (HSD) in his cockpit. The crew did not see raw video, but a picture optimized by computer. Now the picture was merely a small dot, recognizably a big aircraft, but just a dot nevertheless.

He looked around. To his right and rear, his wingman's plane hung motionless, suspended in space. The clouds above were too indistinct to give an impression of motion. Far below, the top of the gray and lumpy stratus layer slowly rolled along from front to rear. It was almost as if the planes were stationary and the earth was moving beneath them. It was an illusion, of course. These machines were really hurling through the sky toward an uncertain rendezvous.

"We're just about to cross their beam, CAG. Turn ninety degrees left."

Jake did so. This course would lead the bombers by forty degrees, necessary since they were moving. He eased the throttles forward, then pushed them into afterburner. The wingman was right with him. He advanced the throttles another smidgen.

The fighter sliced through the sonic barrier with only the barest jolt. Mach 1.3 . . . 1.4 . . . 1.5, 605 knots indicated, true airspeed 820 knots.

Now Jake could recognize the target on his HSD. It was a Soviet Bear bomber, a huge four-engine turboprop. But at which one was he looking? The lead or the wingman? The second plane might be a mile or so away to the left or right. Bomber pilots weren't known for flying tight formation, not over the distances they covered. These bombers were out of Murmansk. They had flown around the Scandinavian peninsula, down through the Iceland-U.K. gap, and then another twenty-five hundred miles south. After hours on station they would return to the Soviet Union or fly on to Cuba.

"Scan the camera, Toad."

In a few seconds Tarkington said, "Got him. This guy is behind the leader. A little farther away, so he's off the lead's right side."

"Okay. Go back to the leader."

As the camera panned sky, the cross hairs on Jake's heads-up display, the HUD, also moved. But squint as he might, the bombers were still to far away to see. The camera settled in on the first plane. Jake corrected his heading.

At fifteen miles he could see the leader under the HUD cross hairs. At eight miles he came out of burner and pulled the nose up, allowing the gentle climb to bleed off his airspeed. Had this been a shooting interception, he would have launched his missiles long ago.

At five miles he gestured to his wingman, sweeping his open hand in a chopping motion to the right, then kissed off the wingman by touching his oxygen mask and sweeping his hand away, splaying his fingers. The other pilot gave him a thumbs-up and turned away to the right. He would join on the second Bear.

Two miles from the bomber Jake said, "Burn 'em, Toad." The RIO turned his radar to transmit. Jake knew the bomber crew would hear the fighter's radar on their ECM equipment, which no doubt they had turned up to maximum sensitivity. At this range the noise should sear their eardrums. And the crew would know that if this had been a wartime intercept, they would be dead.

The F-14 climbed rapidly toward the stern quarter of the bomber, Jake reducing power to decelerate to equal airspeed. He turned to the big plane's heading and joined up just below and behind it. The bomber was the color of polished aluminum, a silver gray, with a red star on the tail and under one wing. Jake could see the gunner in the tailgun compartment looking out the window. The barrels of the 23-millimeter twin tail guns were pointed aft and up, at the limit of the gimbals. They didn't move, Jake noticed, which was nice. The two governments had promised each other that their servicemen wouldn't point weapons during these encounters, since the person on the wrong end of the weapon tended to get nervous and jittery and had a weapon of his own. But it was a long way from the diplomatic conference table to the skies over the Atlantic and Pacific.

Jake turned right and came up alongside the bomber's right wing. He could now see into the copilot's side of the Bear's cockpit. The copilot was staring across the hundred feet of empty air that separated them.

"Just stay here, CAG," Toad said. "I'm getting pictures." In the rearview mirror Jake saw Toad focusing a 35-millimeter camera.

In the cockpit of the Bear a camera was being pointed this way. "They're taking our picture, too," Jake said.

"Not to sweat, sir. I have the sign against the canopy." Jake knew the sign Toad was referring to. Printed in block letters on an eight-by-ten-inch piece of white cardboard was the word "Hello." Under it in letters equally large was the word "Asshole."

When Toad had six shots of this side of the bomber, Jake dropped below the plane and Toad kept snapping. Then they photographed the left side of the plane and the top, ending up back on the right side, where Toad finished out the roll. These pictures would be studied by the Air Intelligence officers for indications of modifications or new capabilities.

By the time Toad was finished with the camera, the other F-14 was joined on Jake's right wing. Jake knew the RIO of that plane was busy photographing his fighter against the bomber. One of these pictures would probably be released by the navy to the wire services in the States.

"Okay, CAG," Toad said. "Our guy's all done. I'll just flip Ivan the terrible bird and we can be on our way anytime."

"You've got real class, Tarkington."

"They expect it, sir. They'd feel cheated it we didn't give them the Hawaiian good luck sign." Toad solemnly raised a middle finger aloft as Jake lowered the Tomcat's nose and dove away.

2

THE USS *United States* and three of her escorts, two guided-missile frigates and a destroyer, anchored in the roadstead off Tangiers around noon after completion of the voyage across the Atlantic. Due to her draft, the carrier anchored almost two miles from the quay where her small boats began depositing sailors in midafternoon. By six that evening almost two thousand men from the four gray warships were ashore.

In twos and threes and fours, sailors in civilian clothes wandered the streets of the downtown and the Casbah, snapping photos of the people and the buildings and each other and crowding the downtown bars, which were relatively abundant in spite of the fact that Morocco is a Moslem nation. Fortunately, downtown Tangiers had been built by the French, a thirsty lot, and the pragmatic Arabs were willing to tolerate the sinful behavior of the unbelievers as long as it was profitable.

In the "international bars" barefoot belly dancers slithered suggestively. The sailors didn't stay long with beer at the equivalent of four U.S. dollars a glass, but when they saw the belly dancers they knew they were a long way from Norfolk, and from Tulsa, Sioux Falls, and Uniontown and all the other places they had so recently left behind. Properly primed, they explored the streets and loudly enjoyed the respite from shipboard routine. The more adventurous sought out the prostitutes in the side streets. Veiled women and swarthy men watched the parade in silence while their offspring gouged the foreigners unmercifully for leather purses, baskets, and other "genuine" souvenirs. All things considered, the sailors and their money were welcomed to Tangiers with open arms.

Just before sunset the Air France flight from Paris touched down at the local airport. One of the passengers was a reporter-photographer from *J'Accuse,* a small leftist Paris daily. The French government was considering a port call request from the U.S. Naval Attaché for a *United States* visit to Nice in June, so invitations to a tour of the ship while she was in Tangiers had been liberally distributed to the Paris press.

The journalist, a portly gentleman in his fifties, took a taxi from the airport and directed the driver to a modest hotel that catered to French businessmen. He registered at the desk, accompanied his bags to his rooms, and returned to the lobby a quarter of an hour later. After an aperitif in the small hotel bar, he walked two blocks to a restaurant he apparently knew from prior visits to Tangiers. There he drank half a bottle of wine and ate a prodigious expense-account dinner. He paid his bill with French francs. He stopped in the hotel bar for a nightcap.

Within minutes an attractive young woman in an expensive Paris frock entered and seated herself in a darkened corner of the room away from the bar. Her hair looked as if it had been coiffed in a French salon. She had a trim, modest figure, which her colorful dress showed to advantage, and the shapely, muscular legs of a professional dancer or athlete. She ordered absinthe in unaccented French and lit a cigarette.

Her gaze met the journalist's several times but she offered no encouragement, or at least none which caught the bartender's eye. When it became apparent she was not waiting for an escort, the reporter took his drink and approached her table. He seated himself in seconds. The couple talked for almost twenty minutes and laughed on several occasions. There were only two other men in the bar, both of whom were apparently French business-men; they discussed sales quotas and prices the entire time they were there. Around 11:30—the bartender was not sure of the time—the reporter and the lady left together. The reporter left French francs on the table sufficient to cover the price of the drinks and a modest tip. At midnight the two businessmen de-parted and the bartender closed up.

The following morning the *J'Accuse* press pass was handed to an American naval officer on the quay as he assembled a group of thirty journalists, about a third of whom were women. At ten o'clock the group was loaded into the captain's gig and the admi-ral's barge for the ride out to the great ship, which was visible from the quay. The journalists had a choppy ride in the invigo-rating morning air.

As the boats approached the ship the photographers were in-vited to the little amidships quarterdecks, where they snapped pictures of the carrier and watched the coxswains steer. The gray hull of the carrier appeared gigantic from a sea-level perspective, a fifth of a mile long and rising over six stories from the water. As the boats neared her she looked less and less a ship and more and more like a massive cliff of gray stone.

At the officer's brow the journalists found themselves under the overhang of the flight deck. Sailors assisted them from the bobbing boats to a carly float, and from there up a ladder to the ceremonial quarterdeck where they were met by several junior officers. Several journalists were struck by how much alike these men, all in their early to middle-twenties, looked in their spotless white uniforms. Of various sizes and racial groups, these half dozen trim, smiling young men still looked as if they had been punched from the same mold as they saluted and welcomed the tour group aboard.

The journalists were led down a series of ladders in groups of five and through mazelike passageways to a large, formal ward-room deep within the ship. Spread on tables covered with white cloths were plates of cookies, a pile of coffee cups and glasses, and several jugs of an orange liquid. "It's Kool-Aid," one of the young officers informed a Frenchman after he sipped the sugary orange stuff and stood looking at the glass as if he had just ingested a powerful laxative.

"Good morning." The speaker was an officer with four gold stripes and a star on each of his black shoulder boards. His white shoes, white trousers, white belt, and short-sleeved white shirt were accented by a yellow brass belt buckle and, on his left breast, a rainbow splotch of ribbons topped by a piece of gold metal. The touches of color made his uniform look even whiter and emphasized the tan of his face and neck. He stood a lean six feet tall. Clear gray eyes looked past a nose which was just slightly too large for his face. His thinning hair was cut short and combed straight back.

"I'm Captain Grafton. I hope you folks had an enjoyable ride out to see us this morning." Although he didn't speak loudly, his voice carried across the group and silenced the last of the private conversations. "We're going to give you a tour of the ship this morning when the cookies are gone. We'll break you up into groups of five. Each group will go with one of these young gentlemen who are standing over there watching you eat cookies. They had some before you arrived, so don't feel sorry for them."

Several of the journalists chuckled politely.

"Captain, why was this group invited to tour the ship?" The question was asked by a woman in her late twenties with a hint of Boston in her voice. She wore a bright red dress and carried an expensive black leather purse casually over one shoulder.

"And who are you, ma'am?"

"I'm Judith Farrell from the *International Herald Tribune.*"

"Well, we often entertain groups aboard, and starting this Mediterranean cruise with a tour for you ladies and gentlemen of the European press seemed appropriate."

"Are you saying the invitations had nothing to do with the American request for a French port visit for this ship in June?"

The gray eyes locked on the woman. "No. I didn't say that. I said a tour of the ship for you folks of the European press seemed appropriate."

"This ship is nuclear-powered?"

"Yes, it is. You may wish to examine the fact sheet that Lieutenant Tarkington is handing out." An officer immediately entered the crowd and began distributing printed leaflets.

"What assurances can you give to the people of Europe in light of the recent revelations about the extent of the Chernobyl disaster?"

13

"Assurances about what?" The captain glanced from face to face.

"That your reactors are safe." Judith Farrell replied as she tossed her head to flick her blond hair back from her eyes.

"The Russians didn't build these reactors. Americans did. Americans operate them."

Judith Farrell flushed slightly as her fellow reporters grinned and nudged each other. She was inhaling air for a retort when a well-dressed woman with an Italian accent spoke up. "May we see the reactors?"

"I'm sorry, but those spaces are off limits except to naval personnel." When he observed several people making notes, the captain added, "Only those sailors who actually work in those spaces are admitted. I might add that, outside of the Soviet Union, you are far more likely to be struck by lightning than you are to become a victim of a nuclear accident."

"Captain . . . ," said Judith Farrell, but Grafton's voice was covering the crowd: "Now if you folks will break up into groups of five, these officers from the air wing will show you around." Everyone began talking and moving toward the door.

"Captain," said Judith Farrell firmly, "I do not appreciate that evasive answer."

"Mister Tarkington, include Miss Farrell in your group."

"It is 'Ms.,' not 'Miss.' "

"Please come with me, Ms.," said a drawling voice at her elbow, and she turned to see a tan face framing perfect teeth. The grin caused his cheeks to dimple and deep creases to radiate from the corners of his eyes. The innocent face was topped by short, carefully combed brown hair.

"I'm Lieutenant Tarkington." The captain was walking away.

In the passageway she asked, "Lieutenant, who is that captain? He's not the ship's commanding officer or executive officer, is he?"

"He's the air wing commander, ma'am. We call him CAG." Tarkington pronounced "CAG" to rhyme with "rag." It was a fifty-year-old acronym from the days when the air wing commander had been known as Commander Air Group, and it had survived into the age of jets and supercarriers. "But let's talk about you. Whereabouts over here on this side of the pond do you live, ma'am?"

"The pond?"

"Y'know, the puddle. The ocean. The Atlantic."

"Paris," she said in a voice that would have chilled milk.

"I sure am glad you're touring this little tub with me this morning, ma'am. All my friends call me Toad."

"For good reason, I'm sure."

Lieutenant Tarkington smiled thinly at the other members of his group, all men, and motioned for the little band to follow him.

He led them through pale blue passageways with numerous turns, and soon everyone except Tarkington—who frequently looked back over his shoulder to ensure his five were following faithfully—was hopelessly lost. They passed fire-fighting stations with racks of hose and valves and instructions stenciled on the bulkhead. Above their heads ran mazes of pipes, from pencil-thin to eight inches in diameter, each labeled cryptically. Bundles of wires were threaded between the pipes. Every thirty feet or so there was a large steel door latched open. When asked by one of the men, Tarkington explained that the doors allowed the crew to seal the ship into over three thousand watertight compartments. He paused by a hole in the deck surrounded by a flange that rose about four inches from the deck. Inside the hole was a ladder leading to the deck below. Above it a heavy hatch on hinges stood ready to seal it.

"When the ship goes into battle," Tarkington said, "we just close all these hatches and this ship becomes like a giant piece of Styrofoam, full of all these watertight compartments. The enemy has to bust open a whole lot of these compartments to sink this bucket."

"Just like the *Titanic*," Judith Farrell muttered loudly enough for all to hear.

"A bucket?" one of the men murmured in a heavy French accent.

Tarkington led them on. The smells of food cooking assailed them. They looked into a large kitchen filled with men in white trousers, aprons and tee shirts. Each wore a white cap that covered his hair. "This is the forward crew's galley." Huge polished steel vats gleamed amid the bustling men, several of whom smiled at the visitors. "They're fixing noon chow. The ship serves eighteen thousand meals a day."

Beside the galley was a cafeteria serving line with steam tables,

15

drink dispensers, and large steel coffee urns. Huge racks of metal trays stood at the entrance. "The men go through here and fill their trays," Tarkington said as he led them into the mess area, which was filled with folding tables and chairs. "They find a chair and eat here." The overhead was a latticework of pipes and wires. Around the bulkheads were more fire-fighting hoses and numerous buttons and knobs to control machinery which wasn't visible. Large doors formed the forward bulkhead.

"What are those doors?" Judith Farrell asked.

"Weapons elevators, ma'am."

"Does the entire crew eat here?" one of the men asked in an accent Tarkington took to be German.

"Couldn't be done. There's fifty-six hundred men on this ship. We've got another galley and mess area back aft. The crew eats in both mess areas in shifts. The officers have two wardrooms and the chief petty officers have their own mess." The group just stood, looking. "It isn't exactly eating at the Ritz, but the chow is pretty darn good," Tarkington added and waved his hand for them to follow.

He led them outboard from the mess area to a ladder that rose steeply. They ascended one deck and followed him through another open watertight door out into the hangar bay.

The hangar was a two-acre cavern crammed with aircraft. The group threaded their way around the myriad of chains that secured each plane to a clear walk area that meandered down the center of the hangar between the planes. Tarkington stopped and the visitors gawked.

"Sort of takes your breath away, doesn't it?"

"All these planes . . ." the Frenchman marveled. F-14 Tomcat fighters, A-6 Intruder attack bombers, and F/A-18 Hornet fighter-bombers, all with folded wings, were crammed in so that not a square yard of space was empty. Tarkington led them to a clear area that divided the space laterally.

"Now this space right here is always kept open, so we can close these big bombproof doors." Massive doors that were as tall as the bay was high—about twenty-five feet—were recessed into each side of the bay. "There are two of these doors, this one and the one back aft. By closing these we can separate this bay into three compartments and isolate any fire or bomb damage. Up there," Tarkington pointed at a small compartment with windows visible near the ceiling, "is a station that's manned twenty-four hours a day. The man on duty there can close these doors from up there and turn on the fire-fighting sprinklers at the first sign of fire or a fuel spill. You will notice we have three of these stations, called CONFLAG stations, one in each of the three bays." In the window of the nearest CONFLAG station, the face of the sailor on duty was just visible. He was looking down at them.

One of the reporters pointed at some racks hanging down from the ceiling which held large white shapes pointed at both ends. "Are those bombs?"

"No, sir," said their guide. "Those are extra drop tanks." When he saw the puzzlement on the reporter's face, he added, "Drops are fuel tanks that hang under the wings or belly of an airplane that the pilot can jettison if he has to." The lieutenant stepped to an A-6 and patted one that hung on a wing station. "Like this one, which holds a ton of fuel."

The German pointed his camera at the lieutenant. Tarkington shook his head and waved his hands. "Please don't take any pictures in here, sir. You can get some shots up on the flight deck. I'll show you where." He herded them around the planes to a large opening in the side of the ship. A greasy wire on stanchions was the only safety line. About twenty feet below them was the sea. On the horizon the group could see the city of Tangiers and the hills beyond. The spring wind, still raw, was funneling into the hangar through this giant door. Above, a large roof projected out over the sea and obstructed their view of the sky. Tarkington nodded to a sailor on the side of the opening and instantly a loud horn began to wail. Then the huge projecting roof began to fall.

"This is one of the four aircraft elevators that we use to move planes and equipment back and forth to the flight deck. We'll ride it up." As the platform reached their level, the safety stanchions sank silently into the deck. When all motion stopped, Tarkington led them out onto it.

The elevator platform was large, about four thousand square feet, and was constructed of grillwork. Several of the journalists looked down through the grating at the sea beneath them as the elevator rose with more sounding of horns, and several kept their eyes firmly on the horizon after a mere glance downward. The wind coming up through the grid swirled Judith Farrell's dress. As she fought to hold it against her thighs she caught Lieutenant

Tarkington looking at her legs. He smiled and winked, then looked away.

On the vast flight deck, they walked around a row of aircraft to a clear area. Their guide stopped at a giant hinged flap that projected out of the deck at a sixty-degree angle. "This is a jet blast deflector, a JBD. The plane on the catapult sits in front of it," he gestured forward to the launching area, "and this thing comes up and deflects the exhaust gases up and away from the planes behind. The JBDs are cooled internally by salt water." He showed them the water pipes on the back of the unit, then strolled forward to the catapult hookup area.

He pointed out the slot in which the shuttle traveled. The slot ran forward to the bow of the ship. "The catapult is about a hundred yards long and accelerates the planes up to flying speed."

"What moves ze shuttle?" a Frenchman asked.

"It's driven by steam. See, the catapult is right here under these steel deck plates. It's like a giant double-barreled shotgun. There is a piston in each tube and they are mated together," he sneaked a glance at Farrell, "and the shuttle sticks up through this slot. The airplane is hooked to the shuttle. Steam drives the pistons forward and tows the plane along." He held up a hand and slammed it with his fist. "Pow!"

"What is that?" Judith Farrell pointed to a glassed-in compartment between the two bow catapults that protruded eighteen inches out of the deck.

"I'll show you." Tarkington led them over and they looked in the windows. "This is the bow catapult control bubble. The cat officer sits at this console facing aft and operates both bow cats. That console facing forward is where the man sits who monitors all the steam and hydraulic pressures and electrical circuits. He's sort of like a flight engineer on a jetliner."

The group proceeded to the bow where they looked back down the length of the ship. The view was spectacular. The island superstructure over two hundred yards aft looked like a goatherder's cottage. Here, Tarkington suggested, was a good place for photographs. Everyone except Judith Farrell began snapping pictures. She turned and stared forward, out to sea.

"That's east," Tarkington told her. "You can't see it, but not too far in that direction is the Strait of Gibralter, the entrance to the Med. We'll be going through there in a few days."

"I know my geography."

"I'll bet you do, ma'am. Just where in Paris do you live?"

"The Left Bank."

"Where all those ol' hippies and crackpots hang out?"

"Precisely there."

"Oh." He was silent for a moment. "Is this the first carrier you've been on, ma'am?"

"Yes."

"Well, what do you think of her?"

"It's a waste of billions of dollars when there are people in the world starving."

"You may be right, ma'am. I always figured that maybe somebody said something like that to Joshua when he was standing there looking at the walls of Jericho and thinking about tooting his horn. But my suspicion is that the folks in Jericho were thinking they hadn't spent enough bucks on the walls. I reckon it all depends on your point of view."

She glanced at him with her brows knitted, then turned and began walking aft. Tarkington followed slowly, and the rest of the group lowered their cameras and trailed after them.

They passed the bow catapult control bubble and the upright JBD and approached the island. It had looked small and unobtrusive from the bow, but as they neared, it took on the aura of a ten-story building festooned with radar dishes and radio antennae.

The lieutenant led his five through an oval door—they had to step over the combing—and into a ladderwell. Their footsteps echoed thunderously against the metal walls as they trudged up flight after flight of steep stairs (ladders, the sailors called them), swimming against a steady stream of people trooping down. The ship was so stupendously large, yet the passageways and ladders were narrow, with low ceilings, and crammed with pipes and wires and fire fighting gear; the ship's interior was incongruously disconcerting to visitors unfamiliar with warship architecture. Some people found themselves slightly claustrophobic inside this rabbit warren of bulkheads and ladders and people charging hither and yon on unimaginable errands. Toad paused on several landings to let his charges catch up and catch their breath.

Six stories up they exited onto a viewing area their guide

quaintly referred to as Vulture's Row. Several other groups of journalists were also there. Everyone with a camera snapped numerous photos of the planes parked neatly in rows on the deck below and the junior officers answered technical questions as fast as they were posed. Several of the tour guides were pilots who expounded with youthful enthusiasm on the thrills associated with flying off and onto the carrier.

"Are you a pilot?" the Frenchman with a Japanese camera asked Lieutenant Tarkington.

"No, sir. I'm an RIO—that means Radar Intercept Officer—on F-14s. Those are the sharky-looking jobs down there with the wings that move backwards and forwards."

The Frenchman stared. "Ze wings?"

"Yeah, the wings move." Tarkington pretended to be an airplane and waggled his arms appropriately. Out of the corner of his eye he saw Judith Farrell roll her gaze heavenward.

"Oui, oui. Formidable!"

"Yep, sure is," the irrepressible Tarkington agreed heartily.

When their turn came, Tarkington led his followers into "Pri-Fly," a glassed-in room that stuck out of the top of the island over the flight deck and offered a magnificent view. Here, he explained, the air boss, a senior commander, controlled the launch and recovery of aircraft. As Tarkington drawled along a helicopter came in to land, settling gently onto the forward portion of the landing area. Several of the group took pictures of the air boss standing beside his raised easy chair with all his radios and intercom boxes in the background.

Tarkington's group then packed themselves into the minuscule island elevator for the ride down to the flight deck level. Somehow the lieutenant ended up jammed face-to-face with Judith Farrell. He beamed at her and she stared at his Adam's apple. The machinery was noisy and the whole contraption lurched several times. "Nobody's died in here since last week, ma'am," he whispered.

"I wish you wouldn't call me 'ma'am,' " Farrell said, refusing to whisper.

"Yes, ma'am."

When the door opened, they went down another ladder to the O-3 level and then through a myriad of turns to a ready room. The tourists were greeted by an officer who gave a little explanation of how aircrews planned and briefed their missions in ready rooms like this throughout the O-3 level. He showed them the closed-circuit television monitors around the room on which the only show playing during flight operations was the launch and recovery of aircraft on the "roof," the flight deck. And he got some laughs with his explanation of the greenie board that hung on one bulkhead. Every pilot in this squadron had color marks recorded for each of his carrier approaches, which his squadron mates witnessed in glorious detail on the television monitors. Green was the predominate color and symbolized an OK pass, the best grade possible. Yellow was a fair grade and a few red spots recorded no-grade or cut passes. Apparently a pilot's virtues and sins were recorded in living color for all to see.

Back in the passageway one of the reporter-photographers delayed the group almost three minutes as he repeatedly snapped an apparently endless, narrow passageway that ran fore and aft. At this level the openings in the frames that supported the flight deck were oval in shape and only wide enough for people to pass through in single file. "Knee-knockers," Tarkington called them. The passageway appeared to be an oval tube receding into infinity. The photographer got a shot of a sailor in the passageway over a hundred yards away that later appeared in a German newsmagazine. The picture demonstrated visually, in a way words never could, just how large, how massive, this ship truly was.

"It's very noisy," one of the visitors said to Toad, who nodded politely. The hum and whine of the fans inside the air conditioning system was the background noise the ship's inhabitants became aware of only when it ceased.

"What is that smell? I've noticed it ever since we came aboard," Judith Farrell said.

"I don't really know," Toad replied as he examined her nose to see if it crinkled when she sniffed. "I always thought it was the oil they used to lubricate the blowers in the air-conditioning system, or the hatch hinges, or whatever." All the other visitors were inhaling lungfuls. "You don't notice it after awhile," Toad finished lamely.

The photographer was finished. They went down another set of ladders and back to the wardroom where they had begun the tour.

"I sure am glad you folks could come out today for a little visit," Tarkington said as he shook hands with the men. "Hope we didn't walk you too much or wear you down. But there's a lot to see and it takes a little doing to get around." He turned and gazed into Judith Farrell's clear blue eyes. "I just might get up Paris way sometime this summer, ma'am, and maybe you could return the hospitality and give me a little tour of Gay Paree?"

She favored him with the smallest smile she could manage as she ensured he had only her fingertips to shake.

"I hope you enjoyed your tour," Captain Grafton said to the group.

"Very much," the Italian woman replied as heads bobbed in agreement.

"There's more Kool-Aid," Grafton gestured toward the refreshment table, "if you're thirsty. Please help yourselves. The boats will be leaving in about five minutes to take you back to the beach. Your tour guides will escort you to the quarterdeck. If you have any unanswered questions, now is the time to ask them."

"Are nuclear weapons aboard this ship, please?" The question came from one of the Frenchmen.

"The American government can neither confirm nor deny the presence of nuclear weapons aboard any ship."

"But what if a war begins?" Judith Farrell asked loudly.

Grafton's face showed no emotion. "In that event, ma'am, we'll do the best we can to defend ourselves in accordance with American government policy and our commitments to NATO."

"Isn't it possible the presence of this ship in these waters adds to international tension, rather than lessens it?" Farrell persisted.

"I'm not a diplomat," Grafton said carefully. "I'm a sailor. You should ask the State Department that question." He glanced at his watch, then at the junior officer tour guides. "Gentlemen, perhaps it's time to take these folks to the quarterdeck."

As his group prepared to descend the ladder from the quarterdeck to the carly float Lieutenant Tarkington again shook each hand. To Farrell he said, "I sure am glad I had the chance to get to know you, ma'am. It's a small world and you just never know when or where we'll meet again."

She brushed past him and was three steps down the ladder when she heard him say loudly, "I'm sure you're a fine reporter, Judith, but you shouldn't work so hard at playing the role." Teetering on her heels, she turned and caught a glimpse of Tarkington's face, dead serious, as the man behind her on the ladder lost his balance and almost sent her sprawling.

"Don't forget the Toad, Judith Farrell."

A week later the Tangiers police received an enquiry from Paris about the *J'Accuse* reporter. He had not returned from his trip nor had he filed a story. At the hotel where he had reservations, the bartender, a retired merchant mariner from Marseilles, identified the reporter from a black-and-white photograph which pictured a middle-aged man with thinning hair and heavy jowls. The bartender gave a tolerably accurate description of the young woman to the police, but he had not overheard any of the couple's conversation. The reporter's bed had not been disturbed and his luggage was missing when the hotel maid entered the next morning. The bartender ventured the opinion that the woman was not a prostitute, and this professional observation caused police to make fruitless enquiries at every other hotel in Tangiers that catered to foreigners. Where the pair had gone after they left the hotel bar was never established.

An official of the French government asked the American embassy in Paris if the *J'Accuse* press pass to the *United States* had been used, and was informed several days later that it had. Two weeks after the event a photo of the missing journalist was shown to the naval officers who had guided the tours. The ship was then at sea in the Mediterranean. None of those who viewed the picture could recall the individual, so that information, for whatever it was worth, was passed via the embassy to the French authorities.

The American embassy CIA man reported the disappearance to his superiors, and U.S. Naval Intelligence was routinely informed. Apparently the incident was too unimportant to be included in the summaries prepared for the National Security Council. After all, the group had not been shown anything classified or anything that was not shown as a matter of course to any visitor to the ship. Notations were made in the appropriate computer records and within a month the incident was forgotten by those few persons in the intelligence community who were aware of it.

The reporter was never seen again. Since he was divorced and his only daughter lived in Toulon with children of her own, his disappearance caused scarcely a ripple. Within six weeks his mistress had another regular visitor and *J'Accuse* had another reporter at a lower salary.

3

EL HAKIM, THE RULER, stood at the window and gazed east in the direction of Mecca. He took a deep breath. Ah, the air smelled of the desert—it smelled of nothing at all. It was pure and empty, as Allah had made it.

"There are enormous risks involved, Colonel Qazi." The colonel sat behind him on a carpet before a low table. A hot dry wind stirred the curtains. El Hakim continued, "The Americans declared war at the end of the last century when one of their warships was merely suspected of being lost due to hostile action. The course you propose is unambiguous, to say the least."

El Hakim turned from the window and glanced down at Qazi, today dressed in clean, faded khakis. About forty, Qazi was dark with European features. Only his cheekbones hinted at his ancestry. The son of a British army sergeant and an Arab girl, Qazi often moved about Europe as a wealthy playboy or businessman, sometimes Greek, sometimes French, English, or Italian. He spoke seven languages without an accent. In a military environment he stood ramrod straight. "You have never failed us, Qazi. And you have never attempted so much."

The colonel remained silent.

El Hakim obliquely examined the seated man. Qazi did not think like most soldiers, he reflected. He thought like the spy Allah must have intended him to be. And his ability to slip so completely into the roles of these people he pretended to be—indeed, to actually become the man his papers said he was—this ability troubled El Hakim, who had heard the stories of Qazi's feats from informants and silently marveled, since he himself had spent his entire forty-nine years in the Arab world, except for one six-month visit to England twenty years ago. On that one foreign excursion he had felt so utterly, totally out of place, among people who seemed to have just arrived from another planet. One just never knew, he told himself now, when Qazi was onstage. He was a dangerous man. A very dangerous man. But most dangerous for whom?

El Hakim reluctantly resumed his seat. "Tell me about the ship."

"Her main weapons are her aircraft. Her deck is crammed with airplanes and to ready them for launch requires many men and a reasonable amount of time. It cannot be done quickly, if at all, while the ship is at anchor and unprepared. Then she is most vulnerable.

"She carries three missile launchers, known as the Basic Point Defense Missile System." Qazi opened a reference book and displayed a picture of the ship. "A battery is located on each side of the after end of the flight deck, below the level of the flying deck, and one is forward of these two aircraft elevators in front of the island, on the starboard side of the ship." He pointed them out. "The reference book says these contain Sea Sparrow missiles with a ten- to twelve-mile range.

"Her only other weapons are four close-in weapons systems, called CIWS." He pronounced the acronym as the American Navy did, "see-whiz." "These are very rapid-fire machine guns aimed by radar and lasers. Two are located on each side of the ship." His finger moved to the prominent little domes that housed each installation. "These weapons automatically engage incoming missiles and shoot them down before they can strike the ship. Maximum range for these systems is about two kilometers. They are for last-chance, close-in defense."

"Is that all the weapons the ship has?"

"At sea, Excellency, the ship is surrounded by surface combatants with modern guns and missiles with ranges beyond ninety miles. These escorts also carry antisubmarine weapons. Occasionally a large surface combatant, such as a battleship, will accompany the task group. When the carrier anchors, several of her escorts will anchor nearby."

"But the carrier? Has she any other weapons?"

"Four machine guns, about 12.5 millimeter, are mounted on the catwalks around the flight deck when the ship is anchored, two on each side. These are constantly manned by marines. These guns could engage any unauthorized boat that comes too close, or a helicopter. The carrier's crew does not carry small arms."

El Hakim arched an eyebrow. "Not even the officers?"

"No, sir."

"And how many men are in the crew?"

"About five thousand six hundred, Excellency."

The ruler gazed incredulously at the photograph in the reference book, *Jane's Fighting Ships*. Although it is a big ship, he thought, with that many peasants crammed into such tight quarters the discipline problems must be stupendous. He remembered the stories he had heard about the slums of Los Angeles and New York, and allowed his upper lip to rise contemptuously.

"Have you any photographs?"

"Yes, sir." Qazi passed across a stack of enlarged prints.

El Hakim took the photos to the open window and studied them in the sunlight. He had a strong, square face set off by a perfect Roman nose. His nostrils flared slightly above sensuous, expressive lips. He had been an army officer when, nineteen years ago, he had organized and led a coup, preaching independent nationalism. Through the years he had stayed on top by ensuring the officer corps received a generous share of the petrodollars from the nationalized oil industry and by using every technological and public relations gimmick at his disposal to enshrine himself as the peoples' savior while he spent the rest of the oil money to keep them fed, clothed, and housed. He postured on his little corner of the world stage under the benign eye of his state media, which portrayed him as one of the world's movers and shakers and flooded every radio and television set in the country with his simple, drumbeat message: American and European imperialism —political, economic, cultural, and technological—were responsible for the dishonor of his people. Harried government bureaucrats were kept on edge with a never-ending avalanche of "revolutionary reforms" decreed from on high, as well as a raging torrent of orders and counterorders and orders changing the counterorders. All the while he goaded his North African neighbors and fluxed the military with rumors of war. The constant confusion created a tense domestic atmosphere, perfect for rooting out real and potential political enemies and ruthlessly destroying them in the name of national security.

El Hakim's methods certainly weren't unique. Military strongmen routinely toppled governments and seized power in other Third World nations, poor nations slowly sinking into hopeless debt and starvation in the effluvium of the great powers' economies. El Hakim knew just how easy it had been for him—he knew how much money he had spent—and through the years he had tired of the footnote role history had assigned him. He wanted glory. He wanted to be the man his propagandists said he was.

El Hakim tapped the stack of photos on his left hand and looked out the window. "The American government," he said slowly, "has never admitted the presence of nuclear weapons aboard any naval vessel. Nor," he added dryly, "has it ever denied it." He thumbed through the photos again, then turned back to the colonel. "We must be very sure, Qazi. Absolutely certain. Once we begin we shall be unable to hide our involvement. We will have laid hands on the very essence of American power." El Hakim paused as the shame of past insults and outrages from the madmen who ruled America flooded him. He threw back his head, a conscious gesture, and spoke authoritatively. "What do we *know*?"

"The weapons are aboard, Excellency."

El Hakim stood waiting expectantly.

"An American sailor told us. We used sodium pentothal. There is no possibility he was lying." Qazi extracted a cassette player from his attaché case and set it on the low table before him. He adjusted the volume and pushed the "play" button.

El Hakim sat and sipped coffee as they listened. He spoke English well enough to follow what was being said, although he occasionally missed a word or two. He identified Qazi's voice immediately. Qazi certainly had been thorough. He had approached the subject from every conceivable angle and discussed details that were far beyond the level of knowledge of El Hakim. Apparently the American knew the answers.

Even with sodium pentothal, the American had needed encouragement to talk, Qazi reflected. He managed to be looking at El Hakim when the man on the tape screamed. El Hakim sipped his coffee.

Qazi had listened to the tape many times, so now as it played he reviewed the kidnapping of the American. Weeks of effort had gone into selecting the proper individual, one whose speciality was aircraft weapons and who would be officially leaving the ship soon. Four agents had worked the bars and nightclubs of Naples under Qazi's supervision during two port calls by the USS *Carl Vinson*. She was a sister ship of the *United States*, slated to leave the Med soon and sufficiently similar to the *United States* that the information obtained was still valid. Qazi finally settled on a second-class petty officer who was going on three weeks leave to visit a brother serving in Germany with the U.S. Army. The team took the man off a train in Rome and drove him to a safe house.

It had been a good operation, Qazi reflected as he watched the cassette reels turn. The sailor had known the answers and his absence would not be missed for a reasonable time. He would appear to be a deserter and only a cursory investigation would be made, one which, Qazi was reasonably certain, would fail to uncover even a hint of the sailor's real fate.

A reasonable time and a reasonable certainty were all he could hope for. This business—one had to be so careful and yet there were so many unknowns. Chance or the unforeseen could betray one anywhere. So one moved in a perpetual paranoid fog, weighing the incalculable against the unknowable, forever tensed against contact with an obstacle that might or might not be there. And the nations that bordered the Mediterranean were awash in foreign agents, as thick as fleas on a camel. The Soviets were the most numerous and the Israelis the most energetic and efficient. Qazi was certain the Mossad had a voluminous file on his activities. If El Hakim approved this operation, it would have to be his last, for he was already a marked man.

El Hakim's fingers twitched and Qazi stopped the tape. The dictator sat silently for several moments before he spoke. "The bombs will alter forever the balance of power in the Mideast." He rose and strolled around the apartment examining objects with eyes that were opaque.

The Jews would have to come to terms or risk obliteration, El Hakim assured himself. That fact alone would make him the strongest man in the Arab world. Perhaps he should drop a bomb on Tel Aviv before he began to talk. Even Egypt would grudgingly yield to his leadership. He would be a hero to the masses and he would have the bomb: that combination would melt the most reluctant heart.

He had thought deeply on this subject. Nuclear weapons were the power base that would allow him to force the world to its knees. The Americans, the Soviets, the French and the British all have these weapons, many of them, and one walked softly in their presence because the weapons could conceivably be used. Even the Israelis had them, though they refused to admit it.

And every time he had tried to obtain them in the past he had been thwarted! Immense quantities of time, money and prestige had been expended, all to no avail. This time there would be no necessity to obtain some foreign government approval for a reactor sale, no secret deals to siphon processed fuel from an Indian reactor, no negotiations with the Chinese—no necessity to reveal information to foreign officials that they could sell or give to the Americans or the British for their own purposes.

He would use one of the weapons as soon as he got it, so the question would not be, Will he use the bomb? The question would be, Will he use it again?

His influence and prestige in the Arab world would rise astronomically.

None of the superpowers has the courage to use the ultimate weapon, El Hakim assured himself, as he had a hundred times before. The Americans excoriate Truman for using two on the Japanese and luxuriate in their guilt. The Communists are too fearful of losing their privileges to ever let one of their number pull the trigger. The French? That nation of decadent sensualists whom the Algerians defeated with rifles and pistols? Conceivably the British under that maniac Thatcher, they might. But not for the Jews. Not for the Americans. And the Israelis? If they ever used nuclear weapons they would have to live with the holocaust as perpetrators, not victims.

No, none has the courage to oppose the man who possesses the weapon and the will to use it, he told himself, believing it absolutely, believing it with all his heart and soul.

I will bring down the decadent unbelievers and the misguided imams, like Khomeini, who understand so little of the ways of the world. Khomeini, that fool! He thought he could build a pure, holy nation on the insatiable thirst of the infidels for that stinking black liquid. The old imbecile is almost as bad as the Saudi princes, Saddam Hussein, and all those others who lust so for the goods of the West. Their greed is a travesty of the Koran.

Praise Allah, I am not like them. I have the courage and strength to live according to the Word. With the bomb will come all power, so I can purchase only what is really needed.

I will defend the Faith.

I will purify my people.

Mecca will be my capital in a united Arab world.

He started from his thoughts and glanced at Qazi, who was examining the photographs. Yes, he thought, Qazi is ambitious and competent and almost as ruthless as I. Unconsciously El Hakim flicked his hand as if at a fly.

"Ring for coffee." He composed himself as the servant moved about, the only sound the faint clink of china.

After the servant departed, El Hakim seated himself across from the colonel. "What is your plan?"

CAPTAIN JAKE GRAFTON held his F-14 Tomcat level at six thousand feet in a steady left turn as his wingman came sliding in on a forty-five-degree line to rendezvous. The other plane crossed behind and under Jake and settled on his right wing. Jake leveled his wings and added power as he tweaked the nose up.

He keyed his radio mike and waited for the scrambler to synchronize. "Strike, Red Aces are joined and proceeding on course."

"Roger, Red Ace Two Oh Five. Report entering patrol area Bravo."

"Wilco."

It was a cloudless night with a half moon, now just above the eastern horizon. To the west a layer of low haze over the sea limited visibility, but Jake knew that there was nothing to see in that direction anyway. The Lebanese coast was a mere thirty miles to the east, and as the two fighters climbed on a northerly heading toward their assigned altitude of 30,000 feet, Jake searched the blackness in that direction. Nothing. No lights. Jake scanned the night sky slowly in all quadrants for the lights of other aircraft. They seemed to be alone.

"Keep your eye peeled for other planes, Toad," he told the RIO in the rear cockpit.

"Uh, yessir," came the answer, sounding slightly puzzled. Normally the pilot performed routine lookout duties while the RIO worked the radar and computer. Well, thought Jake Grafton, let him wonder.

"What's on the scope, anyway?"

"Not a daggone thing, CAG. Looks like one big empty sky to me."

"When's that El Al flight from Athens to Haifa scheduled to be along?"

In the back seat of the Tomcat, Lieutenant Tarkington consulted the notes on his kneeboard. "Not till twenty-five after the hour." He slid back the sleeve of his flight suit and glanced at his luminous watch. He matched it with the clock on the panel in front of him. "About fifteen minutes from now."

"When will we reach area Bravo?"

Tarkington checked the TACAN against the chart on his kneeboard. "About two minutes."

"We'll make a turn west then, and you see if you can pick up that airliner. Let me know when you see him."

"Yessir."

"In the meantime, let's get some data link from the Hummer." The Hummer was the slang nickname for the E-2 Hawkeye radar reconnaissance plane that Jake knew was somewhere about.

Toad made the call as Jake checked the Tomcat on his right wing and noticed with satisfaction that Jelly Dolan was right where he should be, about a hundred feet away from Jake. Jelly was a lieutenant (junior grade) on his first cruise and flew with Lieutenant Commander Boomer Bronsky, the maintenance officer for the fighter squadron that owned these airplanes. Jake knew that Boomer liked to complain about the youth of the pilots he flew with—"Goddamn wet-nosed kids"—but that he had a very high opinion of their skills. He bragged on Jelly Dolan at every opportunity.

"Battlestar Strike," Toad said over the radio, "Red Ace flight entering Bravo at assigned altitude."

"Roger."

Jake keyed the mike. "Left turn, Jelly."

Two mike clicks was the reply.

One minute passed, then two. Jake stabilized the airspeed at 250 knots, max conserve. He scanned the instruments and resumed his visual search of the heavens.

"I've got him, CAG," Toad said. "Looks like a hundred and twenty miles out. He's headed southwest. Got the right squawk." The squawk was the radar identification code. "He's running about a mile or so above us."

Jake flipped the secondary radio to the channel the E-2 Hawk-eye used and listened to the crew report the airliner to the Combat Decision Center (CDC) aboard the carrier. He knew the radio transmissions merely backed up the data link that transmitted the Hawkeye's radar picture for presentation on a scope in CDC. The watchstanders aboard ship would watch the airliner. If the course changed to come within fifty miles of the carrier, Jake's flight or the flight in area Alpha would be vectored to intercept. They would close the airliner and check visually to ensure that it was what they thought and that it was alone. The fighters would stay well back out of view of the airliner's cockpit and passenger windows and would follow until told to break off.

Jake yawned and flashed his exterior lights. Then he turned north. Jelly Dolan followed obediently. In a few moments he turned east to permit Toad and Boomer to use their radars to scan the skies toward Lebanon. If any terrorists or fanatics attempted a night aerial strike on the carrier task group, it would more than likely come from the east.

"Nothing, CAG. The sky's as clean as a virgin's conscience."

"How come you're always talking about women, Toad?"

"Am I?" Feigned shock.

"After three months at sea, I'd think your hormones would have achieved a level of dormancy that allowed your mind to dwell on other subjects."

"I'm always horny. That's why they call me Toad. When are we going into port, anyway?"

"Whenever the admiral says."

"Yessir. But have you got any idea when he might say it?"

"Soon, I hope." Jake was very much aware of the toll the constant day-and-night flight operations had taken on the ship's crew and the men of the air wing. He thought about the stresses of constant work, work, work on the men as he guided the Tomcat through the sky.

"We're approaching the eastern edge of the area," Toad reminded him.

Jake glanced toward Jelly. The wingman was not there.

"Jelly?"

He looked on the other side. The sky was empty there, too. He rolled the aircraft and looked down. Far below he saw a set of lights.

"Red Ace Two Oh Seven, do you read?"

Jake rolled on his back and pulled the nose down. "Strike, Red Ace Two Oh Five, I'm leaving altitude." The nose came down twenty degrees and Jake pointed it at the lights. "Jelly, this is CAG. Do you read me, over?"

"He's going down," Toad informed him.

"Boomer, talk to me." Jake had the throttles full forward: 450 knots, now 500, passing 21,000 feet descending. The aircraft below was in a gentle right turn, and Jake hastened to cut the turn short and intercept.

"Red Ace Two Oh Five, Strike. Say your problem."

"My wingman is apparently in an uncontrolled descent and I can't raise him on the radio. Am trying to rendezvous. Have you got an emergency squawk?"

"Negative. Keep me advised."

Now he throttled back and cracked the speed brakes. He was closing rapidly. Passing 15,000 feet. Goddamn, Jelly's nose was way down. In the darkness Jake found it extremely difficult to judge the closure, and he finally realized he was too fast. He cross-controlled with the speed brakes full out and overshot slightly.

"Thirteen thousand feet."

Jake slid in on Jelly's left side as he thumbed the boards in. Toad shone his white flashlight on the front cockpit of the other fighter. The pilot's helmeted head lolled from side to side. In the back cockpit Boomer also appeared to be unconscious. Both men had their oxygen masks on.

"We're steepening up, CAG." Toad said. "Twelve degrees nose down. Fifteen-degree right turn. Passing nine thousand."

"Jelly, talk to me, you son of a bitch." No good. *"Wake up!"* Jake screamed.

He crossed under the other plane and locked on the right wing. He moved forward as Toad kept the flashlight on Jelly's helmet. He flipped the radio channel selector switch to the emergency channel and turned off the scrambler.

"Wake up, Jelly, or you're going to sleep forever!"

"Six thousand." Toad's voice.

"Pull up!"

"Five thousand."

"Eject, eject, eject! Get out Jelly! Get out Boomer!"

"Four thousand. Fifteen degrees nose down."

Jake began to pull his nose up. As the descending Tomcat fell away he lost sight of the slumped figures in the cockpit. He rolled into a turn to keep the lights of the descending plane in sight.

"Pull up, pull up, pull up, pull up, pull . . ." He was still chanting over the radio when the lights disappeared.

"Sweet Jesus," Toad whispered. "They went in."

"Strike, Red Ace Two Oh Seven just went into the drink. Mark my position and get the angel out here buster." The "angel" was the rescue helicopter. "Buster" meant to hurry, bust your ass.

"Red Ace, did the crew get out?"

"I doubt it," Jake Grafton said, and removed his oxygen mask to wipe his face.

"How heavy are the weapons?" El Hakim asked.

"About two hundred kilos," Colonel Qazi replied.

El Hakim stood in the apartment window and let the warm, dry wind play with the folds in his robe. Already the great summer heat had begun. Here in this retreat deep in the desert he did not wear the military uniform that he was obliged to wear in the capital before the Western diplomatic corps and press. He hated the uniform, but it gave him an air of authority that he felt essential. Soon, very soon, he would burn the uniform. He closed his eyes and faced the rising sun. He could feel it through his eyelids. The power of the sun would soon be his. Praise Allah, he would make the unbelievers kneel.

"So no matter how many weapons are there, we can only take a few."

"Correct, Excellency. Our goal shall be to obtain six. Even half that many will make us a formidable political force to be reckoned with."

El Hakim left the window reluctantly and returned to his seat on the carpet. "If you destroy the ship, the Americans will not know for sure how many we have."

"True, but they will be able to estimate the number with accuracy. Destruction of the ship will merely ensure our escape. The Americans will undoubtedly leap to the proper conclusion without evidence."

"No doubt." The dictator snorted. "They have demonstrated their capacity for that aerial feat numerous times in the past."

"So when the mission is complete, we must inform the world promptly in order to forestall any rash action on the part of the Americans. They are very sensitive to public opinion, even when goaded beyond endurance."

El Hakim tilted his head back and narrowed his eyes. "The political and military exploitation of your mission is my concern, Colonel, not yours."

"Of course." Qazi lowered his gaze respectfully. "But still, Excellency, our mission will be for naught unless the Americans are sufficiently delayed to give us time to escape and alter the weapons."

"Time? How much time?"

"The Americans have built numerous safety devices into each weapon. That information was part of the interrogation of the American sailor you did not hear. It was extremely technical. The only real danger from an unaltered weapon is that fire or an accident will split the skin of the weapon and cause nuclear material to be spilled. If one were handled carelessly enough, a conventional explosion of low magnitude could occur. But there can be no nuclear explosion unless and until a variety of sophisticated devices within the weapon have all had their parameters satisfied. For example, the devices must be initially stimulated by precisely the right amount of electrical current for precisely the proper length of time for the triggering process to begin. And that is only the first safeguard. But these safeguards must all be overcome or bypassed."

"How will you do that?"

"We'll need the cooperation of an American expert, one who helped design and construct the safeguards. Fortunately we are well on our way to obtaining the cooperation of just such an individual right now. We have identified him with the help of Henry Sakol."

The left corner of El Hakim's mouth rose slightly in a sneer. He knew Henry Sakol far too well. A former CIA agent, Sakol supplied weapons which El Hakim could obtain nowhere else, thanks to the American government, Mr. Sakol's former employer. Sakol was a ruthless and greedy man, a godless man without scruple or loyalty. "When we have the nuclear weapons, we will have no further need of Sakol."

"Truly."

"Do you intend to use him for this operation?"

"Yes, Excellency. He knows much that will be useful."

"He will betray you if given the slightest opportunity. The Americans would reward him well, perhaps even forgive his crimes."

"He'll have no opportunity. I'll see to it."

"And the weapons expert?"

"A fat fool with a very rich, very stupid wife and a fondness for small boys. He would serve the devil himself to preserve his filthy secret. I'm allowing him a quarter hour in the plan for him to alter just one weapon. But for our purposes, five or six hours must pass before the Americans are in a position to generate a military response to the incident. We need that time to escape. Then they must face the fact that we have also had sufficient time to alter the others. Of course, we don't actually have to do it. The Americans must merely be delayed until they see that we have the personnel, the equipment, and the time to accomplish the task."

Qazi searched El Hakim's face. "The beauty of these weapons is that one never has to use them. They accomplish far more by simply existing, ready for use, than they could ever accomplish by exploding."

The ruler smiled. "What course do you recommend?"

"An announcement by you to the world press immediately after the operation. This will cause alarm throughout the Western world and create confusion in Washington, where all the decisions will ultimately be made. The confusion will give us time while the Americans assess how they should react. We want a thoughtful reaction, not a knee-jerk lashing out by the American military. When they pause for thought, the Americans will realize the implications of our deed and will accept the new reality. The new reality will be that we are now a nuclear power. They will accept it! They have no alternative."

They discussed it. The dictator prided himself on his understanding of the decision-making processes of the American government and his ability to predict its policies. The Americans would be greatly embarrassed, he thought, but the critical factor would be the hysterical fear of Western European governments that a military response to his acquisition of nuclear weapons would lead to a nuclear conflict on their soil or in their backyard. After all, they would scream at the Americans, "You are four thousand miles away from El Hakim, with an ocean between you. We are *here.*" So the Americans would wring their hands and suffer the humiliation. It would be a bitter pill, but they would swallow it. Finally El Hakim sighed. "Fortunately we are smarter and more determined than the Americans, praise Allah, even if we cannot match their technology. When can we proceed?"

"That we do not know, Excellency. The *United States* is now patrolling off the coast of Lebanon. How long she will be there no one can say. As you know, the Moslem factions, with Iran's backing, will do all in their power to embarrass the Americans. And embarrassment is about all they can accomplish."

El Hakim nodded his head a thirty-second of an inch and his jaw tightened. He did not appreciate being reminded of the limited options open to a group with few political assets and still fewer military ones. He had spent too many years in that position. "We must be ready when the ship enters port, whenever that is."

"We'll be ready, Excellency. We are monitoring the commercial hotels and airports at various possible ports of call. The longer the ship is at sea, the greater the likelihood that many wives will come from America to visit their husbands when the ship enters port. Advance hotel and airline reservations will give us ample warning."

"We must not fail, Qazi. We cannot fail." El Hakim's voice was soft, yet hard, like a thin layer of sand over desert stone.

"I understand, Excellency."

"The stakes are too high to allow my genuine personal affection for you to have any bearing on my decisions."

It was Qazi's turn to clench his teeth and nod.

"Keep me advised of the state of your preparations." El Hakim rose and left the apartment, leaving the door open behind him.

5

HOW MUCH LONGER before we go into port?"

Jake was still in his flight suit and stared at the admiral, Cowboy Parker. They were seated in the admiral's stateroom on the O-3 level, immediately below the flight deck.

"I don't know." As usual, Cowboy's angular face registered no emotion. In his mid-forties, he had been identified years earlier as one of the finest young officers in the navy and had been sent to nuclear-power school after his tour as commanding officer of an A-6 squadron. He had served two years as executive officer of a nuclear-powered carrier, then as commanding officer of a fleet oiler. When he finished his tour as commanding officer of the *Nimitz,* he had been promoted to rear admiral. In spite of that, Jake thought, his ears still stuck out too much.

"We can't keep flying around the clock like this. We've just lost one plane, and if we keep it up, we're going to lose more. These men have been working like slaves."

Cowboy sighed. "I know that, Jake."

"If we can't go into port, at least let's pull off a couple hundred miles, say down south of Cyprus where we can get some sea room, and stand down at five- or ten-minute alert. It's keeping airplanes aloft around the clock that's wearing these guys down to nothing."

"Jake, I don't have that option. You know that! As soon as I get that authority, we'll go down there."

Grafton stood up and began pacing the little room. "Well, maybe we can drop our nighttime flights to just the E-2, a tanker, and a couple fighters. Maybe use the Hornets as fighters during the day and the Tomcats at night. Keep the A-6s in five-minute alert status at night, armed for bear."

"Sit down, Jake."

Jake eyed Cowboy. They had served together during the Vietnam War in an A-6 squadron aboard the *Shiloh* and had remained good friends ever since. When Cowboy had had his tour commanding an A-6 squadron in the late seventies, Jake had been his assistant maintenance officer.

"Sit down. That's an order."

Jake sat.

"This is like Vietnam, isn't it?"

Jake nodded. "Yep," he said at last. "Just another set of damn fools pulling the strings. And we're grinding people into hamburger. It's frustrating."

The telephone rang. Cowboy picked up the receiver. "Admiral Parker." He listened for a moment or two, grunted twice, then hung up.

The two men sat in silence. A plane slammed into the flight deck above their heads and the room vibrated slightly as it went to full power. Then the engines came back to idle and faded into the background noise. A minute later another one hit the deck. On the television in the corner the landing planes were depicted in a silent show filmed from a camera high on the island and one buried in the deck, aimed up the glideslope. The picture alternated between the two. The only audio was the very real sound of the planes smashing into the steel over their heads.

Jake massaged his forehead and ran his fingers straight back through what was left of his hair.

"You don't look very well," Parker said.

"Hell of a headache."

"The head quack tells me you're over a month late getting your annual flight physical."

"Yeah. He's been after me."

"Go get the physical."

"Yessir."

"What do you think went wrong with that plane tonight?"

"Don't know. My guess is a malfunction in the oxygen system, but we may never know. Depends on how much wreckage that destroyer pulls out."

"They haven't found much." Parker jerked his thumb at the phone. "Just a few pieces floating. Most of it went to the bottom."

"Did they find the bodies?" A postmortem on the bodies might reveal an oxygen malfunction.

"Nope." Cowboy searched the younger man's face. "What are you going to do now?" Jake knew he was referring to the leadership problem.

"Remember the last month of the war in Vietnam, after I was shot down? Camparelli hung a helmet in the ready room and said anyone who couldn't hack the program could throw his wings into it."

"I remember."

"I'm going to hang up a helmet."

"As I recall, no one quit."

"Yeah. That's why Camparelli did it. He was smart. I'm going to give the helmet a try, but with my luck I'll have a dozen crews quit on me."

Cowboy laughed. "Your luck will hold, Cool Hand. Keep rolling the dice." He stood up. "I better get back to flag plot." That space, a part of the combat decision center, depicted the task group's tactical situation to the admiral on computerized presentations. It was his battle station. "They get nervous if I'm gone too long. Hell, I get nervous if I'm gone over ten minutes." He paused at the door and turned back toward Jake. "If it'll make you feel better, I have a 'Nixon in '88' T-shirt I can let you steal."

"It may come to that."

Admiral Parker stuck out his hand and Jake pumped it.

When Jake entered the air wing office, Chief Harry Shipman was sitting at his desk.

"Heard we lost one."

"Yeah. Call Mister Cohen and ask him to come to the office."

"Aye aye, sir."

Jake walked between the desks and entered his office. For some reason known only to the ship's architect, he had a sink in his small office. He took three aspirin from a bottle in the desk drawer and washed them down by drinking from the sink tap. Then he soaked a washcloth in cold water, raked the papers away from the middle of the desk, sat in his chair and tilted it as he arranged his legs on the desk. He draped the wet cloth over his forehead and eyes.

He tried not to think about Jelly Dolan and Boomer Bronsky. His office was on the O-3 deck, immediately beneath the flight deck, so he could hear the sounds of aircraft being moved about his head. He tried to identify each sound.

He had just drifted off to sleep when someone knocked on the door. "Come in." He threw the washcloth in the sink. He felt better.

Lieutenant Commander William Cohen and Chief Shipman entered and sat in the two empty chairs. Cohen was the air wing aircraft maintenance officer. Shipman worked for him.

"Who went in?" Cohen asked.

"Dolan and Bronsky. They were flying my wing. I didn't see them eject, and the angel and the destroyer haven't found them. They passed out in the cockpit and the plane nosed over."

"Oxygen problem?"

"Probably, but who knows? Maybe the accident investigation will tell us." Jake removed his feet from his desk and sat upright in his chair. "How well are the squadrons maintaining the planes?" Jake asked this question looking at Cohen.

"Availability is very good. Only three planes down awaiting parts, one F-14 and two A-6s. F-18s are doing fine. That F-18 is one hell of a fine airplane to maintain." Cohen had started in the navy as an enlisted man and received his commission while a first class petty officer, Jake knew. After twenty-two years in the navy, Will Cohen knew aircraft maintenance better than he knew his children.

"Are the squadrons taking shortcuts to keep the availability up?" Jake found his cigarettes and set fire to one.

"I don't think so." Cohen draped one leg over the other and laced his fingers behind his head. "If they are, I haven't seen it."

"We're going to find out," Jake told them. "Will, I want you to check the maintenance records on every airplane on this ship. Are the squadrons missing or delaying scheduled inspections? Are they really fixing gripes or merely signing them off? Look for repeat gripes signed off as 'could not find' or 'could not duplicate.' You know what I want."

"Yessir."

"Chief, I want you to check their compliance with proper maintenance procedures. Select gripes at random and watch the troops work them off. See if the manuals are up to date and being used. Check to ensure the supervisors are supervising and the quality-control inspectors are inspecting. Check their tool inventory program."

"Aye aye, sir. Do you have a deadline on this?"

"Make progress reports from time to time. Start with the Red Rippers, then move around at random."

Cohen flicked a piece of lint from his khaki trousers. "CAG, this is gonna look like we're trying to close the barn door after the horse has shit and left."

"I don't give a fuck how it looks." Jake put his elbows on the desk. "The troops are tired and morale is low. Shortcuts and sloppy work become acceptable when you're tired. We're going to make everyone, from squadron skippers to wrench-turners, absolutely aware that the job has to be done right. We're going to reemphasize it. We're going to make sure we don't drop a plane in the future because of sloppy maintenance."

"I understand."

"I want you guys to be visible. I want everyone to know just exactly what you're up to. Let it be known that I intend to burn anyone who's slacking off."

Both men nodded.

"Finish your night's sleep, then get at it. Chief, before you go back to bed, call the squadron duty officers and tell them I want to see all the skippers here at 0800."

"Yessir." The two men rose and left the office, closing the door behind them. Jake retrieved the washcloth from the sink and rearranged his feet on the desk. In moments he was asleep.

Jake sat in one of the molded plastic chairs in the sick bay area. He watched the corpsmen in their hospital pullovers moving at their usual pace, coffee cups in one hand and a medical record or specimen in the other. They came randomly from one of the eight or ten little rooms and strolled the corridor to another. The atmosphere was hushed, unhurried, an oasis of routine and established procedure.

At last the door across from him opened and a sailor came out tucking his shirttail into his bellbottom jeans. Seconds later Lieutenant Commander Bob Hartman stuck his head out and waved at Jake.

The little room had one desk and a raised examination table. "Good afternoon, CAG. Glad you finally paid us a visit down here in the dungeon."

Jake grunted. Doctor Hartman was assigned to Jake's staff and liked to while away off-duty hours in the air wing office, yet whenever anyone suggested he look at a sore throat or toe, he told them to come to sick bay. This was his turf.

"Strip to skivvies and socks, please, and take a seat on the table." As Jake hung his khakis on a convenient hook, the doctor pored over the notes the corpsmen had made when they ran Jake through the routine tests.

At last he left his desk, arranged his stethoscope in his ears, then held it against Jake's chest. "You failed the eye examination, you know." The doctor was about thirty-five, had a moderate spare tire, and a world-class set of bushy eyebrows. When he looked at you, all you saw of him were the eyebrows. Then the nose and chin and all the rest came slowly into focus.

"Please cough." Jake hacked obediently. "Now turn and let me listen to your back." He thumped vigorously. "You need to quit smoking."

"I know."

"How much do you smoke?"

"A pack or so a day."

"Your lungs sound clear." Hartman turned to the X rays on a viewing board and studied them. "No problem there," he said finally and came back to Jake. "Stand up and drop your drawers." After the usual indignities were over and the doctor had peered into all of Jake's bodily orifices, he told him to get dressed and resumed his seat at the desk.

"Your eyes are twenty-forty," the doctor said as he scribbled. "You need glasses."

"Okay."

He flipped through the medical file. "You've gained ten pounds in the last ten years, but you're still well within the weight standards. Have you been having any headaches?"

"Occasionally."

"Probably eyestrain. The glasses will cure that." Doctor Hartman laid his pencil aside and turned in his chair to face Jake. "But you've been having some other vision problems." Jake said nothing. Hartman cleared his throat and toyed with the papers in the medical file. "Captain, I know this is going to be damn tough for you. It's tough for me. I'm sorry I have to be the one to tell you this, but your flying days are over."

"Bullshit."

"Captain, you flunked the night-vision tests. Glasses won't cure that. Nothing can. Your eyes are aging and you just don't see well enough to fly at night."

"Gimme some pills or shots."

"I can give you some vitamin A that may help. Over time." He shrugged. "Everyone's vision deteriorates as they age, but at different speeds. Yours just happens to have started faster than most people's. The nicotine you have been poisoning yourself with for twenty years may also be a factor. Sometimes it has an adverse effect on the tissues inside the eye." He found an envelope on his desk and sketched an eye. "When light stops stimulating the eye, the tissues manufacture a chemical called liquid purple, and this chemical increases the sensitivity of the rods inside the eye. In your case, either the chemical is no longer being manufactured in sufficient quantity or the rods are becoming insensitive. . . ." He droned on, his pencil in motion. Jake thought he looked like a flight instructor sketching lift and drag vectors around an airfoil.

"Listen, Doc, most people don't command air wings. I do, and I have to fly to do my job."

"Well, I'll have to send in a report. My recommendation is that you be grounded, but maybe we can get permission for you to just fly during the day."

Jake finished dressing in silence and sat in one of the molded plastic chairs. "That won't hack it," he said at last. "I have to fly at night and I'm going to continue to do so. This cruise will be over in four months and I can turn in my flight suit then. But until we get back to the States, I have to fly at night to do this job."

"They could send another officer out here to replace you."

"They could. But even if they do, he won't be here for a while, and I'm the man with the responsibility."

Hartman toyed with his pen. "Are you ordering me not to make a grounding recommendation?"

"No. I'm telling you I am going to keep flying at night and I don't give a damn what you do."

"You can't fly if I recommend you be grounded," Hartman said aggressively. "I know where I stand."

"You know all about sore throats and clap and which pills are which. But you don't know a goddamn thing about the navy. How long have you been in? Three years?"

"Three and a half. But that's beside the point."

"No. That *is* the point. I was flying navy airplanes and scaring myself silly coming aboard while you were still in junior high school. I've been riding these birdfarms for twenty years. *I* know what naval leadership is and I know my own capabilities. The navy picked me for this job because I know how to do it. And I intend to do this job the best way I know how until I'm relieved by another qualified officer."

"I'm going to send a message to BUMED."

"Before you do, I want you to talk to the admiral. You give him your opinion. I work for him."

"And you're going to keep flying?"

"Unless Parker says not to, that's precisely what I will do. You whip up some of those vitamin pills. Order the glasses and call me when they come in."

Toad Tarkington was standing by the wardroom door when Jake approached carrying a helmet bag. Toad stepped through the door and announced, "Attention on deck." The men were still rising when Jake went by Toad and said loudly, "As you were." He still couldn't get used to officers snapping to attention when he entered a room.

By the time he reached the portable podium placed on a table at one end of the room, most of the men were back in their chairs. Jake waited until everyone was settled before he spoke. It had been over three hours since he had a cigarette. He noticed that there were ashtrays on the tables and several people were stubbing butts out.

"Good evening." He looked at the eight squadron skippers sitting in the front row. "Have we got about everyone?"

"Except for the guys flying, sir."

"Fine." Jake took an envelope from his hip pocket on which he had made some notes. He looked at the sea of faces looking at him. Most of the faces were young, in their twenties. Just looking at them made him feel over the hill.

"How many of you guys are on your first cruise?" Almost a third of the men raised their hands. "Well, this is my ninth one, and I have never before been at sea for three months straight. We didn't stay out like this during that little fracas in Vietnam. Ain't peace wonderful?"

Titters.

"I'm not here tonight to give you any little patriotic pep talk. The politicians that drop in do it a whole lot better than I could."

More chuckles. The ship had recently been visited by several congressmen and a senator, and those worthies had insisted on addressing the sailors from their home states. As they told it, the sailors were the equals of Washington's troops at Valley Forge.

"A couple of guys died last night. We don't know why they died, and we may never know. But they are indeed dead, and dead forever. No one shot them out of the sky. The hazards inherent in naval aviation killed them.

"Now that doesn't mean that we are not going to try to find out why they died, or that we are not going to do everything humanly possible to prevent further accidents. We are going to do both. I had a discussion with the squadron skippers this morning, and they tell me they are going to conduct safety reviews in every squadron." Jake had ordered them to do so. "We're going to ensure these planes are being properly maintained and you guys who fly them haven't forgotten how.

"But what I can't do is give you and your sailors some time off. We're going to have to keep our noses to the grindstone. We've got to keep the planes up, to guard this task group."

A hand shot up several rows back. Jake pointed and a lieutenant he didn't recognize stood up. "Sir, we wouldn't have to keep flying around the clock if we pulled off a couple hundred miles and gave ourselves some sea room. Then we could go to an alert status. Sitting here thirty miles off the coast just cuts our reaction time to incoming threats."

"We may be thirty miles off the coast right now," Jake replied, "but just before dusk we were seven miles offshore so everyone in Lebanon could get a good look. Every wacko in Lebanon knows we're here. The orders to steam seven miles off the coast came from the National Security Council."

The lieutenant sat down and spoke from his chair. "We'll just get those fanatics stirred up."

"Maybe. What's your name?"

"Lieutenant Hartnett, sir. I just think that if we had more sea room, we would have a little more reaction time if and when Ahmad the Awful cranks up his Cessna or speedboat and comes roaring out to sink us."

"Do you think we can handle a threat like that?" Jake asked with a grin.

"We'll send him to that big oasis in the sky, sir."

"I'll sleep better knowing that."

Laughter swept the room. Jake grinned confidently, though he was well aware of the real problems involved in defending the task group. The admiral, his staff officers, and Jake had spent many hours discussing alternative courses of action in the event of a terrorist threat from Lebanon. It wasn't a laughing matter. The rules of engagement under which the American ships operated severely limited the options available. This was the main reason Admiral Parker was rarely more than twenty feet from Flag Ops.

"Seriously, we are here to make our presence felt. That's why we parade around right off the coast. Doing damn fool things because politicians tell you to goes with the uniform. And every man in this room is a volunteer. But I don't want anyone killing himself or his crewman because he kept flying past the limit of his own capabilities." He unzipped the helmet bag and took out a helmet. He held it out by the chin strap, so it hung upside down.

"I'm going to hang this thing in my office. Anyone who thinks that he has had all of this bullshit he can stand can throw his wings in it. Put a piece of tape around your wings with your name on it so I'll know who to talk to." All eyes were on the helmet. "Flying the schedule we do demands the best you can give it. I hate to see guys turn in their wings, but I like it even less when people kill themselves. Each and every one of you knows what your personal limit is. I am relying on you to call it quits before you go beyond that limit.''

He picked up the helmet bag, tucked the helmet under his arm and headed for the door.

"Attention on deck," Toad roared.

Everyone in the room snapped to attention while Jake walked out.

Up in the air wing office Jake handed the helmet to Yeoman First Class Farnsworth. "Get a coathanger," he said, "and hang this thing from the ceiling right here by the door. I want anyone who opens this door to see this helmet."

"Why?" asked Farnsworth, slightly baffled.

"It's for wings," Jake said and tossed the helmet bag on a table. "Go get a coathanger and do it now. Someone may want to use it sooner rather than later."

"Yessir." Farnsworth laid the helmet on his desk and started for the door.

"Any new messages on the classified board?" Jake asked before Farnsworth could get out the door.

"Yessir. A bunch. There's even another intelligence report about a planned raid on the ship by some group or other using an ultralight."

"Again? How many air raid warnings have we had?"

"I think about nineteen, CAG. Thank God for the CIA." Jake waved Farnsworth out the door and took the message board into his office. He thought about having a cigarette. There should be a pack in his lower right desk drawer. He remembered putting it there two or three days ago. Well, maybe it was still there. He opened the drawer and glanced inside. Just papers. He stirred them. Aha, the pack of weeds had fallen under this little report with the blue cover. Hiding there, weren't you, little fellow. Don't try to get away like that. He closed the drawer and began thumbing through the messages, trying to sort the important ones from the usual reams of computerized goo that constituted the vast bulk of the classified traffic.

He found it difficult to concentrate on the messages with that pack of cigarettes lying down there in the drawer, just waiting. Shit, how long had it been? He looked at his watch. Three hours and fifty-one minutes. No, fifty-two minutes. Almost four hours!

□ □ □

The black Mercedes rolled through the dusty streets on the edge of town as if the streets were empty, which they most certainly were not. Children and men leading laden mules and camels scurried to clear the path of the speeding vehicle with army flags on the front bumper. Dark glass prevented anyone outside the vehicle from seeing the passengers, but most of the people on the street averted their gaze once they ensured they were not in danger of being run over.

The limousine stopped momentarily at two army checkpoints on the outskirts of the city, then rolled through the open gate of an enormous stucco building.

In the courtyard two men stepped from the rear of the car. Both wore Western clothes. A waiting officer wearing a major's uniform led them through a small door and up a flight of stairs lit only by a naked bulb hanging above each landing. High, narrow windows without glass lined the lengthy corridor at the top of the stairs. Dirt from the desert lay accumulated in corners. Their footsteps echoed on the slate floor. After several turns, the major opened a door and stood aside. The two men from the Mercedes entered a well-furnished apartment. The late afternoon sun shone in the one window, a window in which glass had been installed at some time in the past but which had apparently never been washed.

"Colonel Qazi, Sakol is in the next room. Is there anything further you need?"

"Tell me about Jarvis, the weapons expert."

"Your instructions have been followed precisely. He was examined by a physician while still sedated after his journey. The physician found him in fair health with no apparent abnormalities, although seventeen kilos overweight. He has been kept naked in solitary confinement and fed precisely one thousand calories a day, with all the water he can drink. The bucket in his cell is never emptied. The light there remains on continuously. No one has spoken to him."

"Very well. Has Sakol been any trouble?"

"No trouble, sir, although he has asked several times when to expect you."

"You have guarded him well?"

52

"Of course. His guards are unobtrusive, but he cannot leave the apartment area where he is staying."

"Thank you, Major. Bring Sakol in." Qazi selected a stuffed chair and sank into it. His companion stood against the wall, a man of medium height with short, dark hair and olive skin. He wore dark blue trousers, a white shirt open at the collar, and a lightweight Italian sport coat that had lost its shape at some point in the distant past. He had a large, square jaw which he unconsciously clenched and unclenched rhythmically, making the muscles in his cheeks pulsate. His restless black eyes scanned the room, then steadied on the door through which Sakol, the ex-CIA agent, would enter.

Qazi placed a pack of American cigarettes and some matches on the table before him, then studied his fingernails.

The door opened and a bearlike man in his fifties entered. He had the broad chest and heavy arms of the serious weightlifter, but now the muscles were covered with a layer of fat that made him look even more massive. He stood at least six feet tall. "Ah, Sakol. So good to see you," Qazi said in English.

Sakol stopped three steps into the room and studied the man against the wall. "Why did you bring this son of a dog?" Sakol asked in Arabic. The expression of the man against the wall did not change.

"Sit here, Sakol." Qazi pointed to a chair beside him. The American turned the chair so he could see both Qazi and the man against the wall and sat. "You know Ali is indispensable to me. I cannot do everything myself." English again.

Sakol sniffed several times and said in Arabic, "Ah, yes, I can still smell him."

"English please," Qazi said firmly and offered the American a cigarette, which he accepted. Qazi had gone to great lengths in the past to ensure Sakol thought Ali could speak only Arabic, and he was not yet ready to drop the deception. Conspirators felt most comfortable when their secrets appeared safe.

"You have succeeded brilliantly with the Jarvis recruitment. I've had good reports."

"I took a lot of heavy risks pulling it off, Qazi, and earned every goddamn dime of the money you agreed to pay. I assume the money is where it's supposed to be?"

Qazi extracted a bankbook from his jacket pocket and passed it to Sakol, who examined the signatures carefully, then placed it in his trouser pocket without comment.

"That's a lot of money, Sakol."

"I've supplied things you could purchase nowhere else. I risked my butt doing it. I earned the fucking money."

"Indeed. Have you enough money now?"

Sakol pursed his lips momentarily. "Jarvis is a nuclear weapons expert." He smoked his cigarette while Qazi sat in silence and watched the dust swirl in the sunbeam coming through the one window.

"Your help on my next project would be worth one million dollars," Qazi said when the burning tip of Sakol's cigarette had almost reached the filter. "Half in advance."

"The agency and the Mossad are after us both. They want us dead. Ding dong dead. Blown away."

"Indeed! What did you expect? Why do you think we paid you so much money?"

"I want two million, half in advance. You Arabs always like to haggle. People eventually forget about stolen antiaircraft missiles and kidnappings, but they won't forget about anything that smells of nuclear weapons. Not ever."

"One million real American dollars in your numbered Swiss account, Sakol, and if you are very lucky, you will live to spend it."

Sakol threw back his head and laughed harshly. "You amaze me, Qazi. You could have killed me anytime, and only now you threaten me. My sheep-fucking Arab friend, you can kiss my ass. I've taken precautions."

"Ah, yes. The letters to be mailed in the event of your death. The ones you gave your sister in Chicago, which she keeps in a safe deposit box at the State Street National Bank. Box number One Five Oh Eight."

Sakol helped himself to another cigarette. He struck a match and held it to the cigarette with twisted and gnarled fingers without nails. The flame did not waver. He inhaled deeply, then blew the match out with a cloud of smoke that engulfed Qazi. "Two million. You know damn well I'm not scared of you."

"One million, one hundred thousand. Half in advance. The Americans will learn of your aid to our cause."

Henry Sakol laughed, a harsh guttural laugh that filled the room. "You really know your bastards, don't you, Qazi? That's right! I want those arrogant, snot-nosed, Ivy League pig fuckers to know I helped you screw 'em. Right in their tight little cherry asses." He slapped the bankbook on the arm of his chair, then handed it over. "What's the job?"

"Has Jarvis seen you?"

"No, he hasn't. The guys you sent to help were competent."

"Then I'll explain." Qazi talked while Sakol chain-smoked. The sunbeam coming through the one window crept up the wall and finally disappeared, leaving the room in growing darkness.

The phone rang. "Captain Grafton."

"Jake, this is the Admiral. I'm here in Flag Ops with Captain James and Doctor Hartman. Would you come over, please."

"I'll be right there, sir."

Jake gave the message board to Airman Smith to lock away and rooted in his desk drawer for his baseball cap. He needed to be covered to salute the admiral, and aboard ship everyone routinely wore ball caps. He found his and settled it on his thinning hair.

In Flag Ops, the commanding officer of the *United States,* Captain Laird James, was discussing a mechanical problem in the forward reactor with Admiral Parker when Jake arrived. Laird James was in his late forties and tall and lean, without an ounce of fat. In those few times Jake had dined with him, James had only picked at his food. His hair was shot through with gray and the skin of his face was stretched tightly around a small mouth. He never smiled, or at least he never had in Jake's presence.

The doctor was looking over the shoulders of several members of the watch team as they worked the displays on the Navy Tactical Data System (NTDS) computer. Jake stopped several steps short of the admiral's raised padded chair and waited. When Parker nodded toward Jake, he stepped over and saluted. The doctor joined them.

"Doc Hartman wants to ground you," Cowboy Parker said without preliminaries. "He says that your night vision is unacceptable."

"Yessir."

"Why don't you want to be grounded?"

"Admiral, we've got these flight crews stretched as tight as rubber bands. We're getting all the flying out of them that anyone has a right to expect. We lost one crew last night. And no matter

55

how careful we are, we may lose another. These men all know that. I can't ask them to keep flying unless I put myself on the flight schedule. It's that simple."

"How long would it take to get a new CAG out here from the States," Parker asked Captain James.

"A couple months, if we're lucky," James said gloomily.

Parker shifted in his chair several times, then stood up and stretched.

"What do you think, Doc?"

"Sir, the regulations say . . . ."

"How many times did you check Captain Grafton's eyes?"

"I didn't, sir. A first-class corpsman did."

"So you don't even know if the corpsman's result, or diagnosis, is correct?"

"Well . . ."

"Assuming the corpsman is correct, could this be a temporary condition that might clear up?"

"I suppose anything's possible, but—"

"He said that maybe nicotine is contributing to the vision loss," Jake put in quickly. "I got a bottle of vitamin pills to take. And maybe quitting smoking will help."

Parker looked at the doctor with one eyebrow raised.

"It's possible nicotine is contributing to the loss," the doctor said.

"You personally recheck Captain Grafton's eyes in two weeks," Parker said, "and let me know the results."

"Yessir."

"Can you live with that, Laird?" Captain James had been ordered aboard the *United States* while she was still under construction, so he knew every frame, every space, almost every bolt and rivet, all ninety-five thousand tons worth. He knew all the systems in the ship better than any other living human. He had no time for incompetents or fools, preferring instead to transfer those officers whom he concluded fell into one or both categories with fitness reports that ensured they were professionally doomed. His department heads scrambled to match his knowledge of their domain and lived in terror of his wrath. Jake doubted that Captain James could lead a horse to water, but as the chief administrator of a fifty-six-hundred-man institution, he was ruthless efficiency incarnate. In short, he was a perfect bastard.

"Yes, sir," Laird James said sourly. Although Jake was not under his command—indeed, under the new air wing system, James actually needed Jake's permission to fire the ship's weapons—still, it was his ship, and if Jake crashed coming aboard, James would be splattered with his share of the blame.

"Thanks, Doctor. And Laird, I'll talk to you later." Both the doctor and the CO saluted and left the space.

"Can you still see to fly at night, Jake?"

"Yessir. Not as well as I used to, but well enough. If I couldn't, I'd be the first to know."

"I'm banking on that. Just go easy on yourself. Do most of your flying in the daytime. Are you flying tonight?"

"No, sir."

"How did it go this evening with the helmet?"

"You should have seen them looking at it. They're thinking. A man or two may quit, but most of 'em will stick like glue since they've been offered an out. They wouldn't be here if they weren't stubborn as hell; they'd have washed out long ago."

"Go get a decent night's sleep."

"Thanks, Cowboy." Jake saluted and Parker returned the salute with a smile.

Jarvis was led into the room naked and blindfolded, in handcuffs, and a rope was lashed around his ample middle to hold him to the chair. A lamp had been placed on the table and shone directly in his face. Qazi and Ali stood in the shadows until the guards closed the door behind them. Sakol was not in the room.

"Welcome, Jarvis." Qazi came forward and sat in the same chair that he had occupied when Sakol was in the room. A portion of his lower legs was in the lamplight, but he knew from careful experimentation that his face was hidden. He crossed his legs and began moving his toe back and forth slightly. He nodded and Ali stepped forward and untied the blindfold. Jarvis screwed up his face in the light and narrowed his eyes to slits.

"We know your little secrets, Jarvis. All of them."

"Who are you? Where am I?" The voice was soft, hesitant, fearful.

Qazi uncrossed his legs, leaned forward and slapped him soundly. The man in the chair began to cry.

"All your little secrets, Jarvis. Each and every one of them."
Qazi slapped him again.

"Please . . ." Another slap.

"Get a grip on yourself, Jarvis, or this will go on all night."
Sniff. Sob. Sniff.

"You are here to help us, Jarvis, and you shall. If you do your
work diligently and well, you may live to return to your wife in
Texas and your Tuesday evening meetings with the woman who
supplies you with little boys. If you fail us, well . . . I need not
go into that."

Jarvis was at least sixty, with several long strands of brown hair
which he normally combed over his bald pate but which now
hung at odd angles and made him look pathetic. His jowls
quivered when he breathed.

"You won't tell my wife about . . . Will you?"

Qazi slapped him again. "You fool. Your wife is the least of your
problems." Wrong response, he thought. He changed tactics instantly. "You will do as we say, or indeed, we will tell your wife, we
will send her pictures of you and several of your little friends,
then we will pass the photographs to several newspapers. Every
man, woman, and child in Texas shall know of your perversions
and your wife's shame. Do you understand me?"

Jarvis blinked continuously and his jowls quaked as he nodded
his head.

"Answer me!"

"I understand."

"Very good." Qazi leaned back in his chair and crossed his legs
again. He sat silently for a moment as Jarvis squinted to see his
face, but finally began speaking when the prisoner began watching the foot that was in the cone of light. Qazi moved his toe
rhythmically.

"I want you to build me seven instruments, Jarvis. These instruments shall be used to bypass the safety devices in Mark 58
nuclear weapons."

"I don't . . ." The toe stopped and Jarvis ran out of steam.

"If you were going to tell me that you know nothing of these
weapons, it is well you saved your breath." Qazi got the toe in
motion again. "Your position as a design engineer at the factory
that assembles these devices is your finest credential. We did not
bring you here because you disgust us. You will build seven in-

58

struments that will bypass the safety devices in Mark 58 nuclear weapons. These instruments shall contain a source of electrical power that will energize the weapon and trigger it. One of these instruments will contain a radio receiver that allows it to be triggered from a distance. Do you understand?" The toe stopped again.

"Yes." The toe began its back and forth motion.

"Are you agreeing with me merely to avoid unpleasantness, or do you really intend to help us and spare your wife the agony we can inflict?"

"You said . . . my wife . . ."

Qazi placed both feet on the floor, leaned forward and slapped the quaking man several times. "Bring in the other man," he said to Ali in Arabic.

A cursing Sakol was dragged in by four guards and lashed to a chair. Ali removed the blindfold and slapped him into silence. He did it with vigor, Qazi noticed. The guards assumed a position at the door.

"Another man with a secret. You Americans seem to be up to your eyes in filthy little secrets."

"Please, mister," Sakol begged. "For Christ sake, let's talk about this. I didn't mean to hurt her. It was an accident—" Ali's open hand on Sakol's face made a dull smack. And another. He began to weep.

"Let me introduce William James Moffet, Jarvis. He is a technician with some experience and a taste for young women. Unfortunately for them, they rarely survive his attentions. Moffet shall assist you in assembling the instruments. Now I am going to have you taken back to your cell where you will be given food and water and a pencil and paper. After you have eaten, you will make a list of the material you will need to construct these devices. Tomorrow morning at nine o'clock you will be brought back here. I shall examine your list and question you about it. You had better have all the answers tomorrow morning, Jarvis, or your wife's humiliation shall begin before the sun sets. Do you understand me?"

"Yes."

"Yes, *sir.*"

"Yes, sir." He snuffled uncontrollably, in little gasps.

"I don't think you do, Jarvis. I don't think you do." He produced a large black-and-white photograph which he held in the light. He watched the man's eyes slowly focus. The picture was of Jarvis and a boy, about six or seven. Jarvis had the boy's penis in his mouth.

"Guards, take them to their cells."

6

THE ROAD ran south through a parched brown landscape. Heat mirages obscured the horizon in all directions. Still Qazi stared out the window at the barren earth as Ali kept the Mercedes at over a hundred and twenty kilometers per hour. They passed an occasional truck, but no other cars.

Qazi's boyhood had been spent in country like this, living with his uncle and his family. They had lived in a small village and his uncle had been a shepherd. Qazi's earliest memories were of dust storms and foul waterholes and the aroma of sheep and camels.

He had been about thirteen when his uncle's only three camels had been stolen. He had never forgotten the look of despair on the old man's face as he examined the camels' leather hobbles, severed with a knife. The family's journey across the harsh terrain, following the flock as it grazed, would be difficult without the camels, if not impossible. A third of the assets his uncle had worked a lifetime for were gone into the desert. The old man had

61

borrowed four camels from his neighbors and, together with Qazi and his two sons, had set off after the thieves.

They rode for a week across the rock and hardpan. The nights had been bitter, the sun merciless. The wind had an edge that chapped exposed skin, then opened it and scoured a bleeding sore. The wind had wiped out the tracks of the fleeing thieves by the second day. They followed the trail of dung thereafter, until it too gave out because the thieves weren't pausing to let the camels graze on thorns. Not that there were very many thorns. The desert had become a hot, empty hell, a wasteland of smouldering stone under a pitiless sun.

His uncle stared at the featureless horizon while the boys fingered their Enfields and looked helplessly about, tired and frightened and desperately weary. "The well at Wadi Hara," his uncle finally said and goaded his camel into motion. "Not the closest waterhole, which is Wadi Ghazal," his elder cousin said, "but the closest uninhabited one. The Mami live at Wadi Ghazal, and they would not steal our camels."

Never before had Qazi rode so long and drank so little. They were baked by day and frozen by night. His tongue became a lump of useless flesh and his lips bleeding sores. But day by day the excitement had increased. The thieves would be at Wadi Hara with the camels.

The men checked their Enfields every evening, and Qazi practiced aiming at rocks. How would it feel to aim at man? How would it be to hear the whine of bullets? How would it be if one struck him? Would he be able to stand the pain? Would he die? The emptiness of the desert now had a new taste, a new feel. He heard the sounds and felt the wind as he never had before. He felt . . .

An hour south of the capital, Ali slowed and turned from the main road to an unmarked track that wound across the natural contours of the land. Immediately beyond the crest of the second ridge away from the highway they encountered a roadblock. Uniformed soldiers approached the car cradling submachine guns. Ali rolled down his window to show his identification. The smoldering air filled the interior of the car.

They rolled on through the sand and rock. After another fifteen minutes a military post appeared. Ali stopped before an unpainted, rambling two-story wooden building and both men got out of the car. Qazi stretched and let the furnace heat engulf him. "It feels good, eh, Ali?"

"Personally, Colonel, I wish we had some rivers and trees and grass."

"Explain the device again." Qazi stared across the waist-high table at Jarvis, who had cut himself several times that morning when he had been allowed to shave for the first time. Pieces of toilet paper clung to the gouges in his jowls. The men stood in a large room. The only illumination was the summer sunlight coming in the three open windows. Even with the breeze it was very hot and Jarvis was sweating.

"The weapon has numerous safety devices placed in the firing circuit. Upon release from the aircraft, a jolt of 220-volt direct current ignites a pyrotechnic squib. The heat from the burning squib is converted into an electrical current that charges a lithium battery. It happens quickly. The safety devices are between the battery and the detonators."

Jarvis picked up a bundle of leads with alligator clips attached. "These attach to the battery. Basically, I have rigged up a timer, so you set these dials," he touched them, "and at the end of the set period, current will run from the battery directly to the detonators." He picked up another wire bundle with alligator clips on the end. "These attach to the detonator circuits."

"What about the weapon's safety devices?"

"Oh, they are still in the weapon, but they are bypassed. Once this thing is properly hooked up, the bomb will go nuclear at the end of the period set on the timer." He pointed to the seventh trigger. "The radio in that one will receive the signal and that will start the timer. So you could initiate the firing sequence by radio and have whatever time was set on the timer to leave the danger zone."

"We don't want this bomb to blow up in our faces while we handle it or as we hook it up. Is there any way to leave the safety devices installed and still allow the weapon to be triggered remotely?"

"No way." Jarvis shook his head and his jowls quivered. "Absolutely no way. The installed circuitry requires that you drop the bomb, let it free-fall for over ninety seconds continuously. Then the radar altimeter in the weapon is enabled, and when the weapon reaches the preset height above the earth, it detonates. There are over a dozen safety devices in all. There is no way to physically satisfy all those parameters unless the weapon is used as it is designed to be used—that is, dropped or tossed by an aircraft. So these safety devices must be bypassed. And once bypassed, there are *no* safety devices."

"And how do we ignite the pyrotechnic squib that charges the weapon's battery?"

"This thing down here." Jarvis led the way to the end of the table. "I've rigged four automobile batteries in series and used a voltage regulator and a capacitor. The juice is stored up and then fired as one brief jolt of direct current."

He paused and looked at the device. "You wire this contraption to the battery in the weapon. The timer triggers it. That's all there is to it."

"Will these things work?"

Jarvis mopped his brow with a shirttail. The bits of toilet paper looked grotesque against his pasty skin. "Yes, they'll work."

"Will they, Moffet?" Qazi asked Sakol.

"They should. Actually both these things are pretty simple."

Qazi bent down and examined the wiring and workmanship on the battery charger. Finally he straightened up. "Show me."

It took only a minute to rig the battery charger to a voltmeter. Jarvis performed the task smoothly, with no lost motion, as Qazi and Ali watched. When all was ready, Jarvis used a portable voltmeter to check the charge on the automobile batteries. Then he pushed a switch on his device. The needle on the voltmeter on the output wire swung and stopped. Qazi examined the reading.

"See, I told you it would work."

"Now the safety bypass device, please."

This instrument took several minutes to rig. All the input wires were connected directly to the battery charge device since Jarvis had no battery capable of storing the energy required in only a few milliseconds. Separate voltmeters were connected to each of the dozen output wires. Colonel Qazi dialed in one minute on the timer and watched it tick down. While it ticked, Jarvis triggered the battery charger. At the end of the minute, the voltmeters on the output wires pegged. Qazi examined each one. "Satisfactory," he said at last. "Now build me six more of each of these. Then we will test them all."

Jarvis mopped his brow again with his shirttail, which by now resembled a cleaning rag. "Listen. You have what you wanted.

Anyone can duplicate these. Moffet here is quite capable." He stopped as his lower lip began to tremble uncontrollably.

Qazi stood silent, expressionless, his hands limp by his sides. Ali moved toward a wall and Jarvis followed him with his eyes.

"Go on."

"I'm Jewish," Jarvis blurted.

Qazi slowly folded his arms. In the silence you could hear the bleats and cries of children coming through the window from the huts across the empty street.

"I don't know where you are going to get these weapons. Maybe you have them already." Jarvis took a step forward. "But for God's sake, man, don't make me a part of it. You can't."

"Get on the floor."

"What?"

"On your knees. On the floor."

Jarvis looked desperately from face to face. Sakol was staring stonily out a window, oblivious to the scene. Ali stood in the shadows with a trace of a smile just visible on his lips. Qazi's face was expressionless, without mercy or emotion of any kind.

"I will not repeat myself," Qazi said softly.

Jarvis slowly sank to his knees.

Qazi stepped forward and looked down on the man. "In this position you forfeited your rights as a man, as a Jew, as a human being. You forfeited your life. Now you will obey my orders or you will force us to smear your wife with your slime."

Jarvis was sobbing.

"You will do as you are told. You will do precisely and exactly as you are told and you will attempt no evasions or subterfuges. You will concern yourself only with performing the tasks I set for you. You have lost the right to make moral judgments on the affairs of men. You have cut yourself off from your fellow Jews and from your family. We are all that you have left."

Qazi seized Jarvis' chin and forced his head up. He stared into the watery eyes. "I'm all that you have now."

At last he removed his hand and motioned to Ali, who seized Jarvis by an arm and jerked him to his feet, then propelled him toward the door. After the door closed behind them, there were only the dusty shafts of the early afternoon sun.

Qazi bent to the devices on the table. "Nicely played, Colonel,"

Sakol said. "Your reputation for manipulating overweight sexual deviates is well deserved."

The amplified call of the muezzin came through the windows and filled the room. "Allah is most great, I testify that there is no god but Allah, I testify that Mohammed is the Prophet of Allah, come to prayer, come to success, Allah is most great, there is no god but Allah." Even here, at this army base in the desert, the call of the faithful was part and parcel of life.

The workmanship was excellent, Qazi decided finally. Each wire was of equal length, each was connected with a conservative little solder dollop, nothing sloppy or makeshift.

"But it's all an act, isn't it, Colonel? Just an act to impress Jarvis and Ali and whoever Ali whispers to. You have no intention of really using a nuclear weapon."

Sakol sensed movement behind him and turned to see that Qazi had an automatic pistol leveled at his face, a lethal little Walther PPK, Sakol noted professionally.

"El Hakim is insane, but you aren't, Qazi. You know that Israel has nuclear weapons and, if pressed too far, will use them. You know that pushing the nuclear button would remove the Arabs from the human race. You know all that, Qazi. So what's your game?"

"You talk far too much, Sakol. I understand now why the Americans left you to die in that prison in Afghanistan."

"They were playing games, too."

"Just one more word and I will finish what the Russians started."

Sakol stared at him. Finally he said, "You would. I believe you."

Qazi stepped forward and slashed the front sight of his pistol across Sakol's cheek, then quickly stepped back. As the blood dripped from Sakol's cheek onto his shirt Qazi pocketed the weapon. "You'll be returned to the cell with Jarvis. You'll ensure he performs as required."

Just then the door opened and Ali stood there, framed in the opening. Qazi issued orders to Ali in Arabic as Sakol walked toward the door.

"How do we know," Ali asked Qazi later in the corridor, "that the electrical outputs those instruments produce are the proper ones?"

"That is why we have Sakol working with Jarvis," Qazi answered offhandedly, his mind still on Sakol and the possibility he might speak frankly to the wrong people. Keeping Sakol alive was a large risk, a much larger risk than he had previously believed. Sakol's attitudes and opinions should have been anticipated. There was just no margin in the plan for errors of that magnitude. "Sakol has assured me Jarvis is giving us the correct voltages."

"Can we not verify the voltages through other sources?"

Qazi stopped on the stairs and faced Ali. The black eyes were not evasive. "That information is classified Top Secret by the Americans. One would need the actual technical data manual for the weapon. That manual is one of the most closely held American secrets."

"So we must rely on Jarvis and Sakol."

Qazi resumed his descent of the stairs. "That would be a very slender reed, indeed. No, I have a source that will supply the manual."

"I suspected as much, Colonel. And what is the source?"

"The traits that make you valuable to me, Ali, are your unquestioning faith and your discretion. Keep exercising both."

The two men stepped into the desert heat and walked across the courtyard to the waiting Mercedes, where Ali slid behind the wheel.

In the car Qazi sat in the front seat with Ali.

"Why does Sakol hate you so?"

Ali laughed. "I call him a whore, selling himself for money. I ask him to do sexual things for me. He is not amused." His face grew serious. "I think when he was a prisoner in Afghanistan, the Russians forced him to do sexual things with other men. Or the Russians did it to him. The Russians are such pigs." He made a spitting motion.

Ali was on the main road now, heading north. To the west the afternoon sun caused the dust-filled sky to glow red. Perhaps they would reach the capital before the dust storm struck. Qazi turned off the air-conditioning and rolled down his window. The heat filled the car. He took a deep breath. He, too, loved the smell of the desert, the smell of purity, the smell of nothing at all.

Along the road ahead he saw a bedouin on a camel. The mounted figure shimmered in the heat as the car approached. As the car went by Qazi saw that the rider did not even deign to give them a glance. Qazi adjusted the rearview mirror on his door and watched the receding figure until it was lost in the heat mirages rising from the stony emptiness.

HOW LONG was Columbus at sea on his first voyage to the New World?" Jake Grafton asked Yeoman First Class Farnsworth, who pushed himself back from his typewriter and thought seriously about the question.

Abandoned by his mother at the age of five, Farnsworth had spent his youth shuttling between foster homes. He had enlisted in the navy at seventeen and earned his high school equivalency diploma during his first tour of sea duty. The navy, with its routine and tradition and comfortable discipline, was the only happy home he had ever known. There were times when Farnsworth wished the captain standing in the middle of the office and gazing about distractedly had been his father. Except that Grafton was about ten years too young. Still, he had an air of quiet self-confidence that Farnsworth found most agreeable. So Farnsworth tried desperately to recall if he had ever heard how long Columbus' voyage had taken.

"Sir, I don't remember."

"Me either. How about running up to the ship's library and looking it up? Better check on Noah, too." And since he was not in the habit of giving frivolous orders, Jake added, "I need a good excuse to ask the powers that be for a day off for the troops. Maybe we could have a deck picnic when we equal Columbus' time at sea."

Farnsworth was out the door almost before Jake finished. The captain went into his office and tackled the contents of his in-basket. He was deep into the preliminary draft of an accident report, Jelly and Boomer's crash, when Will Cohen knocked and entered.

"Sit down, Will."

"Thanks, CAG. Thought I'd give you a report on the maintenance inspection."

Jake leaned back and propped his feet on the open top drawer of the desk. "How's that going?"

"We've finished both the F-14 outfits and one of the F/A-18 squadrons. Still working on the others. One of the fighter squadrons"—he named it—"has been cheating a little. They've been robbing parts from down birds to keep the others flying."

Jake knew about that dodge. You kept your aircraft available to fly by shuffling components, which increased the work load on the sailors. For every bad component that needed replacement, the mechanics had to remove two parts and install two more. The practice, known as cannibalism, increased the opportunities for a maintenance error, and it certainly didn't help morale.

"Are parts all that hard to come by?" Jake asked as he watched Cohen take out a pack of cigarettes, Pall Mall filters, and light one.

"Supply says no. But that skipper and maintenance officer are doing their damnedest to keep their availability looking as good as possible."

Jake grunted and watched Cohen look around for an ashtray. The maintenance officer settled on the trashcan and pulled it over.

"That's a lot of work for the troops for a damn small increase in availability."

"Yep," Cohen agreed. "But when everyone wants a 'walks on water' fitness report, you want the numbers as good as possible."

Jake knew all about the fitness report game, too. But this, he realized, was more complex than the natural desire of the skipper to look good. The skipper was under intense pressure to keep the maximum number of his aircraft ready to fly, and if the supply system failed to spew forth spare parts quickly enough, the temptation to cannibalize an aircraft that couldn't be readily repaired was almost irresistible. The real challenge was making the supply system work properly. Jake Grafton's primary responsibility was making the entire system—including supply—function as it should, and the effort absorbed the bulk of his time. There were moments when the sheer inertia of the bureaucracy daunted him. "I'll have a little chat with that skipper. You give me a list of the parts he's been cannibalizing. What else have you found?"

"Not a whole lot. Little screw ups here and there, but the repair work seems to be getting done properly and quickly. At times they get behind on the documentation, which is par for the course. Overall the quality of the work is excellent."

"They only have to fuck up once and somebody dies." He picked up the draft accident report and perused it again as a thin blue fog of cigarette smoke filled the small compartment. The exact cause of the accident was unknown, but the investigators opined that the probable cause was an oxygen system malfunction that the crewmen had not noticed in time. The equipment used to fill the aircraft's tank with liquid oxygen had checked out perfectly. The aircraft had flown almost a hundred hours without an oxygen system gripe. The crew was current on their low-pressure chamber training and their masks had been inspected recently. Jelly had five hours sleep in the twenty-four hours prior to the crash and Boomer had slept for six. Both men had eaten within six hours of flying, food from the wardroom that had not affected anyone else.

Jake sighed and tossed the report onto the desk. He eyed Cohen. "Gimme a cigarette."

"I thought you were trying to quit."

"I am trying, asshole. But you came in here and fumigated the joint and now I want a fucking cigarette. So gimme one."

Cohen scrutinized the captain carefully. He decided he was serious and passed one across the desk. Jake sniffed it, then placed it in his mouth. "Now a match."

"You shouldn't do this, you know."

Jake glared.

Cohen passed over his lighter. Jake lit up and exhaled slowly, through his nose. "Keep going on the inspection. And tell Chief Shipman to drop in the next time you see him. I want to hear how he's doing too."

Cohen stood up. "Yessir."

"Thanks, Will." Cohen closed the door behind him on the way out.

Jake took another drag on the cigarette. It tasted terrible and made him light-headed, yet he wanted it. He held it up and stared at the glowing red tip. I'm addicted to these fucking things, he told himself slowly. He stubbed it out on the inside of the gray metal trashcan, only to see several red coals fall on down toward the bottom, under the paper. He poured cold coffee into the can and sloshed it around.

Farnsworth opened the door, paused, and sniffed. "You've been smoking."

"Eat shit and die," Jake Grafton snarled.

The yeoman wasn't fazed. "Columbus was at sea continuously for only thirty-four days before he landed in the West Indies. His whole first voyage, including a few weeks in the Canary Islands, only took sixty-two days."

"That quick, huh? How long have we been at sea?"

"One hundred five days."

"So that's out."

"Noah might be a better bet. It's a little confusing, but it looks like he floated around for a hundred and fifty days. And lots of ships have made longer voyages, sir. Maybe ol' Noah set the record when he did it, but he wouldn't even be close now. I'll bet I could find someone who went to sea a bosun third and came home an admiral."

Down in the wastebasket half the cigarette remained unburned, though it was slightly bent. Jake pushed it off the paper wad where it rested and watched it turn brown in the coffee at the bottom of the can. "Another voyage from yesterday to the day after tomorrow," he muttered and sat back in his chair. "Forget it, Farnsworth. It was just an idea. I'll ask for the day off anyway."

"Can you imagine ol' Noah mucking out under all those animals for a hundred and fifty days? And I think I have to shovel shit around here!"

"How about seeing if you can find me a clean trashcan," Jake said, nudging the offending container with his foot.

"Sure."

"Thanks, Farnsworth."

A heavyset sailor wearing a filthy jersey that had once been yellow stood against the bulkhead outside the XO's stateroom, facing the marine sentry in dress blues. The marine, a corporal, was at parade rest, his eyes fixed on infinity. For him the sailor was beneath notice, not worth the effort to make his eyes focus. On the sailor's jersey, just barely visible amid the grease and gray pall of jet exhaust, were the words "Cat 4 P.O."

"What are you doing down here, Kowalski?"

"Uh, waiting to see the XO, CAG," the sailor said with an embarrassed little grin. He held his flight deck helmet in both hands and twisted it nervously.

Jake nodded and spoke to the marine. "Tell the XO I need a few minutes of his time."

The corporal snapped to attention, then picked up the telephone receiver on the bulkhead and waited until the executive officer in his stateroom answered it. "He'll be with you in a few moments, sir," the corporal said as he hung up the phone and resumed his parade rest stance. Jake leaned against the bulkhead beside Kowalski.

"Are you ready for Naples, Ski?" Captain James had announced an hour ago on the public address system that the ship would dock in Naples in ten days.

"Uh, yessir." Kowalski's forehead and two large circles around his eyes were spanking clean, as white as the top of the corporal's hat, but the bottom half of his face, which was unprotected by his helmet and goggles, was tanned and grimy. The grime was as nothing compared to his hands though; the grease had become permanently embedded in the crevices of his skin and no amount of scrubbing would make them clean. He reeked of jet exhaust. He was so nervous he could not hold still, so Jake gave him a reassuring smile.

The door opened and the XO, Commander Ray Reynolds, motioned to Jake, who went in and closed the door behind him. "What's the problem with Kowalski?"

The XO grinned, a ludicrous effort since his four top front teeth were missing and when he grinned, he tried to hold his upper lip down to hide the hole. The effort caused his entire face to contort, and as usual, Jake politely averted his eyes at this demonstration of Reynolds' vanity. Jake liked Reynolds immensely.

"Ski has a habit of getting drunk and getting into a bar brawl every time he goes ashore. He's an alcoholic." Grafton nodded. "And he's the best catapult captain we have. If we could just keep him aboard ship all the time, he'd do fine. I told him last time that his feet weren't going to touch dry land until the end of his enlistment, but that isn't fair. So I'm going to let him ashore in Naples. If he gets carried back to the ship one more time by the shore patrol, he's on his way to the drunk farm, and maybe out of the navy." Reynolds shrugged. "But what did you want to see me about?"

"I want to have a deck party for the crew on Saturday if we can get a day off. We will have been continuously at sea over three times longer than Christopher Columbus, and I think we ought to play it up and let the crew know they've done something big."

"I'm all for it. I think I can get Captain James to approve it. You talk to the admiral. It'll depend on whether we can pull off the coast long enough to go to alert status that day. Admiral Parker'll have to ask the big poo-bahs." He was referring to the people in Washington. "Three times longer than Columbus, huh?"

Jake nodded and Reynolds crossed his arms on the desk in front of him. He waited expectantly. He was waiting for Jake to light a cigarette. Reynolds was the driving force behind a rigid antismoking campaign that was rolling over tobacco users with the relentless power of a mountain avalanche; indeed, Reynolds was waving the banner of purity with the awesome zeal that he brought to every task. So whenever Jake visited the XO's office, he lit a cigarette and deposited the ash in a neat pile on the front edge of the desk. Reynolds' fulminations were quite gratifying.

Jake patted his pockets dramatically. Sighing, he said at last, "Oh gee, I almost forgot. I quit."

"A sinner saved! Hallelujah!" Reynolds clasped his hands together and looked up. "Thank you, Lord, for saving this poor ignorant fool sitting here before me from the evils of tobacco and impure women and bad whiskey and marked cards and . . ."

Jake couldn't help himself. He laughed. Most of the berthing compartments and working spaces aboard ship were now nonsmoking. The ship's smoke shop, where cigarettes and pipe tobacco had been sold, was now a free-weight gym. The only place aboard a man could still buy cigarettes was in the ship's store under the forward mess deck. And the wise and the weary knew its days were also numbered.

"I had to quit. They stopped carrying my brand."

Reynolds feigned surprise, his hand on his chest and his mouth in a little *o*. He leaned across the desk and lowered his voice conspiratorially. "I'm only letting them stock seven brands from now on, the least popular brands on the ship. When the smokers complain, I'm just going to look surprised and tell them it's the supply system. It'll work sort of like the no-smoking sign caper." No-smoking signs had appeared magically one night in a grab bag of spaces where smoking was traditionally allowed, and the ship's master-at-arms force had ruthlessly enforced the prohibition. Protests about the signs' legality fell on deaf ears. "The little people must be made to suffer."

Reynolds screwed his face up and giggled. In spite of himself, Jake joined in the laugh. Reynolds was one of the few men Jake had ever met who truly loved stress. Not excitement or danger, but pure fingernails-to-the-quick, heart-attack stress. He thrived on it, reveled in it, lived for it. Once Laird James had figured that out, Reynolds could do no wrong. In his mind's eye Jake could see the two of them huddled like thieves on the bridge, plotting every detail of the antismoking campaign and the subsequent disinformation cover-up to deflect the outrage of the addicted.

"One of the reasons I came down here to see the Knight of the Busted Ashtray," Jake said, "is because I'd like to send a message to Oceana." NAS Oceana was the air base where the air wing had its headquarters when the ship was not deployed. "My wife and four or five of the other wives wanted to come to Europe sometime this cruise, and I figure we'd better do it now. May not have another chance."

"No sweat. You draft up the message. I think there are six or eight officers in ship's company who want their wives to come over, too. I'll ask around and we'll put it all in the message."

"Okay." Jake stood up.

Reynolds held out his hand. As Jake passed through the open door, Reynolds roared, "Get your miserable ass in here, Ski, and tell me some more of your pathetic lies."

□ □ □

The old man had difficulty making the first step up into the bus. A young man in a dirty undershirt and smelling of wine steadied him. The old one's back was hunched and he moved slowly, carefully, with the aid of a walking stick. A woman gave him her seat. He sank down with a sigh. *"Grazie!"* His hair was gray, his face lined, and his glasses had an obvious correction. In spite of the June heat, he wore a shabby black suit and leather gloves that had been expensive when new.

As the bus wound its way through the Naples business district, Colonel Qazi ignored his fellow passengers and stared out the window, which was covered with grime. The glasses strained his eyes, so after a few minutes he closed his eyes and nodded as if drifting off to sleep. Every so often he started at a car horn or a severe lurch, glanced around with eyes blinking vacantly, then he napped again. The bus slowly made its way into the suburbs.

It had taken several hours to dye his hair gray, and two hours more to get the makeup just right. He wore cotton plugs between his cheeks and lower teeth to appear more jowly, and the upper front teeth were covered by a false cap that made them look yellow and slightly twisted.

He left the bus at an intersection of a tree-lined street. No one got off with him. He looked about in all directions, examined the fronts of the nearest houses as if unsure of where he was, and began walking slowly.

In a few moments a car stopped beside him and a middle-aged man exited from the backseat and held the door for him. He got in unaided and sat with his walking stick between his knees, both hands resting on the handle. Neither the driver nor the man in the backseat spoke.

Twenty minutes later the car turned off the two-lane country road and swept through an open iron gate. After fifty meters of gravel, a large villa appeared. The car circled the house and eased to a stop on the lawn in back. Qazi's backseat companion helped him from the car and pointed toward the garden.

A man in a white dress shirt with rolled-up sleeves was pruning leaves from tomato plants. He greeted Qazi and watched him settle into a wrought-iron chair with a padded seat.

"Buon giorno, Signor Verdi."

"Signor Pagliacci, with respect, it is indeed a pleasure," Qazi replied, keeping his voice soft and husky.

The Italian produced a large handkerchief from his hip pocket and mopped his brow. He was at least sixty, with an ample girth, though he didn't look fat. He poured two small glasses of wine, held them up and examined them against the sky. He grunted after a moment, then set one glass on the small table on Qazi's right. He, too, took a chair.

Qazi took a tiny sip of wine. It was dry and robust.

"You had a good trip?"

"*Si.* The jet airplanes are much better than the old ones. Really, it is the airports now."

Pagliacci smiled politely and drank from his glass. If he knew Qazi was thirty years younger than he looked, he had never even hinted at it in the five years Qazi had known him.

"Is he well?" the Italian asked.

Qazi knew he was referring to El Hakim. "Oh, yes. He is a bull. It is the women." Qazi chuckled dryly.

Pagliacci smiled again and used the handkerchief on his brow. He sipped his wine in silence and frowned at his tomato plants. Looking at his clothes and hands, one would think him a gardener or perhaps a captain of industry who had taken early retirement and burned his business clothes. Pagliacci was neither. He was one of the most powerful mafiosi in southern Italy, and he was very well connected in the international cocaine trade: four of his sons were in the business—two in New York, one in Colombia, and one, the eldest, here in Italy. Qazi had never met the sons, preferring to do business with the father.

"He agreed," Qazi said at last, after he had lowered the level of the wine in the glass half an inch and set the glass on the table.

"I hoped he would. You see, I have many friends, and I like to help them out as best I can. I help you because you are a friend and I help them because they are friends. Friends help each other, right?"

"It is so."

"And a man cannot have too many friends, friends he can count on in times of trouble, for favors and aid. Aah, sons and brothers, we have too few. So friends are the next best thing, friends who are as brothers and who help each other."

"I have taken the liberty of preparing a list," Qazi said and slowly felt in his jacket pocket. He passed it across.

Pagliacci held it out, almost at arm's length, and scanned it. "The uniforms will not be a problem. The vans are, of course, no problem. The helicopters . . ."

"They must be fueled and ready. Every night, all night, for the entire ten days. And I cannot guarantee their safe return."

Pagliacci reached and flipped a slug from a tomato plant. Finally he nodded, "We can do it," and looked again at the list. At last he folded it and put it in his shirt pocket. "We can help you. The telephone items"—he waved his hand to show their insignificance—"and all these other things. But the airport surveillance at both Roma and Napoli? That will take many people. They will have to be paid."

He belched and poured himself another glass of wine. "People for a month? And a safe office at both airports, with passes to get through security? These things will be expensive. It is our organization and expertise your cocaine is compensating us for, so we should not go out of pocket on your behalf." He gestured for understanding to his guest. "Do you agree?"

Qazi had expected this. The old pirate would squeeze him for every lira. "Signor Pagliacci, we value your friendship. What do you think is fair?"

"First we must know just what is it that you are planning. What are our risks?"

Qazi rested both hands on the head of his cane. They were badly palsied. Next time he must remember to half the drug dosage.

"I will be frank with you," Pagliacci said. "I will tell you my problems. You must explain carefully to El Hakim. If an . . . event . . . happens at an airport, then the authorities will place such pressure on my people that they might be compromised." He gestured again, hugely. "I must watch out for their interests."

"It will cost more?" Qazi asked disingenuously.

"Truly. I must take care of them."

"El Hakim is looking for several enemies of his regime," Qazi lied. "He is irrevocably committed to removing these people as threats to our political system. We will provide your watchers with photographs of these misguided ones. When they are found, of course they will die." The colonel needed a reasonable explanation for the equipment and services he needed from the Italian, and the best way to provide a plausible one was to expand the list of goods and services required to fit a fictitious story, the cover. This was the cover. The entire airport project was designed to keep Pagliacci's people occupied while Qazi was busy elsewhere.

"Here? In Italia?"

"Probably."

Pagliacci named a figure which both men knew from past experience was twice as much as he wanted.

They discussed it like two pensioners relating recent surgical experiences, with gusto and mock sympathy. Pagliacci came down. Qazi came up. They sipped wine and finally compromised.

Qazi was apologetic. "El Hakim expects me to haggle. You know the Arab mind."

Pagliacci was gracious. "No man likes to pay too much. And sometimes what sounds right in one place will sound too expensive in another. Do not concern yourself."

"As long as you understand." Qazi wet his lips with wine and set the glass down with finality.

"When can I tell my friends in New York to expect the first shipment?"

"It will arrive at our embassy via the diplomatic pouch the day after tomorrow. Your man should call at the embassy and ask for this man." Qazi produced another scrap of paper from a pocket and passed it over. They settled on a recognition phrase. "I am sorry we must deliver it there in the embassy, but it has become too dangerous for our man to carry it in the streets." This was an understatement. Should a diplomat accredited to the United Nations be involved in an accident, or be detained by police, and be found in possession of several kilos of cocaine, the diplomatic consequences would be catastrophic. Even El Hakim understood that.

"Getting it into the U.S. is the problem," Pagliacci said. "My friends can handle it from there." His sons, he meant.

"We will deliver two kilos of pure, uncut cocaine on the same day every other week until you have the quantity we have agreed upon. If your man does not show on the appointed day, he will be expected two days later. If he does not appear then, it will be assumed that he is never coming and all deliveries will cease."

Qazi leaned back carefully in his chair. "Money would have been easier."

Pagliacci ignored that comment. Years ago, when Qazi had first approached him for aid on another project, cocaine was the only currency which Pagliacci would discuss. The money was secondary, icing on the cake, for the local soldiers.

"But now I must go back to El Hakim and inform him that money is also required." Qazi had made this comment on other occasions. Both men knew it was pro forma.

"He will understand. I have great respect for him."

"I suggest that we pay you the money when we are ready to take delivery of the goods." Qazi was apologetic again. "It is no reflection on you or on our relationship, which is an excellent one of long standing, with mutual satisfaction, but a necessity due to my position with El Hakim."

Pagliacci nodded slowly. Qazi always insisted on this point, too.

Qazi used his cane to rise from the chair. "Signor Pagliacci, I salute you. You are a man of wisdom and discretion." He looked slowly about, at the grass, the tall palm trees, and the rows of olive trees across the back of the lawn. "It's so beautiful here. So peaceful."

"It is perfect for an old man like me. With my wife gone"—he crossed himself—"and with the children in homes of their own, I am left with the pleasures of old men. And the summer is not being kind to my tomatoes. Like all old men, I complain, eh?"

"*Arrivederci.* Until we meet again."

The two men shook hands and parted. Qazi made his way toward the waiting car without looking back.

When Jake walked into the air wing office, one of the A-6 squadron bombardiers was sitting in the chair by Farnsworth's desk. Jake tried to match the name to the face but couldn't. He was too far away to read the leather name tag on his flight suit. "What can we do for you today?"

"I need to talk to you, sir."

Farnsworth nodded toward the helmet hanging by the door. Jake tilted it and a bright piece of metal fell into his hand. Naval Flight Officer's wings. A piece of white paper with a name was taped to it. Lieutenant Reed.

"Better come into my office." Jake led the way.

When both men were seated with the door closed, Jake tossed the wings in the middle of his desk.

"Okay."

Reed swallowed several times and wet his lips with his tongue. He was about twenty-five, with short blond hair. His features were even, as if eyes, nose, lips, and chin had been carefully chosen to make an attractive set. A fine sheen of perspiration was just visible on his forehead. His name tag proclaimed he was Mad Dog Reed.

Jake pulled out his lower desk drawer and propped his feet on it. The desire for a cigarette was very strong, so he rammed both hands in his trouser pockets. "What's the deal?"

"I want to turn in my wings."

Jake grunted and stared at his toes.

"Uh, you know . . ."

"No, I don't."

"Well, you said if we got to feeling that we couldn't do our best up there, we ought to turn our wings in. That's the way I feel," he said defensively. When Grafton didn't respond he added, "I've had all of this bullshit I can stand."

"By chance, do you have a personal computer on board?"

"Yessir." Reed brightened. "I do all my paperwork on it. I've written a few programs. We can now track . . ." and he rambled on enthusiastically.

Jake wiggled his toes. Almost every junior officer these days had a computer in his stateroom. The flight program had become so competitive that one almost needed an honors engineering degree to have a chance for the limited slots available. As a result, the pilots and naval flight officers today were the cream of the college crop, brilliant youngsters with stock portfolios and spread sheets that the navy couldn't keep beyond the first tour. Over half of them turned down career-retention bonuses that approached fifty thousand dollars and left after their first tour. Rocket scientists, one admiral called them. "I see," Jake murmured.

"I submitted my letter of resignation from the navy, but it won't be effective for six months. I just don't think I should keep flying if my heart isn't in it." Reed's words were carefully enunciated, respectful but not apologetic.

Jake searched for something to say. "How'd you get that nickname, Mad Dog?"

Reed flushed. "There was a big party at Breezy Point." Breezy

Point was the name of the officers' club at NAS Norfolk. "I had too much to drink and . . . made something of a fool of myself. When the CO of the base called the squadron a few days later to complain, the skipper told him I was just a mad dog."

The A-6 skipper was John Majeska. "What does Commander Majeska say about all this?"

"Well, sir, he and I fly together and I've talked it over with him."

"And . . ."

The door opened and Farnsworth stuck his head in. "You better start suiting up now, CAG. You have a brief in ten minutes for a five-minute alert bomber. With the A-6 outfit." His eyes swiveled to Reed.

Jake stood up. "You're my bombardier tonight, Reed. See you at the brief in ten minutes."

"But, sir—"

"No fucking buts, Reed. Ten minutes. Now get out of here so I can change clothes."

When Reed was gone, Farnsworth said, "That was a good line, sir. 'No fucking buts' . . ."

"Go fly your word processor, Farnsworth."

"A very good line, sir. I may use it as the title for my memoirs, which will chronicle my lifelong crusade to promote heterosexuality."

Jake Grafton laughed and slammed the door in his face.

An hour and a half later Jake stood in Flight Deck Control and stared out the bomb-proof porthole at the flight deck. Misting rain and water trickling down the glass distorted the planes and men on the flight deck and made them look grotesque in the weak red light.

He turned and watched the aircraft handling officer, the "handler," who was seated in a raised chair, direct the spotting of the planes that were landing. As each aircraft announced its arrival on deck with a full-power bellow of its engines as the arresting gear dragged it to a halt, a sailor wearing a sound-powered telephone headset placed a cutout of the plane in the landing area of the table-sized model of the ship, which stood in front of the handler's chair. Taxiing out of the landing area, the pilot visually signaled the aircraft's maintenance status to a man on the deck, who relayed it by radio to another sailor here. This man placed a colored nut or washer on the model aircraft. The handler then announced the parking spot, which other sailors wearing radio-telephone headsets relayed to the taxi directors on the flight deck.

Four sailors wearing headsets surrounded the table and pushed the aircraft models around it in response to the observations of spotters stationed high in the island or on the hangar deck. The scale model and the cutout aircraft allowed the handler to instantly ascertain the location of every aircraft on the ship. Although he had four and a half acres of flight deck and two acres of hangar to work with, the handler fought a never-ending battle against gridlock.

Against the far wall the squadron maintenance chiefs shouted into their headsets and intercom boxes and wrote with grease pencils on a large plexiglas board that showed the maintenance status of every aircraft on the ship. Almost everyone was shouting, at someone else or into a mouthpiece, and the muffled whine of engines at idle or full power provided symphonic background. The airmen in flight gear waiting to man the alert aircraft crammed the rest of the space. Grafton turned back to the window when a sailor near him lit a cigarette.

"Okay. That's the last one," the handler finally roared over the hubbub. "You alert guys give me your weight chits and man 'em up."

Grafton passed him a printed form with his aircraft's weight computation penciled in. The launching officer would need this weight to calculate the proper setting for the catapult in the event the alert birds had to launch.

The handler glanced at the form, ensuring it was signed by the pilot, then scribbled the number in grease pencil on a status board beside him. The crews donned their helmets and waddled toward the door in pairs—it was hard to walk normally wearing forty pounds of flight gear and a tight torso harness that impinged upon your testicles.

Grafton opened the hatch to the flight deck and stepped through. He and Reed walked between two aircraft and stopped at the foul line, the right edge of the landing area. The wind and misty rain gave the air a chill, and Jake shivered. The rescue helicopter, the "angel," came out of the gloom over the fantail and settled onto the forward portion of the landing area. The crewman tumbled out the side door of the SH-3 and began installing tie-down chains as flight deck workers in blue shirts rushed in to help. In moments the chains were installed and the engines died. The rotors spun slower and slower, until finally they came to rest.

A yellow flight deck tractor towed an F-14 with wings swept aft past the helicopter and spun it around into the hook-up area of Number Three Catapult. When the blue-shirts carrying chocks and chains had it secured, the tractor was unhooked and the nose tow-bar removed. In a few moments another tractor came aft from the bow towing the A-6E that Jake and Reed were to man and parked it just short of the foul line on the port, or left, side of the landing area.

Tonight the alert aircraft consisted of the two F-14 Tomcats spotted just short of the waist catapults and two A-6 Intruders spotted clear of the landing area. Only one aircraft was aloft now in the night, an E-2C Hawkeye early-warning radar plane. This twin-engine turboprop could easily stay airborne for four hours. The radars aboard the various ships would also be probing the night, but the Hawkeye's radar, from its vantage point six miles up, had a tremendous range advantage. The information from all these radars was data-linked to the NTDS computer and displayed in the Combat Information Centers aboard every ship in the task group. In the half-light of computer-driven display screens, amid the murmur of radio speakers, the CIC watchstanders coded, analyzed, and identified every object within hundreds of miles. And if any unidentified plane appeared whose course might take it so near the task group as to constitute a possible threat, the alert fighters would be launched. If the bogey was an unidentified surface target, a ship or boat, the A-6 bombers would follow the fighters into the air.

Tonight the handler had his alert bombers spotted clear of the landing area, so he would only have to respot the two alert fighters when the time came to launch another Hawkeye and trap the returning one.

Jake Grafton began his walk-around inspection as the tractor backed up to the starboard side of the aircraft and a high-pressure air hose was attached to the plane. Another man dragged a power cable across the deck from the catwalk and plugged it into the aircraft.

Jake examined the ordnance hanging on the A-6's wing stations. A Harpoon air-to-surface missile was mounted on the right inboard wing station, station four; a pod of flares hung on the left inboard wing station, station two; and four Rockeye cluster bombs hung on each of the outboard wing stations, stations one and five. The centerline station, station three, contained a two-thousand-pound belly tank, as usual. He checked each weapon to see that it was properly mated to the rack and the fuses were correctly set.

Jake also examined the grease-penciled numbers in the black area on the port intake to ensure the plane captain had written in the proper weight of the aircraft, including fuel and ordnance. This was yet another check for the catapult officer, whose calculation of the catapult launch valve setting had to be correct or the aircraft would not get enough push from the catapult to get safely airborne.

One mistake, Jake mused, by any of the dozens of men involved in a launch, if not detected and corrected, would be fatal to the men in the cockpit. Every man had to do his job perfectly all the time, every time. The launching ballet had come to symbolize, for Jake, the essence of carrier aviation.

Satisfied at last, he mounted the ladder to the cockpit, pre-flighted his ejection seat, removed the safety pins and counted and stowed them, then maneuvered himself into the seat. The plane captain scurried up the ladder to help him strap in. Reed was busy strapping into the bombardier-navigator's seat immediately to Jake's right. Unlike most military planes where the crew sat in tandem, in the A-6 they sat side by side, although the BN's seat was several inches aft and slightly lower than the pilot's.

The pilot's hands flew around the cockpit arranging switches for the start. All the cockpit lights and dials came alive as electrical power was applied to the plane from the deck-edge cable. As the plane captain twirled his fingers and the huffer bellowed, Jake cranked the left engine. When it was at idle, 60 percent RPM, the plane captain disconnected the huffer, which supplied high-pressure air to the plane, and advanced the left engine to 75 percent. Now he started the right engine using bleed air from the left one. With both engines at idle, he turned on both of the A-6E's radios and watched Reed complete his set up of the computer and inertial. Finally he gave a thumbs-up to the flight deck bosun who stood in front of the aircraft. The bosun cupped his hand around a lip mike on his headset and informed flight deck control that the alert bomber was ready. Then the engines were shut down and the plane captain closed the canopy and snapped the pilot's boarding ladder up into the fuselage.

Now the crew relaxed. They would sit here like this for two hours until they were relieved by another crew. Unless the alert planes launched, it was all very boring, a typical military exercise in hurry up and wait.

Jake surveyed the cockpit as if it were the front seat of a familiar and treasured automobile. The A-6 had changed significantly in the years since he flew the A-version in Vietnam. The search and track radars of the A-6A had been replaced by one radar that combined both search and track functions. The rotary drum computer was gone, and in its place was a solid-state computer that rarely failed. The old Inertial Navigation System (INS) had also been replaced by a new system that was more accurate and reliable.

Above the bombardier-navigator's radar scope was a small screen much like a television screen. This instrument displayed a picture from a Forward-Looking Infrared (FLIR) camera mounted in a turret on the bottom of the fuselage, in front of the nose gear door. Also in the turret were a laser ranger designator and receiver, which the crew could use to obtain very precise range information on a target within ten nautical miles.

Jake used a rheostat to adjust the level of the cockpit lighting, then he looked around at the other airplanes and the men moving around the deck on random errands. He had difficulty distinguishing features of the other aircraft and the colors of the jerseys worn by the men on deck. He squinted. The island floodlights didn't seem to help much.

This is just an alert, he told himself. Nothing will happen. We won't launch. He breathed deeply and exhaled slowly, trying to relax.

"So why do you want to turn in your wings?" he asked Reed over the intercom system, the ICS, as he watched little droplets of rain adhere to the canopy plexiglas.

"I'm tired of night cat shots," Reed said finally. "I'm tired of drilling holes in the sky and risking my butt for nothing. I'm going back to school for an MBA, and I don't see why I should keep doing this until Uncle Sam kisses me good-bye."

The fine rain droplets on the canopy occasionally reached a critical mass and coalesced into one large drop, which slid slowly down the glass.

"After you get your degree, what are you going to do?"

"I dunno. Go to work for some company, I suppose. Make some money."

"Is that what you want? Nine to five? Same shit, different day—everyone in the office creeping toward retirement one day at a time."

"The civilians can't be as fucked up as the navy. They have to turn a profit."

Jake listened awhile to the airborne Hawkeye talking to the ship on strike frequency. Only ten days to Naples. He wondered where he would be and what he would be doing if he had left the navy after Vietnam. Should he have resigned years ago? The thought of all the time he and his wife, Callie, had spent apart depressed him. And his parents were getting on without their eldest son around to check on them. Too bad he and Callie had had no children, though, Lord knows, they had wanted them.

Maybe it's time for me to pull the plug, too, he thought. Forty-three years old, eyes crapping out, maybe it's time to go home to Callie. He thought about her, the look and feel and sound and smell of her, and he missed her badly.

"Shotgun Five Zero Two, Strike, are you up?"

Jake started. He picked up his mask from his lap and held it to his face. "Battlestar Strike, Shotgun Five Zero Two's up."

"Go secure."

"Roger." Jake threw the switches on the radio scrambler. When the synchronization tone ceased, he checked in with Strike again.

"CAG, we have been tracking a group of six boats near the Lebanese coast since dusk this evening. Apparently fishing boats. Three minutes ago one of them turned toward the task group and increased speed significantly. If he doesn't resume course in two minutes, we're going to launch you. Stand by to copy his position, over."

Jake turned toward Reed. He was still sitting there, slightly dazed. Jake keyed the ICS. "Copy the posit, Mister Reed, and put it into the computer."

Reed grabbed a pen from the kneeboard strapped to his right thigh and asked Strike for the coordinates. Without realizing he was doing it, Jake tugged his torso harness straps tighter.

"Steering to the target is good, CAG," Reed told him.

Jake read the readout on the panel. Only forty miles. The task group is too goddamn close to the coast! This guy is almost here and he just started. Wonder what kind of weapons he has? He looked at the heading indicator. The ship was steaming southwest, away from the coast. That was a help. But the ship would have to turn into the northerly wind to launch, which would stop relative motion away from the coast and the threat, which was to the east. He felt his stomach tighten.

The deck loudspeaker blared. "Launch the alert five! Launch the alert five!"

Jake heard the flight deck tractor come to life and the high-pressure air unit, the huffer, winding toward full RPM as the catapult crewmen came piling out of the catwalk and raced toward the Tomcats in the hookup areas. Kowalski was there, small and chunky, waving directions to his men. The blue-shirts broke down the tie-down chains on the chopper and the rotors engaged. He could feel the ship heel to port as it started a starboard turn into the wind.

The plane captain twirled his fingers at Jake, signaling for a start. Jake pushed the crank button and advanced the starboard throttle to idle when the engine reached 18 percent RPM. The engine lit with a low moan and the revolutions slowly climbed.

He had both engines at idle when the chopper lifted off and the two F-14s began to ease forward to the waiting catapult shuttles. The large jet-blast deflectors (JBDs), came out of the deck behind each aircraft and cocked at a sixty-degree angle.

The taxi director waved his yellow wands at Jake. He released the parking brake and goosed the throttles. The Intruder began to roll. He applied the brakes slightly to test them, felt the hesitation, then released the pedals. He pressed the nosewheel steering button on the stick and followed the taxi director's signals toward Catapult Three.

Now the engines of the fighter on Cat Three were at full power. With its new, more-powerful engines, the D-version of the Tomcat no longer needed the extra thrust of afterburner to launch. The roar reached Jake inside his cockpit, through his soundproof helmet, as the Intruder trembled from the fury of the hot exhaust gas flowing like a river over the JBD. The Tomcat's exterior lights came on. Two heartbeats later it was accelerating down the catapult as the JBD came down. In seconds the catapult officer had the fighter on Cat Four at full power, then he fired the second plane into the waiting void.

A red-shirted ordnanceman was holding up the red safety flags from the weapons for Jake to see as the yellow-shirt waved him forward toward the cat. As he taxiied, Jake used his flashlight to acknowledge the ordie, okayed the weight board being held aloft by a green-shirted cat crewman with another flashlight signal, and eased the airplane right, then left, to line it up precisely with the catapult shuttle. It looked like utter chaos, this little army of men in their different-colored jerseys surging to and fro around the moving planes, but the steps and gestures of every man were precisely choreographed, perfectly timed.

Wings spread and locked, flaps to takeoff, slats out, stabilizer shifted, trim set, parking brake off, Reed read off the items on the takeoff checklist and Jake checked each one and gave an oral response as he eased the plane toward the shuttle. He felt the jolt as the metal hold-back bar stopped the aircraft's forward progress. Then he felt another tiny jolt as the shuttle was hydraulically moved forward several inches to take all the slack from the metal-to-metal contact—"taking tension," the catapult crewmen called it.

He released the brakes and jammed both throttles full forward and wrapped his fingers around the catapult grip, a lever that would prevent an inadvertent throttle retardation on the catapult stroke.

The engines wound to full power with a rising moan. EGT, RPM, fuel flow, oil pressure, all looked good.

He flipped the external lights on and put his head back in the headrest as the plane trembled under the buffeting of the air disturbed by its engines. His eyes were on the green light in front of the launching officer's control bubble in the port catwalk. Now the light went out—the cat officer had pushed the fire button.

Oh lordy, here we go again! The Gs pressed him back into the seat and the forward edge of the angled deck rushed toward him and swept under the nose. As the G subsided he slapped the gear handle up and locked the nose at eight degrees nose up. The rate-of-climb needle rose and the altimeter began to respond. No warning lights.

Log another one.

8

SHOTGUN Five Zero Two's airborne."

"Radar contact. Your squawk One Three Zero Two. When safely airborne, your vector Zero Niner Five for surface bogey and switch to Strike."

"Squawking and switching." Reed dialed the radio channelization knob to Channel Nine, which was preset to Strike frequency. Jake checked in.

"Shotgun Five Zero Two, Vector Zero Niner Eight for surface bogey. Make an ID pass at two thousand feet and report. Avoid Lebanese three-mile limit, over."

"Wilco."

Accelerating through 180 knots indicated he raised the flaps and slats and concentrated on flying the plane as the aerodynamics changed. He leveled at 2,000 feet on course and accelerated toward 400 knots. "Get the FLIR fired up, Reed. We're gonna need it real soon." Jake secured the aircraft's exterior lights. No sense in giving anyone with an itchy trigger finger an illuminated target.

"I've got the target, CAG. Steering's good."

The infrared screen was mounted above the radar screen on the BN's side of the instrument panel, and both were concealed inside a dark, collapsible black hood that shielded the displays from extraneous light. "This mist in the air is degrading the IR, CAG. Maybe if we go lower . . ."

"Strike, Shotgun is gonna make that pass at a thousand feet."

"Roger."

Jake shoved the nose down. Only eighteen miles to go. "Are you ready, Dog?"

"Uh . . . Yeah. . . . He's a nice little target, easy to see. System's tight." Reed adjusted the presentations on the displays without removing his head from the scope hood, while Jake set the radar altimeter to give an aural warning if he descended below 800 feet.

"Have you got the ECM on?" Jake could see that the electronic countermeasures panel was still dark.

"Oh, shit. I forgot."

Reed turned it on. It would take a while to warm up. Better be safe than sorry, Grafton decided, and dropped the left wing. "Strike, Shotgun is doing a three-sixty to get set up."

"Jeeze, I'm sorry, CAG," Reed said. "I guess I got too busy." He checked all his switches again. Jake visually checked the master armament switch to ensure that it was off and examined the symbology on the Analog Display Indicator (ADI), a television-like screen mounted in the center of the panel in front of him. This instrument had replaced the Vertical Display Indicator of the A6-A and presented all the information the pilot needed to fly the plane. At the top of the presentation, compass headings moved from left to right as the aircraft turned.

As Jake rolled out of the turn back on course the ECM was on the line and gave them a visual and audible warning of an X-band radar dead ahead. Jake punched off two bundles of chaff and the warnings flickered out. "What do they have that transmits in X-band, Reed?"

"Uh . . ."

"This is for fucking keeps, kid. You have to know this shit."

Ten miles. Reed was tuning the IR screen.

They would never see the boat in the mist at this altitude with the IR, Jake decided, and lowered the nose as he advanced the throttles. He reset the radar altimeter warning for 450 feet and dropped quickly to 500, where he leveled. 480 knots. Five miles. The plane felt sluggish, no doubt because it was still full of fuel.

"The bastard will probably turn, Reed."

The bombardier dropped his gaze to the scope and reached for the cursor control. "He's turning left." Jake's steering slewed left slightly and he eased the plane left to follow.

"I see him," Reed announced. The X-band was back. More chaff. The X-band radar stayed with him.

"I don't seen any missiles."

"Nothing?"

"Well, there's something on the deck, but it's covered up with something and I can't tell what it is." Reed sounded frustrated.

Jake pulled the commit trigger on his stick grip to the first detent and instantly the usual symbology on the ADI was replaced by the infrared video.

There was the boat! They were almost on top of it, looking straight down at it. There was something under a dark cover on deck, all right, but Jake couldn't tell what. Even as he looked, the boat was changing aspect as the turret under the plane's nose swung to keep the boat in view. Now the boat appeared upside down, as if the plane were diving over it.

The radar altimeter warning sounded. The pilot's eyes flicked to the gyro. Inadvertently he had eased the nose over. He released the stick button and pulled the nose back to the artificial horizon as it replaced the IR video on the ADI.

Jake reported what they had seen to the strike controller. No doubt the admiral, Cowboy Parker, was listening to the radio conversation. He couldn't be enjoying what he was hearing. Under the rules of engagement dictated by Washington, the admiral could not use weapons except in self-defense. As currently interpreted by the Pentagon, this rule meant that U.S. ships could not open fire unless the target "demonstrated hostile intent," i.e., shot first. One was left with the frail hope that the evil in the rascals' hearts would spoil their aim, a straw that apparently gave the politicians some comfort.

"He's back on his original course," Reed reported. No doubt

the admiral was moving his destroyers and frigates forward to intercept the intruder and keep it away from the carrier.

"Shotgun Five Zero Two, Strike. We have just launched another A-6. In the interim, drop a flare on the bogey and attempt a visual ID."

Which means, Jake thought grimly, the admiral wants us to troll and see if the bastard will open fire. "Shotgun wilco."

Reed turned the safety collar on wing station two and pulled the station selector switch down. Then he set the armament panel to release one flare. Jake turned the aircraft back toward the boat. He decided to drop the flare at a thousand feet to give himself a little time to look around underneath as the flare parachuted toward the water.

A minute from the boat, he turned on the master armament switch, which put electrical power to the panel. "Let's drop the flare about five hundred yards in front of the boat," he told Reed.

"Roger." Reed's head was firmly against the scope hood as he slewed the radar cursors.

The X-band warning squawked. Jake eyed it as he continued inbound. He squeezed the commit trigger as far as it would go, authorizing the computer to release the flare. The release marker marched relentlessly down the ADI display as they approached the boat, then dropped off. The flare was gone.

A few seconds later a brilliant light illuminated aft and below them. "Strike, flare's burning," Jake reported as he dropped the nose and left wing and began a descending spiral turn.

He was below the clouds a few seconds before the flare came out. The naked white light, a million candlepower, reflected from the black sea and the ragged tendrils of dirty cloud which covered it. He saw the boat.

He contented himself with glances at the boat as he constantly rechecked his altitude and nose attitude. It would be desperately easy to fly into the water under that artificial sun, which fooled his sense of the natural order of things and gave him vertigo, the aviator's name for spatial disorientation.

"Do you see any guns, Reed," Jake asked as he concentrated on the attitude instruments and fought the temptation to roll the plane to put the flare directly overhead.

"Nope." Reed had never removed his head from the hood. He

was staring at the IR scope, using the camera's lens magnification to see much more than Jake could with the naked eye.

The flare was drifting beneath them now, which increased Jake's disorientation. He kept the plane circling and limited himself to peeks at the boat. He toggled the stick trigger and glanced at the IR display, remembering to cross-check the gyro and the other flight instruments as he did so. He was perspiring profusely. This was hairy, dangerous flying. Any mistake would be fatal.

"Strike, Shotgun," Jake said. "The surface bogey has something we can't identify on his deck. No guns visible. He's headed your way, over."

"Concur." The ship also had him on radar. "Drop another flare."

Jake put the plane in a climb while Reed reset the armament panel. Dropping flares was not going to solve the admiral's problem. If the boat had a missile and got within range of the American ship, their close-in weapons systems, the Phalanxes, would have to knock the missile down before it reached its target. These automated guns were aimed by computers and each of them fired fifty very heavy bullets a second at the incoming missile.

The Phalanxes had better work, Jake whispered to himself. He knew Cowboy Parker was at this very moment thinking the very same thing as he stared at the NTDS displays, weighed the options, and maneuvered his forces. Aircraft, ships, guns, missiles, and lives—many lives—men with moms and wives or sweethearts, men with pasts and maybe futures, all packed into these gray ships on this dark sea. And Rear Admiral Earl Parker was the officer responsible for them all. To shoot or not to shoot? Justified or unjustified? Decisions made in seconds would be weighed for weeks by men who had never made a life-or-death decision in their lives, politicians who read the newspapers and keep wetted fingers permanently aloft.

When the second flare was burning, Jake carefully descended again and circled the boat at 500 feet, about four miles away, just as he did the last time. He was far enough away that he was invisible to the men on the boat, hidden in the darkness beyond the flare's light.

The boat maintained its course toward the task force.

Jake thoughtfully fingered the wing fuel-dump switch, checked the small needle on the fuel gauge, then toggled it. He watched the gauge as three thousand pounds of wing fuel ran out into the atmosphere. He listened to Strike directing the other A-6, now airborne, to a holding fix. When the wing fuel was gone, Jake closed the dump valves. Without the wing fuel the plane would maneuver better, and there was less chance of an explosion if a flak shell went through the wing.

"You ready?" Jake asked Reed.

"For what?"

Jake turned on the exterior lights. He cranked on a four-G turn and pointed the plane's nose at the boat. The radio altimeter warning sounded. He didn't have time to reset it.

Down they came, 400 feet, 300, the throttles forward against the stops. He leveled at 250 feet, two miles from the boat. Above them shone the ghastly white light of the magnesium flare.

A string of tracers reached for the cockpit from straight ahead. "He's shooting!" Reed shouted in disbelief.

Jake rolled hard right and flipped off the lights with his left hand. He kept the nose coming up and the turn in. The tracer stream weaved, trying to correct. It was a belt-fed weapon, maybe 14.5-millimeter.

The shells reached for them, crossing just under the plane. Jake was rolling and jinking, turning hard to get away from the boat and the gun.

The gunner was shooting bursts of five or six shells. God, they were close!

Jake jammed the stick forward and they floated under negative G as the streaks crossed above the cockpit. As the end of a tracer string went by he hauled the stick aft and began a four-G pull up, toward the clouds above.

Reed was on the radio, "He's shooting." His voice had gone up an octave.

Now they were up into the clouds, which glowed from the flare underneath.

Jake kept climbing. "Well," he said to the bombardier.

"It sure as hell ain't no fishing boat."

"Battlestar Strike, Shotgun. We took some tracer fire from the bogey, which appears to be some kind of speedboat. It has no fishing gear or missiles that we could see, but it's carrying an X-band radar, which it's using occasionally. Tracers were probably fourteen point five mike mike, over. Looks like he's laying his gun with some kind of an optical night-sight, over."

"Roger. Your vector One Eight Zero degrees." Jake pulled the throttles back and soared to 3,000 feet, where he leveled and turned to southern heading.

"Do you think we'll have to bomb it?" Reed asked.

"I suspect so," Grafton replied. He didn't think the admiral had any other choice, except possibly sink it with naval gunfire. And every mile the boat closed the task group increased the missile threat to the ships.

Twenty miles south of the target Jake swung the plane around and Reed checked that the computer crosshairs, the cursors, were still on the boat. The boat was still on a westerly heading.

"What's the bogey's speed?" Jake asked.

"About nineteen knots, sir." At last, Grafton noted, Reed thought he was worth a 'sir.' "

"Shotgun Five Zero Two, Strike."

"Go ahead."

"Sink the bogey. I repeat, sink the bogey. Use Rockeye, over."

"Understand sink it with Rockeye."

"That's affirmative." Apparently the admiral didn't want to expend this million-dollar Harpoon missile Jake was carrying. A penny saved . . .

Jake set up the armament panel to train off all eight of the Rockeye canisters, two at a time. He deselected the flares on station two and selected stations one and five, where the cluster bombs hung. Each of the Rockeye canisters contained two hundred forty-six 1.7-pound bomblets. After the canister was dropped, it would open in midair and the bomblets would disperse into an oval pattern. Each bomblet contained a shaped charge that could penetrate nine inches of cold-rolled steel. Reed was watching him. The BN inadvertently keyed his ICS mike and Jake could hear his heavy breathing. He was muttering to himself, "Jeesuss, ooooh Jeesuss . . ."

"You ready?" Jake asked as the nose came around toward the target.

"Yessir."

Jake jammed the throttles to the stops and centered the steering. "Shotgun's starting the bomb run," he reported to Strike.

"He's still heading west and I'm in attack," Reed said.

"Expect him to turn as we close. Go for a radar lock. Forget the FLIR."

The X-band warning lit as they passed ten miles inbound. Jake punched chaff and held the plane steady.

The ADI on the panel in front of him was alive with computer symbology which gave him steering commands, time to go to release, drift angle, and relative position of the target. Jake concentrated on keeping the plane level and the steering centered. At five miles to go he pulled the commit trigger on the stick and held it. The weapons would be released by the computer when the aircraft arrived at the release point, that precise point in space where the computer calculated the bombs would fall upon the target given the aircraft's height, speed, and heading.

The glare from another string of tracers reflected through the clouds. The weaving yellow finger probed for the aircraft, searching like the antennae of a hungry insect, as Jake punched chaff and checked the computer steering against the glow of the rising fireballs. Dead ahead. The gunner was firing blindly, Jake decided. He concentrated on the ADI as the release symbol on the display marched down.

We'll make it! The bombs were released in a quick series of thumps, and he rolled hard right away from the rising tracers and pulled as the Rockeye canisters flashed open to disperse their bomblets.

"Weapons away," Jake told the ship.

"Roger."

In about twenty seconds the antiaircraft fire ceased abruptly. Jake eased the nose down and slid below the clouds. The pilot turned the aircraft slightly and looked back. Gleaming through the darkness was a smear of yellow light. Fire!

"Where's the coast?" Jake asked the BN.

"Twenty miles east."

The pilot checked his heading. "Get the FLIR humming. We'll turn back at eight miles and make another low pass to see what we hit."

The yellow glow of the fire was the only light visible in the dark universe under the clouds when they turned back inbound. Now a brilliant flash split the night, a fireball that grew and blossomed on the water ahead, then faded almost as suddenly as it appeared.

98

Jake turned away to avoid the debris that he knew would be in the air.

"He blew up," Reed breathed, amazement in his voice.

"Tell the ship," Jake Grafton said, and pulled the throttles back to a cruise setting.

At ten miles inbound to the ship Jake Grafton coupled the autopilot to the Automatic Carrier Landing System, the ACLS. He felt the throttles move slightly in response and kept his finger-tips lightly on top of them. Now the computer aboard the ship would tell the plane's autopilot where the plane was in relation to the glideslope and centerline, and the autopilot would fly the plane down, all the way to the deck.

Jake stared at the crosshairs display on the ADI in front of him and watched the horizontal line representing the glideslope de-scend toward the center of the display. As it reached the center the throttles moved aft and the plane transitioned to a 600-foot-per-minute rate of descent. They were exactly on speed, the angle-of-attack needle frozen in the three-o'clock position. The plane was still in clouds, yet it was rock-steady, descending nicely.

"You're on glidepath, on centerline," the approach controller said, confirming what the instruments were telling the pilot.

As far as Jake was concerned, these coupled ACLS approaches, known as Mode One, were the greatest thing to happen to naval aviation since the invention of the tailhook. He had been making these automatic approaches at night all the way to touchdown for the last month, since his night vision had begun to noticeably deteriorate. And my eyes have probably been going downhill for years, he told himself bitterly, and I just haven't noticed.

He was feeling rather pleased with himself until, at one mile from the ship, under the clouds, the crosshairs disappeared from the ADI and the autopilot dropped off the line.

The angle-of-attack needle rose slightly, so Jake added a smidgen of power and stared into the darkness for the meatball and the deck centerline lights. They were very dim and far away.

He had to see the meatball, the yellow light between the two green reference, or datum, lights of the optical landing system. This visual aid defined the proper glideslope. And he had to see the landing area centerline lights and the red drop lights extending vertically down the fantail of the ship. These lights gave him his proper lineup. "Oh fuck!"

"Three-quarters of a mile. Call the ball."

Reed made the call. "Five Zero Two, Intruder ball, five point zero."

"How'm I doing?" Jake asked the BN.

"You're high."

Jake made the correction. The lights were still too dim. He fought the controls.

When he glanced away from the angle-of-attack indexer lights on the cockpit glare-shield, he had trouble focusing on the meatball on the left side of the landing area. Then when he looked back at the indexer, it was fuzzy unless he stared at it. So he missed the twitching of the meatball as he approached the ship's ramp, and by the time he saw movement, the ball had shot off the top of the lens system and he touched down too far down the deck to catch a wire. The Intruder's wheels hit and he slammed on the power and continued on off the angle as the landing signal officer, the LSO, shouted "Bolter Bolter Bolter," over the radio.

The next pass was better, but he boltered again. He couldn't adequately compensate for the twitches of the ball when he just didn't see them.

He caught the four wire on his third approach, mainly because he assumed he was high and reduced power hoping it was so.

They debriefed in the Strike Operations office, surrounded by Air Intelligence officers, the strike ops staff, and a half-dozen senior officers from the A-6 squadron. The crowd was happy, laughing. They had met the enemy and "taught 'em not to fuck with the U.S. Navy," in Reed's words. Reed was the happiest of the lot. Jake Grafton sat in a chair and watched Reed explain every detail of the bomb run to the A-6 skipper, John Majeska, whom his peers knew as "Bull."

"That tracer was so bright you could read a newspaper in the cockpit," Reed proclaimed. "And the CAG didn't even blink. Man, that system was humming! Those fucking A-rabs had better stay perched on their camel humps or they're all going to sleep with Davy Jones."

When Bull Majeska turned to Grafton and asked quietly how

Reed had really performed, Jake smiled and winked. "He did okay. Let him crow. They were trying to kill him."

One of the strike ops assistants answered the ringing phone. "CAG, the admiral wants to see you in his stateroom when you're finished here."

"Thanks." Jake gathered his helmet bag and shook Reed's hand.

"Uh, sir," Reed said softly. "About that subject we were discussing earlier. Uh, maybe I could come see you tomorrow?"

"Sure, Mad Dog."

As Jake went out the door the crowd was rigging up the video-tape monitor to watch the tape from the aircraft that recorded the radar and IR displays, the computer readouts, and the cockpit conversations. Maybe they could learn more about the sunken boat.

"So how did it go?" Cowboy Parker asked. The two men were in the admiral's cabin. Jake sat beside the desk watching Parker shave at the little sink.

"They must have been packing a boatload of explosives. It was one big blast. Either the Rockeyes or the fire set the stuff off, or they blew it up themselves. They were on a suicide mission." Jake took a deep breath. "Good thing for us that someone got trigger-happy."

"That lot would have been pretty spectacular going off against the side of a ship." Parker rinsed his razor and attacked his chin. He eyed Jake in the mirror. "Damn good thing for us that some-one got shook when you turned on your lights and headed right at them."

"Hmmm. Even I was surprised when I did that." Jake chewed on a fingernail. "We don't have any evidence except our word that it was a terrorist boat. They may announce that the U.S. Navy just offed some poor fishermen, all good Moslems on a sailing pil-grimage to Mecca by way of Gibraltar and the Cape of Good Hope. And if those guys had succeeded in damaging an American ship, well . . ."

"You boltered twice tonight." Cowboy was examining his face in the mirror, trying to find if he'd missed a spot.

"Yeah. I couldn't see jack." Jake stared at his toes.

"Mode One didn't work, huh?"

"Quit on me at a mile." Jake sighed. "I'm going to ground myself at night and send a message asking to be relieved. The good part is that this little incident will improve morale on this tub. Everyone can see what we're up against and they'll keep their noses firmly on the grindstone."

"Quitting smoking hasn't helped the eyes?"

"Not that I can tell."

"A tough way to end a flying career." Cowboy rinsed his face and dried it on a towel.

"Cowboy, if I didn't ground myself, you'd ground me. I know you. You're yuks and giggles and Texas corn off duty, but you can slice the raw meat when you have to, whether it's living or dead."

Parker snorted and sat down at his desk. "I wish you were writing my fitness report."

Jake rubbed his chin. Over eighteen hours had passed since he had shaved and his face felt like sandpaper. "Those Arabs. Suicides earning their way to Allah's big tent in the sky. Damn, that's scary. What would you have done if he hadn't started shooting?"

Parker stroked his forehead with an index finger. "I'm not going to take a missile hit before I open fire. I don't give a damn what Washington thinks or how it reads in the newspapers. Every ship in the force was at general quarters tonight. Every gun was ready to fire. The battlewagon was ready with sixteen-inchers and Harpoons. If one of these boats uses a radar on the proper frequency, points its nose at a ship and holds that heading to stabilize the gyros in a missile, I'm going to blow him out of the water. Right then and there."

"The next guy won't panic and start shooting," Jake said. "They learn real fast."

"We never suck it up and go after these guys. For the life of me, I can't see why it's better to drop bombs from an airplane or shells from a ship's gun than it is to just hunt the terrorists down and execute them on the spot. Our response to hijackings and murder is to merely send some more ships over here to wave the flag. And salt a bomb around every now and then."

"Where is all this going, Cowboy?"

The admiral scowled and his right hand became a fist. "Israel wants us in bed with them. The terrorists are trying to push us there. The Soviets are hoping to catch us there. Iran claims that's where we've been all along." His hand slowly opened. "It's Vietnam all over again, Jake. Our politicians have gotten sucked into taking sides, so our diplomatic options have evaporated. Now the only American card left is the military one, and sooner or later Washington is going to play it. Just as sure as shootin'. " The hand was a fist again, rapping on the desk. "And the politicians aren't going to do any better here than they did in Vietnam. Those people never learn."

Jake Grafton's shoulders rose a half inch, then subsided. "Everybody but us will have God on his side. And we'll be in the middle."

"If only we *were* in the middle," the admiral mused, drumming his fingertips on the tabletop. "And everyone knew it."

Jake stood and stretched. "Thanks for giving me the chance to ground myself."

The admiral's lips curved into a hint of a smile. "I know you, Jake."

9

THIRTY SECONDS after Colonel Qazi stepped onto the sidewalk in front of the terminal at Leonardo da Vinci Airport with his jacket hanging over his shoulder and his tie loosened, a sedan slid to a halt near the curb. He tossed his valise on the backseat and climbed in. The woman driving had the car moving in seconds.

"How was your trip?" she asked as she deftly worked the vehicle through the gears. Her hair was cut in a style common in Europe this year, medium length and swept toward one side. She was wearing a modest, medium-priced tan dress and casual shoes.

Qazi scanned the back window. "I was recognized at the airport." He checked the road ahead. "Drive on into Rome."

The driver glanced at her rearview mirror. "How do you know you were recognized?"

"I saw it in his eyes. It was the gate attendant, as all the passengers filed past him." He sighed. "Ah, Noora. I'm too well known. It's time for me to retire."

Noora concentrated on her driving, checking the mirror regularly. The daughter of a rich Arab carpet merchant, she had grown up in Paris. She had studied dance seriously, and chucked it all after the allowance from her father dried up when her affair with a fellow female student became common knowledge in the Arab expatriate community.

She was belly dancing in a cabaret in Montmartre when Qazi recruited her. He had had misgivings then, and they still nagged at him occasionally. She was physically attractive, though not too much so, and she meshed into her surroundings anywhere in Europe, but try as he might, he could not break her of her distinctive heel-and-toe dancer's walk, the smooth, muscular flow of which made her stick in an observer's memory. While high heels helped her gait, they also emphasized the molded perfection of her legs. He used her sparingly, only when he had to.

"Your pistol and passports are in the glove compartment." The weapon and passports had come into Italy in the diplomatic pouch and Noora had picked them up at the embassy.

Qazi removed the Walther PPK from its ankle holster and checked the magazine and the chamber. It was loaded. He pulled up his right trouser leg and strapped the holster on. The silencer went into a trouser pocket. Then he carefully scrutinized both the passports, especially the photographs.

One passport was British, for Arnold MacPhee, age forty-one, six feet tall, residing Hillingdon, Middlesex. Inside was an international driver's license and a membership in the British Automobile Association. The other passport was for an American, occupation priest, one Harold Strong of Schenectady, New York. This passport contained a New York driver's license and a medical insurance card from a large American firm. The passports were genuine. They had been stolen, of course, and all the pages were genuine except for the pages that contained the physical description of the bearer and the photograph. The paper for the new pages had been stolen from the manufacturers who supplied the very same paper to the governments involved. No cheap forgeries, these; they had been manufactured in the state passport office by men who had spent their adult lives printing genuine passports.

The documents contained in the passports were forgeries, but good ones. They would pass the scrutiny of immigration officials whose expertise was passports.

Qazi slipped the documents into his jacket pocket and sat back in the seat. He adjusted one of the air conditioning vents to blow the air on him. The heat here was less oppressive than in North Africa, but the air-conditioning of the airplane had lowered his tolerance. "Where will Yasim meet us?"

"The parking garage under the Villa Borghese."

They came into Rome on the main thoroughfare from the airport, which was on the coast, near the mouth of the Tiber. The hills around Rome were partially obscured by thick haze. A typical September day in Italy, Qazi thought.

Soon the car was embedded in heavy traffic—buses, trucks, automobiles, and motor scooters. The exhaust fumes pumped through the car's air conditioning system made his eyes sting. They passed the Circus Maximus and circled the Coliseum, then weaved through boulevards until they were on the Via Veneto. Ahead, the tall umbrella pines and huge oaks punctuated the open expanse of the Villa Borghese, the Central Park of Rome.

"I don't think we are being followed by a solo vehicle," Noora said.

Qazi said nothing. With enough vehicles and two-way radio communications, a surveillance team would be almost impossible to detect. One never knew if the airport watchers had enough time to alert such a team. The only safe course was to always assume the surveillance team was there, undetected and watching.

Immediately after crossing the Piazzale Brasile, Noora slipped the car into the lane that led down to the entrance to the underground parking garage under this section of the Villa Borghese. On the second level down, near the back of the garage, Noora slowly crept by a parked limo. A uniformed chauffeur was dusting the vehicle. He wore a cap and did not look up from his task. Noora continued on, apparently hunting for a parking place. She descended to the third level of the garage, drove up and down the rows, and returned in about five minutes to the second level. This time the chauffeur's cap was on the fender. No one was in sight. Noora stopped as the limo backed out of its parking slot and the trunk sprung open.

Qazi leaped from the sedan and tossed his valise into the open trunk. Noora threaded the sedan into the vacant parking space.

Then Qazi and the girl laid down in the trunk and the chauffeur slammed the lid closed. The transfer had taken forty-five seconds.

The trunk was dark and their positions were cramped, although they were lying on a blanket. Qazi and Noora tried to ease themselves into comfortable positions as the vehicle swayed and bounced. The safe house was only three miles away, but the circuitous route the driver would take would stretch the ride to almost an hour.

"Welcome to Rome, Colonel," Noora whispered as he helped her unfasten the buttons on her dress. She wore nothing under it. As she fumbled with his trousers, Qazi tried to decide if wearing a bra would make Noora more or less noticeable in a major European city. He lost his train of thought when her lips found his.

The man in the gray wool suit cut in the English style paused briefly in the door of St. Peter's and quickly scanned the tourists, then stepped to his right and let the people behind him enter. He moved further right and scrutinized each person coming in while he pretended to consult a guidebook. Finally the book went into his pocket. He stood with his left arm folded across his chest, his right hand on his chin, raptly examining the architectural features of the great basilica as if seeing them for the first time. On his right, near the *Pietà,* he saw a man in a rumpled black suit, with close-cropped hair and fleshy lips. This man was also engrossed in a guidebook.

After another minute of wondrous contemplation, the man near the door crossed to the left side of the basilica and strolled slowly toward the high altar. He circled it completely, appearing to examine Bernini's bronze baldachin from every angle, his restless eyes actually scanning faces and the niches and cornices above where conceivably a man might observe the crowd.

The crowd was thin today, perhaps owing to the summer heat outside. Colonel Qazi checked his watch as he consulted his guidebook again. With the book closed in his left hand, he walked slowly back toward the main entrance, his eyes moving, his pace slow and even.

The man in the black suit with the fleshy face was still near the *Pietà,* yet he was well behind and away from anyone using a camera to photograph the sculpture. Qazi paused near him and opened the guidebook.

"I see we are using the same book," the man said in English.

"Quite so," Qazi replied. "Most informative."

"Thorough, although there are not enough illustrations." He had a slight accent, hard to place.

"Yes." Qazi placed his book in his pocket and walked toward the nearest door.

Crossing St. Peter's Square, the man in the black suit was fifty feet behind. Qazi paused at the colonnades on the north side of the square until the man joined him. Then he turned and proceeded north through the colonnades, the other man at his side.

"Where are we going?"

"You will know when we get there. What should I call you?"

"Chekhov."

"Someone in the GRU has a sense of humor. This shatters my preconceptions. One hopes the rot has not spread too far. As it happens, I am called Solzhenitsyn. You are perspiring, Chekhov."

"It is very warm."

"They should let you leave Moscow more often," Qazi said as he glanced over his shoulder. "And how have you found the Roman women?"

The Russian did not deign to reply. In a few minutes they reached the entrance to the Vatican Museum and Qazi paid the admission fee with lire for both of them. Once inside he paused where he could watch the door and consulted his guidebook. The Russian looked about dourly and stepped across the room, where he became absorbed in a dark medieval painting with little to recommend it.

Finally Qazi replaced the book in his pocket and wandered away, the Russian a few paces behind. After five minutes of this he entered a men's room. Qazi stood beside a heavy Italian at the urinals while Chekhov used a stall. When the Italian departed, the door to the stall opened and the Russian exited to find Qazi pointing an automatic pistol with a silencer screwed into the barrel.

"Very slowly, Chekhov, lean against the door. We don't need any visitors." The Soviet's face reddened and he started to speak. Qazi silenced him with a finger. "Do it, or this will be a very short meeting." Chekhov slowly placed both hands against the door. "Feet wider apart. That's right. Like in the American movies." Satisfied, Qazi patted the man down. "What, no gun? A GRU man

108

without a gun . . ." Qazi carefully felt the man's crotch and the arms above the wrists. "First humor and now this! The GRU will become a laughingstock. But of course there is a microphone."

Qazi lifted all the pens from the Russian's shirt pocket and examined them, one by one. "It had better be here, Chekhov, or you will have to part with your buttons and your shoes." It was in the third pen. "Now turn around and sit against the door."

The Russian's face was covered with perspiration, his fleshy lips twisted in a sneer. "The shoes."

Qazi examined them carefully and tossed them back. "Now the coat."

This he scrutinized minutely. From the uppermost of the large three buttons on the front of the coat a very fine wire was just visible buried amid the thread that held the button on. Qazi sawed the button free with a small pocketknife, then dropped the pen and button down a commode. He tossed the coat back to Chekhov. "And the belt."

After a quick glance, Qazi handed it back. "Hurry, we have much to say to each other." He unscrewed the silencer and replaced the pistol in his ankle holster. He opened the door as the Russian scrambled awkwardly to his feet.

An hour later the two men were seated in the Sistine Chapel against the back wall, facing the altar and Michelangelo's masterpiece *The Last Judgment* behind it. On the right the high windows admitted a subdued light. Qazi kept his eyes on the tourists examining the paintings on the ceiling and walls.

"Is it in Rome, as General Simonov promised?"

"Yes. But you must tell us why you want it."

"Is it genuine, or is it a masterpiece from an Aquarium print shop?" The Aquarium was the nickname for GRU headquarters in Moscow.

The Russian's lips curled, revealing yellow, impacted teeth. This was his smile. "We obtained it from Warrant Officer Walker."

"Ah, those Americans! One wonders just how long they knew about Walker's activities."

The Russian raised his shoulders and lowered them. "Why do you want the document?"

"El Hakim has not authorized me to reveal his reasons. Not that we don't trust you. We value the goodwill of the Soviet Union most highly. And we intend to continue to cultivate that goodwill.

109

But to reveal what you do not need to know is to take the risk that the Americans will learn of our plans through their activities against you."

"If you are implying they have penetrated—"

"Chekhov, I am not implying anything. I am merely weighing risks. And I am being very forthright with you. No subterfuge. No evasion. Just the plain truth. Surely a professional like you can appreciate that?"

"This document is very valuable."

"Perhaps. If it is genuine, it certainly has some potential value to El Hakim or we would not desire to obtain it. If it is genuine, El Hakim will no doubt be grateful in proportion to the value it ultimately has for us. If it is not genuine, the Americans have made very great fools of you. And of us, if we do not factor in that possibility."

The Russian slid his tongue out and moistened his lips. "El Hakim has yet to approve the treaty granting the Soviet Navy port facilities. Anchoring privileges are very nice, but we need the warehouses and dock space provided for in the treaty."

"Your masters should reconsider their position. A strong, united Arab people friendly to the Soviet Union and hostile to American imperialism would certainly fulfill many of the Soviet Union's long-range diplomatic objectives. Yet, you ask for the politically impossible now as your price to assist in a great effort which will benefit you in incalculable ways."

"If it succeeds."

"First you must plant the potatoes, Anton."

The Russian sneered. "We have it and you want it. The treaty must first be approved."

Qazi stared into the Russian's eyes. Then the Russian felt a sharp pain on the inside of his thigh. He looked down and saw the knife, ready to open an artery. "Your belt," Qazi said.

"What?"

"Take off your belt and give it to me."

Chekhov complied slowly, his eyes reflecting dismay. Qazi knelt as if to pray with the buckle a few inches from his lips. His eyes swept the chapel. "General Simonov, I would like to take delivery of the manual for the Mark 58 device tomorrow. I shall call the public telephone on the north side of Piazza Campo dei

110

Fiori at ten o'clock. Please follow the directions you are given and come alone."

Qazi laid the belt in Chekhov's lap. The Russian watched him join a group of American students and leave the chapel. Chekhov slowly worked the belt with the transmitter in the buckle through the loops in his trousers as he wondered what General Simonov was going to say.

Qazi sat on a bench watching the lovers and office workers eating lunch near the lake. Through the trees he could see the Galleria Borghese and traffic in the Piazza le Brasile. This great green park in which he sat, the Villa Borghese, was one of his favorite places in Rome. The magnificent pines and oaks, the strolling lovers, and the squealing children seemed to him to epitomize the best of European civilization.

He sat on a bench under the trees. This walking area was covered with a mixture of dirt and pea gravel. When someone walked through a shaft of sunlight, he could see the little dust clouds rising every time a foot came down. Beyond the walkway there was grass, but it was spotty; the city didn't water the grass and it suffered from the heat and too much traffic.

He wondered idly what his uncle would have said if he could have spent a few hours here watching the ducks upon the limpid blue water and feeling the soft breeze as it eased the effect of the heat and rustled the tree leaves.

Waterholes in the desert are always brown, and the sheep and camels wade in and urinate and stir the tepid mixture until it resembles thin mortar. Then in a few days, three at most, the water is gone, leaving only brown mud cracking and baking in the sun. Then one must dig, dig, dig, and haul the water from the well with skin bags. Could the old man have even fathomed wealth like this?

His uncle had insisted he join the army. Even though the old man had read only the Koran, had seen only that one book in his entire life, he sent Qazi to the city to join the army, the boy who loved the desert and the eternal wind and the free, wild life.

They had lain in the sand and stared into the blackness toward the waterhole. He heard only the wind and the whisper of sand moving across stone. But his uncle had announced, "They are there," and told him to go

111

around the wadi onto the escarpment, where the old man said he would be able to look down into the waterhole when the light returned. He could still remember leading the camel through the darkness, stumbling over stones while the animal strained against the leash, smelling the water, grunting against the rag tied around her muzzle. After an hour he saw the looming bulk of the escarpment on his right, darker than the surrounding night. It had taken hours to feel his way up leading the reluctant animal. Once on top, he tied the camel securely to a stone and waited for her to lie down. He snuggled against her side, his rifle in his hands, exhausted, yet too excited to sleep. The stars wheeled in the sky above him and the wind sighed restlessly.

He had spent countless nights watching the stars and listening to the wind. He had tried to count them once, spent all night on just one segment of sky, numbering faithfully as the stars wheeled above him, on a night so black the stars were just beyond reach in the clear desert air. With his back against the earth there were only the stars and he was one with them, alone and yet not alone, a part of the undying universe. He had finally given up the counting. There were too many stars, flung like grains of sand against the eternal void.

Tonight he glanced at the heavens, but his thoughts were on the darkness around him. He gripped the rifle and rubbed the smooth metal, the blueing long worn off, and the scarred wood of the stock. He fingered the notch of the rear sight and the bolt handle and the trigger. His uncle had told him not to chamber a cartridge until daylight, and he obeyed. Yet the cartridges were in the magazine; all that remained was the opening and closing of the bolt. He caressed the rifle and knew its power, its tension, as he waited impatiently for the stars to complete their nightly orbit. The tension and the fear and the anticipation . . . of what he knew not, gave life a pungency that he had never known existed. At this time, in this desolate wilderness beneath the eternal stars, here and now he was alive.

A thick figure emerged from the back of the limousine in the Piazza le Brasile and set off alone down the sidewalk toward the entrance to the mall under the Villa Borghese, which also contained the parking garage where Qazi had changed cars on his arrival in Rome two days before. The man carried an attaché case.

Qazi checked his watch, then scanned the park in every direction. The lovers on the blanket near the lake had been there since he arrived and were sharing wine. A woman was walking her dog. Most of the office workers had finished their lunches and were leaving the area. Fifty feet away a middle-aged woman sat on a bench and watched two small children play in the dirt with plastic automobiles.

Qazi watched the traffic in the piazza to see if any more vehicles were going to stop to discharge passengers. None did. After five minutes he arose and began strolling slowly toward the upper mall entrance, his hands in his pockets, checking everyone in sight. He was perspiring, perhaps because he was wearing three shirts in this heat. On the sidewalk he stopped at a mobile ice cream stand and paid fifteen hundred lire for a cone, which he licked as he stood in the shade watching the pedestrians and the traffic. The ice cream melted faster than he could eat it. It dripped on his fingers. When he finished the cone, he returned to the stand and used one of their napkins to wipe his fingers and mouth.

Waist-high circular concrete walls sat amid the grass and trees on the other side of the street. Beyond these walls, which looked like the ends of huge concrete pipes set vertically into the earth, he could see the track and stables where wealthy Roman girls learned to ride. That area was known as the Galoppatoio. Qazi knew the concrete walls encircled shafts that opened on the underground mall and admitted air and light. Several of the shafts had stairs to the mall below. He noted that there was no one standing near the shafts. Without benches to sit on, that area of the park had only a few strollers.

Satisfied at last, he went down the stairs from the sidewalk into the mall.

The man from the limousine was standing on the side of the corridor directly across from an office of the Bank of Rome. He wore an ill-fitting suit and his tie was pulled away from his throat, his shirt collar open. When Qazi was near, he could see why the suit did not fit. The man's shoulders and chest were massive, rising from a too-small waist. He was about sixty, with a tanned head that made his cropped gray hair almost invisible.

"*Buon giorno*, General," Qazi said.

"Aleksandr Isayevich, huh? A priest today." He was looking at Qazi's clerical collar, black short-sleeved shirt, and trousers.

"When in Rome . . ."

"Your man ran me all over the city."

"He enjoys his job."

"So what do you and that fanatic fool, El Hakim, plan to do with

113

this?" the general asked, nodding toward the attaché case near his feet. His Russian accent was muted but detectable.

"I thought I might read it."

"You picked a nice place for this little meet. As I recall there are at least eight nearby exits from this rabbit hole."

"Eight or nine."

General Simonov removed a packet of American cigarettes from his pocket and lit one. He inhaled deeply and blew the smoke out through his nose. "The Israelis want you very badly. They did not enjoy reading about their underground weapons facility in the press."

People were walking by. A young man with a backpack walked through the double glass doors from the main entryway and stood behind a gray matron using the automatic teller. To the right, through the floor-to-ceiling windows and across the air-shaft, Qazi could see the entrance to the parking garage and, beyond that, the entrance to the pedestrian tunnel that led to the subway station and on to the Piazza di Spagna.

"And you?"

"I'll admit, that was one of your better shows. A triumph."

"Thank you."

"The CIA is also very unhappy about the disappearance of one Samuel Jarvis, weapons engineer. Should I tell them to see you for the particulars?"

"Come come, General. You didn't drive all over Rome on this warm summer's day to have an idle chat."

The general's eyes were as gray as Moscow in winter. "What are you up to, Qazi? Why did you want the manual delivered in Rome?"

Qazi had thought long and hard about the wisdom of seeking the Soviets' help. He had not discussed it with El Hakim because if the ruler had approved, the manual would have been delivered in the capital by a Soviet diplomat. General Simonov was no-body's fool. He would have several working hypotheses to explain the delivery in Rome, one of which would be very close to the truth.

"I needed a short holiday on the expense account, old boy," Qazi replied lightly.

Simonov's fingers flipped rhythmically at the cigarette filter. He glanced at a man in a dark business suit who had joined the line to use the money-dispensing machine. "No doubt that's why you just spent three days in Naples, Qazi. Ah, and you thought I wouldn't know about that. We have many, many friends in Italy. Old boy."

No doubt, thought Qazi bitterly as he once again scanned the area. Naples has a communist city government. Every garbageman and street sweeper is probably on the GRU payroll. And that is where the Americans anchor their aircraft carriers! "It must be pleasant to have a post that takes you to the sunny climes for a change."

"What do you intend to do with a nuclear weapon?"

Qazi glanced at Simonov. "We do not have a nuclear weapon, but if we did, its employment would be strictly our business."

"That is what El Hakim told our ambassador this morning." The general dropped the cigarette on the floor and ground it out with his shoe. "Moscow would be very unhappy if any such device were used in a way that conflicted with Soviet interests in the Mediterranean." He extracted another cigarette from his shirt pocket and flicked a lighter. The youth with the backpack was punching the buttons of the automatic teller machine. He wore jeans and running shoes and had unruly, short black hair. "We're concerned about El Hakim's activities. It would be a great mistake to think otherwise. A very great mistake."

The teller machine rejected the young man's card. He slapped the machine, then fed the card in again and pushed buttons. "I think El Hakim is aware of your position," Qazi said, "but I'll tell him you voiced it, again. But I didn't know the Kremlin used you to deliver diplomatic notes to third-world fanatics, General. I thought they had better uses for you."

The man in the suit behind the youth at the machine was looking around impatiently. The machine had rejected the youngster's card for the third time.

"Your El Hakim has spent too many nights dressed up in women's clothing. Tell him *I* said that."

The backpack was now under the young man's left armpit. His head moved slightly. Qazi realized he was looking at the reflections in the shiny metal of the machine.

Qazi bent and lifted the attaché case with his left hand. The youth at the machine was spinning, falling on one knee, reaching into the open backpack. The Russian started.

Qazi lunged through the open door to his right, knocking aside a woman coming in. He ran down the ramp toward the entrance to the tunnel. Over his shoulder he saw the youth coming through the door, a weapon in his hands.

Qazi ran.

The tunnel had a flat roof about eight feet above a floor covered with a rubberized mat. The mat improved his footing. The walls were concave, giving the illusion of more space. The lighting was indirect, from the ceiling.

Not too many people. Qazi scrambled through them and sent a few sprawling. He ran past the turnoff to the Galoppatoio exit, and before he reached the next turn, he glanced again over his shoulder. The gunman was still coming.

The low ceiling gave Qazi an illusion of great speed. He shot past an exit to the Via Veneto on his left and raced toward the moving sidewalk ahead. He almost lost his balance when he hit it, but he pushed off on a pedestrian who didn't hear him coming and kept his balance. The moving sidewalk also had a rubberized coating. It descended ahead of him, seemingly endless. He felt as if he were literally flying. After fifty yards he glanced back. The gunman was gaining.

He was running faster than he ever had in his life. The end of the sidewalk was coming up. He leaped for the platform and lost his balance and careened onto the down escalator, into a group of men and women, bowling them over. He was up before they could react and taking the moving stairs downward four at a time.

At the bottom the tunnel ended in a cross-corridor. He turned left, toward the entrance to the Metropolitana, the subway, and buttonhooked against the wall.

He scanned the corridor. Just pedestrians, walking normally.

When the gunman rounded the corner, Qazi shot him three times with the Walther before he hit the floor. The falling man lost his weapon, an Uzi, which bounced off the concrete wall. Someone screamed. A young man reached half-heartedly for Qazi and he threw a shot over his shoulder.

Then he ran, away from the subway entrance, down the corridor toward the Piazza di Spagna. As he ran he ripped off the clerical collar and the black shirt. He literally tore the shirt from his left arm.

When he reached the tunnel exit, he slowed to a walk. He could hear several sirens growing louder, a penetrating two-tone wail. The piazza was full of people strolling and sitting and pointing cameras in all directions. Qazi walked purposefully but unhurriedly the hundred feet to the Spanish Steps and began to climb it toward the obelisk at the top. The stairs were lined with flowers. He paused and watched a police car with blue light flashing proceed through the scrambling people at the foot of the white marble staircase.

He transferred the attaché case to his right hand, wiped the perspiration from his forehead with a handkerchief, then continued climbing the stairs. Two carabinieri in khaki uniforms, wearing berets and carrying submachine guns on straps over their shoulders, ran down the stairs past him.

Qazi stood on the sidewalk in front of the entrance to the zoo. A dirty brown sedan, much battered, stopped at the curb. Noora was at the wheel. Ali was beside her in the front seat and another man, about twenty-five, sat in the rear. He opened the door for Qazi.

As soon as the car was in motion, Qazi opened the attaché case. It was empty except for a stack of paper almost two inches thick, held together with rubber bands. He pulled away the top sheet, which was blank, and examined the next. He was looking at a copy machine copy of a photograph. The photo was of the cover of a document marked "Mk-58" and "Top Secret" in inch-high black letters. On the lower right was a printed four-digit number and a hand-lettered inked notation "2 of 3."

Qazi placed the document in an empty shopping bag that sat waiting on the floor. He passed the attaché case to the man beside him. "Wipe it off."

In the front seat, Ali turned and watched with raised eyebrows.

"A man watched my meet with the general. He chased me. I shot him."

"We heard the sirens."

"Who?" Ali asked.

"I don't know."

The car stopped shortly thereafter and Ali walked over to a large green trash barrel near a cross walk, deposited the attaché case, then returned to the car.

At the next traffic light, Ali looked over his shoulder at Qazi and said, "The *United States* will anchor in Naples seven days from now."

"For how long?"

"The hotel reservations are for eight nights."

"Any particular hotel?"

"Over a dozen reservations at the Vittorio Emanuele. Some reservations elsewhere."

"Noora," he said to the girl, "get us two rooms at the Vittorio. Suites, if possible, doubles at least. And stay out of sight." She nodded.

Qazi turned to the young man beside him. "As soon as you learn which rooms will be assigned to the Americans, Yasim, wire as many as possible." Yasim was a rarity, an Arab with mechanical talent. He had been the star pupil of the national university's engineering department when Qazi had discovered him.

"Ali, you set the plan in motion. I will join you at home tomorrow." Qazi kept checking the rear window as Noora threaded through the traffic onto the Via Tiburtina eastbound. When they came to the limited-access highway that circled Rome, Ali merged with the traffic in the high-speed lane headed south as Qazi checked behind them repeatedly.

An hour later Noora dropped Qazi near Castel Sant'Angelo and sped away. The colonel now wore a short-sleeve, open-neck pullover shirt with a little alligator on the left breast. He walked west on the Via della Conciliazione. Old medieval buildings rose four and five stories above the street on either side, while ahead of him he could see the facade of St. Peter's. Several blocks short of St. Peter's Square, he turned right into a side street. He walked under the ancient Roman wall that arched above the street and kept going, into one of the more expensive quarters of Rome. After several blocks, he entered a quiet hotel with a tiny lobby.

"I say, old chap," he hailed the desk clerk. "Have you any messages or calls for me? Name's MacPhee. Room 306."

"No, Signor MacPhee," the clerk said after looking in the key box. "There is nothing." Qazi would have been astounded if there had been. No one, not even Ali, knew he was here. He had checked in this morning, before he walked the three miles to the Villa Borghese.

"Grazie!" the new Signor MacPhee murmured as the clerk handed him the key.

Dusk had fallen and the street below his window was lit with lights from the bar across the street when Qazi finally tossed the last of the photocopied pages on the bed and gazed out his window. Without conscious effort his gaze moved from figure to figure on the sidewalk below, then roved over the parked automobiles.

His eyes ached from four hours of reading. He stretched, then slouched down in a chair and stared at the manual lying on the bed. After a few moments he picked up his pistol from the writing desk where he had been reading, turned off the light and stretched out on the bed. He laid the pistol on top of the manual.

When he awoke, the room was illuminated only by the glare of streetlights coming in the window. He checked his watch. Eleven o'clock. He lay in the darkness listening.

After twenty minutes he arose, tucked the pistol into its ankle holster, and placed the manual back in the shopping bag. He locked the room door behind him and descended the maid's staircase all the way to the basement. The hallway was silent and dark. The eyes of a scurrying mouse reflected the glare from his pocket flashlight. The coal furnace was in the second room on his right. It looked exactly as it did two months ago when he selected this hotel because it had this furnace.

He opened the chimney flue and the firebox door. He placed a dozen pages inside the firebox. Soon the fire was burning nicely. He fed the pages in a few at a time. It took half an hour. When all the pages were cold ashes, Qazi latched the furnace door, closed the flue, and climbed the stairs back to his room.

There was a telephone book in the nightstand beside the bed. Qazi looked up a number and dialed it. After two rings a man's voice said in English, "You have reached the Israeli embassy. May I help you?"

Qazi cradled the receiver. He stared at the listing in the telephone book and repeated the number several times to himself. Then he replaced the book in the nightstand.

"But he did not have the manual when he got off the airplane this afternoon," Ali protested.

El Hakim set his jaw. "What did he do with it?"

"Your Excellency, he must have read it and destroyed it."

"Why?"

"He obviously has no further use for it, Excellency." Ali shrugged helplessly.

I'm sure he doesn't, El Hakim thought savagely. Qazi has just made himself the indispensable man. This little episode is his life insurance. El Hakim smote the table with his fist, then rose and went to his large world globe. He twirled it with a finger and watched it spin. He hated to be thwarted by anyone, but especially by one of his lieutenants whom he did not trust. It was infuriating. He slapped the globe and it spun so fast the colors blurred. He adjusted the collar of his fatigue shirt and his pistol belt as he watched the globe spin down. He pinched his nose between his thumb and forefinger and tried to think like Qazi. Qazi was a devious man, a dangerous man. A far too dangerous man.

"Jarvis," he muttered finally under his breath. He turned and grinned wolfishly at Ali. "Jarvis," he repeated aloud.

10

WHO WROTE this piece of shit?"

The three officers on the other side of the desk sagged visibly.

Jake Grafton arranged his brand new glasses on his nose and read from the accident report in front of him. " 'It is believed that a failure in the liquid oxygen system led to the loss of this aircraft. However, due to the loss of the airframe at sea, the precise cause of this accident will never be known.' " Jake looked up. The three faces across the desk were blurred. He took off the glasses. "I won't sign that."

None of the three said anything.

"Has the Naval Safety Center got any record of any other F-14 lost this way? Have you torn down a LOX system and tried to identify possible components that might fail? What does the Grumman rep have to say? Maybe the connection from the oxygen container and the aircraft's system wasn't hooked up right. What connectors or filters or whatever could have failed and

121

allowed ambient air to dilute a flow of pure oxygen? You guys have got to answer these questions."

"Yessir."

"Dolan and Bronsky are dead. I want to know what killed them."

"A defective oxygen system killed them, CAG."

Jake picked up the report and waved it at the officer who spoke. "This report doesn't say that. This report hasn't got enough facts in it to say that and make it stick. Right now this report is merely a guess."

"We're going to need more time, CAG."

"Write an interim message report and send it to the safety center and everyone on the distribution list. Tell them what you think and what you're working on and tell them when you hope to get finished. Then get cracking. I want answers. Not bullshit. Not guesses. Real answers." He closed the report and pushed it back across the desk.

"Sir, the captain's office says there will be some reporters out here in a few days to interview you about that boat you sank." Farnsworth was standing at the office door.

Jake looked up from the maintenance report he was reading. "When?"

"About 1400 Wednesday, sir. They should arrive on the noon cargo plane from Naples."

"Okay."

"Lieutenant Reed is waiting out here to see you. Oh . . . and some congressmen are going to arrive on Tuesday. The XO is going to talk to you about it. I think he wants you to host them."

Farnsworth always saved the worst for last. "Who stimulated that think?"

"YN2 Defenbaugh in the captain's office." The captain's office was the administrative heart of the ship, sucking in paper and pumping it out in quantities that awed Jake. And still the yeomen there found time to tell Farnsworth everything aboard ship worth knowing!

"When should I expect the XO's call?"

Farnsworth looked at the insulated pipes in the overhead and pursed his lips. "In maybe thirty minutes or so, sir. There'll be three congressmen and a senator, and the captain's office is gonna bunk 'em in the VIP quarters. Four squadrons will each furnish one junior officer as an escort. Captain James will meet 'em on the flight deck when the cargo plane arrives, then a trot to the flag spaces to meet the admiral. After that, lunch with the XO. Then I thought you might start them on a tour of the ship with the escort officers. We'll set up a deal that afternoon down in the mess hall where they can meet their constituents. Politicians always want to shake hands with voters. Finally, dinner with Admiral Parker in the flag mess."

"That schedule should let them find a ton or two of facts," Jake agreed. "Firm it up and brief the escorts."

"Aye aye, sir."

"Send Reed in."

Jake motioned the bombardier-navigator into a chair and leaned back in his own. He pulled out a desk drawer and propped his feet up on it. Wait. Where were Reed's wings? He rummaged through his top drawer and took out the gold-colored piece of metal. He tossed it on the desk on top of the maintenance report and resettled his feet on the drawer.

Reed stared at the insignia. You could buy one in any navy exchange for about $4.50.

"You wanted to see me?" Jake prompted.

"Uh, yessir. I've been thinking and all. About our conversation. Maybe I should stay in the cockpit, at least until I get discharged."

Jake grunted. He picked up the metal insignia and tossed it across the desk. It landed in front of Reed, inches from the edge. The bombardier palmed it.

"Still going to get out, huh?"

"I'll have to think about it. Talk to my wife."

Jake found himself searching his pockets for cigarettes and consciously grasped the arms of his chair to keep his hands still. "You may spend another twenty years in the navy and never get shot at again. It'll be train, train, train, bore a lot more holes in the sky, kiss your wife good-bye for cruise after cruise."

"It sounds like you think I should get out."

"What I'm telling you is that this job isn't Tom Cruise strutting along with his balls clicking together, ready to zap some commie before breakfast." The movie *Top Gun* was going through the ready rooms, for about the fourth or fifth time.

"We need people with brains and ability to fill these cockpits, but there's no glamour. None. And you aren't ever going to be the guy who helps win the big one for our side. If there ever is another major war, the first and last shots are going to be fired by some button-pushers in silos or submarines. Then the world will come to an end. Everyone who isn't vaporized by the explosions, or who doesn't die from burns, shattered skulls, or asphyxiation, is going to die slowly of radiation poisoning. And who in his right mind would want to survive? Civilization will be over. The birds and animals will all die, the seas will become sterile as the fallout poisons them . . . about the only creatures that will survive will be the cockroaches."

Jake was feeling for cigarettes again. He stared at Reed dolefully. "What the navy has out here on these carriers are jobs for warriors. It's an ancient and honorable profession, but just about as obsolete today as horse cavalry. The button-pushers who are preventing a nuclear war, and who will wage it if it happens, aren't warriors." Jake shrugged. "Maybe they're professional executioners. Hangmen. Whatever the hell they are, they're not warriors."

He settled his new glasses on his nose and flipped a few pages of the maintenance report.

"I understand," Reed murmured.

"I don't think you do." Jake closed the report on a finger and eyed the younger man. "The people in the navy are first-rate. Our enlisted men are the smartest, best educated, best trained on the planet. You'll never work with better people. The flying is pretty good. The pay is adequate. The family life sucks. Most officers get squeezed out of the service after twenty years or so because they can't all be captains and admirals. Now that's the stuff you should be talking over with your wife. But . . . while you wear that uniform I expect you to fly when you're scheduled and to give it the best you've got. Use every ounce of knowledge and brains and ability you have. You owe that to your country."

Jake gestured toward the door. "I have work to do." He spread the report open on the desk and began to read as the lieutenant departed. When the latch clicked shut, the captain leaned back and stared over the top of the glasses at the gray metal door. At length he shook his head slowly, wiped the perspiration from his forehead, and picked up the report.

□ □ □

Ali held the door open for Colonel Qazi. Ali wore a chauffeur's uniform, and after Qazi had passed into the real estate office, he went back to the limousine, took a rag from the trunk, and began to wipe off the few flecks of dust that had accumulated on the car in the ten-minute drive from the agency where he had just rented it.

Inside the real estate office, Qazi stood impassively as the receptionist whispered hurriedly into her telephone, then gave a barely perceptible nod to the office manager when he came rushing out. He was a breathless, corpulent man with only a fringe of hair remaining, one lock of which had been carefully placed so as to run back and forth across his shiny pate. The manager guided him into his office while the receptionist stared after him.

As Qazi sat on the overstuffed sofa and removed his sunglasses, the manager settled behind his desk. The manager saw the visitor staring at his overflowing ashtray, so he whisked it away. He placed it in a bottom drawer of the desk, then crossed his hands and beamed at his visitor.

Qazi wore a white caftan and burnoose. Black whiskers flecked with gray adorned his chin. He looked, he hoped, like a young King Faisal.

"I wish to rent a villa, Signor Livora," Qazi said in very British English.

"Ah, you know my name."

"You are highly recommended, sir."

"You have come to the right place," Livora beamed. "We have several fine villas to rent, from . . . how you say? . . . modest? To quite large. What are your requirements, Signor . . . ?"

"Mister Al-Sabah. The villa is not for me, you understand. I am merely an executive secretary." He flicked his right hand, on which he had three rings with rather large, conspicuous stones. The real estate man's shiny, decorated head bobbed knowingly. Ah, yes. He had heard all about those filthy-rich Arab sheiks and all the money they threw around. No doubt he even dreamed of them, sitting here in Naples surrounded by poor Italians and vacationing Europeans and Americans who watched every lira.

Qazi outlined his needs. His master needed ample quarters. Perhaps an estate. Something with grass and gardens. Of course he had his own staff of servants, including a gardener. Something in the country, available for at least three months, beginning next week.

"What are you going to say to these congressmen and reporters?" Vice-Admiral Morton Lewis asked.

Jake fought the impulse to squirm in his chair. Admiral Lewis was the commander of the U.S. Sixth Fleet and had flown out to the carrier with the congressional delegation. He and Jake sat in the flag offices beneath the flight deck. The Public Affairs Officer from Lewis' staff had earlier provided Jake with a list of probable press questions and suggested, "sterile" answers.

"I'm just going to tell it like it was, sir."

"They're going to grill you on policy." With even, regular features, perfect teeth, and a trim stomach he maintained with a forty-five minute ride on a stationary bicycle every morning, the admiral looked every inch the professional sea dog, 1980s edition. His three stars gleamed on each collar. It was no secret that he wanted a fourth star.

"Yessir. But I plan to refer them to Washington for questions about policy."

"Don't be evasive. We've nothing to hide and we don't want these people inputting that we do. Don't reference them anywhere."

"I understand."

"The distance the task force maintains from the Lebanese shore, that's a policy matter. It will be questioned. As the air wing commander and as a professional aviator, your opinion as to the wisdom of the employment of this task group will be asked. There is just no way to avoid the fact that if this task group was two hundred miles away from Lebanon, that boat attack would have been impossible. Or at least highly impractical."

"Yessir." Jake grasped the arms of his chair with both hands and kept both feet on the floor. "But isn't that a matter for Washington to comment upon?"

The admiral rubbed his lips with his forefinger. "I recommend the location of this task group in light of the results Washington expected, and Washington concurred. The reasons for the recommendation don't concern you."

"If I'm going to have to give an opinion, I should know your thinking, Admiral."

The admiral's forefinger tracked back and forth along his chin. "I think that what you are going to say is this: 'U.S. Navy ships have an absolute right to navigate freely in international waters, and they will defend themselves against attack in international waters, attack from anyone, any time.' "

"Yessir." Jake couldn't object to saying it, since it was true. "But that isn't going to satisfy the reporters. They'll want to know why we chose to navigate where we did."

"And you will repeat your answer."

"Yessir." Because if Jake told them to ask Washington, someone there just might say that the ships were where they were because the navy recommended it. Which would put Vice-Admiral Lewis rather firmly on the spot. Of course, the folks in Washington had approved the recommendation—they could have ordered the ships to any location on the map—but Admiral Lewis well knew the games that could be played when Important People did not wish to publicly defend their policies, the very same Important People that he had tried to please—or impress—with his recommendation. There were sure a lot of ins and outs to the admiral business, Jake reflected.

"By the way, you handled that boat attack well."

"Someone on that boat got trigger-happy. Lady Luck won't spread her legs like that for us again."

A look of distaste flickered across the distinguished face above the admiral's stars. Jake felt grubby. "Is the accident report finished on that F-14 loss?"

"It's about finished, sir."

"Hmmm. Pilot error?"

"Probably an oxygen system failure. The crew obviously didn't recognize it, if that was what it was."

"Have someone transcribe your press conference. I'll chop the transcript, then forward it to Washington."

"Aye aye, sir."

"My PAO has a statement about the boat incident that was just released in Washington. You interface with him."

"I understand."

"Don't contradict anything in the press release." The admiral's gaze held him pinned. "And don't go beyond it except for personal data that these reporters always want, like hometown, names of children, etc. Use the PAO's prepared answers whenever you can. The less the bad guys intel our operation, the better off we'll be. Read the press release and strategize your conformity."

Jake nodded.

The admiral traced a pattern on the desk with a forefinger. "Senator Cavel fancies himself as something of an expert on naval affairs." He made a steeple with his fingertips. "He's on the Senate Armed Services Committee and wants to be president." His top front teeth came to rest on his fingertips. He looked at Jake speculatively.

"I've read about Senator Cavel."

The admiral snorted. "Don't contradict Cavel unless you have to. He's an egotistical, self-righteous bastard who would walk five miles without his trousers to even a score. Right now he's fulminating against the way the administration is using this task group here in the Med. One of his allies who'll be with him on this trip is a representative from a conservative district in the Deep South. His name is Victor Gilbert. He's on the House Armed Services Committee. He's also unhappy about the Middle East, but he votes right on most defense issues. The other two are big-city congressmen looking for ways to chop the military budget. I wouldn't turn my back on any of them."

"Yessir."

"You're the pilot who just sent a boatload of fanatics to Paradise and you're the air wing commander, so you're getting a turn on the hot seat. Don't forget you may be worth more to them dead than you are alive. That's all." Which meant Jake was dismissed.

Senator Cavel was fiftyish, graying at the temples. His fluffed, teased hair was coiffed tightly over ears hidden from sight, and when viewed from the front, he looked, Jake thought, like a man of distinction in a whiskey ad. In profile, the hairdo looked like a football helmet two sizes too small. His slightly sagging abdomen and rounded shoulders were expertly encased in a dark-gray wool suit with flecks of red and blue that Jake suspected had set him back the better part of a grand. The senator was tall, about six-three, and had a booming voice that dominated the congressional delegation and the group of officers in the flag lounge. He treated everyone as voters, hail-fellow-well-met, and even shook hands with the admirals' aides. His handshake had the polish of years of practice. It wasn't crushing and it wasn't wimpish, just dry and quick with a hint of firmness.

"Damned nice ship you fellows have here, Admiral. Damned nice. Great to see what all those taxpayers' dollars bought. Three billion and some change, I seem to recall."

Parker nodded. "Yessir. She's . . ."

But Senator Cavel wasn't listening. "Just why do these things have to be so damn big? I never did understand that." He shook his head ruefully, as if he had never seen the engineering and design justifications on *Nimitz*-class carriers that the navy had spent a year and several million dollars completing, at his insistence. "I get letters from all over, wondering why we can't build these things cheaper. Are you aware that 95 percent of the American public has never even laid eyes on an aircraft carrier? Lots of letters . . . Ah, so you're Grafton?"

He had finally zeroed in on Jake's name tag. He had apparently ignored the introductions. Jake was shaking hands with a stout, florid congressman, but the senator put his hand on the representative's shoulder and addressed Jake as if the other man weren't there. "You're the air wing commander?"

Jake admitted he was as the senator glanced at the four rows of ribbons on the left breast of his white uniform shirt, under his wings.

"I see you've been shot at before, Captain," he said, then turned back to the admirals.

"Yessir," Jake Grafton told Cavel's back. But only by guns and missiles, he added to himself, then tried to pay attention to whatever it was this representative was telling him about sailors from Ohio.

With the pleasantries over, the delegation surrounded the admirals and tossed questions about the use of the task group in the waters off Lebanon. Jake eased toward the door. A glance from Admiral Parker froze him in his tracks.

In addition to the senator, Congressman Victor Gilbert also considered himself a heavyweight. It was quickly evident Gilbert was looking for ammunition to take back to Washington and fire at his colleagues in the never-ending political battle over Mideast policy. It was equally apparent that the admirals had no desire to give aid and comfort to either Gilbert or his opponents. Lewis' answers didn't satisfy the vociferous congressman, but the senator said little. Perhaps he's saving himself, Jake mused.

The tour of the ship began in the waist catapult control cab, known as the waist bubble. A similar control cab was on the bow, situated between the cats. Here on the waist the bubble sat on the catwalk outboard of Cat Four. The cabs were unique to *Nimitz*-class carriers. This innovation removed the launching officers from the flight deck and placed them in actual control of their giant steam-powered slingshots. The bubbles also provided a terrific place for tourists to view the launch.

Jake led the congressmen into the waist bubble from the O-3 level, the deck just below the flight deck. The catapult officer triggered the hydraulic system which raised the bubble into position for the upcoming launch. Now the top of the armored cab, which consisted of windows of bulletproof glass, extended eighteen inches above the flight deck. The visitors stood packed into the only open area, their eyes exactly at flight deck level. The launching officer sat in a raised chair in the aft end of the cab in front of the control panels for both the Number Three and Number Four catapults.

The cat officer muttered greetings. He was a lieutenant aviator assigned to the ship's air department for a two-year tour. After he had shaken hands all around, he ignored the visitors and devoted his attention to the yellow- and green-shirted crewmen on deck who were hooking planes to both cats.

Jake explained the launching evolution to the congressmen. The first plane to be launched would be the KA-6D Intruder tanker on Cat Three. The F/A-18 Hornet, a twin-engine, single-seat fighter-bomber sitting on Cat Four, would be shot next while another plane taxied onto Cat Three. Up on the bow a similar bang-bang sequence would be occurring on the two catapults there.

The launching officer gave a thumbs-up to the yellow-shirt director on Cat Three. He signaled the pilot to release his brakes and add power. The engines began to roar as the green-shirted hookup man checked the fittings, then tumbled out from under the plane with his thumb in the air. He joined his comrades squatting in the safety area between the catapults. The Intruder pilot saluted the bubble. He was ready to go. He put his helmeted head back into the headrest on his seat, bracing himself for the acceleration of the coming shot.

Jake pointed out the signal light on the ship's island that the air boss used to initiate the launch. It turned green.

The launching officer glanced down the catapult to ensure it was clear, then back to the Intruder at full power. He lifted the safety tab covering the fire button and pushed it. The Intruder leapt forward, its left wing sweeping over the heads of the men squatting in the safety area, and raced for the edge of the angled deck three hundred feet away. The plane covered the distance in less than three seconds and shot out over the sea, flying.

When the visitors' gaze came back to the Hornet on Cat Four, it was already at full power. They were looking at this plane almost head-on. The catapult track ran parallel to the edge of the angled deck, so the Hornet's left main wheel was almost against the deck edge, its left wing extending out over the side of the ship. Upon launch it would pass right in front of the bubble with its wing sweeping over the top. Now the river of hot gases blasting from the plane's twin exhaust pipes and flowing up over the jet blast deflector shimmered as the blast-furnace heat distorted the light. The fighter appeared stark and crisp against this mirage backdrop.

The cat officer lifted the protective safety cover and pushed the fire button on the Cat Four console. The Hornet seemed to shimmy slightly under the terrific acceleration as it raced toward the bubble. In a heartbeat it went by in a thundering crescendo that shook the control cab.

The congressmen laughed nervously and shouted comments to each other above the background noise. "Impressive," Senator Cavel told Jake, who grinned and nodded.

But as spectacular as the planes were, the visitors' attention was soon on the catapult crewmen. One of them crawled under each jet as it taxied onto the cats, lowered the nose-tow bar and installed the hold-back fitting. He waited under the plane until the engines were accelerating to full power before he scanned its belly, checked the fittings one last time, then tumbled out from under. These men reminded Jake of circus roustabouts tending angry elephants.

"That job looks damned dangerous," one of the congressmen remarked.

"It's that," Jake agreed. "It's dirty and dangerous for not enough pay." He recognized Kowalski, the Cat Four cat captain, in his filthy yellow shirt and radio headset. Each cat crew had a captain, a ringmaster who ensured each man understood his job and performed it perfectly.

When the launch was over, the congressmen shook hands again with the cat officer and his engineer, who sat at an instrument panel at the forward end of the bubble. Then Jake led them through the hatch and down the short ladder into the O-3 level. The four junior officers who had been volunteered for escort duty were waiting in the passageway, since there hadn't been room for them in the bubble. The air here was cooler, and calm.

Senator Cavel got down to cases that evening after dinner in the flag mess. The admiral's chief of staff, operations officer, and aide left after dessert. Vice-Admiral Lewis had flown from the ship that afternoon, telling the congressman he had to get back to Naples. Now just Admiral Parker, Jake, and the four congressmen were sitting around the table. One of the representatives lit a cigar, and Jake greedily inhaled some smoke. It made him slightly dizzy. With a wry grimace, he pushed his chair further away from the table to avoid the fumes.

The senator played with the spoon beside his coffee cup. It was real silver, and under the cup was a real white linen tablecloth. Admirals rated the good stuff.

"How come, Admiral, you people had to sink that boat?"

"It was running without lights and closing the task group in a suspicious manner. It refused to identify itself or change course. It shot at one of our planes."

"Would you have sunk it if it hadn't opened fire on Captain Grafton's plane?"

Cowboy Parker scanned the faces gathered around the table. "Has everyone here got a clearance?"

"Yessir," Senator Cavel boomed. "We all do. Top Secret. And we've read the classified action report. We know Captain Grafton turned on his aircraft's lights—apparently no one in the eastern Mediterranean is very fond of lights—and pointed his plane directly at that boat. At a very low altitude. Only then did the crew of the boat open fire. Now what we are trying to find out is whether or not his actions caused the captain of that boat to feel he was under attack." The senator looked at his colleagues. None of them spoke. He resumed, "You do think the men in that boat had the right to defend themselves in international waters, don't you?"

"Yes, Senator, they had that right." Parker picked his words carefully. "But only if they were under attack or had reason to believe an attack was imminent. We know that boat wasn't under attack, and the appearance of a low-flying plane with its position lights on is not what I would call an indicator of an imminent, forthcoming attack."

"We'll be the judge of that, Admiral."

"I'm sure," Parker said. "You people can debate it for weeks. I didn't have weeks. I'm responsible for a lot of lives and ships out here, Senator. You gentlemen have read the Rules of Engagement we operate under. You know that at some point I have to use my own judgment."

The representative with the cigar spoke up. This was Victor Gilbert, from a dirt-poor conservative district in the Deep South. He was the same one that found Admiral Lewis a tad too slippery earlier in the day. "Admiral Parker, we don't want you people to start a war out here." He pronounced "here" as "hyah." "I understand that the navy is just obeying orders from the administration. I think the orders are misconceived, not in the national interest, but I'm not the president. However, I am a congressman. My constituents don't want a war. I can't make it any plainer, Admiral."

"Sir," Parker said. "I agree wholeheartedly with your constituents. I don't want a war, either. I'm doing everything I can to prevent one from happening. On the other hand, I have to protect these ships."

"Captain," the senator said, looking at Jake, "why did you turn on your lights and fly right at that boat?"

Every eye in the place was on Jake Grafton. "I was trying to spook him. If he was hostile, we wanted to know it sooner rather than later. We can't sit here like bumps—"

Senator Cavel gestured angrily. "In my twenty years in the senate, I've found that a man who goes looking for a fight usually finds one. *That's* the problem."

"The men on that boat were looking for the fight," Jake shot back. "We can't wait until they pop a cruise missile against a ship before we decide what we're going to do about it."

"Admiral, you never answered my question. Would you have sunk that boat if it hadn't opened fire on Captain Grafton?"

Parker sipped his coffee and took his time before he spoke. "If they had continued on course toward the task group, I would have had the nearest screening ship fire warning shots. Yes, I'd have been forced to the conclusion that attack was imminent if they had ignored the warning shots, and I'd have defended this task group."

"Do your superiors know what you would have done?" Cavel pressed.

Parker set his cup firmly in its saucer. "My superiors sent me here with written guidelines, called Rules of Engagement. I follow them. If anybody threatens to kill my people or sink my ships, I'll shoot first. That's in the ROE."

"But it all hinges on whether or not there is a threat. You alone determine that, and nobody elected you to anything. If you're wrong, we may be in a war."

Parker turned his hand over and inclined his head an inch.

"Pretty goddamn convenient if you ask me, Admiral, that your air wing commander just happened to be flying the plane that needed to zap somebody," Senator Cavel said. "That doesn't look so good. You can bet your pension that the pundits in the States are pointing to that as proof positive that you and the administration are up to something sleazy."

Parker explained that the air wing commander routinely flies missions with his crews. He concluded, "I can't worry about how this looks on the front pages back in the States on Monday morning. My problems are here and now."

"It strikes me, Admiral," Victor Gilbert said, "that you've got a damn tough job." He puffed his cigar three or four times quickly, then took a deep drag and blew the smoke down the table, toward Jake. "You fuck this up and the navy will hang you by the balls. If they don't, we will."

A trace of a smile flickered on Parker's lips. "I think we understand each other, gentlemen."

After Jake finished answering questions at the press conference in the wardroom, the congressional delegation trooped into the

134

lights of the television cameras. They spoke as a group, then individually. Representative Gilbert, sans cigar, was mouthing a string of one-liners for the evening news shows when Jake joined Farnsworth at the door and opened it as quietly as he could. Farnsworth had operated the tape recorder. In the lounge Farnsworth told Jake, "You did fine, sir."

"I strategized my conformity," Jake Grafton muttered.

Farnsworth nodded sagely. "Why couldn't you have woven my name in there someplace? I always like to see my name in the paper."

"I want to read that transcript before it goes anywhere." Two can play this game, Jake thought.

"Should I put in all the 'uhs' and 'ands' and sentence fragments, or should I clean it up so that it reads like English?"

"Farnsworth . . ."

"An excellent choice, sir. It'll be on your desk in two hours."

11

IT WAS FIVE MINUTES to four in the morning when Jake Grafton walked into the Carrier Air Traffic Control Center (CATCC) space and dropped onto the vinyl-covered couch beside the air operations officer, Commander Ken Walker. As usual, he surveyed the plexiglas status boards that lined the front of the compartment and listed all the aircraft waiting on deck to be launched and all the aircraft airborne awaiting recovery while he bantered with several of the squadron skippers and executive officers who were trailing in. The launch was scheduled to go on the hour, and as soon as the launch was complete, the recovery would follow.

CATCC, pronounced "cat-see," was the nerve center of carrier operations at night. Two monitors suspended near the overhead displayed the video from the island and flight deck cameras continuously. Enlisted "talkers" wearing sound-powered telephone headsets stood behind the status boards and updated the information with yellow grease pencils. The air ops officer sat on the vinyl couch where he could see it all and dictate orders to his assistant, who sat in front of him at a desk surrounded by a battery of intercom boxes and telephones.

The room was dark except for a minuscule light over the desk and red lights that illuminated the yellow words and numbers on the status boards. Behind the couch where the heavies sat, junior officers from each of the squadrons with planes aloft stood shoulder to shoulder. They were there to give advice and answer questions, if asked.

The status boards tonight listed twelve airplanes to launch and thirteen to recover.

"How's tricks?" Jake asked Walker when he finally got off the telephone.

"Terrible. There's about fifteen knots of wind and it's shifted sixty degrees in the last hour. We've meandered all over compass trying to get it down the deck." On the bridge the officer-of-the-deck would be ordering course changes as he chased the wind. This would cause havoc with the air controllers' efforts to stack, or marshal, the planes to be recovered aft of the ship, somewhere near the final recovery bearing. No one knew what the final bearing would be.

"And Five Oh Six hasn't checked in to Marshal yet."

Jake glanced at the status board again. 506, Majeska. No fuel state was given. Majeska was the commanding officer of the A-6 Intruder squadron.

Jake stood. "I'm going next door." As he walked away he heard the assistant air ops officer on the phone to Captain James.

The adjoining compartment housed the radar displays, communications equipment, and status boards to control airborne aircraft. The scopes cast an eerie green light on the faces of the specialists who sat before them. Dim red lights shone down from the ceilings. A senior chief petty officer wearing a headset that allowed him to listen to all the radio transmissions walked back and forth behind the scopes, listening and looking and occasionally issuing an order. The senior chief was a chain-smoker who carried his own ashtray. Consequently the area near the door was a haven for refugees from the clear air of the air ops compartment next door. Here in the inner sanctum amid the scopes the smoke wafted about visibly, alternately green and red, swirled constantly by the ineffectual air-conditioning.

The conversations between the airborne pilots and the controllers came over a loudspeaker and provided the background noise. The same conversations could also be heard next door, in air ops.

The chief saw Jake standing near the door and came over, his headset cord trailing after him. "Where's Five Oh Six?"

The chief led Jake to one of the radar consoles, where together they stared at the large scope, searching for the coded blip of Majeska's aircraft. Jake fumbled in his shirt pocket for his glasses. Even with the display expanded to show the airspace within a fifty-mile radius of the ship, the correct blip wasn't there. "We've been calling him for ten minutes," the chief said to Jake. "Ask Strike if they hold him," the chief told the controller.

The sailor did as ordered. The chief listened to the conversation. The strike controller hadn't talked to the A-6E for almost fifteen minutes. He broadcast the Intruder's call sign over the air several times, but received no reply.

"Could he be just outside the range of your radar?" Jake asked.

"No, sir. And Combat doesn't hold him either." The operators in CDC would be querying the NTDS computer.

"Skin paint?" If the aircraft's IFF gear had malfunctioned, it was no longer coding the radar energy it received and broadcasting it back to the ship. The shipboard radars could also look at raw blips—that is, uncoded energy bouncing off the skin of the aircraft.

"No, sir. We tried. We can't find him up there."

Jake felt the swoosh and thud of a catapult firing. He glanced at the monitor. The launch had started.

An officer stepped up to Jake's elbow. "Sir, Commander Walker wants you." Jake thanked the chief and followed the lieutenant through the smoke.

Walker had a telephone to his ear when Jake sat down. "A Greek freighter called on the commercial net. Says he thinks a plane crashed near his ship about twenty minutes ago. You want to go over to Combat and see what they know?"

"Yeah." Jake heaved himself up. Every eye in the place was on him. He walked out, feeling very tired. The door to Combat was only forty feet or so forward, on the same starboard O-3 level passageway as CATCC. As Jake walked he could feel catapult pistons thudding into the water brakes. More airplanes aloft.

The NTDS computer consoles and their operators were scattered all over the compartment. The watch officer, a lieutenant, was also sucking on a cigarette. Jake wanted one so badly he could taste it.

"Any sign of survivors?"

"The freighter hasn't found any."

"What was that plane doing out there?"

"Surface surveillance. Their last transmission was that they were going to check out that freighter that's in the vicinity. The freighter says it is looking for survivors, but it can't find any. We're sending the fighters that just launched to that position to orbit overhead. Maybe they'll hear a survival radio or see a flare."

The two men discussed the situation; the location of the destroyer steaming toward the crash site, how long the fighters could hold overhead, the estimated time en route of the helicopter which would be launched from the carrier in a few minutes, when the current recovery was complete. Jake called his deputy air wing commander, Harry March. When he arrived the recovery was in full swing and the compartment vibrated as the planes smashed down on the flight deck, which was the ceiling of all the O-3 level compartments. Jake and March went out in the passageway and walked the fifty feet to the strike ops office, whose denizens wrote the daily air plan, the document that created missions for the ship's aircraft. A plan for a wreckage and personnel search at first light by air-wing aircraft was quickly put together as the strike operations officer conferred on the telephone with the admiral's operations officer. Everyone, Jake reflected, had a finger in the pie.

"This would have to happen just before going into port," one of the strike ops officers said glumly.

"Is that chopper still on deck?"

"Yessir." Everyone looked at the monitor. The chopper was spreading its rotors. "Harry, tell Walker to hold that chopper on deck until I get there," Jake said. "I'm going with them. In the meantime, I want you to get all the people you need, right now, and check out the liquid-oxygen system of every A-6 on this boat. And check all the lox servicing gear. If any of those systems are contaminated, seal them." March nodded. "Go. I'm going to get on that chopper."

Jake borrowed a filthy flight suit in flight deck control and dashed across the flight deck toward the waiting helicopter, an SH-3 Sea Knight. The men around it began breaking down the tie-down chains when they saw him coming. The breeze down the flight deck was brisk and the sky clear. The first pale hint of the coming dawn was just visible in the east.

Inside the chopper, one of the two rescue crewmen passed him a helmet which trailed a long black electrical lead. He pulled it on and the crewman plugged the end of the lead into a socket on the forward bulkhead. Now he could hear the pilot and copilot running through the pretakeoff checklist. Jake sat on the floor and wiggled into the flight suit, pulling it on over his uniform. Then he donned an inflatable life vest which the second crewman passed to him.

Even with the helmet, the noise level was extremely high as the helicopter lifted off and transitioned to forward flight. Out the open door, Jake saw the lights on the bow of the ship pass from view. Then there was nothing to see in the featureless darkness of night sea and sky. He motioned to the crewman who had given him the helmet and, when he was close enough, shouted in his ear. "How long until we reach the crash site?"

The crewman spoke into his lip mike and Jake heard the answer from the cockpit. An hour and twenty minutes. As the crewmen closed the sliding side door to improve cruising aerodynamics Jake found a kapok life vest to lay his head on and tried to relax. He gnawed a fingernail already into the quick from too much chewing and half listened to the cockpit crew chanting the litany of the post takeoff checklist on the ICS. Why in the name of God had Bull Majeska crashed, a man with three thousand hours in jets, over twenty-five hundred in A-6s? What could have gone wrong? Was the wreckage afloat or had it gone down? Could it be recovered?

Disgusted at himself for his impatience, he finally spit out the fragments of fingernail and forced himself to close his eyes and breathe regularly.

After ten minutes he gave up trying to sleep and stood behind the pilot and copilot where he could see the flight instruments. He exchanged pleasantries with the crew as the dawn chased the stars away and gradually revealed the restless gray sea and blue-ing sky.

The new day had completely arrived when the radio gave them the news. One of the orbiting jets had located a survivor. He was talking on the radio. It was Bull Majeska.

"Ask them to ask Majeska if the bombardier ejected."

The chopper pilot spoke into his mike. In a moment he turned back to Jake. "The pilot doesn't know, sir."

"Tell the guys in the jets to search for the second man. And tell them to be careful. I don't want anyone to fly into the water on a search-and-rescue."

"I see you," the tinny voice on the radio shouted. "I'm gonna pop a smoke." Orbiting jets overhead had guided the helicopter toward Bull Majeska in his life raft.

"There he is!" The copilot pointed toward eleven o'clock. A trace of orange smoke was just visible rising from the surface of the water. The swells were running three to four feet, and there was enough wind to break a whitecap occasionally. From a thousand feet up you could just see the tops of the low mountains of Cyprus peeping above the northern horizon and the superstructure of the freighter, hull down to the east.

The helicopter pilot approached the little raft from downwind, flying about forty feet above the water, coming up the trail of orange smoke toward the tiny bobbing figure.

Jake moved back into the cargo compartment and watched the hoist operator run the orange horse-collar down toward the sea. The rescue swimmer in full wetsuit adjusted his goggles and leaned out the open door. He would only go into the sea if the survivor could not get into the horse-collar.

Majeska had trouble getting out of his raft, so the helicopter sagged toward the water and the swimmer slipped out of the door. In less than two minutes the crewman pulled Majeska onto the floor of the cargo area and Jake helped get the collar off him. He was so exhausted he just lay there streaming water.

"Did Reed get out?" Jake shouted.

"I don't know."

Jake helped Majeska out of his survival gear and wrapped him in a dry blanket. When the swimmer was back aboard, he gave him a blanket too.

"CAG," the helicopter pilot called on the ICS.

Jake leaned into the cockpit.

"There's no sign of the other guy and we're running low on fuel, CAG. We're going to have to break off and get back. There's another chopper on its way here." He jerked his thumb over his shoulder. "That guy may need medical attention."

"Has anyone spotted the wreckage?"

"An A-6 has spotted a few pieces. The destroyer will be here in about three hours and they will pick up everything they can find."

"How come that freighter didn't wait around until dawn and help look for survivors?"

"I don't know."

"Tell one of the guys upstairs to make a low pass over it and get some pictures. Then let's get back to the carrier." Jake went back to check on Majeska.

"Are you hurt?" Jake shouted at Majeska over the noise.

"Don't think so."

"What happened?" He was referring to the crash.

Bull Majeska shook his head. "Don't know. I blacked out."

"Did Reed eject before you did?" Since the A-6 lacked command ejection, each crewman must eject himself.

"Don't know. I didn't hear him on the radio when I was in the water. I called and called."

Jake wrapped another blanket around the shivering A-6 pilot. He stood in the door and looked at the gray ocean, thinking about the bombardier and watery death. Later the crewman derigged the hoist and shut the side door.

Doctor Hartman hovered over the patient, listening to his lungs and heart. They were in a two-man room in sickbay, but the second bed was empty. Majeska had already been X-rayed and had urinated into a bottle. Now he was sitting on the side of the bed.

"So just exactly what happened?" Jake asked.

"Like I said, CAG, I don't really know. We were making a low pass by that freighter and the next thing I knew, I was in the water. I don't know if the ejection seat fired when the plane hit the water or whether the plane broke up on impact and tossed me out. I just don't know! And I don't know if Reed got out."

"Were you in the seat when you came to?"

"No. My life vest was inflated and there were parachute shroud lines everywhere. I had to cut my way out of them and get my raft deployed. Jeez, I haven't worked that hard in years, and I swallowed a couple gallons of salt water. I must have cut every shroud line three times."

The life vest, Jake knew, had two carbon dioxide cartridges that automatically activated when immersed in salt water and inflated the vest. But the parachute should have deployed only if the ejection seat had fired.

"Did you see the freighter after you were in the water? They said they looked for survivors."

"I saw it. But I was so wrapped in shroud lines I couldn't get my flares out for a while. And when I finally did, they left anyway. At least I think they did; after the first flare burned out I spent at least a half hour trying to get into the raft, puking my guts out all the while. There were shroud lines everywhere and the raft kept getting hung up. I kept thinking the parachute might pull me under. I was flailing away with that shroud cutter and swallowing water and heaving my guts."

"CAG," Doctor Hartman said, "I can't finish this examination with you two talking. Could you . . ."

"Come back after a bit, Doc," Jake said. The doctor opened his mouth, thought better of whatever he was going to say, and left the room, closing the door behind him.

Jake sat on the other bed, facing Bull. "I don't believe you," he said.

Majeska set his jaw. "Just what the hell do you mean by that?"

"I mean I don't believe you. I think you know a lot more than you're telling and I want to hear it. Now."

"You're calling me a liar."

"Don't you puff up on me, you sonuvabitch. There's one man dead and a thirty-six million-dollar airplane at the bottom of the ocean. Now I want the whole fucking truth."

Majeska lowered his gaze. "There's nothing we can do to bring Reed back," he said softly.

"I want it all, Bull. Now."

"I've said everything I'm gonna say to you, Jake. I've told you how it happened. Now I'll tell it again to the accident board, but I'm not saying anything more to you. Sir."

"I'm your boss, Bull. I write your fitness report. That accident

143

report will come to me for my comment before it goes off this ship." Jake took a deep breath. "You idiot, I'm responsible for all these airplanes and every swinging dick that gets in them. I don't want any more people dead." Majeska's face was covered with a fine sheen of perspiration and he was biting his lip. "I'm not here to just chew on your ass. If you fucked up, you fucked up. But I need the truth!"

"You already have the truth, sir." Bull Majeska said at last.

Jake rose and walked out of the room.

Will Cohen was waiting for him in the CAG office, along with Harry March.

"We checked out all the liquid-oxygen servicing equipment and the lox system in the A-6s, CAG. Couldn't find anything wrong, except one A-6 had a leaky seal. We downed it for that. Take a couple hours to fix."

"One leaky seal. Could a seal leak have contaminated the system?"

"No way." Cohen shook his head.

"Do every other airplane on this ship. And have the senior parachute rigger check every oxygen mask on this boat."

"Gee whiz, CAG. If some fighter puke has a mask that wasn't inspected when it should have been, that doesn't have anything to do with why Majeska crashed."

Jake just looked at Cohen.

"You want it, you got it, Toyota," Cohen said and made for the door.

Jake headed for his office. "What do you have, Harry?"

"Photos of that Greek freighter, the *Aegean Argos*. It seems she probably came from a North African port and is on her way to Beirut now. She's headed in that direction at twelve knots. Making plenty of smoke." When Jake was behind his desk, March tossed the photos in front of him.

Jake examined them. There were no visible weapons, but the deck cargo was covered with a tarpaulin. "What do the Air Intelligence guys say about this?"

"They say there are no visible weapons."

"Send off a message. Somebody should check that ship out when it docks."

"Beirut isn't New York. The port authorities aren't going to be falling over each other trying to help us."

"I know that. And I know that half the people in Lebanon are probably on the CIA payroll or would like to be. Send the message."

"You think maybe the *Argos* shot Majeska down?"

"I don't know what to think. Maybe they nailed him with a hand-held missile or a machine gun mounted on a rail. Maybe a wing fell off, catastrophic failure. It's happened before. Maybe the plane just blew up. I don't have the foggiest. Bull says he blacked out and came to in the water. One thing is sure, the captain of that freighter didn't want to give us a real close look in the daytime. It's almost as if he started to look for survivors, then realized if he found any we'd come aboard to get them, so he sailed away."

"A real nice guy."

"There's a lot of them here in the Med. Majeska says he had a flare going and the freighter left anyway. They should have seen him. There wasn't that much of a sea running and visibility was good. Go talk to the strike ops guys. And see what the admiral thinks of all this."

"I'm on my way."

As the officer departed, Farnsworth came to the door. "Admiral Parker wants to see you, at your convenience."

"What about?" Farnsworth had probably been talking to the yeoman in the admiral's office. The yeomen usually knew more about what was going on than the officers did.

"That little shindig you have planned tonight in the wardroom."

Jake had forgotten. After every at-sea period he liked to get all the aviators together in the wardroom. The LSOs gave out certificates to the crew with the best boarding average and the catapult officers put on a little skit about the worst mistake they had witnessed on the flight deck. Tonight Admiral Parker was supposed to present centurion patches to the crews that had logged a hundred landings aboard this ship. And he had asked Cowboy to participate in a skit. He had also forgotten about the skit.

"That will have to wait. Since the skipper of the A-6 squadron had the crash, I think I'll probably have to convene the accident board." Normally the commanding officer of the squadron that had the crash convened the board.

Farnsworth held up his hand. He stepped out the door and returned with a large, black binder, which he laid on Jake's desk. Farnsworth opened the binder to the accident instruction. Between the pages was a draft of the appointing order for Jake's approval.

Jake looked it over. It was complete, except for the names of the officers who would do the investigation. Jake gave Farnsworth the names. "Type them in. You know, someday you and I are going to have to trade jobs for a day or two. I want to see if I know as much about running an air wing as you do."

"Thanks anyway, sir. But I just type."

"Any ideas on the A-6 crash?" Cowboy Parker asked. He was seated in his raised easy chair on the left side of the flag bridge. From this vantage point, he could see the activity on the flight deck without rising from the chair. A stack of paperwork lay on the window ledge in front of him.

Jake told him what Majeska had said. "I think he's probably lying," Jake concluded. "We've checked these lox systems from here to Sunday and they're perfect. Jelly Dolan may have had the oxygen system in his Tomcat go out on him, but I don't think Bull did. The probability of that happening twice without defective shipboard oxygen equipment is astronomical."

"And you're damn sure the shipboard equipment is okay?"

"Positive."

"Did you tell Majeska you think he's lying?"

"Yes, sir. I did."

"And he stuck to his story." Cowboy Parker cocked his head and scratched it. "So if he lets it lay like this, he'll get hammered in the accident report. And he knows you'll rip him on his fitness report. He might even be relieved of his command. He's finished in the navy."

"That's about the size of it."

"Yet for him that's preferable to telling the truth."

Jake held both hands out. "If he's lying."

"What the hell could he have done in that cockpit?"

"It's probably something he didn't do."

"But what?"

Jake shrugged helplessly.

"If you know he's lying, why don't you relieve him now?"

"I don't know anything. I have a hunch he probably is. He even hinted he was. But you don't can a guy on hints or hunches."

"We have a missing bombardier. What's his name? Reed? He's undoubtedly dead. I expect some answers. We aren't going to flush this down the john and go on our merry way." Cowboy Parker's face was devoid of emotion. "If you can't get the truth out of Majeska, you send him up here to me."

"Give me some time, Admiral."

Cowboy turned his face toward the deck below. Sailors in blue and yellow jerseys were busy moving aircraft. The snorting of the flight deck tractors was inaudible this high in the island.

"Has the *Wedel* recovered any of the wreckage?"

"Some skin panels. A piece of the radome. Half a flap."

"What do you want me to do in this skit of yours tonight?"

"Let's cancel the skit. I'm fresh out of chuckles. Just plan on presenting those centurion patches. Maybe make a few remarks."

Cowboy picked up a document from the stack on the ledge. "See you there."

"Yessir." Jake saluted.

Jake stopped in a berthing compartment on the O-3 level, aft of the arresting gear machinery spaces. The passageway went right through the compartment, which berthed over eighty men. In one small area where two passageways met, the sailors in their underwear sat on folding chairs around a metal cruise box, playing cards. Jake leaned against a bunk support and watched the game. Several of the men acknowledged his presence with a nod, then ignored him. This was their territory and he was a senior officer, an outsider.

The air was musty, laden with the tang of sweaty bodies and dirty clothes. Air circulation in here was impeded by the curtains that isolated the various bunks. The place resembled an old railroad Pullman car. In the last few years the upper echelons of the navy had devoted much thought to improving habitability in sailors' berthing compartments and getting rid of these curtains, yet the curtains remained. A curtain on his bunk was all the privacy a sailor had. Only in his bunk could a man write a letter or read a magazine without someone looking over his shoulder.

Soft music came from one of the top bunks. A male voice sang slowly, clearly,

147

It was way past midnight,
And she still couldn't fall asleep,
This night her dream was leaving,
She'd tried so hard to keep,
And with the new day's dawning,
She felt it drifting away,
Not only for a cruise,
Not only for a day.

"Turn that damn thing off, Willis, you jerk." The speaker was one of the cardplayers, about twenty, with intense eyes and sandy hair that needed trimming.

"I live here too, Ski," came the voice from the bunk. The piano was light and haunting.

Too long ago, too long apart,
She couldn't wait another day for
The captain of her heart.

"Don't you have earphones for that blaster?" called the black man seated beside the sandy-haired guy.

"Yeah."

"Then either use them or turn the damn thing off, man. We don't want to listen to that crap." The saxophone wailed plaintively.

As the day came up she made a start,
She stopped waiting another day for
The captain of her heart.

"I ain't gonna ask you again, Willis," the black man said ominously.

The music died abruptly.

"Who's dealing the fucking cards?"

An endless army of small clouds drifted across the face of the sea. Jake stood on the forward edge of the flight deck with his hands in his pockets and braced himself against the motion of the ship's bow as she met the swells. The clouds were puffy and white and cast crisp shadows that turned the water a darker, deep intense blue that was almost black. The clouds and shadows moved from starboard to port, spanking along in a stiff breeze.

The Mediterranean under an infinite sky with the clouds and shadows cast by a brilliant sun—this had been the inspiration for poets and singers ever since the days of Homer, and probably even before. Odysseus had sailed these waters on his way home from Troy, as had Phoenician galleys, Roman traders. This ocean was the living heart of Western civilization.

And now another man lay beneath the waters in a sailor's grave.

Twenty-three years in the navy, nine cruises, one war—he had seen it and lived it so many times. Flight deck accidents, crashes, lives twisted and smashed and snuffed out . . . bloody threads woven into this tapestry of young men far from home, young men trying to grow up in a man's world.

And what of you, Jake Grafton? Have you made a contribution? Has the price you paid made a difference? To whom? What have you done that another couldn't have done in your place?

Tired and depressed, he walked over to the port side and went down the short ladder into the catwalk. At the forwardmost portion of the catwalk was a mount for a set of binoculars which a lookout could use when the ship entered or left port, or in foul weather. He leaned against the binocular mount and watched the cloud shadows move across the whitecaps.

Being a navy wife had not been easy for Callie. She had grown up in a family where the father had come home every night, where the rituals of dinner and socializing with neighbors and colleagues and going to church on Sunday had all been complied with. Married to Jake, the only rituals scrupulously observed were good-byes and homecomings. Not that he and Callie had ever really had a home, of course, what with two years here and two years there.

Maybe he would have left the navy if there had been children. They had wanted children, and it never happened. It was in the third year of their marriage that they decided to have a child. After six months off contraceptives, they had consulted a doctor. Jake recalled the experience vividly, since he had been required to take a bottle to the restroom and masturbate into it. Never in his life had he felt less interested in sex than he had at that moment, with his wife on the other side of the door and fully aware of what was going on in here.

When at last he emerged from the little room with his semen sample in hand, slightly out of breath, Callie and the woman doctor were discussing the sexual act in graphic, explicit terms—clinical details that somehow sounded more obscene to Jake than any locker room comment he had ever heard. He had handed the sample to the nurse and sat at attention in the chair beside Callie while the women plowed the territory—ovulation and timing and body temperature and the position of the penis in relation to the cervix—with only occasional glances in his direction. "Be fruitful and multiply," the doctor had said, and sent them forth armed with a complex chart that Callie posted on their bedroom wall and annotated diligently.

He had received telephone calls from Callie in midafternoon at the squadron, joyous proclamations that now was the hour. He remembered whispering embarrassed excuses to the operations officer, dashing madly home, and ripping off his clothes as he charged through the door.

Callie collected a library of sex manuals. He could still see her sitting naked in bed, legs folded, studying an illustrated manual he had purchased from a giggling female clerk whose eyes he had been unable to meet. Their lovemaking became desperate as they experimented with positions, Callie's hunger a tangible thing. He suspected she was continuing to see the doctor, but he didn't ask and she didn't volunteer.

Then, finally, the crying began, hysterical sobbing that continued for hours and he could not console. He had felt so helpless. After almost a month the crying jags stopped. Their lovemaking became relaxed, less athletic, more tender. Those gentle hours he now treasured as the high points of his life. One day he noticed the wall chart was gone. The sex manuals were also missing from the closet. He pretended not to notice.

And he had spent so many months, so many years, away from her!

For what?

Tired beyond words, Jake Grafton turned and walked aft along the catwalk.

The squadron skits were over and the centurion patches handed out that evening when Jake finally stood up at the air wing officers meeting in the main wardroom. Apparently no one noticed that the air wing staff officers hadn't seized this opportunity to make fools of themselves. Every chair in the room was taken and people stood along the bulkheads. Bull Majeska sat in the front row with the other squadron skippers. Admiral Parker had excused himself earlier and left for the flag spaces. The dinner service had been completed an hour before the meeting started, yet the stained tablecloths remained on the tables. The combined body heat was overloading the air conditioning system.

"Okay, gentlemen. Now we find out who the real carrier pilots are and who just talks a good line. Without further ado, the LSOs." Jake clapped as he sat down, but he was the only one. A resounding chorus of boos made the walls shake.

Lieutenant Commander Jesus Chama, the senior landing signal officer—he was attached to Jake's staff and flew F/A-18s—stood up with a wide grin and motioned for silence. He was of medium height and sported a pencil-thin mustache on his upper lip. "Thank you. Thank you all. I can't tell you how gratifying a welcome like that is. It warms our teeny little hearts." More boos.

"The list, please." Chama held out his hand with a flourish. One of his fellow practitioners of the arcane art of "waving" aircraft, of scrutinizing an approach to the ship from a small platform beside the landing area and helping the pilot via radio when necessary, handed him a sheet of paper. Chama held it at arm's length, squinted, and slowly brought it toward his face. When he had the paper against his nose, he lowered it with a sigh and took a set of glasses from his trouser pocket. The glasses were a prop Chama had slaved on for hours in the air wing office. The bottoms of two Coca-Cola bottles were inserted in the frame in place of lenses. Chama had had to heat the plastic frame and bend it to make it hold. He had destroyed three frames in the process. Now he carefully placed his masterpiece on his nose, hooking the earpieces behind each ear.

As the laughter rose to a roar Chama started the list at arm's length again and slowly worked it inward. When it reached his nose, he shouted, "Third place, squadron boarding average, the Red Rippers." The VF-11 skipper stood up beaming while his officers cheered and clapped behind him. Everyone else hooted derisively.

The LSOs graded every approach to the ship, and a running score sheet for every pilot was posted in the ready rooms. A squadron average was an average of the individual scores of every pilot attached to that squadron.

151

Chama handed out the second- and first-place squadron awards, then began on individual awards. After third and second were handed out, he motioned to Jake. "Sir, maybe you better give this last one out. I don't have the stomach for it." Jake stood and looked over Chama's shoulder at his list.

"Him?"

"Yessir."

"Couldn't you have fudged it up or something? Everyone knows you guys rig the scores, anyway."

"Sir!" Chama feigned outrage.

"This is very painful."

"You must do your duty, sir."

"I suppose." Jake sighed and looked through the faces in the crowd for the one he wanted. When he found it, he said, "Okay, Wild, get up here and collect your award."

A storm of applause followed as Major Wild Blue Hickok, an exchange pilot from the U.S. Air Force, made his way through the crowd. By the time he arrived beside Jake, his face was flushed.

"Wild here, in his grungy air force flight suit, had a boarding average for this at-sea period of 98.2. That's figured on ninety-two passes over almost four months. Gentlemen, that is one hell of an accomplishment and, so far, stands as a record for *United States*. Wild, have you ever given any thought to an interservice transfer?"

"No, sir. Not since the air farce announced it's going to issue leather flight jackets again."

Howls of glee greeted this remark. After forty years of nylon and nomex, the air force had recently announced leather jackets would soon be issued to combat-qualified flight crewmen as a career retention measure. The navy men were suddenly extremely proud of the fact that the navy—their navy—had never abandoned its World War II policy of issuing leather jackets to its aviators. Wild had been ribbed unmercifully by his navy comrades, many of whom had taken it upon themselves to personally inform Wild that anyone who would stay in any military service to get a leather jacket was a damned fool.

When Wild Blue and the LSOs were finally seated, Jake had the floor to himself. He waited until the crowd was silent. "We've been at sea for almost four months, flying every day but three, and you guys have done an outstanding job. You've kept the airplanes properly maintained and in the air. We've met our commitments. We've done the job the navy sent us here to do. I'm proud of each and every one of you."

He faced the squadron skippers. "I want you gentlemen to let every enlisted man in your squadrons know that I am equally proud of them. Without our troops the planes wouldn't fly."

He directed his attention back to the faces in the crowd, the bulk of whom were young pilots and naval flight officers on their first or second cruise. "This profession of ours requires the best that we can give it. Three men who were here for our last little soiree aren't here tonight. Sometimes your best isn't good enough, and you have to live with that. Sometimes nobody's best is good enough. Those are the hazards."

Out of the corner of his eye Jake saw Bull Majeska staring at the floor. Jake picked out a young face he did not recognize about ten rows back and tried to talk to him. "In wartime officers are promoted due to their ability to lead in battle. In peacetime, too often, they are promoted because they are good bureaucrats. In case you guys haven't figured it out, the navy is a large bureaucracy." Chuckles stirred the crowd.

"Pushing paper isn't enough. And driving an airplane through the wild black yonder isn't enough. There is something else, something that's a little difficult to put into words." All this had seemed so simple this afternoon in his office as he doodled and thought about what he wanted to say.

He put his hands in his pockets and walked to a new position, then searched again for that anonymous, smooth young face he had been talking to. "You have to have faith—faith in yourself, faith in the guy beside you, faith in your superiors, and faith in the people who work for you.

"You see, a military organization is a team of people who have to rely on each other. The more complex our equipment becomes, the more intricate our operations, the greater the reliance has to be. We can't function unless every man does his job. We must all do the absolute best we can, each and every one of us. We'll each do our part. We'll stick together. We'll accept responsibility. Not for personal gain, not for glory, not for promotion, not for . . ." He ran out of words and searched the faces looking at him.

Did they understand? Could they understand? It sounded so

trite when he said it aloud. Yet he had believed it all his adult life and had tried to live it.

"You must have faith. And you must keep the faith." The faces, these faces, tan, black, brown; he had been looking at these faces for twenty years. Even the names were the same, American names, from every dusty, weary corner of the earth. And the nicknames—Slick, Box, Goose, Ace—all the same. He felt old and worn. He walked toward the door and a lieutenant standing near it called the room to attention.

12

JAKE GRAFTON hurried to keep up with Captain James as he loped along over the knee-knockers and down the ladders. Behind Jake trailed the ship's Damage Control Assistant—a lieutenant commander—and a first-class petty officer with a clipboard. The captain's marine orderly followed them all.

The official weekly inspection of the ship for cleanliness and physical condition was accomplished by junior officers—lieutenants and below—who each received a group of twenty to thirty compartments, a "zone," which they toured and graded and commented upon. But Captain James liked to inspect random compartments from several zones, then compare his observations with the written comments of the junior officers assigned those zones. When the official inspectors missed serious discrepancies caught by the captain, or gave a satisfactory or above-average grade to a compartment the captain judged unsatisfactory, lively, one-sided discussions ensued on the bridge near the captain's chair, with the offending young officer standing at nervous attention and saying "Yessir" or "Nosir" at the end of every one of the captain's sentences. Consequently, aboard *United States* the junior officers hunted through the compartments for discrepancies like starving rats searching for crumbs, and the harried sailors worked like slaves to keep the ship clean, with all her myriad of systems in good working order.

The air wing commander didn't usually participate in these weekly exercises in high-stress, power leadership. Today, however, Captain James had requested his presence and was leading him through compartments assigned to the air wing. Jake felt like a parent being shown damage his children had caused.

The captain stopped outside a closed door and rattled off the compartment number from the plate near the door as he seized and held the doorknob.

"VF-143 airframe shop, sir," chirped the petty officer with the clipboard.

The captain twisted the knob and shot through the door as it opened. Someone inside called a hasty "attention on deck."

James ignored the sailors rising clumsily to their feet. "Deck's dirty. Lightbulb out." He stopped beside a desk and examined the top. He brushed the paper aside. There were gouges in the soft material that formed the writing surface. "See that?" He looked at the nearest sailor, a third-class petty officer. "See that? That's an expensive desk and it's damaged. You people will want another one pretty soon and you won't get it. I won't approve it. You've got to learn to take care of this equipment. Move the desk."

Two sailors picked it up and moved it away from the bulkhead. The linoleum was discolored. The captain bent down and scraped at it with a fingernail. "Look here, son." The third-class bent down obediently. "This stuff comes off. Just move the desk and strip this old wax off and rewax it. Clean it up before it discolors the linoleum."

"Yessir."

"Compartment's unsat. Get this deck in shape." Without another word Captain James led the inspection party through the door and along a passageway toward the outside skin of the ship. He paused before a rest room, a "head."

"VF-11 space, sir," the clipboard man informed him.

In the captain went. The enlisted man in charge of keeping the space clean snapped to attention. Urinals lined one wall and stalls the other.

The deck was clean as a wedding dress. Jake nodded at the sailor, who appeared to be about nineteen. James looked into crannies on the bulkhead formed by the angle iron. Nothing there. This place shone like a new penny. The captain stuck his head into the nearest urinal and looked around under the porcelain lip. "Corrosion," he announced, straightening. "Take a look, sailor."

To his credit, the sailor didn't hesitate. He stuck his head in just like the captain, held it two seconds, then straightened and said, "Yes, sir. I see it, sir."

"Captain Grafton, come look at this." The Old Man was checking all the others. "Corrosion in all of them. These men aren't cleaning the inside of these urinals. That corrosion will eat through the porcelain if it's not removed, and then we'll have to replace the urinals. We've got a brand new ship here, three billion dollars' worth, and unless we take care of it, it's going to fall apart around us. I want these urinals kept clean. Get some soft brushes for these men to use, Captain. The men will do a good job if they have the proper tools."

"Yessir."

"Other than that, you have a good space here, sailor," Captain James said to the man, whose chest swelled visibly. "Above average."

"What's your name," Jake asked the sailor, who was wearing a T-shirt instead of his uniform shirt since he was on a cleaning detail.

"Zickefoose, sir."

"Keep up the good work."

Back in the passageway the captain went over the results on the clipboard of all the spaces he had looked at this morning. He had been in portions of seven zones and he had graded ten compartments unsatisfactory. "CAG," he told Jake, "Tomorrow I would appreciate you and your staff reinspecting every failed compartment the air wing owns." Jake would need to use most of the officers on his staff or he would be at it all day. "I want more emphasis put on cleanliness and material condition."

The captain's eyes fell on the watertight doorway in the bulkhead. He ran his finger along the knife-edge, the bronze edge that the heavy door sealed against. The knife-edge met a rubber grommet on the door when the door was closed and formed a seal. "This knife-edge is nicked. Is it on the list for the DCA?" The Damage Control Assistant, the officer standing behind Jake, was in charge of maintenance on all watertight fittings and fire-fighting gear. The damage control petty officer in each squadron or ship's division reported discrepancies to the DCA, who used his own staff to make repairs.

The first-class flipped to a list on the bottom of his clipboard. "Yessir," the petty officer announced, and read off the hatch number.

"When was it reported?"

The date was over two months ago. The captain merely looked at the DCA, turned, and walked away.

He paused at the first red fire bottle he came to and flipped the inspection tag up so he could read it. "How much does a fully charged CO_2 bottle weigh?"

"Fifty-two pounds, sir," the DCA told him.

"How much does it weigh empty?" The captain began unstrapping the red bottle from the bulkhead bracket.

"Thirty-five pounds or so, Captain." A look of foreboding crossed the DCA's face and he shot a glance at Grafton.

"The VF-11 airman who has been weighing this bottle has been diligent. He has correctly noted it weighs 35.1 pounds. Every inspection, every month. It's empty."

Laird James hefted the bottle, then passed it to Jake. "CAG, I want a report from you. I want names and dates. Explain to me how a sailor can perform his duties diligently and thoroughly, and still accomplish absolutely nothing. Explain to me how his efforts contribute to the combat readiness of this ship. This sailor's chief, his division officer, his department head, and his commanding officer are about to get charged with dereliction of duty. I want the report in twelve hours."

"Aye aye, sir," Jake Grafton said. "But these people work for me. I'll decide when and if they get disciplined."

Laird James cocked his head slightly and his mouth got even smaller than it usually was. He stared at Jake. In the navy these two officers had spent their careers in, the air wing commander was an officer with the rank of commander, and he answered to the captain of the carrier for a variety of things both operational and administrative. The CAG used to be subordinate to the ship's captain. But not anymore. The navy had just recently made the air wing commander a captain's billet—Super-CAG was the acronym currently popular—and had given him almost complete control over the ship's airplanes and weapons. Laird James and Jake Grafton were still feeling out this new relationship. Laird James made no secret of the fact he didn't like it very much. His lips barely moved when he spoke. "I won't tolerate incompetence on this ship, CAG. Anyone's incompetence. It may be your air wing, but this is my ship. There had better not be any more empty fire bottles in spaces assigned to your squadrons." His eyes flicked to the DCA. "There had better not be any more empty fire bottles on this ship."

The captain whirled and loped away for the bridge. His marine orderly strode along behind, trying to keep up. As he watched them go, the DCA muttered to Jake, "That's the first time I ever saw a captain in the U.S. Navy stick his head in a urinal. The—"

Jake cut him off. "He *is* a captain, and for some damn good reasons, one of which is he pays attention to detail. Another is he doesn't ask the men to do things he wouldn't do."

The skipper of the VF-11 Red Rippers, Harvey Schultz, was short and built like a fireplug. He was on a permanent diet after a series of confrontations with medical officers over his borderline noncompliance with the navy's body-fat guidelines. He argued his neck was too skinny, but the doctors said his waist was too big and their opinions were the only ones that counted. Behind his back, his junior officers called him Jack Spratt. The face above the stocky body was lined and seamed and looked like a hundred miles of bad road. The bags under his eyes even had their own bags. He was so ugly he was handsome, or so Callie had once told Jake after she met him.

"Find out why Airman Potocky doesn't know the difference between an empty fire extinguisher and a full one," Jake told Schultz after relating the incident. "I have to write a report for the captain. Gimme the names of chief, division officer, and department head."

"Aye aye, sir."

"Check every fire bottle that kid is responsible for. Have it done and report back to me within an hour. By the way, your man

Zickefoose had the cleanest head I've ever seen. You tell him I said that."

"Is this fire bottle business going to be a flap, CAG?"

"Nothing like it would have been if there had been a fire and someone had tried to put it out with that extinguisher."

"That's comforting."

Jake gulped the air when he stepped out onto the flight deck. He always thought he could detect the smell of oil in the processed air inside the ship. The air inside had a distinctive odor and right now he had had enough of it.

The sky was laced with broken clouds. The sea looked almost black, except for the few spots where the sunlight touched it. The task group was steaming west around the southern edge of Sicily. The two alert fighters were sitting in the hookup areas of the waist catapults, and the crews in the cockpits waved as he went by, then resumed reading their paperback novels.

Jake saw Ray Reynolds standing by the port catwalk near the optical landing system and walked over to him. Reynolds was watching four marines in camouflage fatigues install a fifty-caliber machine gun in the catwalk. Jake knew that two of the guns would be mounted on each side of the ship during her upcoming port call.

"Afternoon, XO."

Reynolds nodded at him, then resumed his supervision of the marines. In a few minutes the sergeant announced the gun was ready and sent a private to the bridge for permission to test-fire it.

"Sergeant, let's see you swivel the gun through its complete field of fire," Reynolds said.

The sergeant did as requested. "Now depress it fully."

"The stern quadrant is completely naked," Reynolds muttered to Jake. "And if they get within a hundred feet of the ship, these guns can't be depressed enough." He spoke again to the sergeant: "Okay. What's the drill on test-firing?"

"Every man who will stand watch on these guns will fire fifty rounds today, sir. We'll throw some cans from the galley off the bow and shoot at them as they float by."

"Try not to put any holes in those cans over there," Reynolds said, and gestured toward the destroyer a mile away on the beam.

"We won't, sir."

Reynolds nodded and turned away. As he and Grafton walked aft on the deck, he said, "I'm going to arm the flight deck security watch this time in port, CAG. Going to give them all shotguns. Wish we had more M-16s." Reynolds threaded his way between two parked Intruders and stopped at the after end of the flight deck. He looked down into the wake, sixty feet below. "I'm putting two marines up here with M-16s. The liberty boats will be coming in to the fantail. . . ." He gestured downward with his thumb. The fantail was the porch-like structure on the stern of the ship, immediately under the flight deck. "And we'll have a couple of armed marines there to augment the master-at-arms force. What else can you think of?"

"Looks to me like you have it covered. Are you expecting trouble?" Which was a polite way of asking if the XO had seen an intelligence summary that Jake was not privy to or had missed.

"Nope. Just worrying, as usual." He grinned, holding his upper lip down. "Don't you do that?"

"All the time," Jake said truthfully. The two men parted, and Jake walked slowly up the deck, examining the airplanes parked in rows.

He paused beside an F/A-18 Hornet and stared at it. Somehow it didn't look quite right. It took him half a minute before he realized the plane had only eight tie-down chains holding it to the deck instead of the requisite ten. He continued up the deck, checking each plane for open access doors and properly installed chains and chocks. His eyes roved freely while he thought about Bull Majeska and empty fire bottles and dead bombardiers. When he left the flight deck, he went through Flight Deck Control and told the handler about the Hornet that needed more chains.

Late that night Jake finished the report on the fire bottle affair and went to the bridge to see Laird James. The captain sat in his raised chair on the port wing of the bridge and read the report. Jake stood beside the chair and watched the officer-of-the-deck, the OOD, discuss the intricacies of a formation turn with the junior officer-of-the-deck. Apparently Captain James was listening to that conversation, too, for Jake saw him glance across at the OOD twice as he perused the report. In the center of the bridge stood the helmsman at the ship's wheel, watching the compass. The navigation table was on the starboard wing of the bridge, and beyond it two lookouts were visible, their binoculars up and sweeping the horizon. The remainder of the bridge watch team were busy with their duties.

"So the chief thought Potocky knew to report empty fire bottles when he weighed them, but he says he didn't, and the chief never checked up on him."

"The chief checked some of the bottles, but he didn't check this one, the empty one. And this *was* the only empty one."

"And the division officer never inspected the bottles to see if Potocky and the chief were doing their jobs."

"That's right."

The captain threw the report on top of a stack of paper which rested on the ledge in front of him. "CAG, I think the chief and division officer are derelict in their duties. I want them taken to mast."

"I think we should leave that decision to Commander Schultz. He's the commanding officer of VF-11 and that's his decision."

"These people hazarded this ship, *Captain* Grafton." He pronounced "Captain" as if the rank had been a gift from a mischievous god. "Their negligence put their shipmates' lives in jeopardy." James turned in his chair until he was looking directly at Jake. "I want every officer and man on this ship to know that such conduct will not be tolerated. I want it punished."

"Skipper, I'm not disputing the seriousness of this. But in my judgment Commander Schultz should have the discretion to handle this matter as he chooses. I'm not going to order him to do anything. Of course, if you want to hold mast . . ."

Both officers knew that Captain James could merely order the ship's master-at-arms to sign the report chit, and the accused would, in a week or two, stand at attention in his dress uniform to hear the charges read and Captain James prescribe the punishment. Mast, a nonjudicial proceeding, was really a means for the commanding officer to enforce discipline, and the only guarantee of fairness was what the commanding officer thought was fair. Both officers were acutely aware of the fact that an officer's or chief's naval career would be irreparably destroyed if either were awarded punishment at mast. They were also acutely aware that under the Super-CAG concept, James had been passing to Grafton all the report chits on air wing sailors generated by ship's personnel for him to hold mast on.

"What does Schultz intend to do about this?"

"I haven't yet discussed that with him."

"Get him up here."

Jake used the nearby telephone to call the Red Ripper's ready room. While they were waiting for Schultz, Captain James said, "I saw you sight-seeing on the flight deck this afternoon, CAG. In the future you might devote your time more profitably to inspecting the material condition of air wing spaces."

"I'm responsible for those airplanes down there, Captain."

"And two of those airplanes have been lost this cruise. This ship is not an airplane, Grafton, that we can afford to crash, then write an accident report on." Laird James picked up a document from a stack on the ledge in front of him and went over it carefully. Jake stood in silence and watched the yellow-shirted aircraft handlers on the flight deck move aircraft.

When Schultz arrived, out of breath because he had apparently run up the ten stories of ladders rather than wait for the elevator, James rested his paperwork on his lap and got straight to the point. "What do you intend to do with Senior Chief Cosgrove and Lieutenant (jg) Slawson for failing to properly supervise Airman Potocky?"

Schultz glanced at Jake. "Captain, Cosgrove has been in the navy twenty-six years. He's one of my two or three best chiefs. Slawson is a Naval Academy grad on his first cruise. He's a damn good young fighter pilot. The navy has made a hell of an investment in both of them and we're getting a hell of a lot in return. I intend to counsel them both, and the rest of my supervisors, and ensure they all know how to be supervisors."

"You inform them," the captain said, his voice so soft that Jake found himself leaning forward a trifle to hear, "that there will be zero tolerance for slovenliness, laziness, negligence, incompetence, or gross stupidity that puts this ship at risk. Zero tolerance. None whatsoever. That includes you gentlemen as well, Super-CAG or no. This is *my* ship."

Jake Grafton and Harvey Schultz saluted and left the bridge.

13

DO YOU KNOW I love you, woman?" Jake whispered.

"I've often suspected it," Callie replied, pretending to examine her nails in the moonlight which streamed through the open door to the balcony and fell across the bed. "But you sailors, with your women in every port! A poor girl must stand in line. And it just doesn't pay to invest much emotion in a 'here today, gone-tomorrow' lover."

Jake chuckled and nuzzled her neck, drinking in the smell of her and luxuriating in the sensuous pleasure of her skin against his, the sleek coolness of the sheets, the ripeness of her body under his hand. "That's me, I guess."

"I guess. So what am I? Number ten for you this month?" She giggled as Jake ran his tongue down her neck and across her collarbone, heading south.

"Eleven, I think."

She hugged him fiercely. "Oh, I love you, Jake Grafton, you

worthless gadabout fly-boy, you fool that sails away and leaves me."

When she released him, he propped his head on one elbow and ran his finger along her chin. She nipped at it.

"Have you been to the beach house lately?" he asked. Three years ago they had purchased a house on the beach in Delaware that they visited at every opportunity, anticipating the day when they would live there permanently.

"Just last weekend. You can still hear the gulls from the window, and the surf hitting the sand when the tide is in. But the upstairs commode stopped up. I had to call a plumber. . . ." She went on, detailing the domestic crises and how much it had cost. He rolled out of bed and slipped a robe on.

From an easy chair near the door to the balcony, he said, "I've been thinking a lot about that house, lately."

Callie sat up in bed and swept her long dark hair away from her face. "Is twenty-three years enough?" That was how long Jake had been in the navy.

"I can't fly at night anymore. I'm half grounded." She left the bed, came over to the chair, and sat on his lap. He wrapped the robe around them both, as far as it would go.

"It's my eyes. I'm losing my night vision. Something about liquid purple and rods and all that."

"My God, Jake, won't you miss the flying?"

"Yeah," he sighed disgustedly.

"And if you can't fly, how can you continue to command an air wing?"

"I can't. They'll send someone to relieve me pretty soon. I'll probably be home in a month or so, and they'll ground me completely. No more flying. Ever."

"Where will you go from here?"

"I don't know. Probably some admiral's staff someplace. We're short on radar repairmen, but we've got a lot of admirals and a lot of staffs."

"So you've been thinking about the beach house?"

"Uh-huh. And about us. About you and your gadabout fly-boy lover and all the time we've been apart. And I've been thinking, maybe it's time. Everybody retires sooner or later, unless they get zapped, and so why not? It's time you had a full-time husband, not some . . ."

Callie put her face inches from his. Her cascading hair framed her dark eyes. She put her hands on his cheeks. "I've been extraordinarily happy married to you. Oh, the separations have been hard to take, but I can endure the days alone because I know that, God willing, you're coming back to me. You are who you are and what you are, and I love you. So don't you dare start talking like you've given me the dirty end of the stick these last fifteen years. You haven't."

He started to speak, but she put her lips on his. In a moment he carried her back to the bed.

They ate a room service breakfast on the balcony, wearing only their robes. From here you could see the sweep of the Bay of Naples and the old Renaissance harbor where the yachts moored. The carrier lay several miles out to sea, foreshortened from this angle. Two surface combatants were anchored near her. The carrier's flat top looked grotesque, but the cruisers with their superstructures looked ominous, powerful—gray warships on a blue sea. And way, way out there, the sea and the sky were married by the summer haze. It was going to be hot today.

"Are you going out to the ship?" Callie asked as she sipped her orange juice.

"Thought I might, after a while. Then maybe this afternoon you and I could go somewhere together. How about Pompeii?" Jake sat looking at the ship and drumming on the glass table with his fingers.

"I'm glad you gave up smoking."

"I haven't made it yet," Jake said, and self-consciously stuffed his hands with their chewed fingernails into his robe pockets.

Callie hid her smile behind another piece of toast. Yes indeed, she decided, she had been extraordinarily lucky when she landed this one. Not that he had had a chance of getting away, of course. She ran a hand through her hair and stretched. Jake was looking down at the patio around the pool three stories below where breakfast was served al fresco.

"What are you looking at?"

"I thought I recognized that girl. But from this angle I'm not sure."

Callie rose and stepped over to the railing. She had her toast in her hand. "Which girl?"

166

"That one with the blue dress."

Callie leaned on the railing and called, "Oh, Judith. Good morning." The girl in the blue dress looked up, grinned, and waved.

"It's Judith Farrell," Callie announced, and popped the last bite of toast into her mouth.

"Where in the name of God did you meet her?"

"On the plane down here from London. She sat right beside me. She's a very nice young lady, an American reporter living in Paris. Gave me an excellent chance to practice my French. She's very fluent. She's going to be in Naples for two weeks. I asked her to have dinner with us tonight."

Jake's startled gaze left Callie and went back to the patio and the top of Judith Farrell's head.

"Who did you think she was?" Callie asked curiously.

"I thought she might be Ms. Judith Farrell of the *International Herald Tribune.* The world is just too goddamn small."

Up in his suite, Colonel Qazi swung his binoculars toward poolside and examined Farrell's profile. He was seated on a chair atop a table well back from the doors to the balcony so that he was invisible to persons in other rooms. After a moment he took his headphones off and handed them back to Yasim. He lifted the binoculars again. His brows knitted as he watched Judith Farrell eat her continental breakfast.

"Judith Farrell. What room is she in, Noora?

The girl checked the chart. "Room 822."

"You and Yasim get it wired as soon as possible. Bugs in her phone, bathroom, and bed."

"Who is she?" Ali asked.

"Ostensibly a reporter. She was on the ship in Tangiers."

"Could she recognize you?"

"No. I was fat and sixty-five years old for that appearance." He handed the binoculars to Ali, who trained them on the girl at poolside.

When Qazi received the glasses back, he swung them to the Graftons' balcony. So Farrell and Mrs. Grafton had side-by-side seats on the flight from London. Very interesting.

The colonel climbed down from his perch while the ex-CIA agent, Sakol, examined Judith Farrell with the binoculars. He fingered the focus knob. After a glance, he placed the glasses back on the table. "I've never seen her before—Mossad, CIA, or GRU."

"It is also possible she is what she seems to be," Qazi said with finality.

"Or she could be one of those amateurs that the Americans are using these days instead of the CIA professionals," Sakol retorted as he resumed his seat. "Perhaps she delivers autographed Bibles and cakes shaped like keys." He yawned and stretched.

"We'll check her room," Qazi said. "It would be an honor to have an opportunity to steal a Bible signed by a president." He turned to Ali. "What did you learn last night about security and antiterrorist precautions aboard the ship?"

"They have armed marines at the enlisted landing on the fantail, and on the officer's brow. Four fifty-caliber machine guns, two on each side of the flight deck, are manned by marines around the clock. Planes are scattered around the flight deck so there is no room for a helicopter to land. The radio masts that surround the flight deck are kept in an up position. Lights are rigged around the ship so that swimmers and small boats cannot approach at night unseen."

"And the communications?"

"He got it all," Sakol sneered. "Your sadistic, camel-fucking assistant enjoyed every minute. He had a hard-on the whole time. I thought his cock was going to rip his zipper out."

Ali's right hand moved toward the pistol he carried in his trouser pocket, since it was too hot to wear a jacket.

Qazi waved his hand at Sakol. "Enough, Sakol. Enough. I can't let Ali shoot you just yet."

"The little prick wouldn't enjoy just shooting me. He would first want to—"

"Enough!"

"I'm going to get some sleep," Sakol said. "You perverts figure out how you're going to rape the world. Put Ali near the crotch." He went into the bedroom and slammed the door.

"He will betray us," Ali said.

"Perhaps, given the opportunity." Qazi sighed and stretched. "Are we on schedule?"

"It will be very tight. I am returning to Africa this afternoon. Noora should return with me. We will need her to handle Jarvis."

"Three days. We must be ready to go in three days. The Americans might sail at any time."

"Their reservations are for another seven days," Yasim reminded them.

"The American government could order the ship to sail at any time in response to events in Lebanon. This would be an excellent time for those Shiite fools to behave themselves, but one cannot expect miracles. We must seize this opportunity before it escapes us."

"Then we must make some changes."

"Yes." Qazi rubbed the back of his neck. Ensuring the painstaking accomplishment of a myriad of small details was the foundation of a successful clandestine operation, and the reason Colonel Qazi was still alive after twelve years in the business. He insisted Ali and his other lieutenants exhibit the wholehearted enthusiasm for detail he preached. Unanticipated events would occur in spite of every precaution, but the less left to chance the better.

"Tell me about the communications."

Jake left the hotel at eight A.M. with four other officers he met in the lobby. All were attired in civilian clothes. Walking down the Via Medina together, they still drew glances from pedestrians and kamikazes zipping by on motor scooters. American sailors on liberty were no longer authorized to wear their uniforms ashore due to the terrorist threat, but their nationality was obvious to everyone, especially when they opened their mouths. Another regulation decreed without even a nod toward reality, Jake mused. He began to perspire as he walked. The exercise felt good after so long without it.

They turned left when they reached the Piazza Municipio and walked down the divided boulevard toward the harbor. Behind them, across the top of the boulevard, was the Municipal Building. On their right the Castel Nuovo jutted upward into the dirty-white morning haze. On the side of the seven-hundred-year-old structure Jake could see a shell impact mark, perhaps a scar from World War II. It appeared as if a shell with a contact fuse had gouged a shallow hole in the stone and the shrapnel had ripped out gouges which radiated in all directions from the center crater. Jake wondered how many wars and sieges and shellings the castle had withstood.

The little group threaded their way through bumper-to-bumper morning traffic to the gate to the quay. The carabinieri on duty gave the little group a salute and received smiles in reply.

They joined other officers and men waiting for the ship's launch. As they chatted they watched the ferries getting under way for Ischia and Capri. People boarded the vessels through the stern, then each moved slowly ahead as a man on the bow took in the anchor cable and, a hundred yards from the quay, the anchor itself. Now the screws bit the water in earnest and the wake began to spread. As each ferry departed, people on the stern waved heartily to the Americans.

When the officer's launch arrived at half past the hour, Jake stood with the boat officer and coxswain amidships rather than sit in the forward or after passenger compartment. He had never gotten used to riding these small craft in the chop beyond the breakwater.

The launch plowed the oily, black water and stirred the floating trash with its wake as it passed the bows of four U.S. destroyers and frigates moored stern-in against the breakwater. At the masthead of each ship the radar dishes rotated endlessly. Most of these ships were part of the flotilla that accompanied and protected the *United States*. At the piers on the other side of the harbor, on his left as the launch made for the harbor entrance, ships of the Italian Navy were moored. Just visible in the haze beyond them was the rising prominence of Mount Vesuvius.

Jake looked aft, over the stern on the boat. Buildings from prior centuries covered the hills behind the Castel Nuovo and the Municipal Building. At the top of the most prominent height stood a magnificent stone castle. This was Castel Sant'Elmo, now a military prison. The flanks of the hill between the Municipal Building and Castel Sant'Elmo formed the oldest, poorest quarter of the city, the tenderloin known to generations of American sailors as "the Gut." The bars and girls there had entertained seafarers for centuries, and the punks there had rolled them and left them bleeding for at least as long.

Even with its smart new residential and shopping districts, Naples remained an industrial port city, not pretty, not spruced up for tourists, but a city of muscle encased in fat and smelling of sweat and cheap wine. It was an old European city that modern Italian glitz and new Roman fashion had yet to transform.

He watched the features of the city merge into the morning haze as the boat bucked through the swells beyond the harbor entrance. The natural breeze was magnified by the boat's speed, so the perspiration dried on Jake's face and his stomach remained calm. He even traded quips with the boat officer, a young F-14 pilot in whites.

Gulls looking for a handout swept over the launch, almost close enough to touch, their heads pointed into the prevailing wind, out to sea. On the boat's fantail the Stars and Stripes crackled at attention.

It was a good feeling, Jake reflected, seeing the gray ships lying there at anchor in the sun with the sea breeze in your face, the coxswain wearing his Dixie cup at a jaunty angle to prevent it from being blown off, his white uniform incandescent in the sun. This was the part of his life Jake would miss the most, this carefree, tangy adventure with the world young and fresh, life stretching ahead over the waves toward an infinite horizon.

But as the launch approached the *United States* Jake Grafton's thoughts were no longer on the scenic quality of the morning. The two linesmen lowered the bumpers at the last moment and leaped onto the float below the officer's brow as the launch brushed against it. At the top of the ladder the officer-of-the-deck saluted Jake, who nodded and rushed on by. He made his way to his stateroom on the O-3 level, right beneath the flight deck, and called Farnsworth as he changed into a khaki uniform. "Have you been ashore yet?" he asked the yeoman.

"Not yet, sir. I'm going this afternoon after I get a few more things done."

"How about having someone bring the maintenance logbook for that A-6 that crashed up to the CAG office. I want to look at it."

"I'll call their duty officer."

"Anything sizzling?"

"Same old stuff, sir. The XO is having everyone do another muster this morning. Seems three guys, one of them a petty officer, didn't show up this morning. So the XO is making the whole ship muster again."

"See you in a few minutes."

He wondered what that was all about. Ray Reynolds must be worried about something.

In the office he automatically reached into the helmet suspended from the overhead. It was empty. He accepted a mug of coffee from Farnsworth and stared accusingly at the helmet as he took the first experimental sips. Finally he retreated to his office, the "cave," where he flipped through the incoming messages and letters. The navy had named an officer to replace him, someone he didn't know. The new man would report in four weeks. No hint as to Jake's next assignment. Perhaps that was just as well. No doubt it would be some staff or paperwork job somewhere. Better he shouldn't know just now, while Callie was here.

The maintenance logbook was delivered by a young airman, whom Jake thanked. The book was a loose-leaf binder. On the metal cover in numbers an inch high was the black stencil "503," the side-number of the A-6 Majeska and Reed had taken on Reed's last flight. Below the large number, in smaller stencil, was the aircraft's six-digit bureau number.

Jake opened the book. On the right side were the "down" gripes for the last ten flights. Each gripe card carried the date of the repair, the name of the man who had performed it, and the corrective action taken. On the left side of the book were all the "up" gripes that had not been repaired. A down gripe, by definition, was one so serious that the aircraft could not fly until it was fixed. An up gripe, on the other hand, was a nuisance problem that could wait until the bird was down for another problem or a planned maintenance inspection before it was repaired, or "worked off."

Jake read the down gripes first and the particulars of each sign-off. The problems struck him as routine; the type of complaints that one expected an aircraft to have, especially if it were used hard, as all the A-6s had been these last few months.

The up gripes constituted quite a stack. The little forms were arranged in order, with the most recent on the top of the pile and the oldest on the bottom. When he had read each one, he went back through and read them all again carefully.

Finally he closed the book. What was there about that aircraft that caused a crash? There was not a single gripe on the oxygen system. Had Bull Majeska really blacked out? At sea level, where there was plenty of oxygen if his mask were not completely sealed to his face? Or was he lying? What revelation could he make that would be so terrible? Terrible to whom? To Majeska, of course.

172

When Jake found himself chewing on a fingernail, he slammed the book on the desk and shouted for Farnsworth.

"Gimme a cigarette."

"No."

"Goddammit! Please!"

"Bust me. Give me a court-martial. No more weeds for you."

"If you shaved your legs, Farnsworth, you'd make somebody a good wife."

"No cigarettes for you, sailor. But you wanna buy me a drink?"

"Go down to the captain's office and find out why we had two musters this morning."

"Yessir."

Up on the flight deck Jake wandered along until he found an A-6 unattended by maintenance troops. He lowered the pilot's boarding ladder and thumbed the canopy switch. The canopy opened slowly, the battery driving a small hydraulic pump that whined loudly in protest. He climbed the ladder and sat down in the cockpit.

He wondered if Reed would still be alive if he hadn't taken him flying that night. Mad Dog, with the regular, even features and the soft voice. Agh, who can say what might have been or should have been or would have been, if only . . . ? That kind of thinking was for philosophers and politicians. But Reed was dead. The kid that had had enough was now dead.

His eyes went from instrument to instrument. ADI, altimeter, airspeed, radar altimeter, gyro, warning lights . . . His gaze meandered to the buttons and knobs on the bombardier's side of the cockpit. He found himself staring at the black hood that shielded the radar and FLIR.

They were looking over a Greek freighter at night. Reed must have had the FLIR on, just as he had done when he and Jake had swooped down on that dynamite boat several weeks ago. And Reed would have had his head glued against the hood. Bull Majeska had been sitting here, flying the plane, close to the water —how high? As they went by the ship Reed would have used the zoom lens on the FLIR in the nose turret to see the detail of the freighter. And Majeska? He would have squeezed the stick trigger and brought the infrared display up on the ADI. And he would have been paying attention to flying the plane. If he got too near the water, the radar altimeter would have given him a warning.

Jake's left hand went to that instrument and rotated the knob that set the altitude at which the warning beep would sound. He watched the little wedge-shaped bug move around the dial. If the pilot had it set too high, when the warning went off he would ignore it. If he had it set too low, when the warning sounded it would be too late.

Say Majeska was watching the freighter instead of flying. Or say he got distracted by something in the cockpit. The audible warning sounds when the aircraft descends to whatever altitude the bug was set to. And then? What? Majeska rights the plane and breaks the descent? No. Not that. They either hit the water or . . . Or what? What made Majeska refuse to talk?

Jake smacked his fist on his thigh and got out of the cockpit. He closed the canopy and strode across the deck. Down in the CAG office, he grabbed the maintenance logbook and flipped through the up gripes. There it was. "Contrast control on ADI intermittent. Went dark once. Possible short." That had been an up gripe. Two fights later, just the night before the crash, a down gripe: "ADI went black. FIX THIS THING." The sign-off was the same as on the previous gripe: "Could not duplicate."

He fired up the office copying machine and shot copies of both gripes. He put the copies in the top drawer of his desk.

"What did you find out?" he asked Farnsworth when he returned.

"They just said the XO told them to take another muster. He didn't say why."

"Here," Jake said, handing the maintenance log to the yeoman. "You can take this back, then go get some chow. It's lunchtime."

Jake called the XO, Ray Reynolds. "This is Grafton, XO. Just curious, why two musters this morning?

"One of those guys who didn't show for muster is a petty officer. Another's a marine lance corporal. I know the corporal. He stands orderly duty for me sometimes. He is one squared-away marine, a damn good kid. Something is wrong."

"Maybe . . ."

"Oh, I know. What officer ever knows what a youngster is thinking, what his wife or girlfriend is writing him? But I would have bet a month's pay on this kid. He's going to the Naval Academy prep school at the end of this cruise. I even wrote a letter of recommendation for his application."

"Terrorists, you think?" Jake asked, chewing again on a finger-nail.

"People see terrorists in every woodpile. I don't know what to think."

"Thanks for filling me in."

"Sure. How's Callie?" They exchanged pleasantries for a moment, then broke the connection.

Jake was sitting in the forward wardroom going over paperwork with four of his staff officers when Toad Tarkington brought his lunch in on a tray and sat down with his buddies at another table.

"Okay, Will. You scribble up responses to these messages," Jake indicated a pile, "and Harry, you do these others." Will Cohen and Harry March gathered up their respective heaps. "Unless a message is marked urgent, we'll answer the rest of them after we sail."

"Yes, sir."

"After Farnsworth gets the messages typed, I want you to put him on a boat for the beach. He deserves liberty and he won't go as long as he thinks there's still something in the in-basket. Kick him off the ship."

"You got it."

"Thanks, guys." The officers picked up their papers and departed. Jake raised his voice, "Mr. Tarkington."

"Yes, CAG."

"Come join me for a minute, will you?"

Toad brought his lunch tray with him. When he had resumed work on his hamburger, Jake said, "Remember that female reporter that came aboard in Tangiers? Judith Farrell?"

Toad nodded and mumbled affirmatively as he chewed.

"How would you like to have another go at her?"

Toad's eyebrows went together and he swallowed hard. "She's here? In Naples?"

"Yep. Going to have dinner with me and my wife tonight. How about you coming along and seeing if you can get her off my hands."

"Geez, CAG . . ."

"Now look, you idiot. I'm not asking you to put the munch on this broad. Just see what you can do to get her away from me. You did a real nice job of that in Tangiers and . . . since you're a sporting lad, I thought you might be willing to try again."

"She didn't think a whole lot of my act, CAG. When I need something hard to pound my head against, I can always go down to my room and bop the bulkhead."

"Hey, my wife tells me she's a very nice lady. Now personally I find that hard to believe, but it might be true. Maybe she was just playing the role for us yokels in uniform. You know, hard-boiled political reporter looking for dirt."

"Or playing a role for your wife."

"Toad, are you going to respond affirmatively to this request for assistance from a senior officer?"

"Uh, yessir, I am, since you put it that way."

"You're a good man, Toad. There's just not much demand for good men these days. Wear a suit and tie. Meet you at seven in the lobby of the Vittorio Emanuele. That's a hotel. Ask a cabbie where it is."

"You're picking up the check tonight, aren't you, sir?"

"Eat a couple hamburgers before you show up. That's an order."

"Has Majeska said anything yet?" Admiral Parker asked.

"No, he hasn't."

"The idiot," Parker muttered, more to himself than Jake. He rubbed his forehead with the fingertips of both hands. "He can't stay in command of that squadron."

"He knows that. But the alternative, for him, seems worse." Jake sipped his coffee.

"Do you have any ideas what happened out there?"

"I've got a theory. But that's all it is. No hard evidence. In fact, no evidence at all." Jake passed Cowboy the copies of the gripes from the lost plane's maintenance logbook. The admiral read each of them twice. He looked at Jake quizzically.

"I think the ADI blacked out on him and he got distracted. Or he had the infrared display on the ADI and the changing aspect angles disoriented him. In any event, he quit flying the airplane, just for a few seconds. Maybe he had the radar altimeter warning set too low. Or too high. Then he realized he was going into the water."

Jake shrugged. "I think he panicked and ejected."

"Leaving his BN sitting there?"

"That's the only thing that would explain his refusal to talk. He'd rather kiss his career good-bye than confess he panicked and punched out without warning his BN. I think he now believes he left Reed there in the cockpit to die."

"Maybe there wasn't enough time to tell Reed. Maybe if he had, they would have both died when the plane hit the water."

"Maybe. But if Bull thought that now, he'd probably be talking."

Parker tugged at an earlobe and read the gripes again, then passed them back to Jake. "I think you should relieve him of his command and notify Washington. Write a message requesting that he be ordered to remain aboard until the accident investigation is completed."

"I already have, sir." Jake passed a draft of the message to the admiral, who read it carefully.

"Have you told Majeska yet?"

"Not yet."

"Do it. If you're wrong, maybe he'll set us straight."

"What if I'm wrong and he's really telling the truth? Perhaps he really doesn't remember."

"Then you've just made a command decision on the best information available and mistakenly cut a good man's throat. You'll have to live with it and so will he."

Jake nodded and placed the message on his lap. He folded the gripe copies and put them in a shirt pocket.

The two men sat in silence. Finally Admiral Parker said, "How's Callie?"

"Fine." Jake chewed on his lower lip.

"Listen, Jake. Majeska has given you no choice with this. You must relieve him."

"I know." Jake's features contorted and he threw the message on the floor. "God damn his fucking ass! God damn him to fucking hell! That kid Reed was going to quit flying since he was getting out of the navy in six months. And I talked him into staying in the cockpit. Damn near ordered him to." He swore some more. "And then that fucker Majeska kills the kid and isn't man enough to face up to it. And now I have to can his ass." He ran out of steam. "Damn it all," he said softly.

Admiral Parker examined a picture on the bulkhead, then stud-

177

ied his fingernails. "What does Callie think about your quitting smoking?"

Jake picked up the message and folded it carefully. He crossed his legs. "She says it's about time."

Parker grunted. "Bring her out to the ship some evening and we'll have dinner together."

"Sure. Which evening? Can't do it tonight."

"Day after tomorrow?"

"Okay."

"Tell her I said hello."

"Sure, Cowboy." Jake got up to leave. "Sure. She'll be looking forward to seeing you again."

"Farnsworth, why the hell are you still here?"

"Uh, I had a few things still to do, CAG." Jake knew he would not go ashore until his boss did. He dropped into the chair beside the yeoman's desk.

"Call the A-6 ready room and ask if Commander Majeska is aboard. If he is, ask them to pass along that I would like to see him here in the CAG office as soon as possible."

Farnsworth had typed the message in Jake's hand, so he knew what this was all about. He dialed the phone and spoke to the A-6 squadron duty officer as Jake stood and stared at the helmet hanging upside down from the ceiling.

"He was in the ready room. He'll be right up."

Jake laid the message on Farnsworth's desk and signed it. "When Majeska gets here, send him into my office. Then I want you to walk out of here with that message, lock the door behind you, and take the message to the communications center for transmission. Then you are to change clothes and go ashore. That is a direct order." Jake stood up.

"Yessir."

Jake tilted the helmet on the coathanger, just in case. Nothing. He gave it a little punch with his fist, then went into his office and closed the door behind him.

When Majeska arrived, Jake motioned to a chair. "Sit down." The A-6 skipper looked exhausted, the creases in his face now deep grooves.

"I'm relieving you of your command, Bull."

Majeska nodded and studied his hands.

"Look me in the face, Goddammit!"

Majeska's gaze came up. His lower lip quivered.

Jake took the copies of the gripes from his pocket and unfolded them. He passed them across the desk.

Majeska read them slowly, unbelievingly, one after the other. When he finished with one sheet, he placed it under the other, and so read them again and again and again. It was as if there were six or eight sheets of paper, not just two. Finally he said, "You knew . . . that speech the other night to the air wing . . . you knew all along."

Jake held out his hand for the copies.

Majeska's chin sank to his chest.

"It was an accident, Bull. You didn't mean to kill him."

"There just wasn't any time. We were going down so fast, the water was right there. . . . I *had* to get out. There was no time to think . . . no time . . ."

14

YOU GOT SOME SUN this afternoon," Jake observed list-lessly as Callie straightened his tie. He was wearing a dark civilian suit. "You look . . ." He kissed her forehead.

She cocked her head. "Do you really want to go to dinner this evening? You don't seem to be in the mood."

"I don't get to take you out very often. If we didn't go, I'd kick myself when I was at sea for missing this opportunity."

She searched his face. Satisfied, she said lightly, "You be nice to Judith this evening."

"Hey, you know me. I'm charm personified. By the way, I asked one of the young bachelors from the ship to join us for dinner." Jake glanced at his watch. "He should be in the lobby now."

Callie eyed him obliquely in the mirror as she checked her lipstick. "I thought you found Judith abrasive when you met her in Tangiers."

"Well, she was probably under a lot of pressure. You said she is very nice. And this kid I invited is a great guy. Maybe they'll like each other."

"Abrasive?"

"All business. She wanted me to comment on things I'm not qualified to comment on and she wasn't taking no for an answer. It was like she was out to write a nasty article about prison camps and had stopped by our stalag for some material."

"She has to do her job." Callie collected her purse and stepped into the hallway. "What's the bachelor's name?"

"Toad Tarkington." Jake turned off the lights and checked that the door would lock behind them.

"That's odd. How did he get a nickname like Toad?"

Jake pulled the door shut with a bang. "He has warts."

"You've met my husband, Judith?" Callie smiled.

"Oh yes. Captain Grafton."

Jake was surprised at the firmness of her handshake. "Good-taseeya again," he muttered just as Toad came out of the bar with a drink in his hand. "Here comes our other dinner guest. Lieutenant Tarkington, this is my wife, Callie, and you may remember Judith Farrell."

"Mrs. Grafton." Tarkington shook Callie's hand perfunctorily, then nodded at Farrell. "Hello."

He received a polite nod and a cool appraisal from Judith Farrell.

"Well, folks," Jake said. "Let's go get some dinner." He took Callie's arm and led them toward the elevators. There was a small crowd waiting for the express elevator to the restaurant on the top floor of the building. The door opened and the people in front of them climbed aboard. There was obviously room for two more, but not for four.

"You go ahead," Judith urged Jake and Callie. "We'll catch the next one." Since a smiling Japanese tourist was holding the door open, Jake led Callie through the door, nodding at the man.

Judith stood silently beside Toad, not looking at him. He kept his gaze focused on the floor lights above the polished metal elevator doors. They waited. Several minutes later the doors opened again. They were the only passengers this time.

On the way up, Judith said, "Nice that you could join us this evening."

"Captain Grafton asked me to," he said matter-of-factly.

"I suppose he's worried that I might ask too many questions. And Callie is such a nice person. I wonder what she sees in him?"

"I'll have you know," Toad shot back heatedly, "that the CAG is one of the finest naval officers I have ever met. He's a gentleman in every sense of the word. He's also a genius with an airplane. He's more than capable of handling a twit reporter who—"

"I'll quote you on that," she said lightly as the door opened, revealing Jake and Callie standing there waiting for them. Judith grinned broadly at the Graftons and murmured to Toad as she stepped past, "Buy a paper."

Toad was still gaping at her back when the elevator door started to close. He elbowed it open again, his face twisted with fury. No one noticed. Jake Grafton and the ladies were already following the maitre d'. The women giggled together as they proceeded toward a table in the corner with a view of the harbor, and he caught Judith Farrell glancing at his reflection in the windows that lined the wall. Only then did it dawn on Toad Tarkington that he had just been had.

"Oh, so you're a linguist?" Judith said, looking at Callie. The two women had been carrying the conversation. Judith had been gently probing Callie about her life without her sailor husband while Toad sipped his wine and poked his fork morosely at the garbanzo beans in his salad. Jake Grafton seemed content to listen, observe, and nibble, speaking only when spoken to. Whenever Callie spoke, however, her husband listened attentively, and whenever she smiled or laughed, his face relaxed into a grin.

"Yes," Callie said, her eyes seeking Jake. "I've taught in several colleges near where Jake's been stationed, and now I'm translating for a government agency in Washington. It's temporary, but with Jake's career that's the way it has to be."

"Is that fair?" Judith asked, looking at Jake, who was gazing contemplatively at his wife. "Captain?" she added.

"What?" Jake said, finally realizing that he had been addressed.

Judith repeated the question and noticed that Callie's hand was now on top of her husband's.

"Probably not," Jake said. "I never thought so. But that's the way Callie wanted it." He shrugged, and turned his hand over and opened it. He smiled at Callie. Their hands remained together.

Judith Farrell grinned broadly and sat back comfortably in her chair. She even found a smile for Toad. Then the waiter brought their dinner.

Over dessert the conversation somehow turned to the political situation in the Mediterranean. "Captain," Judith said, "what will the president do about the kidnappings in Lebanon? Will he use the navy?"

"Is this off the record, or on?"

"Background. Not for attribution."

"Nope. If you want background, go to Washington. They pay flacks to give reporters background. I don't want you to even hint in print that you have ever heard of Jake Grafton, or even know who he is."

"Jake," said Callie. "She's just doing her job."

"So am I."

"Okay. Off the record. A never-said-it noninterview."

"I haven't the slightest idea what the president or anyone else in government will do," Jake said and sipped his coffee.

Toad chuckled, then swallowed it when Judith glanced at him.

"Do you know anything about the terrorist boat incident several weeks ago?"

"You mean the one where the boat tried to attack the task group off Lebanon?"

"Yes."

"I know about it."

"What can you tell me about it?"

"Judith, I think you're being coy. You know very well I flew that mission and later answered questions at a press conference. You've undoubtedly read some of the stories. You should have been at the press conference. We missed you."

"Nothing else to say? Is that it?"

"I'm not going to sit at the dinner table and tell war stories. That's a bad habit old men fall into. Ask me some questions about something I am qualified to comment on, off the record." The waiter delivered the check and Jake palmed it.

"I'll help with that," Judith said and reached for her purse.

"My treat," Jake said.

"We should go dutch. I can pay my way."

"Hey, if you aren't spending a dollar a minute, you aren't having any fun. Tonight I'm having fun. This one's on me."

183

"Is he always like this?" Judith asked Callie.

"When he's on good behavior," Callie told her.

"Okay, I have a question you are qualified to comment on. Do you think the law should be changed so that women can serve on all navy ships, in all career specialities?"

"Why not? There isn't a job in the navy that a woman couldn't do."

"Come on, CAG," Toad scoffed. "You can't mean that! Can you imagine having women in the ready rooms? In the wardroom? The navy would never be the same."

"It would be different," Jake acknowledged. "But so what? We need their talent and brains, same as we need the abilities of the blacks and Chicanos. Sexual segregation is the same as racial segregation. People use the same arguments to justify it. People will see that someday."

"You surprise me, Captain," Judith Farrell said softly.

"Me, too," Toad sighed gloomily.

Judith picked up her purse and stood. "Thank you for the lovely evening, Callie, Captain Grafton." She walked away without a glance at Toad.

"Toad Tarkington," Callie said. "You owe Judith and me an apology."

"Oh, I didn't mean anything by that, Mrs. Grafton," Toad said, reddening slightly. "But the CAG wanted me to get rid of her and I wasn't making much progress on the romantic angle."

The whites of Callie's eyes became very noticeable and her lips compressed to a thin, straight line. "Thanks a heap, Toad," Jake said disgustedly.

"Uh, well, I guess I'd better be shoving off." Tarkington rose hastily. "Thanks for the fine meal. 'Night, Mrs. Grafton." He tossed the last phrase over his shoulder as he marched for the elevators.

"Callie, I'm sorry. I thought Judith and Toad would hit it off."

"Oh no you didn't. You don't like her."

"She's okay. A little strident. But she's a reporter and I don't need any reporters. I was hoping Toad could waltz her off for drinks and whispers, and you and I could be alone."

Callie giggled. "She had you stereotyped."

"Yeah, as a Mark One, Mod Zero military Neanderthal. All Toad did was act like one."

□   □   □

Judith Farrell sat in a stall in the ladies' room off the lobby with her purse on her lap. She smoothed a thousand-lire note and wrote on it in block letters, "The rabbit was good. You must try it soon." She placed the pen back in her purse and made some noise with the roll of toilet paper. She flushed the toilet, and after washing her hands, handed the thousand-lire note to the rest room attendant on her way out.

The street was too dimly lit. Jake swore to himself when he realized his eyes were not going to adjust. He stumbled twice and felt Callie's arm on his elbow.

"Ha! How does it feel to lead a blind man?"

"You just need some practice in this light."

"Like hell. I just need more light."

"Don't we all," she said mildly and tightened her grip on his arm.

"Why are we out here, anyway?"

"Because we both needed a walk."

He relaxed a little when he realized he could see, though not very well. How the devil had he flown like this? It was a miracle he was still alive. He snorted again.

"Maybe it would be better if you put your hand on my arm and let me stay about a half step ahead." They tried it, and it did work better. "See, you can feel me step up or down."

"Yeah," Jake said sourly.

"Don't you wish you had eaten your carrots all these years?"

Jake found himself smiling. He swung her around and hugged her. Four blocks further on they came to a small bistro and sat at one of the outside tables under an umbrella labeled "Campari," after a local wine. They each ordered a glass. Light from the window behind them fell upon the table and traffic rattled by.

"Do you want to stay in the navy now that you can't fly?"

"I don't know. That beach house sounds awfully good right now. But I'm not sure how it would wear in six months or a year. I'm afraid I'd go stir crazy."

"You could always find something to do. Perhaps open a shop. Or go back to school for a master's. Don't think you're going to sit and wait to grow old." Her tone implied that if he did think that, he had better rethink it. "Perhaps you could teach classes at some civilian flight school."

"I don't want to see and smell and taste it and not be able to touch it." He sipped the wine. "But I guess I've nothing to complain about. Flying has been pretty good to me."

"I guess it has," she said. "You're still alive, in one piece, reasonably sane."

"Hmmm," he muttered, seeing Mad Dog Reed sitting in his office, explaining why he should go on to other things. God, how many of those faces had he seen in the last twenty years? So many dead men, so many withered, malnourished, blighted marriages, so many kids with only part-time fathers or no father at all, so many talents squandered and dreams shattered when careers went on the rocks or promotions failed to arrive. What had all this . . . waste . . . what had it bought?

And Jake Grafton? What had he spent the last twenty years doing? Driving airplanes! Dropped some bombs in Vietnam, and we lost that one. Taught a bunch of guys to fly, pushed a few mountains of paper, and drilled a lot of holes in the sky. Made a lot of landings. Got promoted. What else? Oh yes, spent fifteen years married to a beautiful woman, but only was there about half the time.

And buried some guys. Attended too many memorial services and too many changes of command, too many retirement ceremonies, made too many false promises about keeping in touch.

"I'm glad," he said at last, "that you think I'm reasonably sane."

An hour later they watched the moon set from their hotel balcony. As it sank toward the sea it appeared embedded in the clouds, which glowed with a golden light.

"You know," Jake said, "I guess it's the flying I've always went back to." The lower edge of the moon slid into the sliver of open space between the clouds and the sea. The sky with all of its moods and all of its faces was always new, never the same twice. But the flying, the flying—the stick in his right hand and the throttles in his left, the rudder pedals under his feet, soaring as he willed it with the engines pushing—the flying was pure and clean and truly perfect. When strapped to an ejection seat, encased in nomex and helmet and mask and gloves and survival gear, sucking the dry oxygen with its hint of rubber, he was free in a way that earth-bound humans could never understand. As he sat here tonight he could feel the euphoria and freedom once again as the flying came flooding back and he flew through an infinite sky under an all-knowing sun. Irritated with himself, he shook the memory off. "For what? I'm no wiser, no richer, certainly not a better person. Why in hell did I keep going back?"

"Because you couldn't leave it, Jake," Callie said softly.

"I'm not going to miss the night cat shots, though. I've had enough of those to last three lifetimes. I'm not going to miss the damned paperwork or all those long, miserable days at sea with no mail. And the ruthless, implacable bastards that make it all happen—the 'results matter, everything else is bullshit' crowd—I won't miss them either." He realized he was feeling his pockets for cigarettes. "I guess the bag is empty. Maybe I just never had any answers and am finally old enough to realize it."

"Whom are you trying to convince?"

"Myself, I guess." He examined his hands with the chewed fingernails, then remembered Majeska doing that not many hours before, so he stuffed his hands into his pockets. "We all go through life making choices, and each of us has to live with his choices, good, bad, or indifferent. But occasionally, every now and then, someone makes a mistake and finds that he can't live with it. And he can't correct it."

"Not you, I hope?"

"A guy on the ship."

"Someone I know?"

"Yes." He slouched deeper into the chair, his chin almost on his chest, and stared at his feet stretched out before him.

"That's what religion is for, Jake. It teaches us to live with mistakes we think we can't live with." She touched his arm. "That's God's grace."

"Well, I'm no chaplain." Jake sat silently watching the moonset, then finally levered himself from his chair and went inside.

Callie sat and watched the moon's glow fade as it slipped lower and lower into the sea. When she heard him dialing the phone, she stepped in through the open door.

"This is Captain Grafton. Who am I talking to?"

She knew he must be on the phone to the beach duty officer at fleet landing.

"Okay, Mr. Mayer. I want you to get on the radio to the ship,

187

talk to the OOD. Ready to copy? Have the senior chaplain aboard tonight go see Commander Majeska immediately. Tell the chaplain it is an urgent request from me. That's it. Got it?" He listened a moment, muttered his thanks, then hung up.

"John Majeska?" she asked.

He nodded miserably and gathered her into his arms.

Judith Farrell was sitting in a corner of the hotel bar facing the door when Toad Tarkington walked in, saw her, and came her way. There were two couples seated at tables in the windowless, paneled room, and several men stood at the bar chatting with the bartender. An opera murmured from the radio on the ledge behind the bar.

"May I sit down?" Toad dropped into a chair before she could answer. "Listen, I owe you an apology. Several apologies, in fact. Tonight I was just trying to move you out so Captain Grafton and his wife could have some time alone together. Honest, I didn't mean to upset you. I've got two sisters who have fought like hell for decent jobs, so I know how hard it is for women to find them."

"Did you come here just to say that to me?"

He nodded. "And to buy you a drink. Please, will you accept my apology?"

"Ah reckon," she drawled thickly.

He leaned back and laughed. "Thanks. Maybe we should start over. I'm Toad Tarkington." He stuck out his hand.

She took it, and he found her hand was dry, warm and firm. "I'm Judith Farrell, Mr. Tarkington."

"Call me Toad. Everyone does."

"What's your real name?"

"Robert."

"Why did you really come back to the hotel this evening, Robert?"

"To apologize. You're a nice lady and I felt pretty miserable."

"Oh. I was sitting here thinking you might have had a romantic motive."

Tarkington flushed. "Well, I confess that the possibility of a little romance might have been lurking somewhere way back there amid the cobwebs in the attic. After all, if you were some ugly old matron with three chins, I would have been nicer to you in the first place and my conscience wouldn't have squirmed and writhed and tortured me so."

She laughed, a deep, throaty laugh, and her eyes twinkled. "You impress me as a man who knows a lot of girls, but not many women."

"I know one or two," Toad said, well aware that he was on the defensive, yet unable to keep silent.

"You see them as girls. Soft, cuddly little things."

It was true. He stared uncomfortably across the table. In the past, one or two of his female acquaintances had thrown down this gauntlet and he had walked away, unwilling to discuss his feelings. The urge to leave was there now, but there was something else, too. This Judith Farrell . . .

The bartender came to the table and they ordered.

Small talk, Toad thought, small talk. Chat with her, man. But for the life of him he couldn't think of anything to say. She broke the silence. "How long have you been in the navy?"

He opened his mouth and his life story came pouring out. In a few minutes he realized he was making a fool of himself. He didn't care. He gestured and tried to say witty things and kept his eyes on her as she smiled appropriately and watched his face.

The drinks came and he paid. By now she was talking and he found her comments deliciously humorous.

Judith Farrell was certainly no girl. She was a mature, adult woman, happy with life. Perhaps contented was the word. He found her enchanting.

Then, in the middle of a vignette about her family, she gathered her purse in her left hand and pushed her chair back a millimeter. She finished the tale with a flourish and as he laughed, stood up.

"Do you have to go?"

She nodded. "I'm glad we had a chance to get to know each other."

"Could we see each other again?" Toad stood. "Listen, I . . ."

She reached out and her fingertips grazed his arm. "Good-bye, Robert." Her high heels clicked on the polished floor as she walked away.

Toad watched her go, then sank back into his chair. She had scarcely touched her drink. His glass was empty. He waved at the barkeeper, and failed to notice the man in his early forties wearing a gray pinstripe suit who set his empty glass on the bar and strolled out, less than a minute behind Judith.

What had he said that struck her wrong? Dejected, he sat contemplating the chair where she had been.

15

THE SEPTEMBER HAZE obscured the sky, except for a pale, gauzy blue patch directly overhead. Here and there the tops of fluffy little clouds could be discerned embedded in the insubstantial whiteness. The haze completely obscured the peaks of the two islands that formed the gate to the Bay of Naples, Capri and Ischia. Looking toward the coast, one could make out the major features of the Naples estuary, but the coastline north and south merged into this gray-white late-summer mixture of moisture, smoke, and North African dust.

Toad-Tarkington strolled along the flight deck of the *United States* and cataloged the day as a partial obscuration, visibility five miles in haze. Then his attention wandered to a more important subject—a woman.

"Women!" he grumped to himself. Just when your life is flowing along like smooth old wine, a woman shows up.

Women are like cars, he told himself as he meandered along with his hands in his pockets, automatically weaving around the

191

parked aircraft and their webs of tie-down chains, looking only at the gray steel deck in front of his shoes. There are the old sedans, he decided, dowdy and faded, the Chevys and Fords of the world that putter along and get you there for as long as you want to go, not too fast and not in style, but dependable. Then there are the racy Italian jobs that can rip up to warp three in a heartbeat, wring out your skinny little ass, and leave you broken and bleeding beside the road. And finally, there are the quality machines, the Mercedes of the world, the ones that go fast or slow in elegant style, that last forever, and you are exultantly happy with all of your days.

Judith Farrell was a Mercedes, he decided. His Ms. Farrell was not some cheap crackerjack hot rod for a flashy Saturday night date, but a quality piece of design, engineering, and workmanship. She had character, brains, wit, beauty, and grace. He thought about the way she moved, how her hips swayed slightly— but not too much—above her long, shapely legs, how her hair accented the perfect lines of her face, how her breasts rose and fell inside her blouse as she breathed. How her lips moved as she spoke. How she smiled. Just thinking about her was enough to make a man sweat.

And you dumped all over her, fool! Not just once, not just the first time you met her. Oh no. You did it twice. Providence gave you a second chance and you blew that too. You idiot!

He descended into the catwalk that surrounded the flight deck and leaned on the rail just above the forward starboard Phalanx mount. Immediately below him a barge lay tied to the side of the ship, but Toad took no notice. He stood with his elbows on the rail and his chin propped on one hand, gazing blankly at the hazy junction of sea and sky, cataloging once again all the charms he now knew Judith Farrell possessed, charms that apparently lay forever beyond his fevered reach.

The barge was a paint scow. It had been towed into position shortly after dawn by a tug. In its hold were dozens of fifty-five gallon drums of paint, and ropes and scaffolds and long-handled rollers and a gang of a half-dozen or so workmen wearing coveralls that displayed the spills and drips incidental to their trade. The scow itself wore the scars of countless accidents involving paint of every color of the rainbow, though gray seemed predominant.

On scaffolds suspended against the side of the warship—scaffolds not visible from the catwalk where Toad moped, since the sides of the ship slanted steeply inward from the catwalk to the waterline—pairs of men wielded long-handled rollers and brushes. After months of exposure to salt air and seawater, the hull of the *United States* resembled that of a Panamanian tramp steamer with a bankrupt owner.

The workmen quickly applied the new gray paint over the orange-red streaks of rust and what fading gray paint remained. However, on the scaffold near the hangar bay opening for Elevator Two—the second aircraft elevator aft on the starboard side and the one just forward of the ship's island—one of the painters worked slower than his comrades. He spent most of his time watching the unloading of a barge moored near Elevator Three, aft of him several hundred feet. That elevator was in a down position.

The sailors used a crane on the flight deck level to transfer cargo from the barge to the elevator. Wooden crates on pallets were gently deposited on the elevator where sailors derigged the wire bridles. Forklifts moved the crates from the elevator platform into the hangar bay. There sailors in blue denims and white hardhats noted on clipboards the stenciled numbers on the crates and directed other forklift operators in their shuttle of the crates to prearranged positions. They worked quickly and efficiently with only occasional shouts from a khaki-clad figure, a chief petty officer.

The painter on the scaffold worked slowly with his roller and observed the scene from the corner of his eye. The sailors should be done in an hour or so, he concluded. Already men were attacking the crates in the hangar, breaking them open and distributing packages to a seemingly never-ending line of men who carried the cargo below. They queued like ants to receive their loads, Colonel Qazi thought. He noticed that the laden porters took orders from another chief with a clipboard before they departed, and they walked away in every direction to hatches around the walls of the two-acre hangar bay. The colonel correctly surmised that the contents of the crates were being carried to many different compartments throughout the ship.

After a while Qazi's companion, Yasim, finished the section they were working on, so Qazi shouted in Italian until he attracted the attention of the sailor on the catwalk above and outboard of them. With much swaying the scaffold was moved until it hung immediately beside the Elevator-Two entrance to the hangar bay. From there Qazi could better observe the layout and activity of the hangar bay.

Even though it was daytime, the bay was brightly lit from an array of lights on the overhead.

"So many men," Yasim commented softly.

"Yes. All trained technicians. Look at the men working on the aircraft. See all the black boxes." The access panels were open on many machines, exposing the myriad of electronic components that filled every cubic inch of the fuselages that did not contain engines or fuel tanks.

"We do not have this many technicians in our whole country," Yasim said, the envy in his voice discernible.

The colonel motioned Yasim back to work and dipped his own roller in a paint tray. They had better stay busy or they would surely attract someone's attention.

"When?" Yasim queried.

"Tomorrow night, Saturday night," the colonel muttered as a fine spray of paint from his roller misted across his face. "It must be then. The crate comes aboard tomorrow morning and it won't sit there forever. These people are too efficient."

"How do we know they won't open it?"

"We don't." The colonel paused and looked again at the men with the clipboards. They appeared to be comparing the crate numbers against preprinted lists. Computer-generated lists, the colonel surmised. "The numbers on our crate don't match anything on their lists. So they will leave it to last."

"But what if they open it?" Yasim persisted.

"Then they will think there has been a mistake."

The real problem, the colonel knew, was where they would put the crate, opened or unopened. He had toyed with the idea of placing a beeper in the crate, but with so many electronic sensors on the ship, he had rejected that option as too risky. Selecting an unmonitored frequency would be pure guesswork, if there were any unmonitored frequencies, which he doubted. He would just have to visually search for the crate when the time came, betting everything that he could find it.

He had bet his life before, many times, but this was different.

What was at stake this time was the Arab people's chance at nationhood. If this operation succeeded, the emotional and political pull toward one nation for the Arabs would be great enough to overcome the centrifugal tribal, economic, and political forces which had always kept them apart.

Although the forces of nationalism had fired humanity for two centuries, the Arabs still had only a patchwork quilt of states with every major type of government—dictatorship, monarchy, anarchy, even token democracy—all of which left the vast bulk of Arabs poor and ignorant, saddled by a religion that focused on a dead past and culturally unable to embrace science and technology, which alone gave promise of adequately feeding, clothing, and housing them.

So they were left in the wasteland with their dictators and demagogues, their passions and their poverty. Left in a desert of failed dreams which they were taught to accept because paradise awaited them. In the next life, not this one.

The Palestinians were a running sore because the system could not expand to take them in. The system could not grant their desire for nationhood because none of the Arabs truly had a nation. So the Palestinians were cast out, as the culturally oppressed in Iran felt they, too, had been cast out.

Would he find the crate? *Inshallah,* "if Allah wills it," his people would say.

I will find it, Qazi told himself. The Arabs have been a long time dying. The crate will be there and I will find it. Because *I* will it.

He pulled his cap visor down to protect his eyes and began vigorously applying paint.

"Is Chaplain Berkowitz around?" Jake Grafton asked the sailor at the desk in the chaplain's office.

"CAG, is that you?" Berkowitz's door opened wide and he stood there smiling. "Come in, please."

Berkowitz was short and wiry, with a luxuriant head of hair that always looked as if he had missed his last appointment with the barber. He was the senior chaplain aboard—the *United States* had three—and held the rank of commander.

"I was aboard last night when the OOD's messenger found me. I was delighted to help out." Berkowitz dropped into one of the visitor's chairs near Jake.

Jake glanced around. The chaplain had painted his office a light beige and procured carpets from somewhere. A Star of David hung on one wall. On the opposite wall was a cross.

"So how is Bull?"

"I can't violate a confidence, of course, but I think he is coming to terms with himself, which is the important thing."

Jake nodded. "I was a little worried. You know how it is with guilt. It's an acid that eats away everything."

"Chaplain Kerin is talking with him this morning. Commander Majeska's a Protestant, and Kerin is about as near to his denomination as we have aboard ship. It was a terrible thing about Lieutenant Reed, but Majeska is only a man and he made a very human decision. It's the same decision most of us would have made had we been in his place. I think he sees that. But until he understands that emotionally and comes to term with it . . ." Berkowitz ran out of words.

"Yeah," Jake said. "Thanks again, Rabbi."

"Umph. You aviators. You all think you are supermen." Berkowitz smiled to take the sting out of his words. "Naval aviation is the home of more titanic egos than any other enterprise I've ever encountered. With the possible exception of television evangelists and congressmen." He grinned again as a smile flickered on Jake's face. "Sometimes it's hard for supermen to face their own humanity."

"Yeah." Jake started to rise but Berkowitz motioned him back into his chair.

"I've wondered how you felt since the doctor grounded you." The chaplain leaned forward. "So this visit is not unwelcome. Perhaps you could tell me how you're handling it and that would help me when I counsel the other fliers. I see more of them than you might suspect."

Jake moved forward in his chair until only three inches of his bottom was on the seat. "I'm not very religious, you know. . . ." The expression on Berkowitz's face forced him to add, "But you guys do great work. We sure do need chaplains—"

"As a safety valve? To keep the pressure cooker from exploding? Every man is a pressure cooker, CAG, including you."

"Call me Jake."

"Jake."

"Yeah. Well, I'm making it."

Berkowitz rose and retrieved several sheets of paper off his desk. "All the men aren't making it, Jake. Five more UAs this morning." UAs were unauthorized absentees. "It's curious. Normally we don't lose men like this, although maybe the four months we spent at sea is a factor. But two of these people are petty officers." He read Jake the ratings: communications technician first and quartermaster third. "Curious."

Jake examined the list.

"One of the nonrated men who disappeared the last time we were in Naples has shown up in San Diego." The chaplain shrugged. "Do we have a problem?"

"Thanks for your time. How about keeping an eye on Bull?" Jake shook hands and left, headed for the XO's office.

Ray Reynolds was on the phone. "Listen, Lieutenant. These men aren't all drunk up in the Gut. Now I want them found." He covered the mouthpiece with his hand and whispered to Jake, "Shore Patrol." There was a permanent Shore Patrol detachment stationed in Naples under a U.S. Navy Lieutenant. Reynolds had undoubtedly reached him on the ship-to-shore telephone. "So what if I give you some more men? Will you search if I sent you some more men? . . . How many do you need?"

He motioned Jake toward a chair and consulted his watch. "I'll have them come in on the noon boat." Reynolds listened a moment. "I know what your responsibilities are. I'm sending these men with their own officer, and I expect you to cooperate with him. And this evening I'm going to be there to have a little face-to-face with you. You'd better have some good news for me."

Reynolds hung the phone up with the lieutenant's voice still coming out. His voice had not risen once during that conversation. He was known as a man who maintained an even strain, a man who never got excited, but you had better listen to what was said and ignore the conversational tone of voice or you weren't going to get the message. Jake wondered if the shore patrol officer had listened carefully enough.

"Jake, I need another dozen enlisted from the air wing and one more officer to augment the shore patrol. Make him a lieutenant commander so he doesn't have to take any shit from that lieutenant on the beach. Everybody in whites. Relieve them every eight hours. Have the officer come see me before he goes ashore."

Jake picked up the phone on his desk and called Farnsworth, relaying the order.

"Something is going on," Reynolds said when Jake hung up. "We're bleeding men like the Confederate army at Petersburg. If we get one more UA, just one, we're securing liberty."

Jake pursed his lips for a silent whistle. Locking the men up on the ship after four months at sea was a drastic step. "Been to see the captain?"

Ray nodded. "Laird James is not happy. He's sending a message to everyone in uniform east of the Mississippi. He's going to get on the PA system in a little while and tell the men what's going on."

"What is going on?"

"Damned if anyone knows." Reynold's massive shoulders moved up and down. "I still think it's the goddamn A-rabs, but guesses are three for a quarter. We've got to protect our men."

"Maybe we oughta go see the local authorities?"

"Admiral Parker already choppered off this morning to do just that. He isn't happy, either."

Jake stood up. "I'll have all the squadron skippers talk to their men before liberty call goes down. At least they can stick together, look after each other."

"Do that." The XO picked up the phone and started dialing. Jake headed for the door.

Colonel Qazi and Yasim were eating lunch with the Italian workmen on the paint scow when Captain James began speaking on the PA system. The bosun's pipe that preceded his remarks echoed through the hangar bay and was perfectly audible to the men on the scow. The workmen stopped talking to listen to the whistle of the pipe, but they ignored the captain since most of them didn't speak English. Qazi, though, listened carefully as he chewed pickled olives and sipped a local red wine.

After lunch he spoke to the painting supervisor, who had one of his men start the engine in the boat moored alongside and take Qazi and Yasim ashore. The workmen would keep their mouths shut, at least for a few days, Qazi knew, because they had been well paid. By one of Pagliacci's men. That fact was probably more important than the money.

As the boat carried them away from the ship, Qazi looked back.

She was so huge he felt a moment's unease. He could see the tails of the airplanes protruding over the edge of the flight deck and the top of the massive island with its arrays of antennas. In the catwalk on the port side he saw one of the fifty-caliber machine guns. The marine wore a helmet and was waving at them.

Qazi waved back.

"Lieutenant Tarkington is out here to see you, sir," Farnsworth said, leaning through the door to Jake's office.

"What's he want?"

Farnsworth managed an off-balance shrug.

"Okay." Farnsworth stepped through the door, opening it wide and holding it. When Toad passed, the yeoman exited and closed the door. The Keeper of the King's Gate, Jake thought. He would have to speak to Farnsworth. His doorman's bit was becoming too theatrical.

"Good morning, sir."

Jake stared at the junior officer standing exactly two feet in front of his desk. "Thanks a lot for your efforts last night, Tarkington. I really appreciated your suave and de-boner performance."

"I'm sorry, sir."

Daggone, Jake thought, he appears sincere. Jake bit a small piece of his lower lip to hold back the smile.

"So why are you here to waste my time?" Jake shook a piece of paper at Toad, who was staring at a spot two feet over Jake's head.

"Uh, I've made a serious mistake, sir. Judith really is a very nice girl."

Jake snorted and pretended to read the paper in his hand.

"She's really not like she seems. She's a highly intelligent lady." He cleared his throat. "I really want to get to know her better, sir."

"Really? Tarkington, that woman could rip the balls off a brass monkey. Why are you standing here in front of my desk?"

"She's a wonderful woman, sir. I see that now. At first I thought she was just another airhead. You know, a great bod and a brain that went into storage overload by the time she was in the fifth grade." His voice fell and he confided, "You know the type, sir— into astrology and screwball causes and long-haired cats. But

Judith's not like that at all. Uh, I guess I've sort of . . . like . . . um, fallen for her."

"Do I look like a chaplain? I don't give a damn about your love life or lack of it. That goddamn witch is probably related to the Borgias. Go write a long letter home to momma and tell her all about it. Get out of my office."

"I want you to get me another date with her, sir," Toad blurted. "Please," he added as Jake stood up so fast his chair crashed against the bulkhead.

Jake leaned across the desk and roared, "I don't procure women for anybody, mister. I'm a captain in the United States Navy. You're a fucking lieutenant and don't you forget it. How dare you come into my office and ask me to *fix you up!*" The last three words dripped off his lips like poison from a snake. "Jesus H. Christ!"

"But—"

"Shut up!" He could have silenced a riot with that shout. "I'm doing the talking here. Now when I finish, you will about-face and march your brassy, sassy ass out of my office. If I ever again lay eyes on you in this office on anything other than official business, you will be the radar intercept officer on a garbage scow in Newark for the rest of your naval career. Are you reading me loud and clear?" He was in fine voice, braying at the top of his lungs.

"Yes, sir."

"Don't you ever again ask a senior officer to assist you in your debaucheries." He lowered his voice: "You ask the senior officer's wife. Mine is still at the hotel." The volume went back up: "Now get out! *Out out out!*"

Toad fled. As the door to the outer office closed smartly, Jake collapsed in laughter into his chair. This was the first good laugh he had had in months. Farnsworth appeared in the door with his eyes wide and his mouth hanging open.

16

COLONEL QAZI AND ALI sat in the car and stared through the chain-link fence at the six helicopters sitting on the concrete mat.

"There's another in the hangar," Ali said. "Pagliacci's man says the choppers will be fueled and ready tomorrow night. The watchman at the gate and the man at the office of the helicopter company have been visited by Pagliacci's men. We are to tie up the watchman."

"We only need three helicopters."

"We may take any three. All will be fueled and ready, so if we have a problem with one, we merely leave it and take another."

"What if none of them are ready?"

"But . . ."

"What if the watchman gets frightened before you arrive and calls the police? What if there is a police car sitting there beside the office? What if the transport company manager has panicked and sabotaged the helicopters and none of them will start? We will already be aboard the ship. We will be committed. What will *you* do then?"

"Well, if it's just a police car, we'll kill the policeman and proceed as planned. If the helicopters won't start, we will go to the backup machines at the military base." Weeks ago Qazi and Ali had examined every airport within fifty miles, and had located acceptable machines they thought they could steal if necessary. "Nothing will go wrong, Colonel. We will get the helicopters."

"Where is our watcher?"

"Over there." Ali nodded toward an abandoned warehouse. "He's in that little room up at the apex. We relieve him every twelve hours and Yasim develops his photographs. If the watchers see anything suspicious, they will let us know immediately by telephone."

"Who are you using as watchers?"

"The pilots. Here and at the military airfield. But the last shift before departure will have to be stood by nonpilots. It's unavoidable. We only have four of them. Still, it's an acceptable risk. Nothing will go wrong, *inshallah*."

"Don't give me that 'if Allah wills it' dung! You will succeed no matter what happens, because you will be very careful, take precautions, and be ready for the unexpected."

"Yes, Colonel."

Qazi sounded weary. "Everything will go wrong. Believe it. Know it and be ready and keep thinking. Now tell me who comes to see the watchman after ten P.M."

"Occasionally, every third or fourth night, a security guard parks his car and they play dominoes. We haven't seen anyone else during the night, except helicopter company employees and passengers. Occasionally rich people arrive just before dawn and are flown to their yachts. And occasionally a chopper goes away and returns with a yachtsman, but those trips are in the morning or early evening."

"I am tempted to forego these machines," Qazi said thoughtfully, staring at the hangars and the black windows that looked down upon the concrete mat and the street. "One wonders about Pagliacci."

"Has he not done everything he promised—the vans, the uniforms, the weapons, the wiretap equipment, the cooperation of the ship-painting firm? For him, this is just good business."

"Ayiee, the faith of the foolish! Help me, Allah," Qazi muttered. "So tell me again how you will take the helicopters."

Ali did so. He had gone over the plan on four previous occasions with Qazi. He had it down. When he was finished, Qazi put on his brimmed hat and motioned toward the gate. Ali spoke to the man in the watchman's booth, the day watchman, then drove slowly on and parked by the door to the office of the helicopter company. He got out of the car with an attaché case and came around to the passenger's side, where he held the door for Qazi. The colonel eased himself out. Once again he was an old man. Ali preceded him and handed him the case as Qazi passed through the office door.

The only person in sight in the offices was a young woman. She had a breathtaking bosom and wide, ample hips. Her hair was yellowish blond, dark at the roots. She stubbed out her cigarette as Qazi muttered, *"Prego,* Signor Luchesi." She rose from her desk and bolted for the manager's door, glancing at Qazi over her shoulder.

He steadied himself with his cane and scanned the room. Aviation magazines lay on the table near the four pea-green chairs where customers presumably waited. Aviation charts of southern Italy and the islands covered the walls.

The door opened and a man in shirtsleeves appeared. The secretary was visible behind him, nervously smoothing her dress. *"Prego."* He gestured and Qazi entered his office, steadying himself several times by touching the wall for support. He carefully lowered himself into the armchair across the desk from the manager. The secretary took three steps toward the door, then stopped and stood, shifting from foot to foot, twisting her hands.

"Grazie, Maria." The manager nodded toward the door. He was at least twenty years older than the woman, bulging badly at the waist. His complexion was mottled, as if he had a heart condition. "I am Luchesi," he said.

Qazi opened his attaché case. He extracted three large manila envelopes and tossed them on the desk. "Count it."

"There is no need, signore." The perspiring manager spread his hands and tried to smile. "I trust . . ."

Qazi took the Walther from the case and laid it on the desk. Then he closed the case firmly and snapped the latches. "Count it."

The manager ripped open the first envelope and shuffled through the bills.

"Count it slowly."

Luchesi's head bobbed and his lips began to move silently. The light from the window reflected on the moisture on his bald pate. When he finished with the third envelope, he said, "Fifty million lire, *grazie*. I will do as promised . . ."

Qazi opened the case and put the pistol back in.

"You may rely . . ."

The colonel lifted himself from the chair. He opened the door and shuffled past the secretary, who sat at her desk chewing her nails. He could feel her eyes boring into his back.

Ali drove through the gate and proceeded toward the heart of Naples.

"He took the money. He's a nervous, silly little man. He'd better plan on making a fast departure from Italy. He'll confess everything within an hour under interrogation."

"Why won't he leave now?"

"Because Pagliacci arranged this. If he runs without earning the money, he'll be a walking dead man. He knows that."

"Perhaps he'll panic and betray us before the time comes."

"Not unless he's suicidal. And his secretary was hovering all over him. He had to tell her to leave the room." Qazi grimaced. "She'll clean him out in weeks. Ah well, every man should learn such a lesson with someone else's money."

Ali drove down the Via Medina past the Vittorio and double-parked in front of the fountains in the Piazza Municipio. Once again, he helped Qazi from the car, then handed him a folded newspaper that lay on the front seat.

The colonel made his way across the sidewalk, inched over the curb, and crossed the grass to the fountains, where he seated himself on the edge of the circular water basin and watched the children kicking a ball on the grass. Dogs drank from the fountains and growled at each other. Soccer balls went awry and were chased diligently while mothers chatted with other mothers and tended infants in strollers.

Occasionally Qazi glanced behind him at the entrance to the Municipal Building. The policemen on duty there ignored the people streaming in and out of the building through the high archway and smoked cigarettes while they talked to each other.

Down the street, past the parking area where Ali had stopped the car, Qazi could see the gate to the passenger terminal and fleet landing at the end of the short boulevard. To the right were the stark ramparts of the Castel Nuovo.

A man in his sixties clad in baggy trousers and a sleeveless undershirt sat down beside him. The man hadn't shaved for several days. He glanced at the two-day-old copy of *Il Mattino* that protruded from under Qazi's left arm.

"Have you finished with your paper?"

"I've only read the front page."

The man nodded absently and rested his elbows on his knees. A child on crutches sank to the grass in front of him. He grinned at her.

"Your daughter?" Qazi asked.

"At my age? I wish. She's my granddaughter."

"Why did you agree to help us?"

The man turned his head and looked straight at Qazi. "I need the money."

Qazi laid the newspaper between them.

"Grazie!" The man never looked at the paper.

Qazi used the cane to get upright. He was almost bowled over by a kicked soccer ball as he made the step down to the sidewalk, but the ball bounced off his legs and shot down the sidewalk toward Ali, who caught it and tossed it back.

Jake Grafton stood on the quarterdeck by the officers' brow and watched Callie step from the launch to the float and climb the long ladder. After the officer-of-the-deck greeted her, he stepped forward with a smile. "Hi, beautiful."

"Hello again, sailor man," she grinned. "What a big ship you have here!" She put her hand on his arm and he led her through the large open watertight door into the hangar bay.

"Did you have a good ride out?"

"Oh yes. The junior officers whispered and told each other that I was your wife. I haven't felt so privileged or admired in ages."

Jake laughed. "Did a junior officer stop by the hotel today to see you?"

Her eyes twinkled mischievously. "One did. He said you had suggested that he ask my help in a romantic matter."

Jake told her about Toad's visit to his office as they walked across the hangar bay and climbed toward the O-3 level, the deck above the hangar, where his office was located. "So did you get ol' Toad fixed up?"

"He and Judith have a dinner date this evening."

"Now that's what I call service."

"He is head over heels about her. It's very interesting. For a moment when I spoke to her, I sensed her hesitation, but she agreed immediately to dinner."

"Maybe she's just lonely, like Toad."

"Perhaps, but . . ." She broke off as they entered the CAG office and Farnsworth snapped to his feet.

"Farnsworth, you remember my wife?"

"I most certainly do. It's a pleasure seeing you again, Mrs. Grafton."

"Farnsworth looks after me when you're not around, Callie."

Jake slipped into his office, leaving the door open, and let the two of them talk. In the three or four minutes they sat chatting, she elicited almost his entire life history. The man positively blossomed under her attention, Jake noted as he dialed the telephone. The admiral's aide answered his call and suggested he could bring Callie to the flag wardroom at his convenience.

Cowboy Parker's taut, angular face cracked into a large grin as Callie entered the wardroom. The chief of staff, Captain Harold Phelps, and the admiral's aide were there, and Callie called each of them by name as she was introduced. Captain Phelps and the aide, Lieutenant Snyder, chattered through dinner, basking in the glow of her attention. Jake was once again amazed at the grace and wit of his wife, who could make anyone she met feel as though they were one of her lifelong friends. After dessert, Phelps and Snyder excused themselves, leaving the Graftons and the admiral alone.

"Callie, it really is great to see you again," Cowboy said. "This is the most pleasant evening I've spent in quite a long time."

Toad Tarkington was leaning back in his chair, a sappy smile on his face, watching delightedly as Judith Farrell talked about her job on the *International Herald Tribune*. Similar conversations were going on at other tables and their waiter was whisking away the dessert dishes, but Toad didn't notice.

The candlelight made her face glow. Her eyes were so expressive. He loved the way she used her hands. She was a goddess. He had had too much wine and he knew it, but she was still a goddess. What a stroke of luck to get another date with her! Hoo boy, you're dancing between the tulips now.

"And the editor—he is a short chubby man with one little teeny-weeny curlicue right here . . ." She pointed at her widow's peak and giggled. Toad grinned broadly. "And he wants to sleep with me. It's so funny. He hints and sighs and prisses about, walking back and forth in front of my door." She put a hand on her hip and tossed her head and shoulders from side to side, knitting her eyebrows and trying to look serious, then breaking up. Her dress was a strapless number that was cut lower than the law of gravity allowed. What was holding them up?

She giggled again and had another sip of wine. She had had a glass too much, too, Toad decided. But, *c'est la guerre*. Her fingertips brushed his hand when she set her wineglass down. He could feel the fire all the way to his elbow.

As she rambled on he tried to decide how he should go about the seduction. Perhaps he should just come out with it. Suggest they both go up to her room for a drink. No. That has no class. And she is a class woman. Perhaps a kiss in the dark on the way back to the hotel, then silently lead her straight through the lobby to the elevator. But would that be too presumptuous, too take-charge?

". . . to pose in the nude, but his apartment was so drafty. He was very French, *très* romantic, into photography and anarchy." The rhythmic rise and fall of her breasts as she breathed fascinated Toad. He found himself inhaling as she inhaled. Maybe he should take her to a bar first for cognac, sit in a booth and nibble on her ear, and wheedle an invitation.

She raised her arms and lazily stretched, pulling the front of her dress drum-head tight. "Do you want to sleep with me, Robert?"

What? What did she say?

She rested her chin on one hand and looked at him with a warm, sleepy look. The other hand moved slowly across the table and touched his.

He felt his head bobbing up and down. He made a conscious effort to close his mouth.

"Let's leave then. I'm ready."

Toad fumbled for his wallet. He was ready, too. In fact, he had never been more ready in his life.

"He's still there," Sakol said when Colonel Qazi got into the car. They were parked under a large tree, well away from the streetlight, with the windows down owing to the warmth of the evening. The entrance to Pagliacci's drive was over two blocks away, but because of a slight dip in the road the view from here was excellent. Across the street from Pagliacci's estate was a park. Sakol passed his binoculars to Qazi. "A chauffeur dropped him, then drove away. He went in alone."

Qazi adjusted the focus. The big lenses seemed to gather the light. There was a streetlight on a power pole near the gate, and he could see the chest-high brick wall. Then he caught the glow of a cigarette just beyond the wall, inside the grounds. "How many of them are there?"

"I think there are at least two of them on duty—one on the gate, then one at the back of the property. There were dogs loose on the grounds last night, so I think the guards go in the house when the old man is alone."

Qazi turned the binoculars toward the park and began to scan. The occasional lamps by the walking paths provided little oases of light, but there were many impenetrable shadows. "I saw the dogs' droppings the last few times I was there."

"Dobermans. I'm surprised he even has two guards. No local in his right mind would dare burgle the place, and two men wouldn't even slow down a team of hit men. I doubt if Pagliacci even has a burglar alarm."

"There's no alarm system. The guards are for appearances, which are so important. One must keep up appearances," Qazi said and handed the glasses back. "So he's in there."

"Yes indeed. Big, mean, and ugly. No doubt paying his respects."

"No doubt."

"This pretty much tears it, huh?"

"Tears what?"

"The whole enchilada. If Pagliacci's spilled it—and there's no reason to think he hasn't—your little deal is gonna go off like a wet match."

"You're too pessimistic. We mustn't assume the worst just because two men are sitting together in that house. But perhaps I should go have a chat with them." Qazi took a pistol from the waistband in the small of his back and a silencer from a jacket pocket. The pistol was a Bernardelli automatic in 380 ACP. The barrel had been altered by a machinist to take a silencer. He screwed the silencer on, then jacked a cartridge into the chamber. After carefully checking the safety, he eased the gun into his trouser belt. "I'll need the glass-cutter, some tape, and the little torch from the boot." Sakol opened the car door. The interior courtesy light did not come on. The bulb had been removed from its socket.

"And get an Uzi for yourself, and the climbing rope."

When Sakol was back behind the wheel, Qazi ran his hands over the rope and steel grappling hook. "Your knife, please." Sakol unstrapped the scabbard from his right ankle.

Qazi examined the six-inch blade, a scaled-down Bowie. "You Americans make good knives."

"It was made in Japan."

Qazi slipped the knife back into the scabbard and pulled up his left trouser leg. His Walther was in its usual place on his right ankle. "If he comes out before I do, use the Uzi. I want him dead. And kill anyone with him."

"With pleasure."

Qazi adjusted the knife scabbard on his left ankle and pulled the trouser leg back down. "Then wait for me. No matter what, wait for me."

Sakol screwed a silencer onto the barrel of the Uzi, then checked that the magazine was full and there was a round in the chamber. He started the car with his foot off the brake pedal and let it idle. "I've been watching the park since I've been here and haven't seen anyone. But there may be a man in there watching the gate."

"We'll have to risk it." Qazi screwed the bulb back into the courtesy light socket above the rearview mirror.

"Turn on your lights and drive down to the gate. We'll use English."

There was a light on the power pole near the gate. Sakol stopped directly in front of the gate. "Do you see the house number?" Qazi asked in a conversational tone of voice.

"No, but this must be it."

Qazi opened his door and stepped out. He left the door standing open. Sakol shaded his eyes against the interior courtesy light and squinted at the gate. Qazi took a few tipsy paces toward the wrought-iron lattice, peered about, then extracted a scrap of paper from his shirt pocket and swayed slightly as he held it away from him so the streetlight fell on it.

The man on the other side of the wall moved.

"Oh, old fellow," Qazi said thickly. "Didn't see you there. Can you tell me, does Colonel Arbuthnot live here?"

The man took three steps up to the chest-high wall. *"Non comprendo, sig—"* The words ceased abruptly as Qazi shot him. The silenced pistol made a little pop. Qazi stepped over to the wall and looked down. The guard lay with his legs buckled under him, his eyes open, a hole in his forehead.

"Quickly, let's get him into the car." The two men vaulted the wall, wrestled the body over, then dragged it to the car and placed it on the floor behind the front seats. As they did this, Qazi said, "Take the car back where it was and park it. Then come back and get the other guard. Wear this one's cap. You know what to do. Then wait here by the gate. Don't let anyone leave alive."

Qazi vaulted the wall again and walked quickly up the driveway, alert for dogs. He heard nothing except the sounds of night insects and, very faintly, the engine of Sakol's car as it proceeded along the street. And he could hear the background murmur of traffic from the boulevard a kilometer or so away.

As Qazi approached the house he scanned the windows. The porch light was out, but several windows on the left corner of the house had indirect lighting coming through the drapes. The rest of the first-floor windows were dark. Any of them would do.

He paused by the front door and gingerly tried the knob. It turned! But what did Pagliacci have to fear? The most powerful mafioso in southern Italy, he was perhaps the man who slept the soundest. Qazi turned the knob to its limit and pushed gently on the door, a massive wooden slab eight feet high. It gave and he slipped through.

He stood in the darkness listening. Nothing. The house was as quiet as a tomb. He flashed the pencil beam about. A large foyer. Furniture centuries old. With the light beam pointed at his feet, he moved lightly across the Persian rug to the hallway and turned left.

There were voices on the other side of the door. He strained to hear the words. Just murmurs. Qazi put the flashlight in his pocket, the pistol in his right hand, and pushed the door open.

Their heads jerked around. General Simonov's shaved head reflected the light, and he glared. Pagliacci looked startled. They were seated in easy chairs, wine on the small table between them.

"Good evening, gentlemen. Sorry to burst in—"

"Who are you?" Pagliacci interrupted, his voice rising.

"It's Qazi, fool," Simonov growled.

"General, you must forgive our Italian friend. He knows me as an old man, quite infirm." Qazi sat down across from them and leveled the pistol at Simonov.

"Now, gentlemen, we have much to discuss and not much time, so let's get right to it. Which of you wants to be first?"

Simonov merely stared. Qazi watched the general's hands, resting on the arms of the chair. As they tensed and his feet began to move back under him Qazi shot him in the left knee. Simonov's motion was arrested almost before it began.

"Why are you here tonight, General?"

The Russian wrapped his hands around the damaged knee. His eyes remained on Qazi, expressionless. Blood oozed from between his fingers and began dripping on the carpet.

Qazi shot him again, in the right biceps. Simonov leaned back in the chair.

"You won't succeed," the Russian said at last. "El Hakim is mad. Surely you know that?"

Qazi nodded, his head moving an eighth of an inch. Blood was flowing freely from Simonov's arm wound.

"The Israelis, the Americans, the British. They'll launch pre-emptive nuclear strikes."

"Only if they think they can succeed, General. Only then. They are careful men."

"You cannot control—" And Simonov was hurling across the ten feet of space between them, driving on both legs in spite of the knee wound, his arms gathered. Qazi's bullet hit him in the neck, and the general collapsed at his feet. Blood pumped onto the carpet. Apparently the bullet had damaged the spinal column, for the Russian did not move again.

Qazi swung the muzzle of the gun to Pagliacci. "Talk or die."

The old man was trembling. Sweat glistened on his face and

dripped from his veined nose. "Mother of God, holy mother . . ."

Qazi stood and walked toward the Italian.

"The Russian wanted to know about the helicopters. When and where. Don't hurt me! I'm an old man. For the love of God."

"And you told him."

"Of course. He pays me much money every month. He has things he wishes to know about the Americans and we tell him. When ships come and go, what weapons are aboard, documents he wants, documents . . ." He was babbling.

"When did you tell him about the helicopters?"

"You will kill me anyway. I will tell . . ."

Qazi placed the muzzle of the pistol against the man's forehead. "When did you tell him about the helicopters?"

"Tonight. Just tonight."

"And the delivery at Palermo? Did you tell him about that?"

"Not yet. We hadn't time to cover everything."

"If you are lying, I will come back and kill you."

"I'm telling the truth, on the blood of Christ. On my mother's grave I swear it. I swear it on my wife's grave. . . ." His words became incoherent.

"And the villa? When did you tell him about the villa?"

"He did not know about that. I was going to get him to pay me more before I told him." He was sobbing.

"Stand up."

"Oh pleeease, you promised!"

Qazi pocketed the pistol and hoisted the old man to his feet. He spun him around and broke his neck with one hard wrench on his jaw.

Qazi grunted as his arms absorbed the now-dead weight. He dragged the don over to the general, taking care to avoid stepping in the bloodstains. He rolled the general over, then pulled Pagliacci across the wet blood smears. He rolled Pagliacci's body over. Good, the blood was still wet. Now he placed the general's corpse facedown, partially on Pagliacci, and gently squeezed the Russian's neck. More blood oozed from the hole in the throat, directly onto Pagliacci's shirt.

The pistol he wiped with his shirttail, then he pressed the Russian's fingers against the gun, then Pagliacci's. The nails of the Italian's fat fingers still had dirt from the garden under them.

He let the pistol fall beside the two bodies and kicked the spent shell casings to random position around the room. How Pagliacci had gotten the gun from the general was, of course, the weak link, but that was unavoidable. Finally Qazi placed the general's right hand behind the don's neck.

He paused and scanned the scene. It would hold up to scrutiny by amateurs for at least twenty-four hours. The police would never see this room. Twenty-four hours would be sufficient.

He wiped the doorknobs on his way out, and remembered to retrieve the climbing rope from the foyer, where he had left it upon entering.

Sakol was standing in the deep shadows as Qazi walked down the driveway blotting his forehead with his sleeve. "Where's the other guard?"

"In the car with the first one."

"Let's go." After they were across the wall, Qazi said, "You dispose of the guards so that their bodies are not found for at least twenty-four hours."

"No problem. You killed the Russian?"

"I hope I die as well when my time comes."

Fifteen minutes after Qazi and Sakol had driven away, a figure emerged from the darkness of the park. Under one arm he carried a medium-sized camera bag. The man crossed the street and climbed carefully over the wall. In ten minutes he was back. He crossed the street again and disappeared into the park.

Toad Tarkington awoke at four A.M. with a raging headache. The pain throbbed above his eyeballs with every beat of his heart. Then he became aware of a weight on his chest and legs.

Judith was sound asleep, her arm across his chest, her right leg across his. He inched up in the bed, trying not to disturb her. The bedspread and blanket were on the floor. Clothes were scattered where they had fallen or been tossed.

He closed his eyes and let the headache throb as he listened to her breathing. Finally he opened his eyes again. She was still there, warm and naked and sound asleep.

Why did you drink so much, fool?

He eased himself away from her and went to the bathroom. Her purse was on the vanity and he rooted in it. She had a tin of aspirin. He took three and washed them down with water from the tap.

He sat in the little chair by the writing table and watched her. She was so lovely.

He retrieved her dress from the floor and draped it carefully across the back of the chair. What would it be like to come home every evening to this woman, he asked himself. This intelligent, fiery, beautiful woman? It would never be dull. Never boring.

Whoa, Toad. You've never thought like that about a woman before. And this is just a one-night stand. One hell of a one-night stand, but that's all it is. She's a lonely woman in a strange city and you just happened to get the nod for stud service. She probably still thinks you're a jerk. She'll walk away in the morning without looking back.

He was holding the drapes apart and looking out the window when he heard her stir.

"What time is it?"

"About four-thirty."

"Come back to bed, lover. There's still some night left."

She captured him in her arms. She smelled of pungent woman and sleep. Her skin was soft, yielding over hard muscle, warm and sleek. She drew him in as if she had waited for years for his tension and power and desire, as if she had searched and hungered all her life just for him.

When he next awoke the sunlight was leaking through the drapes. He sat up in bed and looked around. Judith was gone.

She had gathered her clothes and tiptoed out while he slept. Oh, he had done that very thing himself—how many times? He had slept in their beds and escaped just as the sun rose. He had fled from the soft, scented sheets and the photos on the dresser and the frilly curtains on the windows. He had stepped over the panties and bra lying on the floor and never glanced back.

He could see himself in the mirror over the dresser. He needed a shave. The bed still smelled of her. The room was as empty as his life.

17

QAZI WAS SEATED on the terrace of the villa drinking orange juice when Yasim joined him and placed several envelopes of black-and-white photographs on the table. Qazi examined them in the morning sunlight. He had had four hours sleep and felt sluggish. This close to an operation, it was difficult to get to sleep, so he had taken a pill, the effects of which had not yet worn off.

The photographs were of people near the helicopters. Qazi sorted them into piles: the shots of each person were stacked separately. When he finished he had nine stacks. "Nine people yesterday, eh, Yasim?"

"Yes, Colonel. And one helicopter flew for two and a half hours. Here are the photographs of the pilots and their passengers." Yasim laid another group of pictures on the glass table.

Qazi carefully examined each picture. Yasim refilled his glass with orange juice. "There is a storm coming, Colonel."

"When?" Qazi did not look up from the photos.

"Rising seas and winds this evening. Frontal passage at four A.M. local tomorrow."

"Terrific. And Ali thinks nothing can go wrong."

"Do we postpone?"

"We can't. Not after last night." He continued to study the pictures. "The same people who have been there for two weeks, on and off," he said at last.

"No known agents," Yasim agreed. "The pictures from the backup site will be ready in an hour."

"And no one has been followed to or from the helicopters?"

"No one."

"No tails that you have seen?"

"That is correct." Yasim frowned. He knew as well as Qazi did how difficult it would be to detect a major tailing operation. "We have taken every precaution."

"Ummm. When does the crate go aboard the ship?"

"The supply barge is tied alongside already. It should be aboard any time."

"No problems at the quay this morning?"

"They took the crate just as we had arranged."

Qazi had a difficult decision to make, one he had purposefully been avoiding. He had hoped these photos would help him make it. The primary helicopters had been identified by Pagliacci, who had arranged for the bribery of the watchman and the transport-company manager. And Pagliacci, Qazi was forced to assume, had told the GRU all about it. Yet no Soviet agents had been seen to visit the site in two weeks, or so it appeared. And Pagliacci had said he had just told Simonov last night. If the GRU intended to thwart Ali's departure tonight, they were being extremely circumspect.

On the other hand, Qazi had kept Pagliacci in the dark about dates. The vans were hired for another two weeks. The villa had been rented for three months. The ship-painting contractor thought his scow was going to be used tomorrow and the day after. And the airport surveillance project was moving along nicely, with lots of Pagliacci's Mafia soldiers involved, costing lots of El Hakim's money and cocaine. Of course, Simonov would have suspected the airport project was a red herring, but only if he were told everything Pagliacci knew. And Pagliacci had dribbled the information out, squeezing rubles out of the Russian for every crumb.

So it was probable—no, certain—that Simonov did not have the big picture when he died last night. But had he already made preparations to act on the information he did have? Certainly the GRU should be checking the helicopters and hangar area if the Soviets intended to act.

Finally, there were the backup helicopters, about which Pagliacci had known nothing because he had not been told and because no Italian or NATO soldier had been bribed or pumped for information. These machines were parked on the concrete mat at Armed Forces South, the NATO base. Ali would literally have to hijack the machines, which might or might not be fueled, which might or might not be airworthy. These machines were guarded. So there would be shooting, and higher authority would be immediately alerted. The success of Qazi's scheme depended upon keeping the American admirals and generals in the dark until he had the weapons removed from the *United States*. He wanted them to see a fait accompli, not an operation in progress. Yet if the Soviets appear tonight at the primary helicopter site, that would be checkmate.

Qazi thought the problem through yet another time as Yasim replaced the photos in their envelopes. Unless something else came up, he decided, he would still go with the primary helicopters.

"Go back to the hotel and monitor the wiretaps carefully this afternoon. If the Americans are warned, they will try to get their men aboard the ship and get underway. I'll be in to see you this evening. We'll sanitize the suite then."

"Yes, sir."

"Assume you are being followed."

Yasim picked up all the photos and went into the house, a large two-story with almost twenty rooms.

There were no certainties in this business, Qazi reminded himself. You felt your way blindly, aware that nothing was ever as it appeared, aware that every action was fraught with hazard, both real and imaginary. And the longer you played the game, the more real the imaginary dangers became. The irony was that you never knew whether or not you had already made the hard, inescapable, fatal mistake.

"Good morning, Colonel." Noora sank into a chair beside him. She was wearing slacks and high heels, and had her hair pinned in a bun on the back of her head.

"Is Jarvis sleeping?"

"Yes."

"What did he eat when he arrived last night?" The two of them had arrived in Rome yesterday evening on a commercial flight. A heavily sedated Jarvis in a wheelchair and Noora in attendance wearing a nurse's uniform had passed through customs and left the airport in an ambulance, which had driven them for five hours to the villa.

"He has not yet eaten. I gave him a shot to counteract the sedative three hours ago. He should be waking soon. I will see that he eats."

"After he has eaten, have him unpack the trigger and inspect it. It's still in the crate in the garage. You and Ali should supervise him. We will repack the trigger tonight."

Noora nodded.

"Has he been cooperative?"

"Yes."

"What is his attitude toward you?"

"He has begun to accord me the respect he gives his wife."

Qazi examined her eyes. "Very good. How did you work that miracle?"

She shrugged. "He wants to be dominated. He needs it." Her eyes stayed on Qazi.

"I want him at peak efficiency in twelve hours."

"He will be."

Noora said only one word to Jarvis as she set the tray in front of him. "Eat." Then she went into the bathroom and locked the door.

She stood in front of the full-length mirror and languidly brushed out her dark hair. She enjoyed the sensual feel of the brush tugging gently at her scalp. She undid the ankle straps of her spike pumps, stepped from them, then slowly eased out of her slacks. She shrugged off her blouse, conscious of every move, watching herself in the mirror.

She was clad only in a thong teddy. She turned and examined her reflection over her shoulder. Yes, the thong strap was com-

218

pletely hidden in the crevice of her buttocks. And her legs, so smooth and sculpted, so perfect!

She effortlessly lifted a foot to the top of the vanity and replaced the shoe, glancing at her reflection as she fastened the strap. The image from the mirror behind her reflected in the glass above the vanity. She put on the other shoe, then stood and examined the way the high heels thickened her calves and raised the curve of her buttocks.

Jarvis appreciated her. How he loved to lick her legs, his tongue caressing and stroking her.

She permitted him to use only his tongue and lips. Already she could feel her nipples harden and the wetness begin in her vagina. She ran her fingertips slowly up her legs and over her hips, then slipped a finger under the teddy, into the wetness. The sensation made her weak.

She checked her reflection again in the mirror and moistened her lips with her finger. Then she unlocked the door and opened it.

On the sixth floor of a downtown building two blocks from the Vittorio Emanuele Hotel—behind a door marked in English and Italian, "Middle East Imports-Exports, Ltd"—another set of photographs was being examined. These photos were black-and-white, but they had been shot on fast infrared film and were grainy.

Judith Farrell selected one of the blowups and taped it on a wall. She stepped back. The photo was of two men standing near a car with a black latticework in the background. There was a heat source above them, to their left, on a pole. It reflected on the faces, changing them somewhat. With infrared film, each face and figure generated its own light, since it generated its own heat.

"It's him," she finally said. "It's Qazi."

"He certainly did a number on Simonov and Pagliacci. Lots of blood." The speaker was a man of about thirty years, tall and pale with stringy blond hair that hung over his ears. He selected a conventional photo of the bodies of Pagliacci and Simonov and taped it to the wall beside the infrared one. He had turned the general's head to try to get some of the face in the picture. Even so, the tanned head and bristle hair were unmistakable.

"Qazi did everyone a service killing Pagliacci. He's been assisting the Soviets too long."

"His successor will pick up where he left off. The Russians have the money and the Mafia has the organization. It's a marriage made in Communist heaven."

Judith sorted through the infrared photos until she found one that showed a three-quarters view of the second man by the car. She held it at arm's length and squinted at it. Too bad it was so grainy.

"Who's he?" the man asked.

"I don't know," Judith said at last and put the print back on the table.

"Should we let the CIA know?"

"I suppose so," Judith murmured. She tossed her head to get her hair back from her eyes and looked again at the prints taped to the wall.

"Why not send copies of these to the Soviet embassy? Maybe the GRU would like to know who rubbed out one of their generals."

"We'd have to get permission to do that. It's an idea. But I think not. Moscow won't be pleased about Simonov's death—or his disappearance—and they'll suspect the Mafia. Qazi set it up rather well. He's very good at that."

"So why is Qazi in Naples?"

"It wasn't to kill these two. He took many chances going in there alone, with only one backup waiting on the street. Too spur-of-the-moment."

"A hijacking? A bombing? Some American sailors have not returned to the carrier. Perhaps he is behind that," the man suggested. "But should we move before we know?"

"We can't let him slip through our fingers again. He won't go back to Pagliacci's. That was just one of the possible places he might turn up. If only we had been ready!" She took a last look at the pictures and turned away. "He's been to the Vittorio every night for three nights. It's going to have to be there."

The blond man shook his head. "Uh-uh. Too many people, too many exits—our team is too small for a place that big. Too many risks."

"Have the team ready. We're very, very close. I can feel it."

"Not the Vittorio."

"Yes. There. Tonight if possible. This may be our only chance."

"Listen, this man is dangerous. He spotted David in Rome. And killed him. We need a better setup, a sidewalk cafe setup. We've got to be able to get in cleanly and quickly, make the hit, and escape."

"David chased Qazi," Judith shouted. "He *knew* better. He had been told a dozen times." She glared at Joel. "But if I had been David, I would have tried to take him then and there too. David's mistake was that he stood and watched, trying to decide, until it was too late."

They stared at each other, thinking of David and the year the team had spent tracking leads and sifting information, chasing a will-o'-the-wisp. "We will never," Judith said, "ever find Colonel Qazi sitting quietly in a public place two days in a row, just waiting for us to walk up and assassinate him by the numbers—one, two, three, bang bang bang—not if we hunt him for a thousand years. He's too clever. And you know as well as I do, we don't have enough people to tail him effectively. It would take a dozen to do the job properly. We're lucky if we know where he is three hours a day, give or take five kilometers."

"If the Italians catch us . . ." The blond man gestured upward. "You *know* that! God in heaven . . . a hotel! Full of people! Taxis with radios parked in front. Police everywhere." He fell to his knees and stretched out his arms to her. "Qazi's here in Naples with his own team. If we're patient, we might get them all."

"No." She shook her head. "He's too clever. And too dangerous. At the first hint that we are closing in—the *slightest* hint that he's being followed or observed or his movements noted—he'll slip through our fingers . . . again. We'll come away empty if we don't grab the chance when we get it."

"Call Tel Aviv. Clear this with the Old Man." As badly as the Old Man wanted Qazi, surely he would not approve such a risky operation.

"I already have." Joel slumped. "Get up off your knees," Judith said. "The position doesn't become you." She turned to the window and looked across the rooftops at the Vittorio. "We were so close in Tangiers. He was aboard that ship."

Beyond the hotel, several miles out on the sea, the long low silhouette of the *United States* was a darker blue against the hazy vagueness of the sea and sky. On the horizon beyond, slate gray clouds were just visible. "He's interested in the carrier." She balled her fist and tapped gently on the window frame. "We're so damned close. We've never been this close."

"What about this American naval officer? Tarkington? What does he want? Where does he fit in?"

"He just wants my body."

"Oh."

She whirled. "Watch your tone of voice, faggot," she snarled. "Some men do like women's bodies. That's why *you* arrived in this world."

The blond man threw up his hands. "Hey, I just asked. If you want him, that's fine with me. I won't lose any sleep. Just as long as the mission isn't compromised."

Judith waved her hand angrily, dismissing the subject.

He approached her and put his hands on her shoulders. "I'm sorry for you that I am the way I am."

"Oh, Joel." Tears ran down her cheeks. "Be sorry for us." She pressed her face against his shoulder.

"What would you like to do today?" Jake Grafton asked his wife.

"You're not going to the ship?" Shock. Amazement.

"I'm going to stay right here with you this livelong day. I may not even get out of bed." He tossed the sheets away and examined her nude body critically.

"It's already ten o'clock, lover. Do you think we could still get breakfast from room service?"

"You're a remarkably well preserved specimen of womankind. Care to share any of your love secrets with an admirer?"

Callie pushed him onto his back and sat astride his midriff. The face on the pillow looking up at her wore a boyish grin. She bent down and began to nibble on his neck.

He picked up the telephone. "Room service, please. . . . Send up two large orders of ham and eggs. Extra toast and a pot of coffee." He gave them the room number and cradled the phone. "They say they'll bring it up in about twenty minutes."

"Twenty minutes," she whispered into his ear. "That's barely enough time to cover today's love secret, Jacob Grafton. But I'll try."

It was noon before they were out on the street, casually dressed and strolling hand in hand. "Let's go catch the ferry to Capri."

"Again? Judith and I went over there yesterday."

"Why not? You'll have more fun with me along."

"Ha! Don't be so egotistical." They turned the corner and began walking toward the ferry terminal.

"What did you and Judith talk about all morning?"

"Well, we discussed young American naval officers and their distressing attitude toward women. And how they must be handled so delicately to avoid bruising their fragile egos. And we discussed our education and careers, and I told her about meeting you in Hong Kong seventeen years ago, and . . ."

When she stopped speaking Jake glanced at her. She was chewing her lower lip.

"And what?"

"There was something troubling about the whole conversation."

Callie slipped her hand from his and hugged herself as she thought aloud. "She's the perfect American career girl, living a fantasy life in Paris. She doesn't let it go to her head, isn't celebrity-conscious, spends her money wisely, never drops names."

"Where is she from anyway?"

Callie stopped dead and turned to face him. "That's it! She's a nonnative speaker! She says she's from New England and has a slight accent to prove it. But she isn't."

"Does that mean English is not her first language?"

"Precisely. She acquired English as a youngster, but there are still subtle traces of her first language—the way she articulates certain syllables, for instance—that she hasn't eradicated. I could hear them but it didn't register." She gestured impatiently. "I accepted her as an American, so I didn't listen."

"What was her first language?"

Callie the linguist walked along deep in thought. "I'll have to think about it," she said at last.

"Perhaps her parents were immigrants who didn't speak English."

"That's rare these days, unless you're Chicano. But no, she didn't learn English at age six when she started school. I think she started later, as a teenager perhaps. The later in life you acquire a language, the more difficult the old patterns of articulation are to change. Many people can never rid themselves of an accent."

They queued for ferry tickets, then stood in the holding area and watched the ferry glide in past the quay where passenger liners and launches for the *United States* docked. The pilot brought his vessel into her slip with just the right amount of closure. The lines and gangplank went over and the passengers from the island disembarked, then the crowd on the wharf streamed aboard.

The ferry was halfway to Capri, and Jake and Callie were standing on the bow with the wind in their faces when she said, "It's a Semitic language, I think. Arabic or Hebrew."

It was noon when Ali came to the terrace where Qazi was sitting. He had been watching the squirrels on the lawn.

"Jarvis says the trigger is ready."

"Take him back to his room and lock him in. Keep someone in front of his door."

"Of course."

"Are Youssef and his men resting quietly?" They had been at the villa for three days now, and Qazi insisted they remain awake all night and sleep during the day. The first day, they had slept little. Yesterday they had slept better.

"They appear to be asleep. I think the lack of sleep finally caught up with them."

"Then they will be rested for tonight. And the pilots?"

"Resting."

"Very well. Check the guards on the perimeter. They must report any—and I mean *any*—vehicles whose drivers do anything but drive straight past. The assault will be hard and fast with no warning, if it comes. And the guards will be the first to die."

When Ali was out of sight, Colonel Qazi walked the hundred paces to the villa's garage. The man lounging in front of the door nodded to him as he went in. Qazi closed the door behind him and shot the bolt.

He walked slowly around the interior of the building, checking the windows to see that they were properly curtained, ensuring the other door was locked and the loft apartment was empty. Three vans sat in the garage bay.

Qazi extracted a small tool pouch from his pocket and opened it on the workbench. The trigger device was housed in an oblong gray box that sat on the floor by the bench. He quickly unscrewed the four screws on the face of the timer, which was a remnant of a modern electric clock, complete with liquid-crystal display. The faceplate came off easily, exposing a circuit board and an amazing amount of small wires.

Three small screws held the circuit board, and when they were removed, the board slid partially out of the timer to the limit of the attached wires. He stared at it a moment, then took a piece of paper from his wallet and consulted it. Using a small pair of wire cutters, he snipped two wires and a diode from the circuit board. Two months ago he had destroyed eight clocks trying to identify this diode. Not trusting his memory, he had sketched a diagram. He had already performed this little operation upon the other six triggers, which were still in North Africa.

He carefully returned the board to its position inside the timer and inserted the three little screws. In less than a minute he had the faceplate back on.

He stood on the workbench and felt along the top of the interior wall, where the plasterboard ended and the rafters sat on top of the studs. Yes, the drywall extended a few inches above the stud. He placed the tool kit there and climbed down, then used a handy automobile polishing rag to obliterate the faint heel mark on the workbench.

He climbed the stairs to the loft apartment. The scrap of paper from his wallet, the diode, and the bits of wire went into the toilet. As the water closet was refilling he heard noises in the garage. Someone was downstairs.

"Colonel." It was Ali.

The diode was still in the bottom of the toilet bowl. "I'm up here." Qazi reached into the water and retrieved it. No towels! Ali was running up the stairs. Qazi wiped his hand on the back of his trousers, dropped them, and sat down on the toilet seat.

"In here."

Ali's head popped through the door. "A car has driven slowly by the access road twice. Four men. They were looking."

"Put four men on the rooftops, out of sight."

Ali disappeared back down the steps. Qazi wrapped the diode in toilet paper and dropped it in the water. It swirled away as the toilet gurgled.

Ali was pointing out the rooftop positions to four men armed with assault rifles as Qazi approached the terrace. "No shooting until you see their weapons," he told them. One man climbed a tree to get on top of the parking garage. Two more went through the villa to the attic exit to the roof. The fourth used a ladder to reach the top of the guesthouse directly across from the villa, then Ali took the ladder away.

Colonel Qazi sat on the terrace and Noora brought him a pistol, a silencer, and a glass of iced tea, then went back inside. Her station was with Jarvis. The rest of the men were still sleeping with their weapons beside them.

Qazi pushed the button and the magazine slipped from the grip of the Browning Hi-Power. It was full. He screwed the silencer to the barrel and replaced the magazine, then chambered a round. After lowering the hammer, he tucked the weapon into his belt behind him. Then he adjusted the volume on his two-way radio and laid it on the table. The guards and Ali also had radios and would use them in an emergency.

It is pleasant here in the dappled shade of the giant trees, Qazi reflected, with the short lawn grass stirring ever so gently to the breeze. The air smelled of flowers, which were still blooming in the beds around the house and walks. He filled his lungs and exhaled slowly. Very pleasant.

Even the pervasive traffic sounds were absent in this pastoral setting. All he could hear were leaves rustling under the wind's caress.

A large yellow-and-black butterfly settled on the toe of his shoe and gently stirred its wings. A shaft of sunlight fell upon the shoe, making the insect's wings appear luminous, almost transparent.

Such a place the Prophet must have envisioned when he described paradise—"a garden beneath which a river flows." And his listeners in their tents under the merciless sun, amid the sand and rock, had known the truth of his message. Yes, paradise will be green and flowering, with pools of clear water and abundant grass and majestic trees that reach deep into the earth and drink of Allah's bounty. And the believers shall spread their rugs on the grass in the shade of the trees and make their prayers to Allah, the all-merciful, all-compassionate. Truly, man loves best what he has not.

□ □ □

The stars had begun to fade one by one. Time dragged on slowly. Then he realized he could distinguish the outline of the top of the escarpment from the lighter black of the sky. Even as he watched, the relief became bolder and the sky beyond began to gray.

He left the camel and crawled toward the edge. The wadi below was still enshrouded in darkness. Behind him he heard the camel rise, then urinate, groaning against the rag around its muzzle.

He stared expectantly into the wadi, trying to distinguish features as the eastern sky changed from gray to a pale, thin blue. He listened intently, trying to hear something, anything, but all he could hear was the pounding of his heart. Finally the top of the sun flamed the stones around him. The wadi was still impenetrably dark.

He saw the flash in the wadi and heard the bullet slap the stone near him at precisely the same instant. Then he heard the shot, a flat crack that boomed off the rock and died, leaving a deeper silence. He couldn't fire back because he might hit the camels. He backed away from the edge and felt his stinging cheek. A piece of stone or shard of lead had caused it to bleed. So this is how it feels!

He changed positions, surprised at how alive and vigorous he felt. He would not die. Even if he did, he was vibrantly alive now, aware of everything, a part of the universe.

When he looked again over the lip of the rock, he could see the hobbled camel in the sandy bed of the wadi, which was lined with boulders larger than a tent. There were four camels. He gently eased the rifle forward and thumbed off the safety.

He saw a head, searching again for him. He lined up the Enfield and tried to quell his rapid breathing. The rifle fired before he was ready.

The weapon slammed back against his shoulder. He crawled backward away from the edge, the barrel of the heavy rifle dragging against the rock.

"You are surrounded!" His uncle was shouting. "Lay down your rifles and step out and you will live. Allah is merciful."

"We have the water." The voice was high-pitched, a boy's voice.

"Surrender or die!"

"You will kill us anyway."

"I swear by the Prophet. If you surrender, you live."

Qazi crawled back to the edge and looked down.

"As Allah wills it," the boy said, barely audible. He and his companion stepped from behind the rocks. Only one of them had a rifle. He tossed it on the ground before them.

227

□ □ □

"I don't think anyone is coming, Colonel," Ali said.

"Perhaps later. Relieve the men on the roofs when you relieve the perimeter guards." This was done every two hours.

"Who could it have been?"

"Anybody," Qazi shrugged. "Even curious neighbors." He glanced at his watch. It was three-thirty. He stood and picked up the radio on the table. "I am going upstairs to sleep. Wake me at five o'clock. Put only men who are not going with us on guard duty. All the others should meet in the dining room at five for a briefing."

Jake threw the telephone receiver onto its cradle with a bang. "The whole damned afternoon wasted, all because of him!"

"Now, Jake," Callie said, "don't be nasty. It's not Toad's fault." They had ridden the same ferry back from Capri that they had ridden over, and Jake had stopped by fleet landing and talked to the ship by radio. He had spoken to the XO, Ray Reynolds, and told him of Callie's suspicions about Judith Farrell, Lieutenant Tarkington's new flame. He had left word that Toad was to personally call Captain Grafton at his hotel. And Jake had asked to be telephoned when Lieutenant Tarkington was located.

In the lobby the Graftons had telephoned Judith Farrell's room, but no one answered. They had even gone to the fourth floor and knocked on the door. All to no avail.

"They say he isn't aboard. They've just figured out that he had liberty all day and cycled through the ready room at ten o'clock, on his way ashore again. No one knows where he is."

"How about the Shore Patrol?"

"Reynolds has already alerted them. If they run across him, they're to secure his liberty and send him back to the ship immediately, after he calls me."

"Surely you don't think Judith is behind the disappearance of those petty officers?"

"I don't know what to think. Goddammit, I don't have enough facts to do any thinking with. Sailors are over the hill. Sailors go over the hill all the time when the ship is in port. The captain has a big mast when we get underway and kicks a lot of kids' butts for overstaying liberty. But petty officers rarely do that. And Judith has a funny accent—a faint, funny accent that only a linguist can

228

hear. She's not what she says she is and she's not in her room and she was aboard the ship in Tangiers. And Toad can't be immediately located. So what does it all add up to?"

"Nothing."

"Maybe. Or it may mean Judith has been a part of a ring kidnapping American sailors. Maybe she's a terrorist. Toad could be her next victim. Maybe she just has a speech impediment. Or that pussy-hound Tarkington may have her flat on her back this very minute and be fucking her silly. Goddamn if I know." He threw himself into a chair.

"So what do we do next?"

"I'm all out of ideas. What do you suggest?"

Callie stood and examined herself in the full-length mirror on the back of the door. She tucked in a stray lock of hair. "Well, let's go have a drink someplace and contemplate where we'll go for dinner."

"Leave Toad to his horrible fate, huh?"

"You've done all you can. But at heart Judith is a very nice young woman and Toad is a nice young man. I'm sure it'll all work out."

"Aaaahg! Women! Why don't you panic like you're supposed to?" She grinned at him. "How men ever managed to keep women from running the world, I'll never know." Jake grabbed the room key from the desk. "Com'on, I'm tired of sitting around the hotel."

As he stabbed the button for the elevator, Jake muttered, "The whole afternoon down the tube. By God, I hope that horny bastard catches the clap."

"Jacob Lee Grafton! You do not! Now calm down and stop that cussing!"

18

TOAD TARKINGTON sat at the bar of the Vittorio and watched the desk in the lobby reflected in the mirror. He had sipped his way through two slow beers and now a third beer sat untouched on the table before him. He was hungry and tired and discouraged. Maybe she would never come. But why hadn't she checked out of her room? Sooner or later she had to come to that desk and ask for messages or check out.

Behind him a crowd was gathering. It looked like a wedding reception. Men in formal dress and women in sharp fashions gathered around a table of hors d'oeuvres against the back wall. The bartender passed drinks across the counter to the lively crowd. The volume was rising. Toad didn't understand a word of it. Couples entering the lounge kept obscuring his view, but he kept his eyes on the mirror anyway.

When he could stand it no longer, he used the house phone on the end of the bar and dialed her room. Perhaps she had come in the back way, avoiding the lobby. He let it ring ten times before he hung up and returned to the bar.

And then she was there, against the lobby counter, looking at the key boxes behind the desk and glancing at the clerk. Toad stood quickly, then eased back into his seat.

Let her read the letter first, he decided. He had spent two hours this afternoon writing and rewriting the two pages, two long hours devoted to the most important letter of his life. The letter said the things that he had never been able to say—had never before wanted to say—to any woman. She should read it first, he concluded, trying to quell his feeling of unease.

She spoke to the clerk and he handed her the envelope. She looked at both sides of the envelope carefully, glanced around the lobby—her gaze even passed over the people going into the bar— before she opened it with a thumbnail.

Her hair was piled carelessly on top of her head. Even at this distance Toad could see stray locks. She was wearing a nondescript dark jersey, a modest skirt, and flat shoes. A large purse hung on a strap over one shoulder.

He watched her face expectantly as she read. Her expression never changed. Her eyes swept the crowd again and returned to the letter. As she finished the first page her attention was back on the crowd. She scanned the second page. Now she was folding the pages and replacing them in the envelope, now looking at the envelope, now tapping it against her hand as she searched the faces of the wedding guests.

He stepped into the doorway and she saw him.

Toad started toward her only to hear the barman's shout. He fumbled in his pocket and found some bills. He threw a wad on the bar and crossed the lobby toward her.

"Judith, I . . ."

"Hello, Robert." Her features softened. "I'll keep this," she said and tucked the envelope into her purse.

"Hey, uh . . ." He couldn't think of anything to say and yet he knew he should be saying the most important things he had ever said. "Listen . . ."

But she was looking away, her eyes tense and expectant. Toad followed her gaze. A lean man with stringy blond hair and carrying a backpack was standing in the door that led to the rear courtyard and looking at her.

231

"I have to go, Robert. You are very, very kind."

"At least give me your phone number, your address. I'll . . ."

"Not now, Robert. Later." She was moving toward the court-yard door and he was moving with her. She put a hand on his chest. "No, Robert. Please," she said firmly. He stopped dead. She bussed his cheek and disappeared through the door.

He stood stock still, unsure of what had happened. She had read the letter. She knew he loved her. He looked around the lobby, at the starkly modern designer furniture, the second-floor balcony, the artsy chandeliers, the bright green drapes, the anonymous dressed-up people coming and going. Of course she didn't love him, but she had to give it a chance. Then he knew. There was another man—a husband or a lover. Oh Christ, he had never even considered that possibility.

He turned and walked down the hall toward the rear courtyard, hurrying.

There was someone lying in the courtyard. Toad froze in the doorway.

Judith and the man with the backpack stood over the prone figure. And there was another man, one wearing a workman's shirt and cap, with a tool case at his feet. He had something cradled in his hands. In the semidarkness it was hard to see. The workman used his foot to turn the body over.

"That isn't him," Judith said softly, her voice carrying very well within this enclosure.

"Uh-uh."

"Well, who is it?" Her voice was tense.

"It's Sakol," the workman said in a flat, American Midwest voice. "We've been after him for a long time. I had to do it."

"You fool," she said fiercely. She took an object from her purse and spoke into it. "Everyone inside. Hit the door. Now." She dashed toward the entrance to the other wing of rooms. As she went under the dim entryway bulb, Toad saw that she was carrying a pistol. The two men were right behind her. Now Toad could see what it was that the workman carried at high port—a sub-machine gun.

Toad crossed the courtyard and stared at the man lying on the stones. He was on his back now, eyes and mouth open, a wicked bruise on his cheekbone. Little circles of blood stained his shirt around five holes in his chest. The holes were neat and precise, stitched evenly from armpit to armpit.

God Damn! Holy Mother of Christ!

He heard muffled, stuttering coughs and the sounds of shattering glass and splintering wood.

A distant shout: "He's on the roof."

Pounding footsteps clattered on the stairway that Judith had gone up. She came flying out, followed by the man with the backpack. He had a submachine gun in his hands and the fat barrel pointed straight at Toad as he moved.

She ran toward the corridor to the lobby. "Get out of here," she hissed at him and the man with her gestured unmistakably with his weapon.

Someone three or four stories up, inside the hotel, was shouting in Italian. Cursing, probably.

Toad looked again at the dead man at his feet. This was the first body he had ever seen that wasn't in a casket. He found himself being drawn toward the lobby inexorably, almost against his will.

The lobby was full of people. A young woman in a white formal gown was wending her way toward the bar, acknowledging the applause and handshakes. Her new husband, wearing a tux, followed at her elbow, shaking hands with the men and bussing the women.

The blond man was bending over near a large potted fern. His backpack lay on the floor near him, by his right hand. Toad looked for Judith. She was behind a group near the elevators, watching the floor indicators above the stainless-steel doors.

The workman faced the elevators, his submachine gun pressed against his leg.

For the love of . . . ! "Look out!" Toad roared. "He's got a gun!" Startled faces turned toward him.

Toad pointed. *"He's got a gun!"*

Women screamed and the crowd surged away from the gunman.

The elevator door opened.

The blond man had the butt of the weapon braced against his hip, spent cartridges flying out. The sound of shattering glass from the elevator was audible, and a low ripping noise and the screams and shouts of the panicked crowd, some of whom were on the floor and some of whom were trying to flee, shoving and pushing and sprawling over those lying on the carpet. The gunman fired one more burst, picked up his backpack, and ran for the courtyard corridor.

Something hard was pressed against Toad's back. "Follow him," Judith ordered, and pushed him toward the archway. Over his shoulder Toad could see a bloody body lying half-in, half-out of the elevator.

The bride stood horrified in the middle of the lobby, staring at the body being crushed by the closing doors of the elevator. A woman somewhere was screaming.

"Quickly," Judith urged.

They were in the corridor. She pushed him hard. "Run." She had a pistol in her hand. It had a long, black silencer on the barrel as big as a sausage. Even in the dim light Toad could see the hole in the end pointed at him.

He ran.

At the street entrance to the courtyard, men carrying weapons were racing toward them, at least four of them. A van careened around a corner and screeched to a stop.

As the men piled in the back Judith shouted, "Him, too." Someone grabbed Toad and hurled him toward the van. He was thrust facedown onto the floor and a heavy foot planted itself on the back of his neck.

The van accelerated at full throttle for fifty feet, then the engine noise dropped. "You asshole," someone said loudly. "You killed the wrong man. You blew it, fucker!" Three or four of them began talking at once.

"Silence!" It was a command. Judith's voice.

He could smell the sweat and hear them breathing hard over the street noises and the eternal quacking of automobile and motor-scooter horns. He could hear the distinctive clicks and hisses of a two-way radio conversation, muted, from the front of the vehicle, the voices low and indistinct. He concentrated on the tinny voice from the speaker and concluded it was a foreign language, one he didn't recognize. Cutting through all the noises was the distant, two-tone panic wail of a siren. Two sirens, moaning out of sync.

He could tell from the road noises, the short accelerations and brake applications, that the van was cruising in traffic. Time passed. How much Toad didn't know. The sirens eventually became inaudible.

When he felt his legs cramping and he could stand it no longer, he said, in as conversational a tone of voice as he could muster, "Take your foot off my neck, please."

The pressure increased. He raised his voice, "I asked you nice. Take your fucking foot off my neck!"

"Okay, let him up." Judith's voice.

"He'll see our faces." It was the flat, American Midwest voice.

"He ought to see yours." Another male voice. This was a heavy accent, perhaps Eastern European. "You agency assholes want to be included, then you fuck it up."

"Shut up, everyone," Judith said. "Let him up."

He was pulled bodily toward the rear of the van and turned into a sitting position. Hands seized his face. They were Judith's hands. Her face was only inches from his. "Don't look around."

The light came through the back windows of the vehicle—headlight glare and occasional streetlights. Her eyes held his as the lights came and went. They were the most intelligent, understanding eyes he had ever seen.

"Don't ever tell anyone what you've seen or heard. Promise me! Not a word."

Her eyes held him.

"Oh, Judith! Why you?"

"If you tell, people will die. Not you. Other people. Good people."

"You?"

"Perhaps."

"I don't even know your real name."

"Don't tell," she whispered fiercely and increased the pressure of her hands on his temples.

"I love you."

The van came to a halt and the rear door opened. "Get out." As he did so, he heard her say, "I'll keep the letter."

The van accelerated into traffic. He was beside a pedestrian island in the middle of a vast piazza. Buses were parked in rows across the street from him. To his right was the central train station, easily recognizable with the black triangles on the low, flat roof. He was in the Piazza Garibaldi.

Then he remembered that he should have looked at the license number on the van. He wildly scanned the traffic, but it was gone. He had been looking at the little rear window when it pulled away. Pedestrians were staring at him.

He put his hand in his pockets and began shuffling along.

Jake and Callie were having dinner in a storefront trattoria on the Via Santa Lucia famous among U.S. Sixth Fleet sailors. Unit patches covered three large mirrors in the crowded dining room. The floor was linoleum and round bulb lamps hung from the ceiling. Pictures of American ships and airplanes in cheap black frames adorned the dingy wallpaper. Two men in their fifties served the noisy customers at the fifteen tables.

An Italian couple at the next table was slaughtering a pizza and demonstrating the proper use of the knife and fork on this delicacy to their daughter, who was about eight. The utensils were used to roll up the triangular slice until it looked like a blintz, then the fork was stabbed through it and the pizza roll raised to the mouth, where one took a delicate bite from one end. The youngster was having her troubles with the technique. Red sauce and gooey cheese dribbled down her chin.

The little brother was peeking at Jake. Jake winked. The boy averted his face, then peeked again. Another wink. The little head jerked away, then inched back around very, very slowly. Jake grinned.

"Kids are great, aren't they?" Jake remarked.

"Oh, you think so?"

"You know what I mean."

"Then you won't mind if we adopt?"

Jake hitched himself up in his chair and stared at his wife. She sipped her wine and gazed innocently around the room with a trace of a smile on her lips, her eyebrows slightly arched, the corners of her eyes minutely crinkled. God, she was beautiful!

He grinned. "Anyone specific in mind, or will a generic kid do?"

Her eyes swiveled onto him like two guns in a turret, then her head followed. "She's ten years old. Her name is Amy Carol. She has black hair and black eyes and a smile that will break your heart."

"And . . ."

"She has diabetes. She's been in four foster homes and she

needs a family of her own. She was sexually abused in her first foster home, and the man went to prison. She doesn't like men."

Jake's smile faded. "Well . . ."

"She needs us, Jake. Both of us. She needs love and understanding and a place of her own and a man who can be a loving father."

Jake took a deep, deep breath, then exhaled through his nose. Callie had mentioned adoption casually in the months before the *United States* sailed on this cruise, but it had been so tentative—newspaper clippings left for him to see, occasional dinner conversations, all of it casual and distant, a social phenomenon worthy of a few minutes of notice. And she had been testing the water! He sat now slightly baffled, trying to recall just when and how he had lost sight of the pea. The little girl at the next table caught his eye. She had tomato sauce smeared all over the lower half of her face and running down her fork, which she held like a sword in her right fist.

"Amy Carol Grafton. When do we get her?"

"Oh, Jake," Callie exclaimed and dashed around the table. She sat on his lap and enveloped him. People at the neighboring tables applauded enthusiastically as Callie gave him a long, passionate kiss. After all, this was Italia.

Qazi leaned back against the sink. Noora and Ali sat at the kitchen table with Youssef and the senior helicopter pilot.

"So Sakol and Yasim are dead?"

"The police radio says they are."

"Sakol is no loss," Ali sneered. "But Yasim is. Who were these people?" Ali asked the question of Qazi.

"I don't know. I heard the silenced automatic weapon in the courtyard. I heard them speaking English. I looked. One of them was a woman, perhaps Judith Farrell. We had finished listening to the tapes Yasim had flagged, and Sakol had left."

"Why did you let him leave?" Ali asked. "He could betray us."

"My judgment. My decision. We shook hands and he left. A few moments later we heard the shots and I looked out the window. We ran toward the stairwell and started down. Then we heard someone running up. So I went up onto the roof. Yasim must have decided to go back through the corridor and take the elevator down to the lobby. He probably figured it would be safe with all the people there."

"So they killed him in the lobby."

"Apparently. He isn't here and the police are telling each other there are two bodies."

"Yasim is a martyr," Youssef said. "He's on his way to paradise." Youssef was a Palestinian, the senior man in the PLO contingent that El Hakim had foisted on Qazi. Political considerations. The PLO needed a success just now, and El Hakim would need the PLO if this operation was to pay the kind of dividends the dictator hoped it would. So the PLO should earn a share of El Hakim's glory. Not too much of it, of course, but an expedient little bit of the shine. Too bad, Qazi thought bitterly, that the Palestinians' primary asset was enthusiasm.

"What do the Americans know?" Ali asked.

"This afternoon Captain Grafton and his wife discussed the fact Farrell is not a native English-speaker. Apparently they were worried she would entrap Lieutenant Tarkington, one of the officers from the ship. Grafton had the Americans searching for Tarkington this afternoon, apparently without success. Then the Graftons went out. Grafton is suspicious and worried, but he really knows nothing."

"Someone knows something," Ali said. "If that assassination team is waiting at the helicopters or the Americans are warned or the Italians are alerted, we won't succeed."

"At last," Qazi said acidly, "you begin to appreciate some of the basic facts."

Ali said nothing.

"I'm worried about the weather," the pilot said. "The winds are going to get gusty, and we'll have rain showers under a low overcast. It may get very rough in the air tonight."

"Is it possible to fly?"

"Yes, it's possible, if the forecast is accurate. But if the weather is worse than forecast, it will be dangerous. There will be no margin for error."

"And in Sicily?"

"The weather should be better there. That is the forecast, anyway."

"So there are many factors we cannot control. We knew that when we were planning."

Youssef spoke. "The PLO does not want this mission to fail. The chairman has given the orders. My men and I are ready to proceed regardless of the danger."

Qazi ignored him.

"Could we wait a day?" Noora asked. "The weather might improve."

"They may dispose of the crate on the ship. The carabinieri or the GRU or the CIA or the Mossad or the Mafia may catch on." Qazi ticked them off on his fingers. "There is already at least one assassination team out there on the hunt. And Yasim or Sakol may still be alive, and the police-radio conversations just a ruse. If either is alive, he can be made to talk. The risk increases every minute we wait. It's now or never. Do we go?"

Noora and Ali looked at each other, then back at Qazi. They both nodded yes.

Qazi slapped his hands together. "Okay. Youssef, load the vans. Noora, get Jarvis to supervise the loading of the trigger. Then line the men up for inspection. Ali and I will check every man. When that is done, we'll pull in the guards and be on our way." He looked at his watch. "We leave in twenty-seven minutes. Go!"

19

QAZI AND ALI sat in the front seat of the van and stared through binoculars at the gate in the chain-link fence and the helicopter pad beyond. Nothing moved under the lights on the corner of the hangars. Qazi aimed his binoculars through his open window at the guard shack. The old man was inside. He still had a two-day growth of beard.

The colonel turned in his seat and examined the tops of the warehouses across the street. No heads or suspicious objects in evidence. He scanned the windows.

"What do you think?" Ali asked.

Colonel Qazi laid the binoculars in his lap and sat watching the scene. "Go," he said at last.

Ali stepped from the van and eased the door shut. He walked past the edge of the nearest warehouse and on across the street, where he was limned by a streetlight. Qazi could hear his footsteps fading. He raised his binoculars and scanned the warehouses again, trying to detect movement. There was none. He swung the glasses to the guard shack and watched Ali walk up to the window. The guard opened it. Ali reached through the window. Qazi knew he was cutting the telephone wire. Then Ali walked on toward the hangar.

"Sentries out," Qazi told the people in the back of the van. He heard the rear door open and saw, in the rearview mirror, a man in black clothing with a submachine gun post himself against the large metal trash box on the edge of the alley. Another man dressed similarly trotted past the front of the van and disappeared around the corner; his post was opposite the gate.

"Anything on the scanner?" Qazi asked over his shoulder.

"No." It was Noora. She was monitoring the police and carabinieri frequencies.

Through his binoculars Qazi could see Ali working on the doorknob to the office of the helicopter company. The hangar windows were all dark. Then Ali opened the door and disappeared inside. In a moment the lights in the office shone through the windows. Since this was normal when the company was waiting for a late-night passenger, it should arouse no comment. One of the two hangar doors slowly slid open.

Qazi raised a hand-held radio to his lips. "Van two, go."

In a few seconds he heard the engine of the other van. It came down the street past the alley and turned in at the gate. Qazi had instructed the driver to pause at the guard shack, and he did so. Then he drove past two parked helicopters and through the open hangar door.

"Van three, go."

Almost a minute lapsed before this van passed the alley where Qazi sat. It also came to a brief halt at the gate, then threaded between the helicopters and entered the hangar. Now the door slid shut.

They waited.

"Nothing on the scanner," Noora told him.

At last the door to the office opened and a man appeared. Qazi could see that he wore the same uniform as the gate guard. This man walked the hundred feet across the tarmac to the guard shack.

Qazi turned in his seat. "Noora, it's time."

She took off the earphones and gathered her shoulder bag.

"Don't kill any Italians unless absolutely necessary. Understand?"

"Yes."

"Shoot any Palestinian the instant he disobeys. And watch Ali's back for him."

She nodded.

"Go."

She stepped between the feet of the men sitting in the back of the vehicle and exited out the rear door. Qazi watched her. The man behind the wheel of the sedan parked behind the van got out and Noora took his place. The engine of the sedan came to life and the car eased past the van, stopping at the sidewalk as Noora looked both ways. Qazi could see the black outline of Jarvis's head above the top of the backseat. Then Noora accelerated into the street and turned left toward the gate. Behind him Qazi could hear the rear door of the van being closed.

In a few minutes five men emerged from the hangar and walked to the helicopter furthest from the guard shack. They began to preflight it with flashlights.

A small two-door sedan came down the street. As it went by Qazi could see a man and woman in the front seat. It passed the entrance to the airfield without slackening its pace and disappeared around the far corner.

Sound carried and echoed through the alleys. He could faintly hear a man and woman shouting at each other, and through some fluke of acoustics, snatches of television audio.

The gentle breeze felt good after the sticky heat of the day. Qazi sat and watched the flashlights move around the helicopter, erratically and haphazardly.

The five men on the other side of the fence spent five minutes examining the first helicopter. When they left it and moved to the next one, a voice came over Qazi's radio. "It's okay. Fuel sample satisfactory."

"Roger."

A small pickup truck came down the street from the north, its headlights almost lost in the black evening. It shot down the street at full throttle, slowing slightly as it passed Qazi so it could make the next corner, which it tore around. He could hear the sound of its engine fading for half a minute after it had passed. A moment later he heard the engine of a large truck. Thirty seconds later it came into view, engine laboring, and drove up the street with its diesel engine snorting.

"This one's okay."

"Roger."

What had he forgotten? What was left undone? As he sat there behind the wheel of the van Colonel Qazi reviewed the operation yet again. He glanced at his watch from time to time, and turned once to check on the men sitting patiently behind him. They looked scruffy in their worn, dirty jeans and short-sleeve knit and pullover shirts. Most of the shirts were filthy. Some of them were torn. Most of the men wore dirty tennis shoes. Satisfied, Qazi resumed scanning the warehouses with his binoculars.

The camel thieves were two young boys, about eleven and twelve years of age. Orphans. His uncle had forced them to deepen the water holes and fill the bags for the camels, which were let out on hobbles to graze. When the work was done, the boys were fed. They had no food of their own. Then the men had lain in the shade as the sun scorched the earth. The two thieves huddled together against a stone below where Qazi and his cousin sat with their rifles across their knees. The old man found a place further away, where he could keep an eye on the camels. Qazi wandered over in late afternoon and found him reading the Koran.

They tied up the thieves for the night. At dawn the next day the animals were watered again and the last of the dried dates and bread were shared.

"Who is the eldest?" the old man asked.

One of the thieves acknowledged that he was.

The old man looked at his son and Qazi. "Seize him. Put his right hand against that rock." He pointed at a large stone.

"No! Allah be praised, have mercy. No! Kill me instead." Qazi had helped drag the sobbing boy to the indicated stone.

The old man took his sword from the saddle of his camel. "You have violated Allah's law. And you know the law."

The sword made a sickening sound as it bit into the boy's wrist. It took the old man three chops to sever the hand. He bound the wrist with a tourniquet and his own undershirt.

They set the two on their own camel, a beast suffering so badly with the mange that it had only half its hair. The old man jammed their rifle into its scabbard and slapped the beast into motion. The young boy held his brother in the saddle as the animal climbed slowly out of the wadi and disappeared over the rim.

"Uncle . . ."

The old man's face was like chiseled stone. He gathered the camels that had been taken and roped them together.

The three had ridden for several miles when they heard the faint echo of a shot.

The old man reined his camel in and looked about wildly. He turned in the saddle and looked toward the west, where the shot must have been fired. Then he dropped the lead rope and beat his mount into a gallop.

Qazi and the cousin followed. They found the lone camel standing amid a patch of lava stones and thorn bushes in a shallow depression. The boy with the missing hand lay on the ground, the barrel of the rifle in his mouth, his toe on the trigger. His brains lay in the sand above the body.

His younger brother sat at his feet.

The old man prostrated himself toward the rising sun.

The sun rose higher and higher into the cloudless sky.

"Allah, I have believed in the words of your Prophet all my days. I have read the book and followed the book. I have kept the faith of my fathers. I have obeyed the law. I have raised my sons to obey the law. But it is not enough."

"Uncle," Qazi said. "Do not blaspheme. He hears everything."

The old man rose from the ground. His face was lined and his beard was gray. "The book is not enough for a simple man like me. Allah knows." He had looked about him at the stones and sand and the merciless sky and the twisted body. "Not enough."

They buried the dead boy. They took the other boy home with them and he was taken in by the old man's eldest son.

Three years later the old man sent Qazi north to the city to join the army.

The small radio crackled to life. "This one is okay."

"Roger."

Qazi started the engine and put the van in gear. As he drove away he looked in the driver's mirror at the hangar lights and the ungainly machines. The rotors were spread now, and they flapped gently in the rising breeze. The wind was gusting.

The book is not enough. His uncle had been right about that. But perhaps, Qazi thought, the Prophet was right and paradise will be better than this life. Perhaps not. Wherever the old man was, that was where Qazi wished to be. If tonight's scheme went awry, he well knew, he would join the old man very soon. Ah well, perhaps it was time.

□ □ □

"You're really serious about adopting?"

Jake and Callie were walking past the Royal Palace, under the white marble statues of the medieval kings of Naples. They looked, Jake thought, appropriately hairy and fierce, clad in their armor with swords in hand. Across the street, around the fountain in the Piazza del Plebiscito, clusters of teenage girls were flirting with the swarms of boys cruising on their Vespas and motocross bikes. Every now and then a girl hiked her skirt up, swung onto the back of the seat, and the boy blasted off into traffic. Apparently this was *the* place if you were young and growing up in Napoli.

"I went to see the agency about four months ago. We would have to wait years for a baby. And these older children who need special love and care, they spend their lives bouncing from foster home to foster home."

"So if we ask for a baby, we really won't be helping."

"Oh, Jake." She squeezed his hand. "That's precisely it. I've met Amy Carol about five times, and she needs a family. And we can be that family for her."

"Tell me about her."

Callie began with a physical description. They rounded the corner of the castle and picked their way through the parking lot, past the entrance to the Galleria Umberto, and around the scaffolding on the front of the opera house. Jake noticed several prostitutes standing on the steps to the Galleria, but Callie was describing the little girl's emotional problems and paid no attention.

A hundred feet further on he saw a tall, willowy woman in spike heels and a black dress standing under the light on the corner across the street. Her low-cut, strapless dress clung to her figure like cellophane and only came down to midthigh. She was busy adjusting her bosom. Callie was reciting Amy Carol's family history.

Callie stopped dead on the sidewalk, in midsentence, and Jake jerked his head from the far corner. Directly in front of them on the sidewalk a woman with exposed breasts stood talking to a man leaning from a car. She wore high heels and some type of black lingerie, but her breasts were completely bare. A transparent robe was draped around her shoulders.

"Keep walking," Jake urged.

Callie looked the woman up and down and gave the man in the car a piercing glance, which he ignored.

Ten paces further on three motor scooters drew to the curb. The young male drivers each had a teenage girl behind him. They chatted excitedly, looking back at the working hooker. Jake and Callie kept walking. The boys eased the scooters into motion and made a U-turn. Jake looked back over his shoulder. The scooters made another U-turn and swung into the curb where the car had been. The woman surveyed the teenagers with disdain and the Italian came loud and fast, audible even above the traffic.

"Stop gawking, Grafton," Callie ordered. "She's a 36 C-cup and needs dental work."

She's lying about the teeth, Jake told himself. Not even Callie had been looking at her mouth. "I wonder where we could get you an outfit like that?"

"Oooh, you men! You like that, huh?" She began to sashay along, rolling her shoulders and hips.

"Just admiring the local color." Callie was still doing it. Pedestrians were staring. "Stop that!"

"Twenty thousand lire."

"What?" If she kept on, she was going to need a chiropractor.

"Twenty thousand lire, sailor, and I no givva da kisses."

"How much for kisses too?"

"More than you gotta, sailor boy. Only da real men get da kisses."

A loafer on the grass whistled at her and she dropped the charade, grasping Jake's arm tightly and laughing.

"Amy Carol's gonna have a real fireball for a mom," Jake said, and led her toward the promenade around the Castel Nuovo.

They stood against the rail of the moat and watched the vendors roasting food in makeshift barbecues on the sidewalk. Working-class families out for the evening sat on the grass and ate roasted ears of corn and pieces of chicken. Dogs with noses to the ground charged through the crowd searching for abandoned delicacies. Jake counted five young couples, three on the promenade and two on the grass, locked in passionate embraces. In front of Jake and Callie three small boys were kicking a ball. With every other boot, the ball bounced off lovers and picnickers, startled the dogs, or caromed ominously toward the busy avenue. Someone

always rescued it and kicked it back to the boys. The tinny beeping cacophony of motor scooter and car horns was the perfect
accompaniment. Napkins and food wrappers were swept away by
the rising wind.

"Saturday night in Naples."

"You enjoy Naples, don't you?" Callie asked, and brushed back
the blowing hair from her face.

Jake grinned broadly and led her on. They crossed the boulevard that led down to fleet landing and strolled down the Via
Depretis, which paralleled the Via Medina, a block to the west.
Sailor bars and pizza shops lined the east side of the street. Jake
and Callie dropped into an empty table at a sidewalk bar and
sipped wine as pairs, threesomes, and foursomes of American
sailors in civilian clothes wandered by, noisy tourists in search of
"action."

The Graftons were walking hand in hand when a young man
shot out of an alley, collided with Jake, and went sprawling. Jake
almost fell, but Callie steadied him.

"Sorry." The man scrambled to his feet.

"What's the rush?" Jake demanded.

The man was four steps down the street when he pulled up and
turned to stare at Jake. "CAG? Captain Grafton?"

"That's me."

"Jesus, sir." He came rushing back. "Sorry I about flattened ya.
But our cat captain is in there," he gestured up the alley, "and
he's loaded and there's gonna be a fight."

"Who are you?"

"Airman Gardner, sir. Cat Four."

"Kowalski your cat captain?"

"Yessir, and he's one drunk motherfucker. . . . Excuse me,
ma'am." The sailor nodded at Callie and flushed. "He's pretty
drunk, sir, and I can't get him outta there and the barkeep is
callin' the shore patrol and I was goin' for help." Gardner didn't
look a day over eighteen.

"Callie, you go back to the hotel. I'll see you there after a
while."

She pecked him on the cheek. "Okay." She winked and began
walking back toward the piazza. Jake watched her go, her skirt
swirling.

"Com'on, sir," Gardner urged. "Them shore patrollers will be along any minute." He tugged at Jake's sleeve.

The bar was a red-light dive that catered to sailors. Several dozen were there when Jake walked through the door. Kowalski was in one corner with his legs splayed out and his shirt ripped, a bar stool in his hands. If he were left alone, gravity would soon conquer his fireplug body. "Alright, you cocksuckers, who's gonna be first?"

Another man wearing a red-and-yellow shirt stood facing Ski and wagging his finger at the cat captain's face. He looked almost as drunk as Kowalski. Behind the bar an Italian in a white shirt with his sleeves rolled up was screaming, "Out out out. They are coming. No fighting, no fighting. Out out out!"

"Excuse me," Jake said to the drunk facing Kowalski, and stepped by him. Jake stood up straight. "Ski, do you recognize me?"

Kowalski stared. The bartender was roaring, "Out out out out . . ."

Ski shook his head.

"I'm *Captain* Grafton." Jake grasped the stool and pried it gently from Kowalski's grasp. He set it on the floor, then shook Ski's right hand and held it while he grasped his elbow and began to move him toward the door. "I want you to come with me."

"Yessir," the petty officer mumbled, and shuffled in the direction he was pointed.

"So long, you windbag motherfucker," the man with the red-and-yellow shirt jeered.

Kowalski roared and tried to turn. Gardner punched him squarely in the jaw and his knees buckled.

"Ooowww," Gardner moaned, and shook his hand.

"I like your style, son," Grafton said, "but that's a good way to break your hand. Now help me get this tub of lard outta here." Gardner grabbed Ski's other arm and they dragged him out the door.

In the alley Gardner said, "I think I busted it."

"They never do in the movies, do they? Come on, Ski, start walking, goddammit, or we'll leave you for the shore patrol."

The petty officer's feet began to move. Jake steadied him on one side while Gardner held him up on the other, his forearm jammed under Ski's armpit with his injured hand sticking out.

"He's a great cat captain, sir. You won't regret this."

"He's a fuckin' drunk. If we get him back to the ship without someone writing him up, he's going straight to rehab."

"Yessir. Come on, Ski, walk."

The cat captain was trying. They came out of the alley and turned for fleet landing just as the Shore Patrol van pulled up. A lieutenant in whites with a Shore Patrol brassard on his left sleeve stepped out and saluted. Jake recognized him. He was a Hornet pilot on the *United States.*

"Want me to take him down to fleet landing, sir?"

"That means you have to write him up, right?"

"I'm supposed to, CAG."

"I'll get him down there, and this sailor here can get him back to the ship. I'll talk to the XO about him tomorrow."

"Yessir."

"Thanks anyway."

The lieutenant nodded.

"But while you're here, there's a bar up the alley you'd better visit. The bozo in the red-and-yellow shirt should go back to the ship in the van."

"Yes, sir." The officer turned and motioned to his men, who got out of the van and followed him up the alley.

Gardner and Jake managed to get Ski back to his feet. After much prodding, he staggered along with one of them on each side.

"Thanks, sir. He's really a fine petty officer and a helluva guy."

"Yeah."

They had to pause several times for Ski to be sick. Some of it splashed on Jake's shoes and trousers. A few drops of rain began to splatter on the pavement.

Just before they reached the boulevard by the Castel Nuovo, another Shore Patrol van pulled up. A chief in whites was driving. He leaned across the petty officer in the passenger seat. "Want us to take him on down to the landing?"

"That's okay, Chief. We'll manage." The van's wipers were smearing the water and dirt on the windshield.

"Bad night for booze, sir. Already got a half dozen drunks in here." The chief jerked his thumb over his shoulder.

"Naw," Jake said. "I appreciate it. But we'll get him there."

"Aye aye, sir." The chief let out the clutch and the van accelerated away.

"Com'on Ski. Walk! I hope to hell you're worth our trouble."

In the van one of the men spoke to the chief. "They took us for Americans, Colonel. We are going to succeed."

Maybe, Qazi thought. If Allah wills it.

The carabinieri on the gate to the quay didn't even look at Jake and Gardner as they marched Kowalski through. They followed the fence around to the right toward the area used by the carrier's boats. The intermittent raindrops were falling steadily now. The Shore Patrol van was parked by the little duty shack and the chief was talking to the embarkation officer. Six drunks in civilian clothes lay facedown in casualty litters under the awning and two Shore Patrolmen were strapping them in.

"Got another basket?" Jake asked, holding Kowalski semierect with one hand and wiping the water from his hair with the other.

"Yessir. We have plenty," said the embarkation officer, a lieutenant (junior grade) named Rhodes. He jerked his head at the chief, who stepped over to the pile of baskets behind the shack and helped Gardner lift one off. The chief helped Jake lower Kowalski into it.

"Mr. Rhodes," Jake sighed as he wiped his forehead with his sleeve and watched Gardner struggle with the litter straps with his one good hand. The chief bent down to help. "There's no report chit on this man. Just take him back to the ship and have him escorted to his bunk. I'll see the XO about him in the morning."

"Aye aye, sir. Oh, I have a message for you. Lieutenant Tarkington left it."

"He showed up, huh?"

"Wandered in about two hours ago and I told him his liberty had been secured. He just nodded and asked for some paper. After he wrote this, he went back to the ship." The duty officer passed Jake a folded square of paper, apparently a sheet from a notebook. On the outside was written "CAPT Grafton."

Jake walked away, unfolding the paper. "Thanks, Chief."

"Aye aye, sir."

Jake glanced back at the name tag. "Dustin." The chief was in his early forties, dark hair flecked with gray, tanned and fit. No fat on that frame. "Aye aye, sir?" He should have said, "Yes, sir" or

"You're welcome, sir." "Aye aye" was used only to respond to an order.

"Where do you work . . ." he started to ask Dustin, but the chief had already turned away as another Shore Patrol van pulled up. The lieutenant that Jake had talked to earlier stepped out and watched two of his men escort the drunk in the multicolored shirt over to the litters. What is that lieutenant's name, Jake wondered. Oh yes, Flynn.

Flynn and Dustin were having a conversation. Jake stepped close enough to hear.

"Chief, where were you this evening when we mustered? I didn't even know you and your guys were out here tonight."

"We got off the ship late, Mr. Flynn. And they sent us out to pick up drunks." The chief shrugged.

"Who is they? I'm in charge of detachment tonight, and I didn't even know you were going to be here."

"Someone screwed up, sir. I'm obviously here."

Jake turned to observe. Flynn was referring to a sheet of paper on a clipboard.

"I don't even see you on this list."

"Sir, they told me to come ashore and bring two men and go look for drunks."

"Who the hell is they?"

"My division officer."

"He may have sent you ashore, but he didn't tell you to go pick up drunks. Who did?"

"Some officer down in the Shore Patrol office. He was there when I arrived on the beach a couple hours ago."

"Lieutenant Commander Harrison?"

"He was a lieutenant commander, sir. But I didn't notice his name."

"Well, he shouldn't have told you that. I didn't even know he was going to be in the office this evening. And with that shooting over at the Vittorio, I can think up better things for you to do than taxi drunks around. Let's walk down to the office and get this straightened out."

"Mr. Flynn," Jake called. "What shooting?"

The lieutenant came over to him, the chief behind him. "There was an assassination tonight over at the Vittorio, CAG. Two guys wasted with submachine guns."

"Americans?"

"Not navy, sir. A couple civilians. I hear one of them looks like he could be an Arab. Maybe terrorists."

"When?"

"About eight." The lieutenant glanced at his watch. "Three hours or so ago, sir."

Jake nodded, and the officer and chief walked away, down the pier toward the terminal building. The Shore Patrol office was at the far end, on the second deck. Jake opened the note from Toad.

"Sir," it read. "The duty officer says you are looking for me. I am going back to the ship. I tried to call you at the hotel but got no answer. I need to talk to you URGENTLY on a very IMPORTANT matter. V/R, Tarkington. 20:50." The "V/R" meant "very respectfully" and 20:50 was the time Toad wrote the note. Jake folded the paper and put it into his pocket.

He leaned against a pole. Seven drunks in litters was unusual. But it's Saturday night, and they've been at sea for four months. Captain James was going to be busy with this lot next week. And some of them are probably air wing men, so he'll send them to me. Jake sighed.

About fifty sailors in civilian clothes were standing, squatting, and sitting under the awning, watching the rain come down. Most had been drinking and they were in a cheerful mood. The banter was loud and light. The mike boat came sliding toward the quay, its diesel engine falling silent as it coasted the last few yards to the carly float.

The boat officer came ashore and went over to the duty officer. Jake followed him. Water glistened on his raincoat and the lower portion of his trouser legs were soaked.

"It's getting bad out there, Rhodes. This may be the last boat tonight."

"How bad?" Jake asked.

The boat officer turned to him. "Lots of swell. We damn near didn't get against the fantail float this last trip. I guess four or five feet of sea. Wind's picking up too. Maybe twenty-five knots out there."

Jake nodded.

"Pretty early in the year for it to get this bad."

The duty officer's assistant, a first-class petty officer, was commandeering sailors to help get the drunks aboard. First they had to be released from the litters, which were used only to prevent unruly behavior on the pier, and placed into orange kapok life jackets for the boat ride, just in case they fell overboard. Then two men had to escort each drunk aboard the mike boat.

"You two guys, you have this man. Get over here and get with it."

The two reluctant men at whom the first-class was pointing rose slowly and walked over. Transporting drunks was a nasty business. "For the love of Christ," one of them complained as they turned their charge over. "This turd has really been drinking, man. Jesus, he smells like he spent the night *in* a bottle."

They jacked the drunk into a sitting position. He snorted and tried halfheartedly to cooperate. "Hey look! This dude has blood on him."

One of the two stepped back. "Hey man," he called to the first-class. "This guy's bloody. Maybe he's got that anally injected death serum."

The first-class, a corpsman, stepped over and made a quick examination for wounds. He stood and struck a thoughtful pose, both arms crossed on his chest. "He looks the type, don't he?"

"Yeah, man. He does. And who knows—"

"Shut up and grab him. You, too, clown," he snarled at the companion. "Let's go," he roared to his working party. "Get 'em aboard."

The two draftees rolled their eyes, glanced at Jake to see how he was taking all this, and finished strapping the life jacket to their shipmate.

Jake read Toad's note again. He folded it slowly and eased it into his pocket.

"Mr. Rhodes, call my wife at the Vittorio and tell her I'm going out to the ship. And I may have to spend the night aboard."

"Yessir."

Jake waited for all the sailors to get aboard the mike boat before he walked down the gangway onto the float and stepped carefully up onto the stern—the quarterdeck. The only light came from the pier and he couldn't see much. He stopped by the boat officer and squinted down into the well of the boat. The last of the drunks were being shoved against the rail and held there, just in case.

"If you're going to stand up here, sir," the coxswain said, "you'll have to wear a life jacket." He handed Jake an orange one

253

and Jake donned it. The coxswain helped him tighten the straps between his legs.

Chief Dustin came striding down the pier from the terminal building. He gestured toward the two Shore Patrolmen from his van, and they preceded him down the gangway and across the float. The Shore Patrolmen went down in the well of the boat. Dustin snapped a salute to Jake.

"Get it straightened out, Chief?"

"Yes, sir. We did." The chief slid down the ladder to join his men in the welldeck.

Lieutenant (j.g.) Rhodes called from the pier, "Shove off."

The boat officer nodded to the coxswain, who called for the lines. The stern line came off first, and as the stern drifted away from the float the bow line came aboard and the coxswain gunned the engine. The boat backed smartly out onto the dark water.

Passing the terminal building and the frigate moored end-on to the top of the quay, Jake could see a halo around each of the lights. The rain drops came into the halos at an angle, driven by the wind. The lights of Naples reflected on the oily black surface of the harbor.

The boat officer fastened the top button of his raincoat and turned the collar up. He wore his life jacket under the raincoat. He loosened the gold strap on his hat and slipped it under his chin. Everyone on this open boat without foul-weather gear would soon be soaked. The boat officer, a lieutenant (junior grade) from a fighter squadron, grinned when he saw Jake watching him. "Great navy night, sir."

Jake Grafton nodded and filled his lungs with the sweet salt wind.

Proceeding down the harbor, they were swept periodically by the circling beam from the lighthouse at the harbor mouth. The boat began to wallow as it entered the turbulent water flowing into the harbor from the sea. The coxswain played with the throttle and helm and coaxed the flat-bottomed landing craft to the right, toward the open sea. Now the square bow rose and fell to meet the incoming swells.

The pitching motion worsened when they cleared the breakwater. As the stern rose, the bow smashed down into the next trough, throwing water out to the sides. But before the boat could rise to meet the oncoming swell, the moving ridge of water smacked into the bow door with a thud and threw a sheet of water aloft, to be sprayed aft by the wind. The men in the welldeck hunched against the sides of the boat in a vain attempt to stay dry. Jake could hear the sounds of retching from the welldeck.

The carrier was several miles ahead, hidden by the rain. Jake watched the coxswain handle the boat. A little red light shone on the compass and RPM indicator. The boat officer held onto a stanchion with one hand and aimed the boat's spotlight with the other. He swept the welldeck and the miserable humanity huddled there. Wet and shivering, Jake tightened his grip on the stanchion in front of him. The wind was quartering from starboard and roared in his ears.

The puny light played on the oncoming swells. The water was black with streaks of white. The swells were at least six feet from crest to trough, and the wind was ripping spindrift from the tops. The view was the same in all directions. Apparently satisfied, the boat officer doused the light.

Over his shoulder Jake watched the glow of Naples fade into the gloom. They were in total darkness. The assault boat plowed on, away from the land, into the heart of the stormy night sea.

20

THE CARRIER loomed like a cliff out of the heaving sea. She had swung on her anchor until her bow was pointed directly into the wind.

The boat officer held the spotlight on the float moored against the ship's stern as the coxswain maneuvered the assault boat in. From the cavernous fantail fifteen feet above the waterline, two more spots were trained on the float, which rose and fell to the rhythm of the sea, water spewing from the steel deck and the tires lashed along the side for bumpers. The stairway up to the fantail had wheels mounted on its base, where it rested on the float, and was tracking madly back and forth across the bucking float like a giant phonograph needle on a badly warped record.

The coxswain threw the screws into reverse and jammed on the power, but the mike boat was in the sheltered lee created by the huge ship and continued to close too quickly on the float, which rose when the boat fell and fell when the boat rose. He slammed the lever for the screws out of reverse and jammed the throttles forward as he spun the helm. He clawed off, barely missing one corner of the gyrating steel float.

The coxswain was no more than twenty. Framed by his slicker, his wet face was a study in concentration as he again brought the boat with its load of sodden, sick men in toward the ship. This time he closed too slowly, and the boat lost headway twenty feet below the float, before it reached the wind shelter created by the ship. The coxswain poured on the power and Jake could hear the engines roaring above the noise of the storm. But the corkscrewing boat was stymied by the wind deflected down the side of the monstrous ship, which pushed it away from the float and the looming stern-quarter of the carrier. The coxswain spun the helm hard over and used full power on just one engine to swing the boat out, away from the ship, for another try.

"Third time's the charm," Jake yelled into the coxswain's ear. The boy's lips parted in a slight grin, but his eyes never left the writhing float.

The boat officer was standing by Jake now. As the senior officer on the boat, Jake was legally responsible for its safe operation. The young boat officer wanted to be where he could relay any order Jake cared to give. Jake knew this, and he also knew that the coxswain was a much better boat handler than either of the officers, so he intended to say nothing at all unless the coxswain completely lost the bubble. Then Jake's only real option would be to order him to return to the beach.

The coxswain had learned from his first two approaches. This time he held his speed until the proper moment, then used the screws in reverse to bring the boat against the float. His line handlers lassoed the mooring bitts on the float and lashed their lines down as the boat and the float ground together, still moving up and down out of sync.

Jake eyed the heaving float, and jumped across when the boat and float established a brief, temporary equilibrium. He held onto the lifeline and made his way to the moving stairway, which he leaped aboard and climbed while holding onto the railing with both hands.

He presented his ID card to the marine sentries at the top of the ladder, then stepped aside to watch the men exit the boat. The boat officer was directing men out of the well, and two men from the ship stood on the float and grabbed as men jumped or leaped across. The drunks were the last to be manhandled from the welldeck and assisted onto the float.

Then it happened. The next-to-last impaired sailor lost his balance and fell backward waving his arms violently. Somehow the men holding him lost their grip, and the flailing man fell against the man behind him and they both toppled over the stern of the mike boat. Their life jackets held them up, but the wind and swells were pushing them away from the float.

"Man overboard, man overboard, from the fantail," the ship's loudspeaker blared.

The boat officer threw a life ring. Then he tossed a saltwater-activated flare.

Jake fought his way through the marines checking ID cards and the stream of sailors coming up the ladder. "Get these people off the float and outta here," he shouted at the sergeant in charge of the marines.

"Keep those lights trained on the guys in the water," Jake roared at the sailors manning the spotlights. He grabbed the bullhorn from the junior officer-of-the-deck and elbowed his way to the rail.

"You in the boat! Take those men there helping on the float and make off. Pull those guys out. Put life jackets on everyone." He turned around. The fantail was full of gawkers. He used the bullhorn again. "You people get the hell out of here. Now!"

Colonel Qazi led his two former Shore Patrolmen and four of the drunks down the narrow passageway that led from the fantail to the hangar bay. He would have to work fast. The men in the water had been instructed to attempt to delay their rescue as long as possible, but once picked up, they would be taken to the ship's sick bay and there it would be discovered they were not Americans. Qazi hoped he had at least fifteen minutes, but that was about all the time he could reasonably expect.

There were many men on the hangar deck, all in soaking wet civilian clothes. They were just passing through on their way to the berthing compartments for dry clothes. Qazi's men in civilian clothes would become conspicuous in just a few minutes. Qazi fanned out his men and they began to search through the crates stacked against the aft end of the hangar bay. Men dribbled past from the fantail passageway. Qazi fought back the urge to help his men search through this mountain of supply crates and stood watching with his arms crossed.

A group of men in working uniform ran past, toward the entrance to the fantail passageway.

The loudspeaker blared to life. "Flight quarters, flight quarters for helo operations. Standby to launch the helo on the waist." Captain Grafton wasn't betting all his chips on the assault boat coxswain, Qazi thought.

A chief petty officer approached Qazi. "What's going on?"

"Couple drunks fell overboard getting off the liberty boat."

"No shit? What a night for it. You better go get some dry clothes on yourself."

"Yeah, Chief."

The chief walked away, headed forward. Qazi turned back to his men. They were still scouring the crates, which were piled four deep on pallets and the pallets were stacked together with narrow passageways all the way back to the aft bulkhead. There must be two hundred crates stacked here. Where was their crate?

"Over here."

It was back in one narrow walkway, on top of one crate, with another stacked on top of it. One of the men grabbed a fire ax from a bulkhead mount and attacked the crate. The planes forward of them in the bay and the piles of boxes sheltered them from observation by other people going to and fro. Yet the ax against the wood made a lot of noise, the wrong kind of noise. Then the wood gave.

They pulled the other crate off the top of it and pushed it up on another pile and disassembled their crate. Two diesel engines were packed side by side.

"Stack the wood neatly against the bulkhead," Qazi directed. As the men quickly cleared up the wood, Qazi examined the two engines. He found the mark he was looking for.

"This one," he said. "Bring the ax." The six men lifted the engine and he led them out of the crate-storage area and between the aircraft which filled the bay to a compartment on the port side. An A-6 with wings folded was parked nearly in front of the door, shielding it from the view of the man in the fire-fighting compartment high in the bulkhead on the other side of the bay. Qazi used the pointed, piercing tool on the back of the axhead to force the door.

The compartment was a damage-control locker. Fire hoses, oxygen-breathing apparatus, fire extinguishers, fire-resistant suits, and other tools of the damage-control party filled the space. With the engine and all the men inside, Qazi shut the door.

When he turned around, the men were opening the container, which really wasn't an engine at all but merely a metal shell stamped to look like an engine. Inside the shell were uniforms and weapons, Uzis with silencers. There were also Browning Hi-Powers with silencers for everyone. The men stripped to the skin and put on the uniforms, bell-bottom jeans, and short-sleeve denim shirts. Over this they added a navy-blue sweater and a jacket. White wool socks and black, ankle-high brogans went on the feet and wool caps on the heads.

"Go get the other shell and bring it in here," Qazi said when everyone was dressed. That shell held plastic explosive and fuses.

The Command Duty Officer relieved Jake on the fantail. Tonight the CDO was Commander Ron Triblehorn, the chief engineer. The mike boat was a hundred yards from the ship making an approach to one of the men in the water. The helo was still on the flight deck. As Commander Triblehorn explained the situation by telephone to Captain James, who was on the bridge and had ordered the helo launched, Jake left the fantail and walked through the hangar bay. He passed Ray Reynolds dogtrotting aft. Jake climbed a ladder amidships and went to his stateroom on the O-3 level. After he stripped off his sodden clothes and toweled himself dry, he called the air wing office.

"Who've you got up there tonight, Farnsworth?"

"Well, sir, one of the yeoman and three of the officers have showed up. I'm getting the yeomen in here to help with the muster." Whenever "man overboard" was called away, every division and squadron on the ship had to muster its people. Since so many men were on the beach tonight, the listing of personnel who could not be accounted for would be time-consuming and tedious. "I was already here when they called man overboard," Farnsworth continued. "Lieutenant Tarkington was looking for you, so I came down to the office to give him a place to sit. He's waiting for you now."

"I'll be up there in a few minutes. I'm changing clothes."

"I'll tell him, sir. And CAG," Farnsworth's voice dropped to a whisper, "Mr. Tarkington's pretty upset."

"If he thinks he's going to rag me about securing his liberty, he'd better have another think before I get there."

"I doubt if that's it. He doesn't look a bit self-righteous."

"Humph. Remind Tarkington to call his squadron to muster."

Jake put on a clean khaki uniform and pulled on his leather flight jacket. The air inside the ship was at no more than sixty degrees tonight. It had been so warm these past few days, perhaps someone had forgotten to turn on the heat. Or Captain James had ordered it left off to save the navy sixty-four cents worth of enriched uranium. Jake toweled his head dry and combed his hair. He grabbed his combination cap, the one with the scrambled eggs on the visor, and locked the door behind him.

"What's your problem, Tarkington?"

"I need to talk to you, sir. And I heard you were looking for me."

"Into the office." Farnsworth and his two assistants were already checking names on muster sheets as the squadrons called in.

Jake closed the office door and motioned Tarkington to a chair. He felt around for the note the lieutenant had written to him on the beach, but he had left it in his civilian trousers.

"They shot two men to death tonight at the Vittorio."

"I heard," Jake said.

"I was there."

"Oh," said Jake, and sank into his chair.

"Judith Farrell was the leader of the assassination team."

Jake Grafton threw his hat on the desk and rubbed his eyes. "Start talking."

His men stood casually. Their handguns were in the back of their trousers, in the small of their backs under their sweaters and jackets. The Uzis were in small gym bags, along with spare magazines and grenades.

Qazi examined each face. "Okay, you know your assignments. The success of our mission depends on each one of you carrying out your assignments exactly as you have been taught. Remember, they do not yet know we are aboard, and the longer we remain undetected, the easier this mission will be. You are now American sailors. Just proceed purposefully, yet unhurriedly, and the Americans will accept you as one of them." Three of them spoke no English and the other three spoke only a little, with heavy accents. They had all been instructed that when spoken to, merely nod, smile, and go on.

Their faces were grim, determined. "Remember to smile." A smile was an American's passport, the visible proof that his heart was pure and his intentions honorable. Since World War II the Americans had grinned at almost everyone on earth. Now even nomads in the Gobi desert were smiling.

"Go."

When everyone had left the compartment, Qazi closed the door and placed a padlock on it. He removed the key from the padlock and put it in his pocket. A close examination would show the door had been forced and the door-handle lock broken, but the padlock would delay them for a few minutes. He picked up his gym bag and, with two of his men behind him, walked between the airplanes until he could look up at the man in the center hangar-deck fire station, CONFLAG 2. He smiled at him and walked toward the hatch immediately below the watch station. He glanced around. One of the red paint lockers stood against the bulkhead. As soon as he finished upstairs, while his men were visiting the other two CONFLAG stations, he would plant bombs on at least four or five of these paint lockers. He took a deep breath and began to climb the ladder.

21

SHE ASKED ME not to tell."

"She knew you would."

Tarkington's face was a study. Lines radiated from the corners of his eyes and his face seemed . . . older.

"She knew you had to tell," Jake said.

"If she knew I was going to spill it, why did she ask me not to? How come she didn't just shoot me?"

"Women are like that," Jake Grafton muttered. "They ask you not to do something they know you're gonna do, and they watch your face while they ask it." He shrugged. "Maybe they're just measuring the size of your heart."

"I think they were Israelis. Mossad."

"Any evidence?"

"They ragged on one guy who sounded like an American. They called him an 'agency asshole.' Apparently he shot the first guy when he wasn't supposed to." Toad looked around desperately.

"They didn't kill me," he said, his voice rising. "The Mossad only kills terrorists."

"Or so you've heard. And you've ratted on them when she asked you not to. Now you feel guilty as hell. Thank you, Judith Farrell."

Jake picked up the phone and dialed Farnsworth. "Find the senior intelligence officer who's aboard tonight and tell him to go to the intel center. I'm sending Mr. Tarkington over there now. I want them to wring out Tarkington like a sponge and draft up a Top Secret flash message. Then find out if Admiral Parker's aboard, or the chief of staff."

When he cradled the receiver, he said to Toad, "I want you to tell this tale to the Air Intelligence guys. Describe every one of those people. Including Judith. What they were wearing, height and weight, facial features, the works." As Toad rose to go, Jake added, "Sooner or later, you may get curious about why I had everyone on this boat looking for you all afternoon. Judith Farrell is not a native speaker of English. She's probably not an American."

Toad looked dazed. "But she said she was!"

"Tarkington . . . ," Jake said, exasperation creeping into his voice, "you got yourself smack in the middle of somebody's heavy operation. Farrell's on someone's team. You're real fucking lucky you didn't get zapped for just being in the wrong place at the wrong time." Toad didn't react, the sap. "Look at it this way, Toad: if you hadn't meant anything to her, she wouldn't have bothered to tell you to keep quiet."

The younger man just stared, his mouth open slightly.

Jake came around the desk and sat on it. Maybe he shouldn't go into this. But Toad . . . Why wait for the guy to figure all this out ten years from now? "You care about her, right? And she was telling you she cares about you. She told you the only way she could. The words weren't the message; it was the way she said it."

Toad nodded slowly.

"Now quit feeling like a shit and go tell the intel guys everything you know." Jake pointed toward the door. "Beat it."

As Toad left the room he glanced back at the captain, who was absently patting his pockets as he gazed at the telephone. Then the door closed.

□ □ □

Private Harold Porter hadn't worn his slicker for this watch. The rain had soaked him and the wind was making him miserable. He huddled against the side of the ship, under the lip of the flight deck curb, and kept his hands tucked under his armpits. The ship's red flight-deck floodlights illuminated the .50-caliber machine gun and the ammo feed box. The sound-powered telephone headset he wore kept his ears warm. At least that was something.

Porter elevated his head and watched the helicopter lift off the angle. Its flashing red anticollision light swept the numbers on the side of the island. The chopper rose several feet off the deck and the tail came up, then it accelerated forward off the angled portion of the flight deck. Porter watched it go, then lowered his head back below the curb of the deck.

Those poor bastards in the water were really in the soup. Too bad the action was on the other side of the ship, where he couldn't see it. The scuttlebutt on the sound-powered circuit was that they were drunk. So if they don't drown, they're going to be shoveling shit when old man James gets through with them. Serves the bastards right, Porter decided. He hadn't been ashore for the last two nights. Envy wrapped its slimy fingers around his heart.

The corporal should be around in a few minutes. Maybe he could get the corporal to go down to the berthing spaces and get his slicker for him. Naw, not Simons, that prick. But maybe Simons would relieve him for a few minutes and let him go get it. He sourly contemplated the odds of talking the corporal into that.

Simons was an asshole, no question. Two little red chevrons and he acted like he'd been promoted to disciple. Why in hell the corps ever promoted a cock-stroking butt-licker like him was a good question to contemplate on a bad night. Aagh, it's enough to make you puke. You work your ass off spit-shining your fucking shoes and polishing your fucking brass and cleaning your fucking rifle, and then Hershey-bar lifer pricks like Simons . . .

Someone was coming down the catwalk. Damn! Couldn't be Simons. Not five minutes early. Oh, it's some dirt-bag sailor, probably drunk, out wandering around after a big night in town, out to give the corps some shit.

"Hey Dixie-cup, you—"

The first bullet from the silenced 9-millimeter hit Private Porter

265

in the throat. The wind swallowed the muffled report. As the marine's hands went to his throat, the pistol popped twice more, and the now-lifeless body slumped down into a sitting position.

The assassin opened the breech of the big fifty and the ammo feed box. He lifted out the belt of shells and fed it over the rail, between the big gray canisters that contained the fifty-man life rafts. The ammo belt fell into the blackness. The killer bent over the open breech. In a few seconds he snapped the weapon's breech and the ammo-box lid closed, and walked forward toward the bow.

Lance Corporal James Van Housen was bored. And when he was bored, he entertained himself with isometric exercises. He strained at the top bar of the catwalk rail, trying to curl it. He counted the seconds: . . . fourteen, thousand, fifteen, thousand, sixteen, . . . When he got to twenty, he relaxed and counted his pulse while he examined the sweep second hand of his watch, just visible in the red lights of the ship's island.

The rest of these guys, they just stand around and get fat while the sergeants kick their asses. Van Housen was staying in shape. He was taking advantage of every opportunity to exercise. That's what the corps is all about, staying in shape, ready to fight. If they wanted to be marshmallows, they should have joined the fucking navy. The sailors all think exercise is what they do to their dicks in the shower.

Van Housen saw the chopper cross the fantail and make its approach to the helo spot on the angle. The sound-powered circuit talker said the angel had picked one guy up from the liberty boat, which had pulled him from the water. A damn bad night for a swim. The talker didn't know about the other guy in the water. Van Housen watched a team of corpsmen with a litter run toward the chopper as soon as it touched down.

The lance corporal seized the top rail and lifted again, counting to himself. He finished this set and was flexing his arms, trying to pump out the fatigue toxins, when he saw a sailor come up a ladder from the O-3 level, fifty feet aft, and turn toward him. He first glimpsed the man from the corner of his eye, then turned to watch him.

What the hell is he doing out here at this time of night?

The sailor had something in his right hand, down against his leg. He was concealing it behind his thigh. A doper? Carrying a joint? Naw, it was an object of some kind.

Van Housen stepped back against the bulkhead, partially out of sight because of the way the catwalk zagged outboard around this nearest ladder up from the O-3 level.

As the sailor in a sweater came around the corner, Van Housen was watching his hand. It swung up. A gun! It flashed—Van Housen heard the dull pop—and the bullet rocked him, but he had already launched himself forward. His momentum drove the sailor back against the rail, stunning him. Van Housen wrestled for the gun. There was a silencer on the barrel. He smashed the sailor's arm against the railing. The pistol fell. Van Housen punched his assailant in the stomach, then again. The man doubled over.

Van Housen could feel himself weakening.

Got to stop this guy! Got to! Before I go down.

He seized the man by the belt and one arm and heaved him up and outboard as he exhaled convulsively from the exertion. The man sprawled on top of a life-raft canister. Van Housen tore the wool cap off and grabbed him by the hair. He smashed his fist into the sailor's face.

No strength. The blow was weak. His legs were buckling.

The marine summoned every last ounce of strength and hit the man again in the face, swinging with his weight behind the blow. The man slid backward off the canister and disappeared, falling toward the sea.

Van Housen collapsed on the catwalk grid. His sound-powered headset had come off in the fight. He felt his stomach. His hand was warm and black and wet. Blood!

He was fainting. He lowered his head to the grid to stay conscious and felt for the headset. He pulled it toward him and fumbled for the mike button. "This is gun one . . ."

Then he passed out. He was unconscious when another sailor in a sweater with a pistol in his hand emerged from between the planes on the flight deck and stood looking down into the catwalk.

Lance Corporal Van Housen never felt the next bullet, which killed him.

□ □ □

Admiral Parker was wearing white uniform trousers and a T-shirt. Apparently he had just pulled the trousers on after his orderly woke him. Jake told him about the incident at the Vittorio, and Judith Farrell and Toad Tarkington's involvement.

"Hell yes, I'll release a flash message. You briefed Captain James on this yet?"

"Not yet, sir. I just heard this from Tarkington and the captain's busy with the man overboard."

"The captain called me just before you knocked. One man's still in the water and one's on his way to sick bay, half dead." Parker turned to his aide, Lieutenant Franklin Delano Roosevelt Snyder. "Get my clothes, Duke. It's time we went up to the bridge." As he dressed the admiral told Jake, "Tonight's Shore Patrol officer has been found dead on the quay. Neck broken."

"What?" Jake said.

"Murdered."

"Where?"

"Right in the Shore Patrol office. He was found just a few minutes ago."

Jake Grafton seized the arms of his chair and leaned forward. "Lieutenant Flynn?"

"Yes."

"I saw him go toward the office just before I boarded the mike boat to come out to the ship. He went down there with a chief who was on Shore Patrol duty tonight. The chief came back down the quay alone and rode out to the ship on the boat with me. He's aboard."

"Did you ever see the chief before? Know his name?"

Jake tried to remember. "Duncan? No . . . Dustin, I think. Dustin. And I can't recall ever seeing him before."

The admiral finished lacing his shoes, straightened and started for the door. Jake and Duke Snyder followed him. "Here we sit," the admiral muttered, "three miles from the beach on the most valuable target in southern Italy. And we may already have an intruder aboard."

"Or more than one," Jake said, recalling the unusual number of drunks on the boat this evening and the confusion on the fantail when the two men went into the water.

□   □   □

Colonel Qazi charged up a ladder on the starboard side of the ship with his two men carrying gym bags right at his heels. At the top of the ladder well, on the O-3 level, they turned inboard to the long passageway that ran the length of the ship on the starboard side. Although this was one of the two main thoroughfares on this deck, it was narrow. Men could pass each other shoulder to shoulder in the corridor, but the knee-knockers were only wide enough for one man at a time to pass through. Qazi consulted the numbers on the little brass plaques near the doors of the compartments as he walked past. He knew the numbering system, but he couldn't readily visualize just where he was from reading the numbers. For the first time tonight Qazi knew a touch of panic. These passageways all looked the same, narrow and full of ninety-degree turns. The place was a maze, a labyrinth of walls and doors and passageways that led off in every direction but the proper one. When the watertight doors swung shut, he would have to fight his way from space to space and he would never know just where he was or where he was going. He would be trapped like a rat.

He touched the arm of a sailor walking aft. "I'm new aboard. How do I get to the communication spaces?"

"Port side, Chief." The sailor gestured toward a passageway that led off to the left, presumably to join with the port-side passageway that paralleled this one. "And forward maybe fifty frames. There's a window to pass messages through. You can't miss it."

"Thanks."

"Sure." The sailor hurried away. Qazi and his men strode down the indicated passageway.

They were in luck. Just beside the window where the clerks accepted messages for transmission, there was a security door which was locked and unlocked by an access device mounted head-high on the bulkhead. The access device had a keyboard into which those who sought entrance tapped a code, which changed weekly. And as Qazi approached, a sailor was tapping on the keys, which were hidden from an observer's view by a black lip which surrounded the keyboard.

The sailor started through the security door just as Qazi reached him and planted his shoulder in the man's back. They crashed through the door together, the two gunmen right be-hind, extracting their Uzis from their gym bags. Black security curtains screened the doorway from the rest of the compartment. Qazi pushed his man through the drapes into the room and Jamail and Haddad, the gunmen following, stepped clear to each side and opened fire. The silenced weapons made a ripping noise. Spent shells spewed from the ejection ports. The sailor who had preceded Qazi spun toward him, and the colonel grabbed his head and broke his neck.

The other five Americans in the compartment died under the hail of bullets.

The office spaces were lit in white light, in contrast to the red light which had illuminated the ladders and passageways. As their eyes adjusted, the gunmen ran deeper into the communications complex, using their weapons on the four other sailors they found there. Qazi went into the equipment room. Banks of panels with dials and gauges and knobs covered the walls. Or did they? There seemed to be lights behind this equipment. Over there was a passage. Perhaps the power cables came in back there. That communications technician Ali had interrogated, what had he said?

Qazi stepped through the gap in the seven-foot-high gray boxes.

He saw the fist and the wrench swinging just in time, and ducked as the wrench smashed into the panel beside him.

The man wielding it was young. Young and black and scared. And quick. He had the wrench swinging again before Qazi could react. The colonel tried to fall, and the wrench struck his head a glancing blow.

He was on the floor, dazed, and the sailor was on his chest, pinning his arms with his legs, drawing back the wrench for the coup de grace, his lips stretched back exposing his teeth, the cords in his neck as taut as wires.

Qazi heard a pop and blood spurted from the side of the Ameri-can's head. The corpse collapsed on top of him. The wrench rang as it hit the linoleum-covered deck.

Jamail rolled the body away. Qazi tried to rise. God, not this!

"Quickly," he tried to say, his tongue thick. He gestured vaguely at Jamail, who nodded and left him there, struggling to rise from the sitting position.

Jamail and Haddad had almost completed the task of setting the charges when Qazi had the cobwebs sufficiently cleared to stand upright and walk out into the equipment room. "Put one on the electrical cables under the raised area of the floor," Qazi told them, "back there." He pointed behind the panels. Haddad seized his gym bag and disappeared into the gap from which Qazi had just come. The colonel inspected the timer on the charge against the power-distribution panel. It was readily apparent what this panel was, because Haddad had opened the metal doors to expose all the switches and connectors. And he had properly armed the magnesium flare, which would ignite thirty seconds after the main explosion. Satisfactory.

"What the fuck?"

The exclamation came from the office, the first compartment they had come through. Jamail heard it too and charged in that direction, his Uzi ready. Qazi was right behind.

The officer in khakis went down under Jamail's bullets. As he fell, the security curtains fluttered and Qazi heard the sound of the passageway door being jerked open. Jamail pumped a short burst into the curtains.

"Intruders in the comm spaces! Intruders . . ." The door clicked shut and the rest of the shout was lost.

"Quick! Let's finish. Arm the fuses and let's *go."*

Fifteen seconds later the three men stood by the door and arranged the straps of their gym bags over their shoulders. Jamail and Haddad put new magazines into their Uzis.

"Jamail, you will lead us out. Clear the passageway left. Haddad, clear it right. Then I will lead you forward—that's to the right—to the first passageway turning left, which will take us out of the ship onto the catwalk and up to the flight deck. Let's go." Qazi nodded and Haddad pulled the curtains aside and opened the door. Jamail went through low. He opened fire as Haddad and Qazi followed him.

In the red-lit corridor a small knot of men were gathered fifty feet aft, most of them facing in this direction. As the Uzi sprayed men dove into open doorways or collapsed onto the deck.

Qazi covered the twenty feet to the outboard passageway and turned the corner when the muffled bursts finally ceased. "The bastard," he swore viciously as he ran. Jamail used a whole magazine on them—unarmed men. He enjoys this!

The passageway turned left, then right, and ended at a dogged-down watertight door. Qazi grabbed the one handle that was mechanically linked to all eight of the dogs and lifted. Each of the eight dogs rotated ninety degrees. Haddad pushed at the door. All three men were through the opening and Jamail was closing the door when the concussion from the explosions in the communications spaces hammered the deck and bulkheads. The heavy door flew out on its hinges and smacked against Jamail. He picked himself up and, with Haddad, dogged it shut.

The wind was fierce here under the catwalk. Through the grid, Qazi could see the streaks in the black sea from the foaming whitecaps. He waited as his eyes adjusted fully to the darkness. So far so good. Phase one almost complete.

The ship's public-address system came to life. A speaker was located on the catwalk just above them. They heard the hum and hiss, then a Klaxon began to wail. The volume was deafening, probably so the announcements could be heard all over the flight deck. Qazi inserted his fingers in his ears. When the Klaxon stopped, a voice came on, equally loud: "General quarters, general quarters. All hands man your battle stations. This is not a drill. General quarters, general quarters. Go up and forward on the starboard side and down and aft on the port side. This is not a drill." The Klaxon resumed its wail, then died abruptly. Even here on the catwalk, Qazi could feel the steel grid under his feet vibrate from the harmonics induced by thousands of running feet.

Time was running out. In three minutes every watertight door and hatch on the ship would be ordered shut. And even now the ship's quick-reaction team—a squad of armed marines—would be on its way to the bridge to protect the captain. He had to get there first.

Qazi led the way up the ladder to the catwalk and up the next ladder onto the flight deck.

Jake Grafton, Rear Admiral Parker, and Captain James were huddled around the captain's chair on the bridge when they felt the shock of the explosion in the communications compartment. High up here in the island it was just a dull thud that jolted the steel deck. A man was on the phone reporting intruders in the comm spaces when the explosion occurred.

"Sound general quarters. Then call away the nucleus fire party and set Circle William," the captain told the OOD, who repeated the order to the bosun's mate of the watch, who announced it on the ship's loudspeaker. The nucleus fire party was a group of damage-control specialists who normally responded to fire reports when the ship's watertight hatches were not closed. They were the most highly trained firemen on the ship, so the captain wanted to use them if possible. The Circle William order was critical to containing the smoke and fumes from a fire. Closure of hatches labeled with a W inside a red circle—Circle William— would seal off the ship's air-circulating system, preventing smoke and poisonous fumes generated by a fire from being pumped throughout the ship.

"Sir," the OOD reported, "No one answers the squawk box or telephone in the comm spaces."

Laird James reached for the microphone of the ship's public address system. "What are you going to say?" Parker asked.

"I'm going to tell the crew what's going on."

"Remember, the intruders can hear you."

James nodded and keyed the mike. "This is the captain. We have just had an explosion in the communications spaces on the O-3 level. Apparently we have at least one group of intruders aboard this ship. Perhaps more that one group. They are armed. Some of your shipmates have apparently already died."

He released the mike button and looked at Parker. "My men don't have guns."

Parker's lips tightened into a grim line. "Don't let them die for nothing."

James keyed the mike again. "Avoid direct confrontation with the terrorists, yet resist the best way you can. Keep the bridge and DC Central informed." He paused again and stared for a moment into the blackness of the night sea. "You men are American sailors. I expect each of you to do his duty. That is all."

James punched the button on a squawk box, an intercom system, labeled "CDC." "This is the captain. You people manned up down there?"

"Yessir."

"Get off a voice transmission, scrambled if possible, on your circuits. Tell our escorts to relay it to Sixth Fleet and CIN-CLANT." CINCLANT was the Commander in Chief of the U.S. Atlantic Fleet.

"Yessir. What do we send?"

"Goddammit, man," James thundered. "Send the substance of the announcement I just made over the 1-MC." The 1-MC circuit was the ship's public-address system. "Tell them we have armed intruders aboard. More info to follow as we get it."

"Aye aye, sir."

Chief Terry Reed stared in disbelief at the padlock on the door to the after hangar-deck repair locker. The men behind him peered over his shoulder, curious about the delay. Why the hell was this door padlocked? The doorknob had an integral lock, and every man in the chief's repair party had a key. This locker was their battle station. Chief Reed took a closer look at the doorknob. It had been forced.

"Somebody get a fire ax and pry this damn lock off."

The chief scanned the hangar bay while he waited. Intruders? Aboard this ship? Captain James didn't throw words around lightly. He must know what's going on. The chief looked at the doorknob lock again. Someone had pried it until it broke. And this padlock—it wasn't navy-issue. Damn. Could the intruders have been here?

A man came running with a fire ax. The chief moved back away from the door. He looked again around the hangar bay, still puzzled. Why would anyone want to get in the repair-party locker? There was nothing in there but damage control gear. The valuable assets were the airplanes, out here in the bay. He stared at them, wings folded and chained to the deck. Some of the machines had access panels and nose domes open, exposing radars and black boxes and bundles of cables. They looked naked. Had they been sabotaged?

Even as the thought occurred to the chief, the paint locker on the opposite side of the bay exploded. In an instant the flammable chemicals stored there were burning fiercely.

The chief looked wildly about for the nearest fire alarm. He saw it against the wall right by the fire-fighting station and lunged for it. His motion galvanized his men into action. They energized the pumps and began dragging the hose out. They had the nozzle half way across the hangar when two more paint lockers exploded.

274

□ □ □

Qazi and his men huddled under an aircraft wing immediately forward of the island. He counted them. Seven plus himself. "Who's not here?"

"Mohammed. Apparently he only wounded one of the marines on the machine guns and they fought. He may have gone overboard."

"Did you set his charges on the antenna leads?"

"Mine and his both." So all the radio-antenna leads of which Qazi was aware had been severed. The damage could be repaired fairly quickly as soon as the Americans discovered where the breaks were, but the search would take time, and time for the Americans was running out.

Qazi looked up at the dark windows of the bridge, eight decks above him in the island superstructure. The glare of the red flood-lights around the top of the island made it impossible to see if any lights were illuminated on the bridge. Of course, the ship's senior officers were there. They had to be. The quick-reaction team couldn't have made it to the bridge yet, but they were undoubtedly on their way. Qazi had to reach the bridge before the marines did or he might not be able to get there at all. Time was running out for him too.

He gestured to two of his men, pointing out the positions he wished them to assume on the flight deck, positions from which they could command the helicopter landing area on the angle, abeam the island. Since the ship's rescue helicopter was airborne, most of the helo landing area was empty and the whip antennas that surrounded the flight deck had been lowered to their horizontal position. Qazi wanted to ensure everything remained that way.

The rest of his men he led across the deck through the wind and rain toward the hatch that opened into Flight Deck Control, the empire of the aircraft handler. E-2 Hawkeye radar reconnaissance planes were parked beside the island, their tails almost against the steel and their noses pointed across the deck at the helicopter landing area. The wet metal skin of the airplanes glistened in the weak red light. The colonel went under the tails and glanced through the porthole into Flight Deck Control. The compartment was full of men. He stopped in front of the entrance door and motioned for two of his men to grab the handle that would rotate the locking lugs.

Reports were arriving on the bridge over the telephones, the squawk boxes, and the sound-powered circuits. Damage-Control Central reported fires in the comm spaces and on the hangar deck. The airborne helicopter had been unable to find the second man overboard. Fully 20 percent of the ship's company was still ashore. Most of the ship's radios seemed to be off the air with suspected antenna problems. As Captain James tried to sort it out, Jake and the admiral stood in the corner and listened to the reports coming in.

Jake looked at his watch. Two minutes had passed since general quarters had sounded.

"What are they after?" the admiral asked, more to himself than Jake. "And where are they?"

The door to Flight Deck Control swung open and Qazi followed two of his men into the space. They had their Uzis in front of them. The rest followed him into the compartment.

"Silence. Hands up," Qazi shouted in English.

A sea of stunned faces stared at Qazi. He waved at the area behind the scale model of the flight and hangar deck. "Over there. Everyone. Over there!"

No one moved. Qazi pointed the Browning Hi-Power, with its silencer sticking out like an evil finger, at the chiefs and talkers near the maintenance status boards. "Move. Headsets off."

They stood frozen, staring. The silenced pistol swung toward the status board and popped, but the smack of the bullet punching its way through the plexiglas and splatting into the bulkhead was louder. Eyes shifted hypnotically toward the neat, round hole in the transparent plexiglas. In the silence Qazi could hear the tinkle of the spent cartridge case as it caromed off a folding chair and struck the metal bulkhead.

"Do as he says. Get over here, people." The speaker was an officer in khakis, a lieutenant commander sitting in a raised padded chair.

The men moved with alacrity, shedding the sound-powered telephone headsets.

When everyone was crammed thigh to thigh in the indicated

space with their hands on the back of their necks, Colonel Qazi spoke again. "You will stand silently, without moving. My men will kill every man who moves or opens his mouth. They understand no English. And they know how to kill." He added, almost as an afterthought, "They enjoy it."

He turned and went through the doorway that led to the ladder up into the island. He would have to hurry. Were the marines ahead of him?

Qazi went past the door to the down ladder, a standard nonwatertight aluminum door, and opened the door to the ladder going up. Although Qazi didn't know it, this was the only place on the ship where the ladderwells were sealed with doors and aluminum bulkheads. This feature prevented fumes and noise from the flight deck from penetrating deeper into the ship.

He heard a thundering noise immediately beneath him. Men running up the ladder beneath his feet! Marines on the way to the bridge! He gestured frantically to the men following him. Just then the door from below burst open and one of Qazi's men triggered an Uzi burst full into the chest of the marine coming through. He fell backward onto the man behind him. The door sagged shut on his ankle.

On the ladder below the marine who had been shot, someone fired his M-16 upward, through the thin aluminum bulkhead. Once, twice, then an automatic burst.

"A grenade," Qazi whispered hoarsely.

The man nearest the colonel pulled the pin and tossed it over the booted ankle trapped in the door as everyone else fell flat on the deck.

The explosion was muffled. "Another," Qazi ordered.

This time the explosion was loud and shrapnel sprayed through the aluminum ladderwell wall.

The grenades would merely delay the marines below. They would seek an alternate route upward, and they knew the ship. He had purchased himself mere seconds. Maybe that would be enough. "Quickly now, let's go."

Two of his men failed to rise. Someone turned them over. One was dead, a rifle bullet through the heart, and the other had a piece of shrapnel in his abdomen. No time to waste. Qazi charged up the ladder two steps at a time with those of his men who were still on their feet right behind. More gunfire. Qazi paused at the top and glanced back. The last man was down holding his leg. The marines had fired through the aluminum sheeting under the ladder. Even as he looked, another burst came through the aluminum and the wounded man lost his balance and fell. But he still had two men on their feet behind him. Qazi circled the open turnaround and leaped onto the next ladder.

O-5 level, O-6 level, O-7 . . . On the O-8 level he passed the flag bridge. No marines in sight. Maybe, just maybe . . .

As he came up the ladder to the O-9 level he saw a marine wearing a pistol belt standing in front of the door to the navigation bridge. The marine had his pistol in his hand and looked apprehensively at Qazi as he took the steps two at a time. Qazi glanced over his shoulder as his head reached the landing coaming—no more marines—and leveled his pistol as he topped the ladder. He shot the surprised sentry point-blank. The body was still falling as Qazi jerked open the door to the navigation bridge and hurtled through.

22

WHEN GUNNERY SERGEANT Tony Garcia reached the bottom of the island ladderwell on the O-3 level, he stood stock still and looked at the carnage, stunned. He had eaten dinner tonight in Naples with two friends and had been sound asleep when general quarters was called away. He had pulled on trousers, shirt, and shoes and raced for the armory, where the corporal on duty had tossed him an M-16 and duty belt. Then he had run for the bridge. Normally he led the squad that guarded the bridge during GQ, but Sergeant Vehmeier had tonight's duty section. Now he stood looking at the five marines lying amid blood and shrapnel. One of them was conscious.

"Grenades, Gunny," the wounded man whispered. His back and side were covered in blood and blood oozed out his left sleeve.

Sergeant Vehmeier lay face down in a pool of gore. Garcia turned him over. The man's hands were gone, only red meat and white bones remained, and his abdomen was ripped open. He

279

had fallen on one of the grenades, probably the first one. Miraculously, he still had a pulse in his neck. Garcia used both hands to scoop Vehmeier's intestines back into his abdominal cavity. He rolled Vehmeier over, then stripped off his shirt and used that as a bandage to protect the wound.

"Quick," the sergeant whispered at a knot of gawking sailors. "Get these men to sick bay, right fucking now! This man first." The sailors leaped to obey.

Garcia wiped his bloody hands on his trousers. "Get tourniquets on these men," he directed. He stepped over the casualties and climbed the ladder, his M-16 at the ready.

The man at the top, with his foot caught in the door and sprawled on his back down the ladder, had taken a half dozen rounds in the chest. He was beyond help. When Garcia eased the door open to peer out, the body slipped, making noise. Just below the sailors were making a hell of a racket carrying the casualties away, but Garcia froze anyway.

He waited for the bullets to come. He was sweating and his heart was pounding. Nothing. He peered again through the crack in the door, then eased it open enough to slip through.

There were two men down in the passageway, here on the flight deck level. Garcia picked up the Uzis and pistols lying on the deck. One man was still alive, but he wasn't going anywhere with that hole in his gut. A gym bag lay near him. Garcia opened it carefully. Grenades and some stuff that looked like plastique. Some fuses.

A crumpled body lay at the bottom of the ladderwell up to the next floor. It had almost a dozen wounds in it. Garcia could see the holes in the aluminum sheeting. One of his marines had fired an M-16 clip through the aluminum and nailed this guy.

The wounded man moved and groaned. Garcia swung the M-16 in his direction. It was tempting. The bastard deserved it. But no.

The sergeant looked up the ladderwell. What was waiting up there? Should he go find out? Or should he take another route? Another route would probably be healthier.

He heard a door opening to his left and leaped right, toward a corner. Even as he did, he heard bullets spanging off the steel. In a corner of his mind it registered that there were no loud reports, and he knew the weapon had a silencer.

He sprawled on the deck and scrambled furiously, trying to ensure his body and legs were behind cover. He rolled over and waited for the gunman to round the turn in the passageway. Slowly, slowly he got to his feet, keeping the rifle pointed. He wiped the sweat from his face with the front of his T-shirt and tried to visualize the corridor that he had just left. The door that opened must have been the door to Flight Deck Control. The bastards must be in there! With all those sailors. He couldn't shoot through the door for fear of hitting a sailor. Damn!

His thigh felt like it was on fire. He looked. A bullet hole in his trouser leg. He felt his thigh. A slug had grazed him, but not too bad. The wound was bleeding some. Those motherfuckers!

He could hear the sound of men running somewhere in the ship, minute vibrations that could be heard for hundreds of feet, and the faint clank of watertight hatches being slammed shut. These were normal noises mixed in with the hum and whine of machinery that was present every minute of every day. He stood listening now for the sound of a door being eased open or shoes scraping on steel or a weapon clinking ever so faintly against a bulkhead. Of these noises, there were none.

It was coming back to him now, those feelings of combat. Always tense, always listening, always waiting . . . waiting to kill and waiting to die. He had not felt those feelings for twenty years. But now they were back and it seemed like only yesterday. He was sweating profusely and his mouth was dry. He was desperately thirsty.

He heard a watertight door being opened somewhere behind him but near. He pointed his rifle and waited. Now someone was coming around the corridor, in from the starboard side of the island. It was only Staff Sergeant Slagle and a lance corporal. What was his name? Leggett. Corporal Leggett.

The 1-MC hissed. "Men of *United States.* I am Colonel Qazi. I have taken over the ship. We have your captain and your admiral with us here on the bridge. Further resistance by you is futile and will result in the deaths of your officers and the sailors here with us on the bridge. If another shot is fired at my men by anyone, I will execute one of the Americans here with me and throw his body down onto the flight deck. Now I want everyone to clear the flight deck. Clear the flight deck or I will execute a sailor."

"What do we do now, Gunny?" Slagle asked.

Garcia examined the silencer on one of the pistols he had picked up from the deck. The slide had been machined to take the silencer by someone who knew his business. He pushed the button on the grip and the magazine popped out into his hand. About ten rounds remained. He reinserted the magazine in the grip and checked that the weapon had a round in the chamber and eased the hammer down. Then he stuffed the pistol in his belt. He gave the other weapons to Slagle. "Get on a phone to Captain Mills—"

"He's on the beach." Mills was the marine officer-in-charge.

"So call the lieutenant," Gunny Garcia rasped. First Lieutenant Potter Dykstra was the second in command and the only other marine officer in the detachment. "Tell him the squad that was on the way to the bridge got wiped out by grenades. And there is at least one gunman in Flight Deck Control. Find out what the lieutenant wants to do. Leggett, you stay right here. If anybody carrying a weapon comes out of Flight Deck Control, kill him. These fuckers are dressed like sailors. I'm going up to the bridge and see what's what."

Slagle turned and trotted away.

"Listen, Leggett. These assholes got grenades. They're liable to toss one out here to see if they can perforate you. Keep your head out of your ass."

"You bet, Gunny." Leggett licked his lips and started to peer around the corner.

"Don't do that, dummy. If you've gotta take a peek, get down on the deck and peek around the corner down low. And don't let him shoot you in the head." With that, Gunny Garcia turned and went up the ladder in the back of the island, his M-16 pointed ahead of him with the butt braced against his hip.

The fires on the hangar deck were out of control almost immediately after the paint lockers exploded. Men came pouring out of the shops and repair lockers and attacked the fires with AFFF (aqueous film-forming foam) from the fire-fighting stations located around the bay, but the burning paint and chemicals from the sabotaged lockers had been sprayed everywhere, on aircraft, in open cockpits, in the drip pans under the planes, and on aircraft tires. The tires ignited almost immediately and gave off a heavy, thick black smoke. When the CONFLAG watches failed to

close the two interior fire doors, the hangar deck officer, a lieutenant, ordered the doors closed manually. And he sent a man up
to the nearest CONFLAG station to light off the hangar deck
sprinkler system.

The men fighting the fires were relieved in shifts to don Oxygen-Breathing Apparatus (OBAs), which were self-contained
breathing systems. Although the fires were producing immense
quantities of toxic gases and smoke, most of it was being vented
out the open elevator doors. And the wind was funneling in the
doors, feeding the fires.

A minute after he had been dispatched to the CONFLAG station, the messenger was back and informed the hangar deck officer that the CONFLAG watchstander was dead, shot, and the
sprinkler control system was shot full of holes.

The hangar deck officer called Damage-Control Central. The
hangar deck sprinking system was turned on from DC Central,
almost four minutes after the paint lockers had exploded. The
sprinklers had little visible effect on the fires, so with the concur-
rence of the Damage Control Assistant (the officer in actual
charge of the ship's minute-to-minute damage control efforts) in
DC Central, the elevator doors on the sides of the bays were
closed too. In seconds the interior of Bays Two and Three filled
with black smoke and toxic gases. The smoke became so thick that
the fire fighters were literally blind inside their flexible rubber
masks. Men worked by feel. They hung onto hoses with a death
grip, and if one tripped and fell, he dragged men down on both
sides of him. A couple men panicked and hyperventilated inside
the self-contained OBAs and let go of their hoses. Lost, blind,
and seemingly unable to breathe, they ripped off their OBAs and
passed out within seconds from the toxic fumes.

Still, the fire-fighting effort continued. In less than ten minutes
the fires in Bay One, the forward bay, were out, although the chief
in charge there didn't realize it for another minute or two.

In Bays Two and Three, amidships and aft, the fires continued.
Since the air was opaque and the heat was building, the fires were
difficult to detect unless someone actually walked into one, so
some fires were not attacked by hose teams. Then an A-6 that still
contained several thousand pounds of fuel blew up in Bay Two.
The concussion and flying fragments cut down almost a dozen
men and severed two hoses. The fires spread. Men staggered out

of the bay almost overcome by the intense heat or passed out where they stood from heat exhaustion.

In Bay Three, Chief Reed made a command decision. On his own initiative he opened the doors to both Elevators Three and Four, on opposite sides of the bay. The wind rushed in the starboard door, El Three, and pushed the smoke and fumes out El Four. Reed's decision probably saved the ship. Although the fires burned more intensely in the draft, the overall heat level was lower and the air cleared. Fire fighters were now able to directly attack the flames.

In the meantime, Bay Two had become a hellish inferno.

In DC Central, which was located on the second deck in the main engineering control room, immediately below the aft hangar bay, the Damage Control Assistant had his hands full. On the wall before him were arranged three-dimensional charts that showed every compartment in the ship. Other charts showed the networks of fuel lines, power lines, fire mains, and telephone circuits. A crew of men wearing sound-powered phones marked these charts as they received damage reports from the various fire-fighting teams.

The DCA was a busy man. He had an extraordinarily hot fire burning in the comm spaces and the fumes were spreading to surrounding spaces, which he had ordered evacuated. Every time someone opened a watertight door to enter the fire-fighting zone, the poisoned air spread a little further. All electrical power to the communications spaces had already been secured by the load dispatcher in the central electrical control station. He and the repair-party leader had already concluded that they were facing a magnesium fire, probably a flare, since nothing in the communications spaces would burn with such intensity or give off such toxic fumes. Consequently the fire was attacked with Purple K, a dry, dust-like chemical propelled by gas that would blanket the burning metal and cut off the oxygen supply. Water or AFFF would have merely caused the magnesium to explode, spreading it. The DCA knew that the electrical equipment in the comm spaces would all be ruined by the fine grit of Purple K. It was unavoidable. The fire had to be extinguished as quickly as possible, before the magnesium melted the deck and fell through to another compartment.

Just now the DCA was checking the chart to locate the compartments that might be beneath the burning flare. He wanted to get
teams in those compartments, ready to attack the flare if it burned
its way through the steel deck it was lying on.

The executive officer, Ray Reynolds, stood looking over his
shoulder, listening to the reports that flowed in and the DCA's
responses, and using the telephone periodically. Since the 1-MC
announcement that the captain was hostage on the bridge, the
DCA had attempted to talk to the captain via the squawk box and
the telephone. Both times there was no answer to his call. As far
as the DCA was concerned, responsibility for the ship had now
passed to the executive officer.

But the DCA had no time to worry about the bridge. He had
fires to fight. A large portion of the communications spaces, the
DCA learned, protruded over the forward hangar bay, Bay One.
He got onto the squawk box to repair locker 1-F, which was
responsible for that bay, and alerted them to the possible danger
from the fire raging above their heads.

Ray Reynolds stared at the charts of the ship and the grease-
pencil marks that adorned them. The first priority, he had already
decided, was to save the ship. Second was to capture the intruders
or thwart them, and third was to free the captain and the admiral.

He stood now absorbing the situation that the DCA faced. Two
bad fires were out of control, and the DCA was marshaling every
man he needed to fight them. He had secured electrical power
near the fires. He had drained the pipes that carried jet fuel to the
flight-deck fueling stations and flooded the pipes with carbon
dioxide. He was monitoring the level of AFFF in the pumping
stations, and he had men relieving the men fighting the fires at
regular intervals. Fire-main pressures were still good, both reactors were on the line, and the engineering plant had plenty of
steam. The auxiliary generators had been lit off and were ready to
take the load if necessary. And the DCA had the repair teams not
fighting fires searching the ship for unexploded bombs.

Someone handed Reynolds a telephone. "XO, this is Lieutenant Dykstra."

"We're up to our ass in alligators, Dykstra. Are you getting the
swamp drained?"

"The quick-reaction squad that was on the way to the bridge

was wiped out. Grenades. I think most of the intruders are on the bridge."

"Keep them there. Don't let them out."

"That announcement. That colonel wanted everyone off the flight deck. We must be getting more company."

Reynolds was aware of that, yet he had had little time to consider the implications. More armed intruders was the last thing he wanted. He turned away from the DCA's desk and walked to the limit of the telephone cord. He had no doubt that the terrorist on the bridge—that's what he was, a maniac terrorist—would do exactly what he said. He would execute people if armed resistance continued.

"Play for time, Dykstra. That's the only option we have. Until we know what they're up to, it's senseless to goad these men and have them kill our people for nothing. What'd their leader call himself?"

"Qazi."

"Put your marines in the catwalks forward and aft so they can control the helo landing area. Have everyone hold their fire. Unless these people are suicidal, they are going to want to leave the ship sooner or later, and we want to be ready when they do. Perhaps then we'll have a better handle on this."

"Maybe they are suicidal, sir. Qazi? Maybe that's a play on 'kamikaze.' "

"You have any better ideas, Lieutenant?"

"Shoot them when they get out of the helicopters."

And the fanatics on the bridge would kill everybody there. Ray Reynolds was a poker player, and just now he wanted to see a few more cards. "No. Post your men. Time's on our side, not theirs."

He broke the connection and called Operations. No one answered. He tried Combat. No answer there either. He reached for the squawk box, then became aware of the DCA's voice. "Get everyone out of that area on the O-3 level." When the DCA saw Reynolds looking at him, he said, "The temperatures are really rising in the spaces above Bay Two, XO. I'm ordering an evacuation. I'm going to have the repair crew up there put AFFF on the deck in all those spaces. Maybe that'll keep the temperature down and prevent flash fires."

So the people in Ops and Combat had probably already left their spaces. With the communications gear in the comm spaces out of action and Ops and Combat uninhabitable, the ship could not communicate with the outside world. She was isolated. "Do it," Reynolds said. There was no other choice. Unless the fires were brought under control, *United States* was doomed.

Gunnery Sergeant Garcia stood in the signalman's locker on the after portion of the O-9 level and peered carefully out the open door. Behind him three sailors shifted nervously from foot to foot. They had extinguished all lights in the compartment, at his request. Garcia looked left, up the length of the signal bridge, past the bin full of signal flags and the signal flashing light mounted high on a post, forward to the closed hatch to the navigation bridge. The signal bridge was open to the weather, without roof or walls. A solid, waist-high rail formed one side of this porch-like area and the island superstructure formed the other. Now Gunny Garcia examined the area to his right. The signal bridge curved around and expanded into a large portico on top of the after part of the island. He looked back left, toward the enclosed navigation bridge.

There were windows beside the entrance hatch to the bridge in that portion of the bridge structure that jutted starboard almost to the edge of the flight deck fifty feet below. The back of a raised, padded chair was visible in the red light that illuminated the interior. That was the navigator's chair, and it was used by the conning officer when he brought the ship alongside a tanker or ammunition ship for an underway replenishment. Garcia wasn't thinking about unreps just now, he was thinking about people. And there were none in sight.

He turned to the sailors behind him, who were staring at the rifle and the pistol butt sticking out of the waistline of his khaki trousers, trousers now heavily stained with Sergeant Vehmeier's blood. "What're you guys doing up here?"

"We're signalmen. This is our GQ station."

"Ain't nobody on the bridge gonna tell you to run up a signal flag tonight. You guys take a hike."

The sailors didn't have to be told twice. They shut the door behind them.

Garcia checked the bridge windows again. Still nobody visible. He looked around the dark signalmen's shack. There was just enough light coming through the door to make out a dark sweater lying on the worn couch. Garcia pulled it on over his white T-shirt, then buckled the duty belt around his waist. The belt had been draped over his shoulder. It contained spare magazines for the M-16.

Too bad he didn't have any camouflage grease, because his face would show like a beacon on the dark signal bridge. He glanced at the coffeepot. Coffee grounds wouldn't help much. The chief's desk. He rummaged through the drawers and came up with a tin of black shoe polish. He smeared some on his face.

A head was visible in the bridge window. The man wasn't looking back this way. The head disappeared.

It was now or never. Garcia swallowed hard, gripped the rifle firmly, and sprinted toward the closed watertight entrance-door to the bridge.

He huddled in the corner, out of the wind and rain, and placed his ear against the door. Nothing. Damn. He tried again. Only the pounding of his heart. He could smell smoke, heavy and acrid. It must be coming from the doors to Elevators One and Two, and being swirled up here by the wind.

The door was heavy and was held shut with six dogs. He moved in front of the door and very carefully raised his head toward the window. Slowly, ever so slowly, careful not to let the rifle barrel touch the metal of the bulkhead or door. More and more of the room came into view, until he was looking directly in the window. Two sailors were visible sitting on the deck with their backs against the forward bulkhead, their arms crossed on their knees and their heads down on their arms. Someone had obviously ordered them into this position and was guarding them. He looked left, trying to see the sentry. No way. There was a little passageway in from this door and window, about four feet in length, and he couldn't see around that corner. And the sentry couldn't see this door.

He could, however, see the navigator's chair and the chart table and the usual compass repeater and ship's clock and, between the windows, telephone headsets mounted in clips. He looked for reflections in the bridge windows. The windows here were all slanted outward at the top so the view down toward the water and the flight deck would be unimpaired. So no reflections.

He lowered his head away from the window and applied pressure to the lower right dog. It moved. Without sound, thank God.

The technician who maintained these fittings apparently didn't want to risk the captain's ire. Garcia turned the dog until it was in the open position.

He peered in the window again, taking his time, inching his head up in case someone was there. Nobody. He opened the two dogs on the upper part of the door. This time the door made a noise as the pressure was relieved. Garcia huddled in the corner, as far out of sight of the window as he could get.

Time passed. He watched the dogs, waiting for a lever to betray the touch of a human hand by a movement, no matter how slight. Nothing.

Where in the fuck was Slagle? That was one hell of a phone call he was making to the lieutenant.

Finally he eased back to the window and ever so carefully raised his head until he could see inside with his right eye. There was a man there. A man with a submachine gun in his hands, the strap over his right shoulder and a gym bag over the other. The man was looking out the windows on the starboard side, searching. Garcia lowered his head and held his breath. If he saw the open dogs, the game was up. The gunman would be waiting for the door to open. Garcia begin breathing again and counted seconds. When a half minute had passed he decided to risk the window again.

A loud screech behind him. Garcia spun, ready for anything. God, it was the loudspeaker.

"You there in the catwalk, down on the flight deck. This is Colonel Qazi on the bridge. Leave the flight deck or I will shoot a man here on the bridge. Go below. Now! Or this man dies."

Gunny Garcia glanced in the window. The gunman was gone. He opened the remaining three dogs and pulled the heavy door open.

"Now, Admiral," Colonel Qazi said as he hung up the 1-MC mike. "I want you gentlemen to understand me. You and I are going upstairs to Pri-Fly. We won't be gone long. My two helpers here will ensure no one on the bridge moves a muscle or opens his mouth. They will cheerfully shoot anyone who is so foolish. Come, Admiral."

Cowboy Parker looked from face to face. Laird James and Jake Grafton had their eyes on him. They were standing with him on the left wing of the bridge, near the captain's chair. The bridge watch team were all seated on the floor in a row across the bridge, facing aft, their heads down on their knees, one of the gunmen watching them while the other pointed his weapon at the three senior officers. "What are you after, Colonel?"

"No." Qazi's voice was flat and hard. "We're not going to do it that way, Admiral. No conversations." The muzzle of the pistol twitched in the direction of the door.

Admiral Parker moved and felt the blunt nose of the silencer dig into the back of his neck.

There was no one in the passageway, no one except the dead marine who lay on his side upon the deck by the bridge door. Parker paused and Qazi dug the pistol into his neck. "Step over him." Parker did so, looking down and feeling very much responsible for the death of that young man. What had gone wrong?

As they climbed the ladder Parker said bitterly, "You're a bastard."

"True. And my father was an Englishman. So you're in big trouble and your next cute little remark will be your last. Believe it. I don't need an admiral."

Nothing in his thirty years in the navy had prepared Earl Parker for this . . . this feeling of despair, frustration, and utter helplessness. He was living a terrible nightmare from which he would never awaken. His men were dying all around him and he was powerless to lift a finger. He was being robbed of everything he had worked a lifetime for, of everything that made life worth living. He was being murdered an inch at a time. Hatred and rage flooded him.

But since he was Earl Parker, none of it showed. He flexed his fists as he topped the ladder, his stride even and confident, his shoulders relaxed, then forced himself to unball his fists. His face remained a mask, an arrangement of flesh under the absolute control of its owner. Don't let the bastard know he's getting to you, he told himself, wishing he hadn't made that last remark. My chance will come. God, please, let it come.

Parker undogged the door to Pri-Fly and pulled it open. Qazi stood just far enough behind him to make any attempt at going for the pistol impossible.

Inside the Pri-Fly compartment, the air boss and assistant boss, both commanders, stood silently and watched Parker and Qazi enter. The three sailors in the compartment kept their eyes on Qazi's pistol. Without a word, Qazi examined the panel that controlled the ship's masthead and flight-deck floodlights. Then he glanced at the air boss. "Where is that helicopter that was searching for the man in the water?"

"We sent it to Naples," the boss said. He named the airfield. Earl Parker was looking at the column of black smoke rising from Elevator Four and being carried aft by the wind. Smaller columns of smoke were coming from Elevators One and Two, forward on the starboard side, and were waffling around the island. On the flight deck below, the planes stood wet and glistening in rows under the red floodlights. Even here, in this sealed compartment, Parker could smell the smoke.

"And the liberty boat?"

"We sent it back to the beach too."

"You." Qazi pointed the pistol at the senior enlisted man, a second-class petty officer. "Come here."

The man looked at the admiral and then at the air boss.

"Do as he says," the boss said.

The sailor moved slowly, his eyes on the gun.

"Turn off the flight-deck floodlights, wait five seconds, then turn them back on." The sailor's hands danced across the switches. The flight deck below seemed to disappear into the night, then reappear. "Again." The sailor obeyed. "Now once more."

With the lights back on, Qazi seized the admiral's arm and backed him up. "All you people leave. Go below. If anyone comes back to this compartment, I will kill them and the hostages on the bridge." After the sailors and officers filed out, Qazi fired his pistol into the radio transmitter that sat on a shoulder-high shelf near the door. He stepped around the room putting bullets into every piece of radio gear he could identify. Then he followed the admiral out of the compartment and down the ladder one level toward the navigation bridge.

Gunny Garcia crouched on the signal bridge and stared at the navy-gray aluminum door that covered the entrance to the bridge, now that he had the watertight door open. His first thought was, That's why the gunman didn't notice the two open dogs. The watertight door was hidden by this aluminum door. A mild piece of luck, in a business where you need every ounce of luck you can get.

His second thought came when he put his hand on the doorknob and started to turn it. There were, he knew, a lot of American sailors on that bridge. The whole watch team, since the ship was at general quarters. And not a one of them armed. How many gunmen there were he didn't know. So he was going to go charging into a firefight where he was outnumbered and some innocent Americans were going to be shot, some of them fatally. Casualties would be unavoidable.

Gunny Garcia took his hand off the doorknob and crouched, thinking about it. The fumes from the hangar fire were in his nostrils and the low moan of the wind in the masthead wires was in his ears. What to do? Where in the name of God was that asshole Slagle? What would the lieutenant want him to do? What would the captain, if he were aboard, tell him to do? If he was going to do anything at all, he was going to have to get to it pretty quickly, before that bunch with the Uzis decided to look out this window again.

When he had been in combat before he had been only twenty, just another rifleman in Vietnam. The sergeants and the officers made the decisions and he laid his ass on the line carrying them out. It was still his ass, but now it was his decision too. That's what you get, Tony, he told himself, for working your butt off for all these chevrons and rockers. Now you gotta earn 'em.

Yet instinctively he waited. You stayed alive in combat by listening to your instincts. The people who didn't have the right instincts died. Combat was natural selection with a vengeance.

What light there was disappeared. Then it came back on. Garcia looked around. And once more. Someone was flashing the big floods on the island.

A signal? To whom?

A minute went by, then another. He risked another glance in the window. Still just the two sailors sitting on the deck.

Damnation! What was going on?

What was that noise? That buzzing? A helicopter! Gradually the noise grew louder. More than one, Garcia decided. He knew where they were without looking. They were coming in with the wind on their nose, across the stern of the ship.

He took the pistol from his trousers and thumbed the hammer

back. One more glance in the window, then he pushed the door open and crept onto the bridge. He eased the door shut behind him.

The sailors didn't look up. Good for them. So far so good.

He would try the silenced pistol first. If he could drop a man without the others hearing the shot, he might get a second or two advantage.

He could hear the choppers even here on the bridge. Now if the guy guarding these sailors is just looking at the choppers . . . He crept to the corner, keeping low, and peered around with the pistol ready.

The gunman was ten feet away walking toward him and looking straight at him! He snapped off a shot. And another. The man was hit! Garcia stuffed the pistol in his pants and stepped out with the M-16 up.

Before he could pull the trigger the bullets from an Uzi tore into his side and he was off balance and falling and the M-16 was hammering and he was desperately pushing himself backward, toward cover.

He was on the floor and he didn't have the rifle. A sailor ran past him for the door where he had entered.

A stuttering hail of lead cut down another sailor charging toward him. The game was up. Surprise was lost; to stay was to die. He scrambled on all fours crab-like for the door, now open. Another sailor careened past and then Garcia was through the door.

He would never make it. The gunmen would come to the door and cut him down. The watertight door was impervious to bullets. He pushed it shut and used the dogs to pull himself to his feet. He cranked the dogs shut with all his strength. There! The bridge windows were thick. Bulletproof. It would take them about fifteen seconds to get this thing open.

He turned and hobbled toward the signalmen's shack as fast as he could go, his side on fire and his back ready to receive the bullets from the Uzis. But the bullets never came.

When the ear-popping roar of the M-16 filled the bridge, Haddad, the gunman on the port wing of the bridge who had been dividing his attention between the captain and the approaching helicopters, dropped to his knees and spun for cover. The jacketed slugs from Garcia's weapon ricocheted off the steel and smashed into the portside bridge windows, crazing them with a thousand tiny cracks.

Admiral Parker grabbed Qazi's gun hand. *"Run, Jake!"*

Grafton was the closest to the door. He launched himself through it.

From behind the helm installation, Haddad fired a burst toward Garcia and another over the body of his downed comrade at a sailor trying to make the door on the starboard wing. The sailor crumpled like a rag doll.

Parker twisted Qazi's wrist with maniacal fury. Qazi drew back his left hand and chopped at the admiral—once, twice—but he was off balance and couldn't get his weight behind the blows. He went to his knees to keep his bones from snapping. The veins in Parker's forehead stood out like red cords. The pistol fell. Qazi flailed desperately at Parker's testicles.

The admiral was a man possessed. They struggled in silence. Qazi went to the floor to deny Parker leverage. His desperation gave way to panic; he had come so far, risked so much, and now this one man was defeating him!

Then suddenly it was over. Haddad struck the admiral on the back of the head with the butt of his pistol and he fell like a tree.

Qazi retrieved his weapon and slowly got to his feet. His right wrist was already yellow and purple. As he massaged it and opened and closed his hand experimentally he glanced at Captain James, still behind the captain's chair, leaning against the wall and looking at him. For the first time in a very long time a smile creased Laird James's leathery face. Then he slid down the wall and rolled face down. A blood stain was spreading across the back of his shirt. One of the ricocheting M-16 slugs, probably.

The helicopters settled into the glow of the island floodlights. Qazi checked his man who lay in a twisted heap in the middle of the bridge. It was Jamail, the man who liked to kill.

The other gunman, Haddad, stood facing the Americans still seated against the wall. Three of them wore khaki. He was swearing at them in Arabic, his Uzi ready.

"No," Qazi told him and walked to where he could see down through the impact-crazed windows onto the angle of the flight deck. The helicopters were just touching down.

There was much to be done. He picked up the microphone for

the 1-MC and pushed the button. "American sailors! This is Colonel Qazi. Three of my helicopters have just landed on the flight deck. If you interfere, more men will die. Someone just tried to gain entry to the bridge. As a lesson to you, the body of one of your sailors will be thrown to the flight deck. If there is any more resistance, any more shooting, if another of my men dies, I will kill your admiral."

He put the microphone back in its bracket. "Watch them," he told Haddad. He walked over to the dead American and dragged his body to the door to the signal bridge. He looked through the window, then eased the door open. Keeping low, he dragged the body through, then wrestled it up over the rail. It fell away toward the deck below, leaving the rail smeared with blood. He went back onto the bridge and dogged the watertight door shut. He propped the interior door open so the dogs were plainly visible. Then he walked the width of the bridge to where the captain and admiral lay on the deck.

James still had a pulse; he was no doubt hemorrhaging internally. He would probably die soon. But the Americans didn't know that.

On the flight deck, sentries had exited the helicopters and spread out to guard them. He could see Noora helping Jarvis out.

Qazi picked up his gym bag and turned to Admiral Parker, who was sitting up nursing his head. He kicked his arm out and rolled him on his back. Then he sat on him and extracted a pair of handcuffs from his gym bag. He snapped them on the admiral's wrists, then rolled him over and placed a piece of tape across his mouth. Finally he helped the man to his feet. "Nice try, Admiral, but not nice enough." He pushed the admiral toward the door. "Stay here," he told Haddad. "And don't let anyone else onto the bridge. Use grenades if you have to. Don't let them take you alive."

23

CALLIE GRAFTON stood on the balcony of her hotel room and shivered in the chilly wind. She ignored the spattering rain-drops and peered into the darkness, across the lights of the city, out to sea. On clear nights she could see the lights of the *United States,* but not tonight. Too much rain, she thought. Too much cloud. She went back inside and closed the sliding glass door. A piece of the drapery got trapped in the door. She freed it and closed the door again.

It was two A.M. She had been lying on the bed still fully dressed, too tense to sleep. She had last seen Jake three and a half hours ago, when he bid her good-bye and followed that sailor into the alley. He must have decided to spend the night aboard ship. The officer at fleet landing had called and said that Jake was going out on the liberty boat, and that he had asked the officer to call and tell her he might be unable to get back ashore tonight. That was so like Jake. The heavens could be falling and Jake would have someone call and say that none of the pieces had fallen on him.

He called her every time a plane crashed. Someone would fly into the ground or eject from a burning plane. Before the news was announced or anyone was notified, if he was ashore Jake would call. He would talk of this and that and nothing in particular, and he would tell her he loved her, and he would somehow find a way to make the time of the call stick in her mind. Later she would hear of the crash. And then she would know that he hadn't been the one injured or killed. She had caught on, of course. Whenever he mentioned the time or asked her what she was watching on television or used any of his other little dodges to make the time of the call memorable, she knew.

She stood at the window and stared down into the street. The puddles reflected the light. God, Naples is such a dreary town in the rain! The dirty stone and mud brown stucco soaks up the light. The place looks as old as it is, old and tired and poor and worn and . . .

The lobby of the hotel had been a mess when she walked through it this evening on the way to her room. The authorities were trundling a body into an ambulance. She had had to wait on the sidewalk while a uniformed man wearing a submachine gun on a strap checked her identification and compared her name to a list of hotel guests. Only then had she been admitted. In the lobby people in formal clothes sat on the black leather sofas without arms and smoked and talked to men with notebooks. The middle elevator had been roped off. She saw the bullet holes in the plaster and the red stains. Another man with a submachine gun had directed her to take the stairs. She had trudged the three flights up the dark staircase with a naked bulb on every landing. Why were all the staircases and buildings painted earth tones? The whole city had that look, that look . . . of an impoverished old age, of . . .

Jake's calls when someone died were his way of reaching out. He wasn't so much reassuring her as reassuring himself. He was still alive. He still possessed the only thing on earth he valued— her.

She fingered the drapes and wiped away her tears. Perhaps she loved him too much. What would she ever do if she lost him?

She opened the door and went out on the balcony again, trying to see through the rain. He was out there somewhere, in the darkness, on that sea.

The *United States* still rode on her anchor with her bow pointed into the wind. Smoke from the fires raging within her seeped out of hatches on the O-3 level forward of the island and from the open elevator doors. Below decks her crew fought desperately to save her.

The magnesium flare Qazi had ignited in the communications spaces melted through the steel deck and fell into the forward hangar bay, Bay One. It struck an aircraft and broke into several pieces which caroomed onto the deck, already ankle-deep in foam. There the pieces exploded. Molten metal was showered around the bay and several fires were ignited.

But the main threat was in Bay Two, amidships. Here the fires were raging unchecked in an ink-black hell of noise and poison gases. AFFF rained from the sprinklers mounted in the hangar ceiling, but the moisture had little effect other than to lessen the heat somewhat. Sailors fighting the fires stumbled from the oven-like bay every few minutes for a soaking from an open hose. Thus cooled, they were given water to drink, the oxygen canisters in their OBAs were checked and replaced if necessary, and they were sent back into the bay.

Ray Reynolds knew the very existence of the ship was at stake. Already the temperature in the compartments above Bay Two on the O-3 level had reached one hundred fifty degrees and fires were spontaneously igniting. The problem was the smoke trapped in the hangar. The fires here were invisible. No one even knew exactly how many fires there were.

Reynolds gathered the repair-locker leaders on a sponson where exhausted fire fighters lay flaked out on the deck. "We're going to have to open the fire doors at both ends of the bay."

The rush of air through the hangar would exhaust the smoke and fan the flames even hotter. Yet if the hose teams formed a line in Bay One with the wind at their backs, they might be able to snuff the fires before they joined and raged into a giant, un-quenchable inferno. Bay Three was already awash in AFFF, so the backline was as ready as it would ever be. The fire leaders rushed away to get their men in place.

Reynolds was betting the ship on this maneuver. If he couldn't get the fire under control, it would only be a matter of time before he must order the ship abandoned.

The magnesium fires were out in Bay One when Reynolds got there. Reynolds was wearing an OBA. The blackened wreckage of burned-out aircraft looked surreal in the stark white light from emergency lanterns, the only lights functioning. Thank God going into Naples he had had the handler move as many planes as possible to the flight deck to clear space in Bay Two for the sailors to play basketball. Reynolds got the hose teams arrayed five abreast amid the wreckage and gave the signal to open the doors. The door in front of him between Bays One and Two opened about six feet, then jammed. It could neither be closed again nor opened any further.

No time to worry about the door. The die was cast. The hose teams crowded together and squeezed through. Already the smoke was going out the aft bay, for the men there had managed to get that door almost completely open before it too jammed. The hose teams laid the AFFF right at the base of the flames as they came to them and kept moving. The bays were littered with smashed, blackened shells of aircraft which the men had to snake around.

The overhead was afire too, and streams of foam were directed upward. A rack holding a half-dozen aircraft external fuel tanks that had been weakened by fire gave way under the pressure of the stream of foam. The tanks, each weighing two hundred pounds, came floating down amid a veritable waterfall of foam. One of them landed on Ray Reynolds and two sailors near him carrying battle lanterns. When the tank was rolled away, Reynolds was dead.

The hose teams continued aft, smothering the fires with foam. One of the men who had been hit by the tank was still alive, so he was carried below to Sick Bay. The bodies of Commander Ray Reynolds and the sailor who died with him were laid on Elevator One with the corpses of fifteen other men who had died fighting the fires.

Jake Grafton stood in the furnace heat of the starboard O-3 level passageway and peered through the murk. The floor was awash with foamy water. The florescent lights were off and the only illumination came from battle lanterns mounted near each knee-knocker and hatchway. The little islands of dim white light revealed a smoky haze full of sweating men wrestling charged hoses. The hoses full of the water-foam mixture under immense pressure had the weight and rigidity of steel pipe. They could only be bent with the combined efforts of several sailors swearing mightily inside their OBAs.

Jake started coughing. "Better get an OBA on," someone shouted, his words distorted by the faceplate on his rubber mask.

Jake pulled his shirttail from his trousers and held it over his face. His eyes were beginning to smart and itch. He stumbled aft, ducking under and stepping over hoses and inching by the busy men until he found a corridor leading outboard. He followed it. He came to a ladder. The watertight hatch was down and dogged into place. In the center of the large hatch was a smaller, round hatch, just big enough to admit one man. This fitting was open and a hose went through it. Jake squirmed through.

The turnarounds were full of men sitting and breathing through rags held before their faces. These men had been evacuated from the compartments above Bays One and Two. There was nowhere else for them to go. If 20 percent of the crew were still on the beach, over forty-four hundred men were aboard.

The central engineering control compartment was still manned and the DCA was at his desk, consulting charts. The engineering department head, Commander Ron Triblehorn, was looking over the reactor control panels when Jake came in, but he strode toward him as soon as he saw him. "How did you get off the bridge?"

"Somebody got onto the bridge and started shooting."

"The admiral and the captain?"

"Still up there."

"Ray Reynolds is dead. He was killed a few minutes ago up in the hangar bay. Something fell on him and broke his neck. You're the senior line officer not on the bridge." The senior officer not a hostage, he meant.

"Ray's dead?" Jake sank into a chair. Triblehorn nodded. "How about the chief of staff?" He was a captain.

"On the beach." Junior officers were gathering, listening and looking at Jake.

Jake looked around the compartment, slightly dazed. He was now responsible for the ship and every man aboard her. Legally responsible. Morally responsible. He was in command.

He rubbed his eyes. They were still smarting from the smoke in the passageways. Ray Reynolds dead! Oh, damn it all to hell. And the poor guy just got his new front teeth!

He tried to think. The terrorists. Helicopters were coming in to land when the shooting started on the bridge. He glanced at the television monitor. The screen displayed a black-and-white picture—from the camera in the television booth just under Pri-Fly—of the helicopters on the flight deck. This was a live picture, real time. He could see people, sentries, some of them lying on the deck and some walking slowly near the machines. The choppers were Italian civilian machines.

"The senior marine officer? Get him down here." One of the junior officers trotted toward a phone. Jake looked up at Triblehorn. "What's the situation in the plant?"

"No damage. Both reactors on line. All boilers on the line." Triblehorn gestured vaguely. "That evaporator that gave us all that trouble last week is acting up—"

Jake cut him off. Evaporators were the least of his worries right now. "Are the marines guarding the entrance to the engineering spaces?" Yes. "Can we get underway?" Yes. "How soon?"

They discussed it. Ten minutes warning. Jake thought hard. "Get things fixed so you can turn the screws within a minute of the decision. Tell the first lieutenant to be ready to slip the anchor chain." They would just let the chain go, leaving the anchor on the ocean floor rather than taking the time to raise it. If they had to.

"Aye aye, sir." Triblehorn turned to his junior officers. "You heard him. Do it."

Jake walked over to the DCA's desk with Triblehorn right behind. He was on the phone. When he hung up, the three of them reviewed the damage control situation. The fire in Bay Two was under control and would soon be extinguished. Power was off throughout the compartments above the bays and on both sides. Above the bays in the O-3 level, the fumes from the fires in the hangar and the communications spaces still contaminated the air. The DCA was opening the watertight hatches on those levels and ordering degassing fans positioned and started to clear the smoke from the ship. Several hundred tons of the water-foam mixture had been used on the O-3 level and was still slopping around in those spaces, but its effect on the trim of the ship was negligible.

Six bodies had been discovered in the communications spaces

and were being removed. At least twenty-six men had been killed fighting fires in the hangar bays, most of them when aircraft exploded. Six marines were dead on the flight deck, shot. And four marines had been killed by grenades thrown by the intruders. Four men were believed to be missing under the rubble in Bays One and Two. Over fifty men were in sick bay being treated for everything from gunshot wounds to smoke inhalation. Last but not least, the DCA reported, all the operations spaces on the O-3 level had been evacuated and the communications equipment in those spaces had been damaged by the heat and smoke and AFFF. It would be a half hour before he could let the operations specialists back into those spaces and get power restored. Meanwhile, the ship was not communicating with anyone. All the radio gear was either smashed or severed from the antenna system.

"Where are the gooks?" Grafton asked as Lieutenant Dykstra joined the group. He was wearing marine battle dress, with helmet and flak vest and ammo belt.

"Three choppers have landed on the flight deck, sir," Dykstra reported, gesturing at the television monitor. "The intruders are on the bridge and in Flight Deck Control and on the flight deck."

"Why didn't you shoot those choppers down before they landed?" Grafton asked the marine officer.

"Commander Reynolds felt that it would be better to wait. With the hostages and all . . ."

Hostages. Yes, that is what the Americans on the bridge and in Flight Deck Control were—hostages. Jake Grafton sagged into a chair and ground his knuckles together helplessly. Do you sacrifice the lives of defenseless people to foil the intruders, or do you passively resist and wait for an opening, perhaps saving innocent lives? What is it the professional negotiators always say? "Play for time: time is on our side, not theirs." Well, in the usual terrorist incident that is true. The terrorist's goal is publicity. But are these people terrorists? Is this crime being publicized? If so, why did they attack the communications facilities? *What* is their objective?

Exasperated, he looked from face to face. The officers were staring at him, waiting for him to make decisions and issue orders. The military system in full fucking flower! "Do you people have any ideas or comments? I'd desperately like to hear some." Blank looks. They were as off balance as he was, but he was the man responsible. "What are these fuckers up to, Dykstra?"

"Maybe they have mines planted below the waterline, sir. Maybe they're planting more firebombs. I think they're going to try to sink us."

Jake snorted. If so, they were taking their time about it, although they were off to a fair start. "Triblehorn?"

"I think it's political, CAG. I would bet the ranch they are making announcements to the media this very minute. It wouldn't surprise me to learn that we have four TV choppers circling overhead right now, with Dan Rather in one of them."

"You think we're all hostages, is that right?"

"Yessir. They're bearding the paper tiger."

Bearding the muscle-bound tiger would be a more accurate description, Jake thought. But no. It's one thing to hijack an airliner full of civilians and wave a pistol in the pilot's face for the cameras. What we have here is quite another thing altogether. This is an act of war. "I think we had better wait and find out what their objective is before we go off half-cocked," Jake Grafton said quietly. "So I'll wait a while. Dykstra, get your men around the edge of the flight deck with enough firepower to drop those choppers in the water if they try to take off. No shooting unless and until I say so. Triblehorn, get this ship ready to get underway. That card may be only a lousy deuce, but I'll play it if I have to. DCA, get the fires out. We'll have no options at all if we sink."

If we sink, Jake thought savagely. Mother of God!

At the same time that Captain Grafton was learning of his accession to command, Gunnery Sergeant Tony Garcia was having his T-shirt and sweater cut off him by two corpsmen in sick bay. They had him stretched out in a passageway on a mobile hospital table equipped with stirrups. They must have got this damned thing from a gynecology clinic, he mused, trying not to dwell on the fire in his side.

A doctor wearing a blue smock splotched with blood stopped and peered at his side. "Nasty. Get an X-ray after you bandage it. May be some internal bleeding. Won't know till we see the film." He paced away muttering about bullet and bone fragments.

The corpsmen rolled the table down the passageway.

"Hey you guys," Garcia said. "When we get done with X-ray, how about putting me in the ward with Sergeant Vehmeier?"

Sailors sat on the deck with their backs against the bulkhead. Many of them were coughing and all had little green oxygen bottles with masks to suck out of. These are the smoke-inhalation cases, Garcia surmised.

The corpsman rolled him under a large X-ray machine and positioned a giant cone above his chest.

Just like fucking Vietnam, Garcia told himself, only the trip to the hospital was a whole lot quicker. No ride in a Huey strapped to a stretcher, absolutely helpless if the damned thing got shot down or crashed. And the wound ain't so bad, either, all things considered. That machine gun round in the gut had been a real dilly. At least he was conscious, which was something. In Vietnam he had hemorrhaged until he passed out and woke up with needles in his arm and a tube down his nose all the way to his stomach and a tube up his dick and ninety-five brand-new stitches. Those doctors had almost cut him in half. Eleven months in the fucking hospital. Never again. He had told himself that about a million times through the years. Never again. The next time he was just going to die. Nothing could be worth going through that again.

Jesus, Vehmeier got blasted by that fucking grenade. That silly shit. Why in hell did he fall on that bastard? That Vehmeier . . . it was enough to make a grown man cry, that a guy like Vehmeier . . .

One of the corpsmen rolled him from the X-ray room and parked the bed along a passageway bulkhead, then hurried away. "Hey, man," he called, wanting to be beside Vehmeier, but they paid no attention. They were busy, he told himself, and Vehmeier wouldn't know he was there anyway. They probably got six IV needles stuck in him and have given him enough dope to supply Los Angeles for a week. Too bad about his hands, but with artificial hands he can do everything except pick his nose.

He wondered if he was bleeding internally. He had seen enough bullet wounds to know that there was no way to tell just from looking. You observed the patient for signs that he was losing blood, and if it wasn't visibly coming out of holes, it must be internal bleeding. And shock looked like hemorrhaging. He wondered if he was in shock. He felt cold, but they had put a blanket over him. Mild shock maybe. He took several deep breaths, trying to see if his lungs were working properly. His side felt as if he had a knife in it. Maybe he shouldn't do that. Maybe a busted rib would penetrate his lung.

Wonder if that foray on the bridge did any good. He had knocked that one gunman down for sure and maybe the other guy. Those sailors had been shot, but there was no other way. They would have approved, he told himself. They would have wanted him to try.

One of the corpsmen returned, the one with the glasses. "The doctor says you have two cracked ribs, but there are no bullet fragments in your chest. Just an ugly surface wound. You were very lucky."

Yeah. Very lucky. That slug could have went into my gut and there is no way my gut could take another, not with all that scar tissue down there. Very lucky. Yeah. "How about wheeling me in with Sergeant Vehmeier."

"Who?"

"That marine that was brought down here a while ago with his hands blown off. He fell on a grenade."

"Oh. He's dead. Sorry." The sailor walked away. It was a busy night.

"Come back here, you fucking swabbie!" Garcia's voice was coldly furious. The sailor paused and turned, uncertainty on his face. "You said Sergeant Vehmeier is dead?"

"Yeah, Sarge. He was dead when they brought him in here."

"I'm 'Gunnery Sergeant' to you, pill-pusher. Now get some fucking tape and put a permanent bandage on this wound." Garcia slid his legs off the edge of the bed and hoisted his torso erect, feeling slightly dizzy and nauseous.

"You can't—"

"Do I have to get the fucking tape and do it myself?"

The sailor scurried away.

Where did they put that fucking rifle?

As the helicopters had settled onto the angle of the flight deck Colonel Qazi marched Admiral Parker down the ladders toward the flight deck with his pistol in his back. He saw no one. The ladderwell was empty. Except at the last flight of stairs before he reached the flight deck level—Qazi's dead Palestinian lay where he had fallen, still crumpled against the door. The door gaped several inches. He made the admiral step over the corpse and push the door open.

He heard a sound to his left and stepped behind the admiral. The barrel of a rifle pointed at him below one frightened eye. "If you pull that trigger, you'll kill the admiral. If you don't, I will. After I kill you."

Several seconds passed, then the eye and barrel disappeared. Qazi listened as the man retreated.

The wounded man had died. The muscles in his face were slack and his eyes stared fixedly at nothing. The other body lay undisturbed. But their weapons were missing. And their gym bags. The door to Flight Deck Control was open a crack. One of his men there opened it wider and nodded.

On the flight deck he met Noora and Ali. They were surrounded by armed men and had Jarvis between them. More men lay in a circle around the helicopters, their weapons at the ready. The engines of the helicopters were still and the rotors stationary.

Qazi set off diagonally up the flight deck, heading for the catwalk forward of Elevator One. Behind him Ali and Noora shepherded Jarvis along. Immediately behind Jarvis was a man carrying one of the trigger devices. It weighed about forty pounds and was slung across his back on straps. Qazi kept the admiral's arm firmly in his grasp. Youssef, the Palestinian leader, carried two backpacks over his shoulders. Two gunmen preceded the party and two followed. Two more were out on each side. "Faster," Qazi told the men in front, and they picked up the pace.

24

THE POWER WAS OFF in the forward mess deck. Emergency battle lanterns provided the only illumination. The unarmed sailors who packed the place gaped when they realized that the officer in whites with tape over his mouth and wrists handcuffed together was Admiral Parker. Ali and his troops pointed their weapons and gestured. The sailors hastily retreated through the watertight hatches into the passageways beyond with many backward glances at Admiral Parker, who watched them go impassively. Qazi's men dogged the hatches shut again behind the last Americans.

The entrance to the forward magazine was a hatch leading downward. It was marked with a warning in red: "Unauthorized Personnel, Keep Out. This Means YOU." Everyone donned gas masks: Noora helped Jarvis with his, and Qazi placed one on Admiral Parker and ensured it was properly positioned on his face and functioning correctly. Then Ali and his men opened the dogs on the magazine hatch and lifted it to the open position.

The first man through the magazine hatch found the compartment below empty. It was merely a security access area. A large vault door stood at the end of the compartment with a television camera immediately above it. The gunman put a pistol bullet through the camera and the red light just below the lens went out. He could hear the muffled sound of an alarm. He quickly set a shaped charge on the door, then stood to one side and detonated it. Within seconds his companion, Youssef, slipped a hose attached to a metal canister through the small hole in the door punched by the explosive and opened the valve on the canister. As the gas hissed through the hole the first man methodically set plastique charges on the vault door. When he had the fuses set, he scrambled away up the ladder. Youssef secured the valve on the canister, pulled the hose from the hole, and scurried after his companion.

The explosion jolted the mess deck. Down the ladder the two men went again.

The access compartment was in total darkness. Shattered glass from the florescent tubes in the overhead and the emergency battle lanterns lay on the deck. The security door was off its hinges and badly warped. Smoke eddied uncertainly. The two men pulled the door free and groped their way into the next compartment.

One of the three marines in the compartment was still conscious, so the intruders shot him. They ignored the others. The gas would keep its victims out cold for several hours. Qazi had insisted on the use of nonlethal gas; not because of any concern for the victims, but just in case one of his key people had a defective mask.

Another hinged watertight door stood against the forward bulkhead of this compartment. It had no locks, but opening the door would be fatal if there were armed marines on the other side. The two gunmen set another shaped charge and backed away. It exploded with a metallic thud.

Youssef approached the hole with his cannister. He never got there. A marine on the other side of the door put his rifle against the hole and opened fire. The M-16 slugs spanged against the canister and tore into Youssef's arm and ripped his throat apart.

The demolition man huddled against the door. He pulled his backpack off and began packing the dogs with plastique, working in the darkness without his flashlight entirely by feel. Bullets sprayed periodically through the one-inch hole blown by the shaped charge as the muzzle flashes strobed the smoke-filled atmosphere. The demolition man cringed under the lashings of the thunderous reports of the M-16, magnified to soul-numbing intensity in this enclosed steel box. Between rifle bursts he could hear an alarm ringing continuously.

In the compartment on the other side of the door, the senior of the three young marines there was trying desperately to inform someone of their plight. The overpressure from the shaped charge that blasted a hole in the door had practically deafened them. Still, the sergeant could hear well enough to learn that the phones and intercom box on the wall were dead. He had already triggered the alarm, which also rang in Central Control, in the main engineering station, and on the bridge. One man was vomiting; he already had too much of the gas. The man at the door changed the magazine in his rifle and sent another burst through the hole. The rifle sounded to him as if it were being fired in a vacuum.

The senior marine was Sergeant Bo Albright from Decatur, Georgia. He groped through the silent, choking darkness for the bulkhead-mounted controls which would flood the magazines. He found them and pulled the safety pin from the lever that energized the system. He pulled the lever down. A row of green lights illuminated above a series of six buttons. He jabbed the first two buttons and held them. In three seconds the lights turned from green to red. He pushed the buttons in succession until all the lights were red.

In the compartment two decks below his feet that ran the width of the ship, the actual magazines, water rushed in from the sea.

"Get away from the door," Albright screamed into the ear of the rifleman. Together they pushed a desk away from the wall and crouched behind it with their rifles. They were as far away from the door as they could get. Albright stuck his fingers in his ears, scrunched his eyes shut, and opened his mouth. He waited.

The plastique around the door detonated. The concussion jolted them with the wallop of a baseball bat.

Albright peered through the darkness, blinking rapidly, shaking his head to clear the cobwebs. They would be coming!

Lights through the gap where the door had been! He triggered a burst. Another. Something was thudding into the desk. He fired again.

He was falling. Slowly, languidly, drifting and falling. The gas! He squeezed the trigger on the rifle and held it down as he went over the edge and tumbled into a black, alien vastness.

"Wake up, Ski. Wake up." The sailor shook the catapult captain vigorously. "Goddammit Ski, wake up!"

Aviation Boatswains Mate (Equipment) Second-Class Eugene Kowalski groaned and opened one eye. "Okay, asshole, I'm awake. We'd better be fucking sinking or . . ."

"We're at GQ, Ski. A bunch of terrorists have landed on the flight deck. No shit."

Kowalski groaned again and sat up. He was on the floor of the waist catapult control station, still in civilian clothes. No doubt someone had carried him here to sleep it off when he came back to the ship drunk. That was what usually happened. He had awakened here on the floor of the waist bubble before—several times, in fact. "Terrorists, huh?"

"Fucking A. And the captain and the admiral are hostages on the bridge and there's a big fire in the hangar and one in the comm spaces." He drew a breath. "And three choppers full of terrorists landed on the flight deck a little bit ago."

"Cut me some fucking slack, Pak. You idiots didn't let me sleep through all of that."

"What could you have done? And this is your GQ station, so when they called it away you were right here. We'd have woke you up for a launch." His voice was so sincere that Kowalski eyed the Korean. Maybe he was telling the truth.

"So how come you woke me up now?"

"You ain't gonna believe this, Ski. One of those choppers is sitting right on top of number-four JBD. Right smack dab on top of it."

Kowalski took his time about standing up. Pak grabbed him under the armpit to help and Ski shook him off. He finally got erect and remained that way by hanging onto the cat officer's little desk.

"Jesus, Ski, you pissed your pants."

"There's some aspirin in my desk. Get me three of them." His desk was in the Cat Four control room. "And some water. A glass of water."

"We ain't got . . ."

"Put it in a coffee cup." Pak dashed out. The cat captain lifted himself into the cat officer's raised chair and rested his elbows on the table, his chin in his hands. After a moment he felt his crotch. It was wet. He tried to remember how he had gotten back to the ship. Captain Grafton was in there somewhere, but the rest was hazy. Maybe the XO was right. Maybe he was an alcoholic.

He slipped off the chair and rushed out the door of the bubble. Here he was on a little sponson on the O-3 level, outside the skin of the ship. He grabbed hold of the safety wire and leaned out and retched. The wind swirled some of the vomit back onto him. He puked until he had the dry heaves, and when they subsided he took off his torn sport shirt, wiped his face with it, and threw it over the side. The stench of something burning was strong. Too strong. It made him feel sick again. He went back into the bubble and collapsed into the cat officer's padded chair.

Pak came back with two other guys. "A committee, huh?" They stood and watched Ski swallow the aspirin and drink the water. "Where's Laura?" Laura was the captain of number-three catapult.

"He didn't get back. He's on the beach."

Ski sat the cup down with a bang. "Okay, let's take a look. Raise this thing."

The three sailors looked at each other in the weak glow of the little red lights here in the bubble. "The terrorists got guns, Ski. They've been shooting people right and left. They have the captain and admiral—"

"This bubble's bulletproof, fireproof, and bombproof. They can't do nothing to us in here."

"Yeah, but they could get into the cat control rooms and—"

"We'll have to risk it. I ain't gonna get out on the catwalk and stick my head up over the edge."

"Pak did. That's how he knows there's a chopper on four JBD. And he went back and checked the fifty caliber on the stern. The marine back there is dead, shot, and the ammo belt is missing." Pak nodded nervous confirmation.

Kowalski shook his head. "And I'll bet the grunt on the port bow gun is dead too and the belt's in the water. Yeah. Well. Pak, you're an idiot. We gotta raise the bubble. But it wouldn't hurt to disable the horn."

One of the men went outside the cab and used a knife to saw through the wire to the warning Klaxon that sounded every time the control bubble went up or down. When he returned, he pushed a button on the bulkhead near the door. As the bubble began to slowly rise in splendid, and safe, silence he dogged down the entrance hatch.

The control cab rose on its hydraulic arms until it protruded eighteen inches above the level of the flight deck. Everything above deck was glass, inch-thick glass that was tilted in at the top so that objects striking it would be deflected upward. Inside the cab, all four men stood with knees bent so only their eyes were above the lower edge of the window. They stared at the helicopters on the flight deck, stark in the island's red floodlights, rotors stationary. The sentries guarding them were also visible. The lights in the control cab were off so the men on deck could not see in, yet when the sentry turned their way, all four dropped their heads down below the window. In a moment one of them raised up for another peek.

"They're civilian choppers. See, that's Italian on the side of that one."

"What'ya expect? Chinese? Look over there. See that guy with the submachine gun? He's one of them."

"He's dressed like a sailor," Kowalski said.

"Yeah. They all are. And they got the captain . . ."

"Sure. Yeah. I got that." Kowalski picked up the phone and held it in his hand. "Maybe we oughta call the office. Maybe the bosun's up there, or one of the chiefs." The office he was referring to was the V-2 division office, where the khaki in charge of the catapults had their desks. He stared aft at the third helicopter. From this angle it certainly looked like it was sitting on the JBD.

"Ain't nobody there," Pak told him. "There's a big fire up in the comm spaces, and the office was inside the fire boundaries, so they ran everybody out. I think they got 'em all fighting fires, either in the comm spaces or down in the hangar."

Kowalski grabbed the ship's blue telephone book and thumbed through it. He dialed a number. It rang and rang. Finally he used his thumb to break the circuit. "The XO ain't in his stateroom," he announced.

A third-class petty officer from the Cat Three crew spoke up. "We figured you're all we got, Ski. There's terrorists in Flight Deck Control. And they're on the bridge. And they made an announcement over the 1-MC about how they're gonna shoot hostages and toss them down on the deck if anybody resists. Maybe the terrorists are in Pri-Fly or over in the air department office. We didn't figure we should take the chance calling them. We tried to call the bow cats and the phones are dead up there. We sent a greenie looking for one of the chiefs or a cat officer, and he ain't come back. The passageways up forward are filled with smoke and they're grabbing guys to fight fires. So you're our man. What are we gonna do?"

Kowalski hung the phone back in its wall cradle. He rubbed his face with both hands. "If I'm all we've got, we're in deep fucking shit." He took one more look around the flight deck, at the choppers and the sentries and the jets sitting with folded wings on the bow and aft of the waist JBDs. Wisps of steam rose from the catapult slots: this would be leakage from the preheaters coming through the gaps in the rubber seals that were placed in the slots when the cats were not in use.

After a moment he asked for a cigarette and someone gave him one. He sat down on the floor and smoked it slowly. "What are these terrorists after?"

The men beside him shrugged.

"But they came on the helicopters, right?"

"Some of them did, anyway," one of his listeners answered.

"And they probably expect to leave the same way." Nods of assent from everyone. "So you guys go get the JBD hydraulic system fired up."

"We thought you'd say that, Ski," Airman Gardner said with a quick grin as he left with the others.

When Sergeant Albright set off the main alarm in the magazine, a red light began to flash on the main engineering panel and an audible tone sounded in the compartment.

"Well, gentlemen," Jake Grafton said bitterly as he and the chief engineer watched the lights indicating the positions of the magazine flooding valves turn from green to red. "Now we know why Colonel Qazi is here."

He had already been informed that Qazi and the admiral were

on the forward mess deck. He and the marine lieutenant had been discussing the possibility of surrounding the mess area and trying to trap Qazi. It was too late for that.

The magazines! Even as they spoke, the lights turned green again. Then the lights went out.

"Goddammit," Triblehorn swore softly. "They've closed the valves and chopped the power."

"Can you flood from Central Control?" Jake asked. The central control station two decks below where they sat actually distributed power and controlled the position of emergency valves. Triblehorn tried the squawk box.

Jake tried to digest it. Qazi and his men were forcing their way into the magazines. To set a charge to detonate the bombs stored there and sink the ship in one glorious, suicidal fireball? If so, why were the helicopters still on the flight deck? No, they were planning to leave the same way most of them arrived. And they were going to take something with them. That something could only be nuclear weapons.

"No way, CAG," Triblehorn said. "We've lost power to those valves."

"Halon. Let's use the Halon system." The magazines could be filled with Halon gas, a system designed to choke off a fire. It would also suffocate anyone in the compartment not wearing an OBA.

Triblehorn paused. "Halon will kill our guys too."

Jake rubbed his eyes. "Do it."

Triblehorn spoke into the intercom box. In seconds the answer came back. The Halon system was also disabled.

Jake slumped into a chair. How will Qazi get out of the magazine through the marines? Hostages won't help Qazi then, and he knows it. Even as he thought of the problem Jake Grafton knew the answer.

"Where's that marine officer? I need to talk to him."

Perhaps he could secure electrical power to the weapons elevator. No good. Qazi will arm one of the nuclear weapons and threaten to detonate it unless he is allowed to leave. And if he is thwarted by marines or inoperative elevators or anything else, he may just carry out the threat. Jake had no doubt that it was technically possible to bypass the safety devices built into the weapon. The weapons were designed to prevent an accidental detonation; of course, a technician who knew what he was doing could intentionally trigger one, given enough time and the right tools. And Qazi probably had enough of both.

The Bay of Naples! Jake rubbed his forehead. It felt like the skin there was dead, as if the blood supply no longer functioned. The explosion would vaporize the ship and everyone aboard her. And the ship was three miles off the coast, in a bay surrounded on three sides by hills and islands which would focus and enhance the concussion, radiation, and thermal pulses from the explosion. And the light and thermal pulses would be reflected off the clouds. How many people are in Naples, anyway? In Pozzuoli, Portici, on the slopes of Vesuvius?

The marine lieutenant was standing beside him, looking at him, waiting.

Will Qazi be bluffing? Can I afford to take the risk of calling him? What if he just lights one of those babies off while he's down in the magazine?

For a few milliseconds a raw piece of the sun about the size of a man's fist would exist here on the surface of the earth. The plutonium's mass would be converted to pure energy. The sky and sea would rip apart. Every human within twenty miles not cremated in the first millionth of a second would see the face of an angry, wrathful God.

"Triblehorn, let's get underway. We'll steer the ship from after steering. Get the navigator to lay a course out to sea. Put some lookouts with sound-powered phones up on the bow and let's slip the cable. Now!"

"Aye aye, sir." Triblehorn stepped away, issuing orders as if he got the ship underway from engineering every other Thursday. Perhaps he was relieved to have orders he found familiar. Jake watched the officers and sailors. They, too, seemed relieved that something was being done.

The marine shifted nervously beside Jake's chair. Jake stood. He felt a little light-headed. "Got a cigarette?" he asked the lieutenant.

"I don't smoke, sir."

Jake nodded vacantly. The alarm from the forward magazine was still sounding. Were the Americans there still alive? What about Parker? At least the fire in the comm space was extinguished and the ones in the hangar were under control and would soon be out. That was a plus. Perhaps the only one.

What kind of man was this Colonel Qazi? Jake had spent a quarter hour on the bridge watching him. He was not the wired-up fanatic one expected after viewing too many terrorist incidents on television. No. He was competent, calculating, intelligent, and, Jake suspected, absolutely ruthless. Not suicidal. Not on a mission for the glory of Allah. But a man who would do whatever he felt he had to do to get the job done.

"What are we going to do, sir, about the intruders?" Dykstra had a stern, square jaw and a wide mouth that just now was set in a pencil-thin line. His nostrils flared slightly every time he inhaled.

"Whatever that asshole wants us to do, Lieutenant. I'm sure he'll be telling us just what that is before very long."

The seawater looked black in the glow of the battle lanterns in the forward magazine. Colonel Qazi waded through the cold, foot-deep water casting his flashlight beam this way and that. Row after row of olive drab sausages met his eye. White missiles hung in racks against the bulkheads. Enough ordnance for a nice little war, he thought as he scanned the compartment. There, a door.

He lifted the single lever that cammed all six of the dogs, then sprung back as the door flew open from the weight of the water behind it. A little waterfall flowed through the doorway until the water in this compartment was equal in depth to the water where Qazi and his companions stood. Qazi stepped through into this compartment. Yes. The weapons were white, about the size of a five-hundred-pound bomb. Each of them was strapped into its own cradle which held it firmly several feet above the deck. Chains and pulleys hung from rails on the overhead.

"Did the water harm them?" Qazi heard Ali say.

"Oh no," Jarvis replied. He tilted his gas mask away from his face and sniffed experimentally, then removed it. "They're water-proof so they can be carried on external bomb racks through rain and snow and still function." He was examining one of the devices under a powerful flashlight. The sheen of moisture on the top of his bald head glistened occasionally in the stray light reflecting from the water's surface. He spread his legs and lowered his gut like a sumo wrestler. He used a screwdriver on an access plate. In seconds he had it off and was shining a flashlight into the interior of the weapon. "Hail wouldn't do the covering on the radar transceiver in the nose any good, of course," Jarvis continued softly, "but a little bath shouldn't hurt anything. As long as these access panels were properly fitted . . ." He knelt in the water and bent his head down so he could get a better view inside the weapon.

He looked up at Noora. She had removed her mask too and was using her hand to fluff her hair. "This one looks fine." He searched her face expectantly and was rewarded. A trace of a smile lifted the corners of her lips. His eyes flicked down and he grinned nervously as he moved toward the next bomb.

"Put this one on a dolly and connect your device to it before you check the others," Qazi said.

They positioned a bomb cart beside the weapon and four of them surrounded it, two on the nose and two on the tail. There were no good handholds, but they were running out of time. Jarvis danced from foot to foot, chanting, "Oh, don't drop it. *Please,* don't drop it . . ."

They got it two inches out of the cradle and set it back down. It was too heavy. "Use a pulley," Qazi said.

On the end of the chain was a piece of metal that fitted into the two metal eyes on top of the weapon. These eyes would fit up into an airplane's bomb rack where two hooks would mate the weapon to the plane. With the mechanical advantage provided by the pulley, it only took two men pulling on the chain to lift the weapon from its cradle and lower it gently onto the dolly.

The water lapped at the bottom of the weapon. Jarvis opened the access panel and used strapping tape to secure the trigger device he had constructed to the top of the weapon. Then he ran two wires with alligator clips on the ends from the device through the access panel. He used the flashlight to attach the wires inside the weapon. When he was finished, he stood back as Qazi bent to look inside.

The interior of the weapon was a maze. Qazi had expected this. He tried to remember exactly what he was looking for. Yes, that clip was on the wire leading from the battery. And this other clip was on the wire bundles that led to the detonators. Jarvis had had to scrape some insulation from both wires to affix the clips.

"Satisfactory." He straightened and found himself looking at

Admiral Parker, whose face was still obscured behind his gas mask. "I'm sorry, Admiral. But we need these weapons."

Parker turned away. He seemed to be listening.

Now Qazi heard it too, a faint rumbling. What was that?

Qazi pointed his flashlight at the water contact with the doorway. The water was moving, ever so slightly. But it should move as the ship rocked at anchor. Parker was looking at the water too. Qazi felt the deck beneath his feet tremble.

Now he understood. The rumble had been the anchor chain running out. The ship was underway!

25

THE OFFICER-OF-THE-DECK of the Aegis-class cruiser, USS *Gettysburg*, anchored three miles north of the *United States*, was momentarily confused. The carrier's lights were moving in relation to him. The lookout on the port wing of the bridge had called it to his attention. The lights of the carrier had only been visible for the last fifteen minutes, since the rain had slackened. He quickly scanned the wind-direction indicator to see if the wind had changed; that would cause the ships to swing on their anchors. No. Perhaps his ship was moving, dragging its anchor—unlikely, since the wind velocity had also eased. But . . . He swung the alidade to the lighthouse at the entrance to Naples Harbor, just visible through the rain, and noted the bearing. He checked another point a little further up the coast. The bearings were the same numbers as in the passdown log, the same numbers the radar operator in Combat had been verifying all evening. His ship was still stationary. But the carrier wasn't.

"Bridge, Combat." It was the squawk box, on this class of ships known as the Internal Voice Communication System which combined a telephone, a speaker system at selected locations, and all of the internal networks in the ship.

"Bridge, aye."

"The *United States* is underway. We have them headed course Two Five Zero at four knots on radar." The watch officer in Combat had established a track on the SPS-55 radar, which was operating.

The carrier was heading directly into the prevailing wind, in the same direction she had been pointing as she rode at her anchor. "Keep tracking her and call her up. Find out if we've missed something. Have someone check the messages." Lieutenant (jg) Epley already suspected the worst. Somehow, some way, a message notifying the cruiser of a planned ship movement had gone astray. If so, he thought glumly, there would be absolute hell to pay. Somebody had dropped the ball rather spectacularly.

"Aye aye, sir."

The OOD looked again through the water-streaked bridge window at the carrier's moving lights as he twirled the handle on the "growler," an old-fashioned intercom box. He could just hear the growler sounding in the captain's cabin directly beneath the bridge.

"Captain." The Old Man sounded half asleep. No doubt he was.

"Sir, this is the OOD. The *United States* seems to be underway. There's no mention—"

"What?" The captain was fully awake now.

"Yessir. She's moving. Combat verifies on radar."

"Have you called her on the bridge-to-bridge?"

"Not yet, sir. Combat—"

"I'll be right there." The connection broke.

Epley pointed his binoculars at the carrier. He could see the masthead lights and the floodlights around the top of the island, though his view was slightly out of focus with all this moisture in the air.

"Bridge, Combat. Her speed is up to seven knots. No answer to our calls on Fleet Tactical or Navy Red." Fleet Tactical was a clear voice UHF circuit. Navy Red, or Fleet Secure, was an encrypted voice circuit.

"Keep trying."

"Watch to see if she turns," the OOD told the port lookout and his quartermaster, who had already noted the time and event in the log.

The captain arrived on the bridge in less than a minute. He carried his shoes in his hand and tossed them on his chair. He wasted only ten seconds verifying that the *United States* was indeed underway, then grabbed the Navy Red radiotelephone. No answer. He called Combat and found they had had no luck either. He stuck his head out of the port bridge-wing doorway and yelled to the signalman to try and raise the carrier with his flashing light, then spent a tense, unhappy minute on the phone with the cruiser's operations officer, who was as mystified as he was. The navigator was equally perplexed.

"Set the special sea and anchor detail, Mr. Epley. We're going to see how fast we can get underway. We can't let the flagship just steam off over the goddamned horizon without us. Then call the communications officer and tell him I want to see him here on the bridge in precisely sixty seconds." He sat down in his chair and put on his shoes, fuming, "The goddamn flagship gets underway in the middle of the fucking night and no one aboard my ship knows jack about it. I'm going to get out of the goddamn navy and buy a pig farm."

The call, when it came, was from Admiral Parker. The chief engineer summoned Jake to the telephone. He had been huddled with the navigator over a chart, plotting a course that would take the ship as far away from land as quickly as possible. The navigator had had to obtain the chart from his stateroom, since he couldn't get up into the island to his office.

"Captain Grafton."

"Jake, this is the admiral. I'm here with Colonel Qazi and he asked me to call you."

"Yessir." Jake listened intently. "Where are you, sir?"

"Uh, I think we'd better skip that. Are you the senior officer in charge?"

"Yessir. I think so." Jake could hear someone whispering, but he couldn't make out the words.

In a moment the admiral spoke again. "Qazi has armed a nuclear weapon. He . . ." Jake heard a muffled phrase, then a new voice came on the line.

"Captain Grafton, I am Colonel Qazi. You have heard Admiral Parker tell you I have armed a nuclear weapon. Do you doubt it?"

"No."

"Unless you and your men cooperate and do precisely as I tell you, I will detonate this device. I will destroy this ship and every living soul aboard her."

He paused and Jake pressed the telephone against his ear.

"Did you hear me, Captain?" His voice was calm, assured, confident.

"I heard you."

"This is what you will do. You will restore power to the weapons elevators servicing the forward magazine. You will call off your marines. You will ensure your crew does not interfere with me or my men as we leave the ship. You will not interfere with the helicopters on the flight deck. If you interfere with me in any way, Captain, if you try to thwart me, I will detonate this device."

"Let me talk to the admiral."

"I think not, Captain. This is your decision, not his. You hold his life, your life, and the life of every man on this ship in your hands."

"Including yours."

"Including mine. I am in your hands. You have the power to decide if this weapon will be detonated. If it is, you will be responsible."

Jake tried to laugh. It sounded more like a croak.

"This is deadly serious, Captain."

"Looks to me like we have a Mexican standoff here, Colonel. You fail if you die here too."

"No, sir. If this bomb explodes I will have shown the world the Americans cannot be trusted. No one will ever know why this bomb exploded, but the evidence will be irrefutable that it did. Your fleets will be disarmed by the American people. Your ships will be banned from the oceans of the world. I will have dealt a mortal blow to American power. I will have accomplished what the Germans and the Japanese could not in World War II. I will have destroyed the United States Navy. And I will have accomplished it very, very cheaply, at the cost of only my life and a few of my men. Think about it, Captain. You have ten seconds."

Jake was acutely aware of the sound of his own breathing. He rotated the phone so the transmitter was up over his head and

Qazi could not hear it. The bastard sounded so goddamn confident, so sure he had all the cards. And he *did.* The U.S. Navy was
finished if a nuclear weapon detonated aboard a ship; Congress
would sink it to the cheers of outraged, frightened voters. And the
Soviets would inherit the earth.

"Your answer?"

"How do I know you won't leave the ship and then blow it up?"

"You don't, Captain. What is your decision?"

"You'll get what you want."

"I thought you would arrive at that rational conclusion. I await
an announcement over your public-address system." The connection broke and Jake was left with a buzzing in his ear. Jake
slammed the instrument into its cradle.

Get a grip on yourself, man! Don't let these sailors see you out
of control. He took three or four deep breaths and tried to ar-
range his face.

"Triblehorn, how long until we can get power restored to the
weapons elevators up from the forward magazine?"

"Oh, maybe fifteen minutes."

"Do it." Jake turned to the marine officer, Lieutenant Dykstra.
"Get your people off the flight deck. Nobody, and I mean *nobody,*
pulls a trigger unless I give my personal approval. If they do, I'll
court-martial them and you."

A sneer of contempt crossed Dykstra's face. "I hope to God you
know what the fuck you're doing. Sir." Dykstra turned and stalked
away.

The navigator was still bending over the chart. Jake glanced
over his shoulder. The navigator was on the phone, probably to
the sailor in the after steering compartment. The emergency
helm was there, below the waterline in the after part of the ship,
near the giant hydraulic rams that controlled the rudder. The
navigator covered the mouthpiece with his hand and looked at
Jake, who asked, "Where are we?"

The navigator pointed. About ten miles southeast of the
anchorage.

"What's our speed?"

"Seventeen knots."

"Let's put on all the turns we can. Work her up to flank speed."

"There may be ships out there. The radar's not in service and
we only have two lookouts. Visibility is poor. I'm DR-ing our

track." DR meant "dead reckoning," drawing a line based on speed and time.

"Flank speed." Jake wanted the *United States* as far from land as possible in case Qazi pushed the panic button. He would just have to pray that Lady Luck kept this blind, stampeding elephant from colliding with another ship. The two lookouts wouldn't help much with this limited visibility; by the time they saw and reported a ship on a collision course, it would be too late to avoid the collision. And Lady Luck seemed to be off duty just now.

Jake picked up the 1-MC microphone from its bracket on the engineering watch officer's desk. The watch officer flipped the switches. This had better be good. Qazi would hear it. He cleared his throat, pushed the button and began to speak.

His announcement was heard all over the ship, except in those spaces where the public-address system was not working because of fire damage to the wires or loudspeakers. As it happened, two of the silent areas were the portside catwalk on the flight deck and the midships area of the O-3 level, where the waist catapult control rooms were located.

On the portside catwalk forward of the angle, up near the bow, Gunnery Sergeant Garcia stepped over the body of Lance Corporal Van Housen and laid familiar hands on the Browning .50-caliber machine gun. He snapped the ammo box open and carefully fed in the belt of cartridges he had so painfully carried up from the ship's armory draped around his shoulders. Then he opened the breech and slipped the belt in. He closed the breech and cycled the bolt. It jammed.

He tried again. No. The cartridge felt like it was hitting an obstruction. Don't tell me! No! He used his fingers to try and seat a cartridge.

They've spiked it. They had pushed a metal plug, probably tapered, into the chamber and his attempts to chamber a cartridge had forced the plug deeper into the barrel, jamming it. And Garcia, you ass, you didn't look first! You should have known!

He looked aft along the length of the catwalk at the helicopters sitting silently on the angle and tried to decide if he had the time to go get a rod to force down the barrel to push out the plug. So near and yet so far! There they sat, and here he was with a weapon that could destroy all three machines right where they were, or better yet, as they lifted off the deck, so they would fall into the sea without damaging anything else. And it wouldn't take ammo.

Van Housen lay face down. Another dead marine.

At least he had had the sense to pick up another weapon in the armory. It was slung over his shoulder, a Model 700 Remington in .308 caliber with a sniperscope. The marines called it the M-40. He hefted it in his hands and stared at the helicopters. No. The best place for this was up in the island. On Vulture's Row. From there he could command the entire angled deck. He turned away from the machine gun and the dead marine and went below.

Captain Grafton's announcement should have been heard in the waist catapult control bubble because the loudspeaker there was functioning perfectly. Or would have been functioning perfectly had the volume been turned up even slightly. As it was, the volume knob had been cranked to its lowest setting by some kind soul earlier in the evening when Kowalski was brought here to sleep it off. Now the loudspeaker didn't even hiss.

Kowalski sat on the floor of the darkened bubble with a headset of a sound-powered telephone over his ears and listened to one of the cat crewmen working on the JBD hydraulic pump in the Cat Four control spaces under the hookup area. The power was off to the pump and the crewmen were trying to tie in a line to another circuit at the main catapult junction box. A man there wearing a headset gave Kowalski an account of their progress when goaded properly.

"How much longer?"

"Goddamn, Ski, we're working as fast as we fucking can. Give us a break, will ya?"

"I just as'd a civil question, peckerhead. Gimme a guesstimate."

"Ski wants an estimate. . . . The Russian says five minutes."

"I'm lookin' at my watch. You tell the Russian he had better hump it."

"Where is the ship going, Ski? We can feel the vibrations here. They must have this mother really cranking."

"You people just worry about your end of the navy."

Ten minutes, Ski thought, maybe fifteen. The Russian always thought he was about finished. Ski checked the clock on the bulkhead behind him. His watch was broken. Probably happened last night at that bar.

He swallowed two more aspirin and inched his way upright. He eased his head level with the deck and surveyed the situation. One of the sentries was walking slowly around the choppers. The wind was whipping his shirt and trousers. The guys below were right; this tub was really bucketing along.

One of the places Captain Grafton's 1-MC announcement was heard was in the fire crew's shack in the after part of the island superstructure, on the flight deck level. The firemen had a watertight door that gave them immediate access to their large fire truck parked just outside on the flight deck. If there had been planes aloft or planes on the deck with engines turning, the bosun would have had his men in asbestos suits and sitting in the truck with the engine running. Now as the bosun listened to the announcement he knocked his pipe out into the ashtray on his desk and slowly refilled it.

He was bone tired and filthy. So were his men, who sat or lay on the floor all over the compartment. They had been down in the hangar bays fighting the fires. That place was a gutted shell now. The bosun and his men had helped the damage-control teams there stack the bodies like cordwood on the elevator when the fires were out. They had helped lay out Ray Reyolds. And they had laid out the waist cat officer and two of the catapult chiefs. They had died when an airplane with a little fuel left in its tank had exploded. The bosun wiped the grime off his face with his shirttail.

"Don't interfere with the intruders," the CAG had said. So the fucking terrorists had the U.S. Navy by the gonads and there was nothing anybody could do. Ha! No doubt that announcement had been made to please the terrorists, because they had heard it too. This Grafton, another over-the-hill, worn-out jet-jock who's pulled too many Gs. A far cry from Laird James. Now there was a real sailor, an asshole to work for and a perfectionist hairsplitter, but the bosun had spent twenty-seven years working for driven men who demanded perfection and were satisfied with nothing less. He was used to them. This Grafton! He'll probably get court-martialed after tonight, the bosun told himself bitterly.

When he had his pipe drawing well, he leaned back in his chair and put his feet on his desk and regarded the no-smoking sign posted on the wall. Yep, Grafton was just like Ray Reynolds. Stick the fucking sign on the fucking bulkhead, Bosun, and don't get caught smoking by the sheriff's boys or by the XO on one of his little jaunts around the boat. Don't get caught breaking any of the chickenshit little rules. Just fight the fires and stack the bodies, Bosun.

Before those terrorists got to the bridge, Captain James made an announcement. Do your duty, he said. That fit the bosun's pistol. He had made warrant officer four, the senior warrant rank, by doing the right thing regardless of what the book said. They couldn't hurt him with a fitness report now. No, sir. It would take a court-martial to rip the gold and blue off his sleeves. And the navy doesn't court-martial guys who do the right thing. It just shits all over assholes like Captain Grafton who earn their rank pushing paper, then fold up when the chips are down.

"Is there fuel in the truck?" he asked his first-class.

"Of course."

"When did you start it last?"

"This morning. No, yesterday, daily maintenance inspection. Started on the first crank."

The bosun puffed on his pipe and stared at the television monitor over the door. The helicopters just sat there. Occasionally one of the sentries moved a little.

The monitor swayed slightly in its mount. Grafton really has this tub cranked up, the bosun thought. Wonder if he knows what the hell he's doing?

"Where in the fuck are those crazy assholes going at thirty-three knots?" The skipper of the cruiser *Gettysburg* roared this question at his navigator, operations officer, and communications officer collectively. All three stood beside him on the bridge and together they regarded the little arrangement of lights several miles ahead in the murk that was the *United States*. "Thirty-three knots, limited visibility, right through the Italian coastal shipping lanes, right through all these little fucking fishing boats and yachts full of rich queers—those crazy assholes must be out of their fucking minds!"

He turned and faced the communications officer. "Why in hell can't you talk to her?"

"They're not answering on any circuit, Captain. We don't think they're transmitting on any frequency. None of their radars are radiating. They're observing EMCON." EMCON meant "emissions control."

The captain picked up the Navy Red telephone and pushed the transmit button futilely. He wiped his forehead and slowly put the instrument back into its cradle.

"They're certainly in a hurry to go somewhere," the ops officer observed calmly. He had always found it best to stay calm when the skipper blew off steam.

"Okay," the captain said, his voice back to normal. "Get on the horn to Sixth Fleet. Tell him what's going on. See if he knows something we don't. Find out what he wants us to do. And get off a flash OPREP to Washington." An OPREP was an "operational report," used to advise naval headquarters of emergencies.

"We're doing all the turns we can, sir," the OOD piped up. "We're not going to catch them if they keep this speed up."

"Thank you, Mr. Epley," the Old Man said sourly. He gestured at the communications officer. "Okay. Call Sixth Fleet and send the OPREP. Ops, you get down to Combat and sort out the surface picture. The *United States* isn't talking to us, she's not talking to anybody. She may run down one of these civilians. Try to call anyone in her way on the civilian emergency nets and tell them to get the hell out of the way. And if that doesn't work, we'll pick up survivors."

"Aye aye, sir."

"Willie," he said to the navigator. "I want to know where we are every damn minute and where we're heading. I don't want to follow those fools smack onto a reef or island at thirty-three knots. Let me see a chart with a projection of this course. They may be running for a launch position." That was the hypothesis that made the most sense, really. The carrier was silently racing to get into position to launch a strike. But against whom?

It's like a nightmare, the captain told himself as he looked at the backs of his departing officers. One day they had a war and nobody told you. Is this the big one? Naw, they would have told *us*, for Chrissake! Maybe Laird James and Earl Parker have gone off their nut. Maybe there's been a mutiny.

Infuriated and thoroughly confused, the captain sat in his chair and tried to get his blood pressure under control as his ship labored into the swells. White water spewed back from the bow, then the bow rose clear of the sea and crashed majestically into the next swell in another thunderous cloud of spray. He pushed his squawk-box button for the chief engineer and warned him to be ready to cut power to the shafts instantly if the screws came out of the water.

He had gotten his ship underway in record time, getting the anchor up in seventeen minutes from the time the capstan had began to turn. Due to the sonar dome under the bow, he couldn't move the ship until the anchor cleared the water. The *United States* had been seven miles ahead, but he had managed to close the distance because she had stayed at seventeen knots for almost twenty minutes. Then she accelerated to thirty-three. Now, with the larger swells here in the open sea, he was hard-pressed just to match her speed. Sooner or later he would close on her; if she turned port or starboard he would turn inside her and close, providing he didn't have to back off some turns to keep the screws in the water and could stay with her.

Something was seriously wrong aboard *United States.* He tried to imagine a combination of circumstances in peacetime that would justify a capital ship weighing anchor unannounced in the dead of night and steaming off alone, without her escorts, at high speed through crowded shipping lanes with radar and radios silent. When, or if, he caught up with her, it wouldn't hurt to be ready for anything. "Lieutenant Epley, sound general quarters."

Meanwhile, aboard *United States,* Jake Grafton was huddled in engineering with the ship's department heads and every squadron skipper who was aboard, plus about half the executive officers. His operations officer and the flag ops boss were also present. Jake had told Qazi when he called the second time that restoring power to the elevators would require half an hour, and Qazi had given him half that time. Still, twenty minutes had passed and the new circuit had not been energized. All that remained was the throwing of a switch by the load dispatcher in Central Control. Jake had not yet told him to throw the switch.

"Goddammit, Captain," the weapons boss shouted, "We can't just let that terrorist take some bombs and fly off this ship. We can't." This statement was merely a rehash of arguments voiced for the last ten minutes by desperate, angry men crowded around Jake.

"Now you listen," Jake said calmly, "All of you. This is going to the the last word. I've listened to all your arguments. We've hashed and rehashed this for ten minutes. *In my opinion,* we've got no other choice. This man has us by the balls. None of you has suggested a viable alternative course of action."

"Goddammit—"

"*No!* Don't you cuss at me! I'm the man responsible and I've made the fucking decision. End of discussion!"

"I still don't see why we can't zap his choppers with missiles when they are about five miles out, after the bomb is disarmed." Everyone assumed that Qazi would leave an armed weapon on deck that he could explode by radio control if he were pursued.

"Bullshit. We've got no radar." Jake pushed his way to the engineering watch officer's desk and picked up the 1-MC microphone. "Central Control, this is Grafton. Energize the emergency circuit to the forward weps elevators." He threw the mike on the desk.

"Now when these people get gone, I want every E-2 and F-14 on the flight deck that can fly fueled and armed for an immediate takeoff. You skippers, get your crews suited up and briefed. Weapons, get ready to bring missiles up from the magazines. And get some senior people to inspect those magazines as soon as the terrorists get out of them. Qazi may leave something ticking down there. Air Department, get your people ready to go. We're going to shoot down Mr. Qazi and his friends when they're the hell and gone away from this ship." They stood and stared. *"Do it now."*

"Jesus, CAG," the weapons boss said. "You should have told us that ten minutes ago. We thought you were just going to let them get away."

Jake shooed them out. He bummed a cigarette and sat down with shaking hands to smoke it. These guys weren't using their heads. Qazi had had all the answers up to this point; he probably had an answer to the possibility of aircraft pursuers. The likeliest answer was just to detonate the bomb aboard ship when he was five or six miles away at fifty feet over the ocean, tail-on to the blast. Still, in war nothing ever goes the way you've planned it, so the name of the game is keeping options open. The ship's officers just don't realize how few options we have. He had decided earlier, when the discussion started, not to stress the fact that there was a 90 percent chance no one on this ship would live another hour. So now they have a straw to grab for, something to do to keep them and the men busy while the last minutes tick by.

"CAG," Triblehorn said after the others had filed out. "Maybe you should let the crew know what this terrorist is up to? Make an announcement on the 1-MC."

"So everyone can have a final moment to polish their soul before they get cremated alive? Nope. We don't need any panic. They'll have to go meet their maker with the tarnish still on. Death's a come-as-you-are deal, anyway."

What a great naval leader you are, Jake Grafton. Here you are, twenty-three years in the navy, presiding over a naval debacle that will make Pearl Harbor look like a minor traffic accident. And if by some miracle you survive, the admirals and congressmen will cram your nuts into a vise and take turns on the handle.

"How come you don't have any ashtrays down here?" he asked the engineering watch officer.

"The XO made us take them out. Smoking's bad for you."

"No kidding. Look where it's got me," Jake said. "Call the master-at-arms shack and have them bring me a big bolt-cutter. One of those things they use to cut padlocks off. Tell them to hurry."

"You sent for me, CAG?" The speaker was a senior chief petty officer wearing glasses. His name tag read "Archer, EOD." EOD meant Explosive Ordnance Disposal.

"Yeah. Pull up a chair and drop anchor." The senior chief did as requested. He was of modest stature, with intelligent eyes and even, regular features. His uniform hung on him as if it were tailor-made. He had fine, delicate hands. He looked as if he were really a banker or an accountant, except for the bare legs of a tattooed woman on his upper arm which peeped out from under his short-sleeved khaki shirt.

"Senior Chief, I need some answers about nuclear weapons. We've got a little problem."

26

THE *United States* pitched gently in the corrugated sea as she charged onward through the night at flank speed, a gentle seesawing of the bow and stern that her crew, accustomed as they were, ignored. They did notice, however, the vibration as her four thirty-three-ton screws thrashed the sea to foam. Inside the ship one could feel the vibration in the decks and passageways and half sense it in the air, a dynamic tension of ominous power and urgency.

The wind had veered more to the east. It was fresh and crisp and empty of rain. Through the opening rifts in the clouds stars were visible, had anyone on the flight deck taken the time to glance upward. From force of habit Jake Grafton did as he stepped on deck trailed by four armed marines in camouflage utilities and helmets. In his right hand he carried a walkie-talkie. Beside him Senior Chief Archer carried his toolbox in one hand and the bolt-cutter in the other. Jake sniffed the sea wind and saw the stars' brightness in the inky tears in the clouds above. The temperature here on the flight deck was fifteen degrees or so colder than inside the ship. He shivered and peered about the deck.

He and his companions stood amid a forest of aircraft with wings jutting upward at crazy angles. Ahead of him on the right the island loomed with its band of red and white floodlights around the top combining to cast a soft, reddish glare on the deck and aircraft. Behind the island and nearer to him a mast reached up into the blackness. On this mast were numerous antennas. He stared at it a second, slightly puzzled. Oh yes, the radar dishes weren't rotating.

He walked forward, toward the bow, between the aircraft until he could see the helicopters parked on the angle. He moved in beside a plane and waited, hoping his night vision would improve. Sentries lay on the deck around the choppers, facing outward. Behind the prone men a supervisor walked slowly back and forth with an assault rifle cradled in his arms. The rotors of the choppers were still and the engines silent.

A row of E-2s were parked athwartships between the helicopters and the island, their noses pointed at the helicopters. Forward of the Hawkeyes, Jake could see the rows of aircraft that were parked atop the bow catapults facing aft, with nose tow bars attached so they could be quickly towed aft and spotted for a launch. Beyond the airplanes on the bow and to the left, outboard, of the helicopters on the angle the blackness of the night made a formless curtain.

Up on the bow between the rows of aircraft, about six hundred feet from where Jake stood, were the upper openings of the forward magazine weapons elevators. Qazi would wheel his weapons down between the parked planes and over to the choppers.

Something smacked the airplane on Jake's right, a stuttering, smacking sound, and Jake's eyes went involuntarily to the plane. He glanced toward the sentries in time to see the twinkling muzzle flashes from the weapons of one of the men stretched upon the deck. The rippling thud of more bullets striking metal came from the airplane beside him.

"Quick, get back! Everyone back."

"Sir," one of the marines said in a stage whisper, "I can take that guy—"

"Get back out of sight. I don't want them shooting up these

333

airplanes, and I told you no fucking shooting without my okay!
Now get back there, goddammit!" Jake followed the retreating
marines. He crouched down under a plane and peered forward
between the mainmounts and belly tanks, trying to see the men
around the helicopters in the glare of the island floods. He could
just make them out. Here under the airplanes Jake and his party
were in darkness, invisible to the sentries.

Son of a . . . All the planes in the hangar destroyed and now
they were shooting holes in the ones here on the roof! God damn
those bastards! He could well understand the marine's frustration. Qazi didn't just have all the good cards; he had the whole
deck!

"CAG! Better come look." It was one of the marines. Jake
moved toward the sound. Three of the marines were checking a
man lying on the deck. "Dead, with a bullet in the head." Jake
looked. "And here's a shotgun." It was one of the men of the
flight deck security watch that Reynolds had armed. The young
man's eyes were open, and to Jake it seemed as if the dead man
were staring straight at him.

"Okay, Ski. It's on and working." Pak and Gardner and three
other sailors crouched beside Kowalski in the waist bubble. He
was sitting on the floor. They slowly inched their heads up to the
windows so they could see the deck and swiveled their heads back
and forth, taking in the choppers and the figures around them.
"When are we going to do it?"

"Not until they're aboard those things and ready to take off. If
we popped them right now, they might come down to the catapult
spaces and gun everybody. We can't take a chance like that."

"How are we going to do it?"

"From the control panel below deck." The primary JBD controls were on a panel in the catwalk, abeam the JBDs for Cats
Three and Four. But it was too risky to have someone crawl along
the catwalk to the panel with that crowd on deck, so this morning
they would use the secondary control panel in the catapult machinery spaces.

"What's that smell?" one of them asked, sniffing loudly.

"I was sick over there behind the panel," Kowalski said.

"Oh."

"Jesus, Ski, you oughta . . ."

"Yeah."

"Boy, we're gonna get those bastards," one of the green-shirted troopers said and giggled nervously.

"Yeah, we'll teach 'em not to fuck with the Uncle Sugar Navy," Pak agreed.

"Them A-rabs is gonna get an edufuckation," enthused the greenie known as the Russian.

"You guys go below," Kowalski said. "Pak, you man the panel in the control room. Don't do nothing until I say, then do exactly what I say. Understand?"

"Hey Ski, can I stay here and watch?" the first greenie asked, elevating his head for another look around. "This is gonna be so good that—"

"Everyone below. You can watch on the monitor down there if it's working."

"Aaaw . . ." They trooped out and dogged the watertight door tightly behind them, leaving Kowalski alone in the darkness with his hangover.

It was the sound of the helicopter engines coming to life that first alerted Jake Grafton. Their low moan rose slowly in pitch until the fuel-air mixture ignited, then it spooled up quickly to a whining howl. When the RPMs were at idle, the main and tail rotors began to turn. The sentries on the deck remained at their posts.

Jake moved until he could see past the noses of the Hawkeyes abeam the island into the parked rows of planes on the bow, the "bow pack." Yes. There was someone! Pushing a weapon on a bomb cart. A sentry was with him. And there comes another.

"Archer?"

"Yessir."

"Take a look." The senior chief moved up beside Jake and peered through the gap between an F-14 mainmount and A-6 belly tank that Jake was using.

"There's the admiral," Archer said. Now Jake saw him too, in his whites with his hands bound behind him, walking with three other people.

□ □ □

335

Kowalski heard the engines of the choppers winding up and donned the sound-powered headset. He adjusted it over his ears and pulled the mike to his lips. "You there, Pak?"

"Yo, Ski. I'm ready."

"Don't do nothing until I tell you. But stay ready. These guys are starting their engines. Let me stick my head up for a look-see." He eased his eyes up to the lower edge of the bulletproof glass. The sentries were no longer lying down; they were milling around smartly. He looked at the last helicopter in line, the one sitting atop the number-four JBD. He could just see the pilot and copilot in the cockpit. Not navy pilots, that's for sure—no naval aviator in his right mind would set one of those eggbeaters down on top of a JBD. Their tough luck.

"What d'ya see?" Pak's voice in his ears.

"A bad accident about to happen. Now keep your ears open and your mouth shut."

The fire-crew bosun watched the helicopters start their engines on the television monitor. He picked up the cards on the desk that he had been using to play solitaire and carefully placed them in their box and put the box in the upper left-hand drawer, right were it belonged. You learned that in the navy, if you learned nothing else—everything in its place.

He stood and stretched, his eyes on the monitor. A figure in white came into the lower right corner of the picture, accompanied by two men, one in khaki and one in sailor's dungarees. There was a fat man in civilian clothes and a figure that looked like a woman. The bosun stepped forward, closer to the screen.

His men crowded around. "Ain't that the admiral?" "Jesus, I think it is." "What *is* going on?" "Beats the living shit outta me, man." "They never tell us nothing."

"What are those things on them dollys?"

The men stood right under the television, as close as they could get, and stared up at the screen. "Holy . . . Those things are *nukes.*"

"You guys sit down." The bosun watched as they took seats on the couch with the stuffing coming out and on the folding chairs. He took down the key to the truck from the hook near the door. "You people stay here."

"I'm going with you, Bosun," the first-class said.

"You heard the last announcement."

"If you're going, I'm going."

"Okay." The warrant officer lifted the lever that rotated the dogs and cracked the door open. He could see the side of the truck a few feet away. It was parked pointing toward the choppers on the angle and there were no planes in front of it. There never were. He snapped off the lights in the compartment with the switch by the door, took a deep lungful of the night sea wind, then pushed the door open and slipped through. The first-class petty officer was right behind him.

Gunny Garcia heard the helicopter engines running as he climbed the ladder into the island, the very same ladder that the gooks had thrown the grenades down, the ones that got Vehmeier and Garcia's marines. The bodies were gone from the passageway at the bottom, though the blood and shrapnel had not been cleaned up. The blood smears were black now, and the place reeked of smoke.

Garcia had had his troubles wending his way through the gutted area of the O-3 level. The sailors still had hoses and power cables everywhere and the only lights were emergency lanterns. The stench was terrible. It was the overpowering odor of burnt rubber and fried meat.

Now, as he heard the chopper engines, his resolve gave way to apprehension. He might well be too late.

He checked the door to Flight Deck Control as he tiptoed to the ladder upward. The three gooks were right where they had fallen. Leggett was nowhere in sight. Garcia continued up the ladder.

On the third level he heard someone coming down from above. He waited grimly, the Remington leveled.

The first thing he saw was the man's shoes, black boondockers, then bell-bottom jeans, then the gym bag and the Uzi. He pulled the trigger on the Remington.

The man tumbled and fell at his feet. He was holding his crotch and screaming. Garcia worked the bolt on his rifle and waited. Apparently this one was alone. He stepped over to the man. The .308 slug had hit him in the pelvis. "That's a nasty wound you got there, fellow," Garcia said and shot him in the head. The head disintegrated. The gunnery sergeant worked the bolt again, then climbed on up the ladder.

□ □ □

Each of the seven weapons was on its own dolly, a little four-wheeled yellow cart with a swiveling tongue that turned the front wheels. One man pushed each cart backward down the deck.

Qazi had one of the weapons, the one with the timer already installed, halted abeam the island. He then handcuffed Admiral Parker to the cart. "As you have probably suspected, Admiral, the triggering device bypasses all the weapon's built-in safeguards. It contains its own battery and can initiate the firing sequence." Qazi held up a small metal box and continued, speaking over the noise of the helicopter engines, "I can activate the trigger with one push on this button. And I will push this button, *if* . . ." He turned and watched the sentries lift two weapons, still on their dollies, into each helicopter.

Standing beside them, Ali removed a small two-way radio from a holster in his belt and spoke into it.

Qazi turned back to Parker. "There is going to be some shooting here on deck in a moment. That's unavoidable. It is necessary that we disable the planes on the flight deck so that your people cannot follow us once they decide we are beyond the range where we could trigger this device. I hope you realize that, in a way, disabling these aircraft is an act of good faith on my part. I certainly hope that we're allowed to depart unmolested and I don't have to push this button. Because I will destroy this ship if I have to, Admiral, so help me God. Do you understand?"

As usual, Earl Parker's face was impassive. He had been watching the bombs being loaded into the helicopters, and hearing the question he glanced at Qazi, then turned his eyes back to the idling machines.

The gunmen who had been in Flight Deck Control ran past them, heading for the helicopters. The woman was helping the fat man in civilian clothes, the weapons expert, into the chopper parked the furthest forward on the angle, the lead machine.

"So long, Admiral," Qazi said and turned away. He and Ali walked briskly toward the lead machine as the sentries fanned out toward the bow and the stern. Almost in unison, they pulled pins from grenades and threw them into the parked aircraft. Then they opened fire with their Uzis.

□ □ □

"Grenades!"

The senior marine, a sergeant, shouted the warning and fell flat upon the deck. Jake Grafton, Chief Archer, and the rest of the marines did the same.

Jake heard the sound of one of the grenades striking a nearby aircraft, then the boom of an explosion. A group of explosions followed, too close together to count.

The shrapnel and bullets sounded like hail on a tin roof as they tore into the fuselages of the nearby planes. Jake looked up the deck. He could see the gunmen and the flashes of their submachine guns. More grenades came raining in.

"What's going on, Ski?" Pak demanded. He and the others were watching the activity on the television monitor, but Kowalski's view was not limited to what the camera was seeing.

"They're shooting the shit outta everything. You ready?"

"Yeah."

Kowalski had hoped to wait until the gunmen were in the helicopter, to ensure they didn't come looking for his unarmed catapult crew, but this was ridiculous.

"Okay, raise it up . . . *now!*"

The helicopter sitting on number-four JBD pitched forward amid flying sparks as its rotors dug into the steel deck. The giant jet blast deflector had risen from the deck on its forward hinge as if the weight of the helicopter weren't there.

The rotors disintegrated. Gunmen fell and sparks flew everywhere as shards of the rotors impacted steel and tore into human flesh. At least one of the gunmen dropped a live grenade and it exploded beside him with a flash.

"JBD down!"

The helicopter collapsed back onto its wheels. Its engines screamed as they overrevved without the load of the rotors.

"JBD up!"

This time the blast deflector turned the chopper over onto its nose. The machine teetered there, then continued over onto its back and caught fire. Flying debris struck the tail rotor of the next helicopter forward and broke it off.

Kowalski heard shouting and laughter in his ears. The guys in the control room were hysterical and Pak had his mike button depressed. *"We did it,"* he screamed at the cat captain in the bubble. *"We did it!"*

The fuel tank in the wrecked helicopter ignited explosively in a yellowish orange whoosh and pieces of the machine showered the deck.

Gunny Garcia stepped out onto Vulture's Row and looked down onto the flight deck. The burning chopper cast a brilliant light on the scene. He wasn't too late! With trembling hands he twisted the parallax ring on the sniperscope to its closest setting and adjusted the magnification ring as he scanned the scene below. Gunmen were shooting into the planes and throwing grenades. He swung the rifle onto a man on his feet near the fire and tried to steady the cross hairs.

The cross hairs danced uncontrollably. He rested the rifle on the rail in front of him and took a short deep breath, then squeezed off a shot. The man collapsed.

Garcia chambered another round.

He had shot three of them when the yellow flight-deck crash truck came bolting from its parking place behind the island, its engine at full throttle audible even above the noise of the chopper engines. There was a man on the nozzle on top of the cab and he had the water-foam mixture spouting fifty feet in front of the truck. The man spun the nozzle and one of the gunmen was blasted off his feet by the water stream. The truck roared across the deck, straight for the helicopter at the head of the angle.

There was a man in front of the chopper, shooting at the truck. Garcia got him in the telescopic sight and jerked off a round. The man went over backward. Muzzle flashes came from the open door in the side of the helicopter. Garcia aimed into the flashes and pulled the trigger. Nothing. The rifle was empty. The truck swerved, its left front tire peeling from the rim.

The fire-truck engine was roaring like an enraged lion as the machine careened left and crashed into the second helicopter in line. The truck slowed, but now the chopper was skidding sideways toward the rail. The chopper's mainmounts struck the flight deck rail and it tilted. Smoke poured from the truck's rear tires. Then the chopper went over the side and the cab of the truck bucked up as the front wheels struck the rail and it followed the helicopter toward the sea, its engine still at full throttle.

Bullets slapped the steel beside Garcia. He crouched behind the rail coaming and feverishly fed more shells into the rifle.

The engines of the only helicopter left, the one at the head of the angle, were winding up to takeoff power. The roar deepened as the pilot lifted the collective and the rotors bit into the air.

Garcia slammed the bolt closed and came up swinging the rifle for the cockpit. He got the cross hairs onto the pilot of the chopper. . . . Something smashed into his left shoulder, jerking the rifle off-target just as he pulled the trigger. He tried to hold the rifle with his left hand and work the bolt with his right, but his left wouldn't work. The chopper lifted from the deck and began traveling forward, toward the edge of the angled deck.

More bullets slapped into the steel near him. His left arm wouldn't work right. Then he lost the rifle; it fell away toward the deck below.

Enraged, he watched the helicopter clear the edge of the flight deck and fade into the darkness. Garcia sank down behind the coaming and sobbed.

Jake Grafton sprinted up the deck as bullets zipped around him and the roars of M-16s on full automatic filled his ears. He ran toward the weapon on the dolly in front of the E-2 Hawkeyes parked tail-in to the island. A man in whites lay by the dolly.

Senior Chief Archer reached the bomb even as Jake did. Archer began examining the weapon with a flashlight as Jake knelt by the admiral. Blood oozed from a dozen wounds in his torso and legs. Shrapnel from the helicopter rotor blades or a grenade.

"Admiral? Cowboy? It's Jake. Can you hear me?"

Behind Jake, the last of the gunmen were going down as the flames from the burning chopper rose higher and higher into the night.

Parker's eyes and lips were moving. Jake bent down, trying to hear.

"Jake . . ."

"Yeah. It's me, Cowboy."

Parker's eyes focused. "Don't let him get away, Jake." His hand grasped the front of Jake's shirt and he pulled him down. "Don't let him get away. Stop . . ." Parker coughed blood.

"You know me, Cowboy. We'll get 'em."

Parker was drowning in his own blood. He was coughing and

choking and trying to talk. In a supreme effort he got air in, then, "Don't let him use those weapons . . ." He gagged and his body bucked as his lungs fought for air. Jake held on as the convulsions racked him.

Finally Parker's body went limp.

"I don't know, CAG." It was Archer. He was looking at the trigger. "I just dunno. It's definitely got a radio receiver built in, and somebody built this that knew a hell of a lot, but I'm damned if I can figure what will happen if I cut this wire here." He pointed.

Jake grabbed the bolt-cutter from the deck where Archer had dropped it and used it on the handcuffs that held Parker's wrist to the dolly.

Jake dropped the big tool and seized the tongue of the dolly. The brake was automatically released when he lifted it. He began to pull the dolly.

"What are you gonna do?" Archer asked.

"Over the side. The radio receiver won't work underwater, and maybe the water will short out this trigger thing."

Archer joined him on the other side of the tongue. They began to trot. "Not too fast," Archer warned, "or this thing'll tip over."

They pulled it around the front of the island toward the starboard rail. "This thing may go off when it hits the water," Archer said.

"We'll have to risk it. We're out of time."

There's a bomb chute somewhere here on the starboard side of the island, Jake remembered. There! He turned the dolly around and backed it toward the chute, which was a metal ramp with lips that extended downward at an angle over the catwalk and ended out in space.

The rear wheels of the dolly went in and then the front and it started to roll. It fell away toward the sea. Jake Grafton turned his face and closed his eyes. If it blew, he would never even feel it.

His heart pounded. Every thump in his chest was another half second of life. Oh, Callie, I love you so. . . .

When he finally realized there would be no explosion, he tried to walk and his legs wouldn't work. He fell to the deck and rolled over on his back. Slowly, slowly he sat up. Archer was sitting on the deck near him with his face in his hands.

□ □ □

Qazi crossed from the open right-side door of the helicopter to the bucket seats that lined the other bulkhead. He had been watching the lights of the carrier recede into the gloom.

"How far away are we?" Ali shouted, barely making himself heard over the engine noise. "When we get to eight miles . . ."

Qazi handed him the radio triggering box. Ali used the telephone by the door to speak to the pilots, then held his watch under the small lamp near the phone, one of three small lights that kept the interior from total darkness. He stepped to the door and leaned out into the slipstream, looking aft.

Noora and Jarvis were huddled in the corner. Noora had Jarvis's head cradled on her breast and was rocking softly from side to side. Jarvis's face was down and Qazi could only see the top of his head.

On Qazi's right, three of the gunmen sat with their weapons between their knees and their heads back against the bulkhead, their eyes closed and their faces slack. They looked totally exhausted. These three had managed to scramble aboard as the flight-deck crash truck charged them, then turned in the door and emptied their weapons at the truck. They were the only survivors of the thirty-six men Qazi had taken to the ship.

Yet he had two bombs. The skins of the weapons were white and reflected the glow of the little light over the telephone near the door. Ali was still leaning out into the slipstream. He pulled himself inside, checked his watch, and grinned at Qazi. He braced himself against the bulkhead and manipulated the controls on the box.

Nothing happened. He tried again with a frown on his face. He leaned out the door with the box in his hand and pointed it aft at the carrier.

Ali hurled the control box at Qazi, who didn't flinch as it bounced off the padded bulkhead and fell to the floor. "Traitor," Ali screamed as he grabbed for his pistol.

Qazi shot him. Once, twice, three times with the silenced Hi-Power. He could feel the recoil, but the high ambient noise level covered the pistol's muffled pops.

Ali sagged backward through the door. The slipstream caught him and his hand flailed, then he was gone.

The gunmen didn't move. Noora continued to rock back and forth with her eyes closed, her arms around Jarvis.

Colonel Qazi slowly put the pistol back into his trouser waistband. He zipped up the leather jacket he was wearing. It was chilly here. He stuffed his hands into the jacket pockets and stared at the white weapons.

27

LAIRD JAMES was in a coma when Jake checked on him in sick bay. An IV bottle of whole blood hung on a hook beside the bed, and two corpsmen were preparing him for the operating room. The blue oxygen mask over his nose and mouth made the rest of his face look white as chalk.

"Is he going to make it?" Jake asked the corpsmen, who didn't look up.

"He's lost a lot of blood. Bullet through his liver. His heart stopped once and we gave it a kick-start."

Jake turned and went back through the ward, looking at the burn, gunshot, and smoke victims. There were more patients than beds and some of the men lay on blankets on the deck. Most were conscious, a few were sleeping, and here and there several were delirious.

One man was handcuffed to his bed. A marine wearing a duty belt with a pistol sat on a molded plastic chair near the bed, facing the prisoner. The man in the bed looked at Jake, then looked

345

away. Jake picked up the clipboard from a hook on the bottom of the bed and read it. Name unknown, no ID. "Can't or won't speak English."

"He's one of the terrorists, sir," the marine said. "He fell overboard from the liberty boat earlier this evening."

Jake nodded, replaced the clipboard on the bed, then moved on. Chaplain Berkowitz was moving through the ward, taking his time, pausing for a short conversation at every bed.

The second-deck passageways outside sick bay were still crowded with men sitting and standing, but the crowd was thinning as the chiefs and division officers got people sorted into working parties and led them off. The 1-MC blared continually with muster information for the various divisions and squadrons.

Jake climbed a ladder to the hangar deck. Foam still covered the wreckage of aircraft and lay several inches deep on the deck. The bulkheads and overhead were charred black. The glow of emergency lights was almost lost in the dark cavern.

In Flight Deck Control the handler was roaring orders over the radio system he used to talk to his key people on the flight deck. Will Cohen, the air wing maintenance officer, turned to Jake when he saw him enter the space.

Every airplane on the flight deck had shrapnel or bullet damage. "All of them?" Jake asked, stunned. "Even the ones clear up on the bow?" Cohen showed him a list he was compiling. They went over it, plane by plane. Jake wanted every fighter and tanker available airborne as soon as possible. He had Harvey Schultz briefing a dozen F-14 crews and a dozen F/A-18 Hornet pilots. But he had to get them some airplanes.

It quickly became apparent that the E-2s parked next to the island would not be flying tonight. One of them had absorbed so much shrapnel from the disintegrating rotors of the upended helicopter that Cohen thought it would never fly again. The others would require rework at an intermediate maintenance facility back in the States. Three of the tactical jets had caught fire, and the fires had damaged two other machines before they were extinguished. All the planes had bullet holes in them, and maintenance crews were checking right now to determine the extent of the damage. "We can't take them to the hangar, and the wind makes opening the radomes and engine-bay doors hazardous," Cohen said. "We're going to damage some planes just inspecting them unless you slow the ship down or run with the wind over the stern."

Jake had the ship heading due south at twenty-five knots, straight at the island of Sicily. *Gettysburg* was a mile away on the starboard beam. Her captain had requested this slower speed to enable his ship to ride easier.

The bullet hole in the plexiglas status board caught Jake's eye. Someone had drawn a yellow circle around it. It looked obscene. "One hour," Jake told the maintenance officer. "We launch in one hour. Get me some planes."

On the bridge Jake ordered the ship slowed to fifteen knots. The reduced wind would also help the crash crews who were trying to clean up the nuclear contamination from the wreckage of the chopper immediately in front of number-four JBD. When the helicopter had turned upside down, the ensuing fuel fire had ruptured one of the weapons, causing the conventional explosive inside to cook off and scatter nuclear material. Most of it had been carried over the port side of the ship, but the wreckage and flight deck were still hot. The crash crew was using high-pressure hoses to wash the radioactive contamination into the sea, where it would soon disperse to harmless concentrations.

Now Jake stood beside the captain's chair and tried to absorb the avalanche of information flowing at him from all over the ship. The information came faster than Jake could assimilate it. The navigator came over to help.

Several long messages were handed to him to approve before they were sent by flashing light to *Gettysburg* for electronic transmission. The first one he looked at was a Top Secret flash message giving the bare bones of the incident. The second one was ten pages long and covered the incident in detail. Jake took exactly one minute to read them both as he listened to someone give him an estimate of how soon various radio circuits could be repaired. Jake handed the short message to the signalman for transmission and used a borrowed pencil to draft a final paragraph for the longer one: "Intentions: Will launch all available fighters ASAP to pursue, find, and destroy helicopter that escaped. *Gettysburg* radar tracked it toward Sicily. Contact now lost. Believe helicopter will land and refuel vicinity of Palermo. Urgently request assistance."

He stared at the paragraph and chewed on the pencil. The

landing near Palermo was only likely because of the chopper's fuel state. There was no way it could fly the width of the Mediterranean without refueling. Perhaps Qazi intended to transfer the bombs in Sicily to another aircraft, a faster one. "All available fighters"—that was a joke: right now he didn't have any. And what assistance could anyone give? Never hurts to ask, he told himself and handed the message to the waiting signalman. Then he pursued the sailor, took the message back, and added one more sentence. "While in hot pursuit, intend to enter foreign airspace without clearance."

The squawk box again. "Bridge, Handler."

"Bridge, aye."

"We have three aircraft on deck with strike damage, CAG. I need room. Request permission to jettison these three aircraft."

"Push 'em over the side?"

"Yessir."

"Have someone take the classified boxes out of them and do it."

For some reason the squawk boxes and telephones fell momentarily silent. The navigator and several of the officers from the flag staff were having a discussion behind him, the OOD and the quartermaster were hard at it, and the junior officer-of-the-deck was briefing the lookouts, yet for the first time since Qazi escaped, no one was talking to Jake. He eyed the captain's chair. He was so tired, exhausted physically and emotionally, and it was tempting. Why not? He heaved himself into it.

Cowboy Parker dead, Ray Reynolds, over a dozen marines and nearly fifty sailors. Major damage to the ship, enough to put her into a yard for a year or so. And forty-some planes lost. That list would grow as the machines were inspected. Any way you cut it, a major debacle. And to top it off, Qazi got away with two nuclear weapons. But this was not the time to dissect the disaster; worry now about winning the next battle. Win the next one and you will win the war. But can we win? So far Qazi has had all the cards; he has prepared and planned and plays a trump at every turn. What has he prepared in the event he is followed? What are his options?

"CAG." Someone was standing beside him.

It was his deputy air wing commander, Harry March. Will Cohen stood beside him with a paper cup full of coffee, which he offered to Jake along with a cigarette. Jake gratefully accepted both and got down from Laird James's chair. Out of the corner of his eye, he saw Harvey Schultz come onto the bridge in his flight gear, with his helmet bag in his hand. He was the senior fighter squadron skipper and would lead the planes after Qazi.

As Cohen lit the cigarette for him, Jake listened to March. "We have three turkeys that can fly, CAG," March said. "Turkey" was the slang name for the F-14 Tomcat. "One KA-6 tanker and two Hornets. We're putting our most experienced people in them and launching in thirty minutes." March spread out a chart of the Mediterranean. "When they get airborne, they'll be talking to the *Gettysburg*. All our radars and radios are out and will be for some hours."

Out the window Jake could see airplanes being towed around the flight deck by low, yellow tractors. The respot for launch was almost complete. March was still speaking: "*Gettysburg* has told us via flashing light that the chopper is headed for Sicily. There is a U.S. frigate that cleared the Strait of Messina twelve hours ago and is now off the eastern coast of Sicily. *Gettysburg* is trying to notify the Italian authorities, but that's all going to take time. Probably too much. They'll be gone by the time Rome tells the local constabulary to drive out to the airport and make an arrest, if possible."

"Can anybody get close enough to shoot down the chopper with missiles?"

"Nope. Not enough time. After we launch, I recommend we take the carrier as far south as we can get her to shorten the flight home for the planes. Fuel is going to be tight. They'll take our one tanker with them, but everyone is going to be watching their gauges pretty close. At least we have Sigonella for a possible fuel divert if necessary." Sigonella was a U.S. Naval Air Station on the eastern end of the island of Sicily.

"That would violate Italian sovereignty," objected an officer from the flag staff who had eased over to listen. He was referring to the fact that bases in foreign nations could not be used for takeoffs or landings of planes on combat missions without the host nation's approval, which they certainly didn't have.

"We're going to violate Italian sovereignty anyway," Jake said wearily. "And if they're pissed they can squawk about it later. That Qazi guy certainly didn't sweat it. I suspect the Italians will have more serious things to holler about when this all comes out in the wash."

"How are we going to do this, CAG?" Harvey Schultz asked. "We talk to the *Gettysburg* and the frigate south of Messina and try to sort out the traffic with their help. Then we arrive over Palermo. Then what?"

"Have someone make a low pass. He can call in an air strike if he sees that chopper on the ground." Jake smote the arm of the captain's chair. "Jesus . . ." It was so weak. It would never work. "You're going to have to use your head, Harve, and do the best you can with what you've got."

"What if they've loaded the weapons on a truck and driven away?"

"Then we're *screwed,*" Jake roared. He swallowed hard and lowered his voice. "It's going to be up to you, Harve. You're going to be the man on the spot. You make the call on the spot and I'll back you up. For whatever that's worth. I'm probably going to get court-martialed anyway. Parker's dead and I'm glad. I'm *glad!* He doesn't deserve to be pilloried for this. Laird James is going to wish he were dead by the time the admirals and congressmen get through with him. Now it's up to you. Don't let those assholes get away with those bombs."

Harvey Schultz kept his eyes on Jake. "I understand."

"Harve, if those people use those weapons on anybody, the United States is finished as a power in the Mediterranean. This ocean will become a Soviet lake. The nations of Europe will be forced to come to terms with Soviet ambitions or face up to another world war, one they can't win. *This is for all the marbles, Harve.*"

Schultz's head bobbed nervously.

"Now get the hell outta here and get those planes into the air. Every minute that passes makes it less and less likely you'll find those people. Get going!" As the officers departed Jake said, "OOD, when those guys start engines gimme thirty knots of wind right down the deck for launch."

Jake slugged off the rest of the coffee and dropped the cigarette butt into the cup. A young enlisted man approached him. "Sir, I'm Wallace, signalman. The chief said to tell you we've established radio contact with Sixth Fleet on the MARS unit. The admiral wants to talk to the senior officer aboard." MARS stood for Military Auxiliary Radio System. The radio set was in a cubby-hole in the signal shack behind the bridge. The sailors used it to talk to their families back in the States with the assistance of volunteer ham radio operators. Jake followed the signalman across the bridge and out the door that Gunnery Sergeant Garcia had worked so hard to get through earlier in the evening.

Jake settled into one of the two chairs in front of the radio. The chief perched in the other and pointed out the switch on the panel that had to be pushed up to receive and down to transmit. "This is a non-secure radio, sir. And people all over the world are probably listening." He pushed the pedestal microphone over in front of Jake, who picked it up.

Jake pushed the switch down. "What's their call sign?" The call sign for this set was written in black Magic Marker on the panel in front of him.

"W6FT, sir," the chief said.

"W6FT, this is W74Y, over." Jake flipped the switch to receive.

"W74Y, W6FT, say your rank and name, over."

"Captain Jake Grafton, over."

"This is Vice-Admiral Lewis. What in hell is going on out there, Captain?"

"I sent you a flash message via USS *Gettysburg*, sir. Have you got it yet?"

"No, and I want to know what the hell is going on. Why did you people sail?" He sounded furious.

"Admiral, this is a non-secure radio link. I'd rather you waited and read the message."

"I want to know *now*, Captain."

Jake stared at the radio. What the hell. The world would probably read all about it in tomorrow's papers anyway, if Qazi's bunch hasn't already issued their own press release. Jake flipped the switch to transmit, held the mike several inches from his lips, and began to talk. It took him three minutes to describe the situation and his intentions. Finally he said, "Over," and toggled the switch to receive.

"Wait."

Jake set the microphone down on the desk and looked at the chief, who averted his eyes. Yeah. Well, I wish I could too, Jake thought.

"Grafton, this is Lewis. I don't want you to do anything. Don't launch. We just received the message from *Gettysburg* and are talking with Washington on the satellite net. This is something the National Security Council needs to make the decision on." You ass, Jake thought, and bit his lip. "Clean up the ship, tend your wounded, and await further instructions. Over."

Jake jabbed the switch to transmit. "Admiral, you don't seem to understand the situation. We have a terrorist on his way God knows where with two nuclear weapons stolen from this ship— stolen from the United States Navy. And he has devices that he can use to trigger them. This man is capable, he's committed, and he's absolutely ruthless. We don't have much of a chance to stop him, but we do have a chance and we had better take it. We may not get another. His attack on this ship was an act of war. We have the right and authority under existing Rules of Engagement to use as much force as necessary to thwart him. We have a duty to do so, sir."

Jake set the microphone on the table and leaned over it. How to say it? "We have a moral obligation to stop this man before he murders innocent people. A lot of innocent people—hundreds of thousands. The world will judge us by our efforts to meet that obligation." The future of the free world is at stake here, Admiral. Can't you see that? "Over to you."

Lewis's voice dripped with fury. He was not used to officers arguing with him. "My orders to you are to wait, Captain. Do nothing! Do not launch aircraft! The president will have to meet with the National Security Council and decide how to handle this incident, which *you* people *let* happen. Outrageous incompetence and stupidity. Never have I seen the like. You have fucked this up from end to end, and there's no chance you'll do any better if you keep trying. Just keep that ship afloat until we get someone out there who is capable of bringing it into port. Over to you for a hearty 'Aye aye, sir.'"

Jake reached for the transmit-receive switch. His thumb hovered an inch above it but then backed off.

Okay, so Lewis is a paper-pusher who instinctively covers his ass rather than stick his neck out on a hard decision. You knew all along he was a pygmy. Okay. What are you going to do?

"I said, 'Over to you,' *Captain*," Lewis snarled.

So you did, Admiral. And Colonel Qazi still has two bombs and he's still taking them somewhere. Jake's eye fell on the on-off switch. He threw it and the static from the speaker stopped.

Jake stood. "Chief, this radio is out of order. Don't turn it on again."

"Aye aye, sir." The chief looked sick.

Jake Grafton stalked out.

The lights on the hangar were off when Qazi's helicopter settled onto the tarmac at the Palermo airport. A group of men came out of the darkness under two high-winged transports parked nearby and walked quickly toward the helicopter as the rotors spun down.

"Where are the other helicopters?" a major asked Qazi.

"The others were destroyed on the ship. This is the only one."

The major stuck his head into the machine for a look. He grinned at Qazi and motioned his men forward. They began unstrapping the restraints that held the dollies on which the weapons rode. The three men who had gone to the ship with Qazi climbed around them and wandered off toward the transports. Noora and Jarvis followed them, arm in arm.

Ten men lifted each dolly from the helicopter to the pavement. Qazi walked behind the weapons as they were pushed the two hundred feet across the tarmac. The rear access doors of both aircraft were open. These were hinged portions of the after fuselage and consisted of two longitudinal doors that folded upward into the fuselage. A ramp led upward into the interior of the plane on the left, which was a Soviet-built Il-76 Candid. In the dim light Qazi could just make out the jet engine nacelles on the wing. The other plane was smaller, a four-engine turboprop, an An-12 Cub.

El Hakim was standing at the rear of the Ilyushin. Two bodyguards with Uzis stood behind him. "How did it go, Colonel?" he asked as he returned Qazi's salute.

"We managed to get the six weapons to the flight deck, Your Excellency, and put two weapons in each helicopter. But the Americans destroyed two of the helicopters before they could take off."

"So we have only these two weapons?"

"Only these two."

"Where is Ali?"

"He was on one of the machines that was destroyed."

El Hakim stood in silence and watched the first weapon go up the ramp and disappear into the interior of the plane.

"And the ship?"

"The weapon we left on deck failed to explode." No doubt El Hakim already knew that. The electromagnetic pulse from a nuclear explosion would announce itself on every radio receiver for hundreds of miles. The pilots of these transports would have reported such an event instantly to El Hakim.

"Why?"

El Hakim was entirely too calm, Qazi thought. He began to feel uneasy. "I suspect the Americans disarmed the weapon before we were far enough away to trigger it. They have weapons experts aboard. That was always a possibility."

The second weapon was going up the ramp. El Hakim said, "We have staked our national survival on your mission, Qazi, and you have succeeded. We didn't gain as much as we hoped for, but we have succeeded. The nation owes you a debt. The Arab people owe you a debt, and it will be paid."

Qazi started to reply, but El Hakim gestured impatiently. "No one else could have done it, Colonel. No one." He sighed audibly. "For twenty years we have struggled to obtain a hammer to strike the chains from our people. Twenty years! Twenty years of frustration and humiliation." His voice cracked. "And now we have it," he whispered, "praise Allah, now we have it."

The second weapon was inside the plane. The engines on the other plane were already turning and the rear door was coming down into place. The three gunmen who had survived the ship had boarded that plane along with the helicopter pilots. Qazi glanced back at the helicopter sitting near the hangar. It would be abandoned here. Not a customs or immigration official was in sight; he had paid Pagliacci a hundred thousand American dollars for the privacy.

"Come," El Hakim said. "We have much to do. History is waiting to be written."

In the transport's interior along the bulkheads was a contraption of ropes and pulleys. Five triggers sat along the walls, and Jarvis was fitting a trigger to one of the weapons. Noora was crouched beside him. Qazi stopped and stared. Two khaki bundles sat behind the rearmost dolly and there were straps flaked out on the floor. These were parachutes, the type used to drop military equipment to troops in the field. The men who had loaded the dollies were busy rigging the straps to the rear dolly. The first dolly, parked as far forward as possible, had been chained to the deck. A hard object dug into Qazi's back.

"Don't move, Colonel." An arm reached around him and removed the Browning Hi-Power from his waistband. El Hakim paused halfway through the compartment and turned to face him.

"What did you plan to do, Colonel? Kill me?" A smile slowly spread across the face of El Hakim. "Don't look so surprised. Come, Colonel. Come up here so we can close the door and depart." He turned and marched forward. The guard prodded Qazi in the back and he followed.

A seating module occupied the forward third of the cabin. The guard motioned Qazi into a seat against the outer fuselage. He was directed to buckle his seat belt, and he complied. With his Uzi against Qazi's neck, the guard snapped handcuffs on his wrists, then used a second pair to fasten the first pair to the armrest of the seat. The guard seated himself across from Qazi, beside El Hakim, and leveled the Uzi at Qazi. Those two had their backs to the radio compartment, beside which was the short stair that led up onto the flight deck.

As the engines started El Hakim chuckled. "You have served us well, Qazi, but your task is complete. You have our gratitude. I express it now." His smile faded. "But that is all the thanks a traitor like you will ever receive." He leaned forward and raised his voice, to be heard above the engine noise. "We are going to Israel now, Colonel, to strike with our hammer. Zionism will not survive the blow. And the debt we owe you for your treason will be paid in full." El Hakim showed his teeth.

Qazi leaned his head back into the seat and closed his eyes. He listened to the creaks and thumps of the taxiing plane, just audible over the whine of the turbojet engines. He heard Jarvis and Noora slipping into seats behind him. He heard Noora speaking to Jarvis, fastening his buckle for him, fussing over him. After a few minutes the transport creaked to a stop, then the engines spooled up. The plane rolled and in a few moments left the earth.

When at last Qazi opened his eyes, El Hakim had reclined his seat and was watching him with a satisfied, contented expression.

□ □ □

Jake Grafton strode across the flight deck toward the F-14 Tomcat sitting behind Cat Three. The boarding ladder was still down and he mounted it. "Get out, Harvey. I'm going in your place."

"What about the ship?" Schultz asked when he found his tongue, his voice bitter.

"The navigator can handle it. Unstrap and get out and give me your gear. You can brief me." Jake lowered himself back down the ladder.

"CAG," came a voice from the backseat. "Do you want me in here?" Jake looked into the rear cockpit. Toad Tarkington was looking back. Jake nodded yes and motioned for him to stay put.

When Harvey Schultz reached the flight deck, he began taking off his flight gear. "None of this stuff will fit you," he muttered.

"No time to wait for my stuff." Jake paused, then continued, "It isn't that I don't trust you, Harve, but I'm the senior man and I'm the one who should take the shit when the fan starts turning."

"I could handle it, CAG."

"I know that, Harve. But I'm not taking you up on the gallows with me. I want you to get with my staff and get as many of these planes ready to fly as possible. Cannibalize if you have to. If Qazi gets away, those weapons are going to crop up somewhere, and whoever ends up with them will have bought a lot of trouble. You get this air wing ready to give them all the trouble it can dish out. Get this ship ready to fight." Jake zipped Schultz's G-suit around his legs. The fit was terrible. Schultz's calves and thighs were much thicker than his; it was as if he wasn't wearing a G-suit at all. He unzipped it. He would just go without one.

Farnsworth came hurrying across the deck carrying a load of flight gear. "I heard you were going flying, CAG."

"Thanks, Farnsworth." Jake pulled his own G-suit from the pile Farnsworth laid on the deck and zipped it around his stomach and legs. Then he wriggled into his torso harness. All this was going on over his khakis, since Farnsworth hadn't brought his flight suit.

"Ask the waist catapult officer," Jake said to Farnsworth as he pulled on his survival vest, "to come over here and talk to me."

Schultz briefed Jake as he completed donning his flight gear. They discussed rendezvous altitudes and frequencies. "Toad knows all this stuff," Schultz said. "You have two Phoenix missiles and two Sidewinders. We had to download the Sparrows—they had shrapnel damage."

Jake nodded. The Phoenix missiles were the big guns and were mounted on a missile pallet on the Tomcat's belly. Weighing almost a thousand pounds each, they could knock down a plane over sixty nautical miles away with a 132-pound warhead when fired from any angle. They were expensive, too, costing over a million dollars each. Although the F-14 could carry six of them, because of their size, weight, and cost, Sparrows and Sidewinders were the usual load. Phoenix was loaded only when you were going hunting for bear—like now. The Sidewinders were heat-seekers and had a limited head-on capability with a much shorter range. They were also a lot smaller and cheaper than Phoenix, weighing only 190 pounds each. Sidewinder was a simple, reliable weapon.

Farnsworth came back with Kowalski and a chief. "Morning, CAG," the chief said. He was in khaki trousers and a yellow shirt, but Kowalski was still wearing grimy civilian trousers. His once-white T-shirt had spots of vomit on it.

"Where's the cat officer, chief?"

"The only one we had aboard is dead, killed in that hangar-deck fire, and the rest of them are on the beach. I'm all the khaki the catapults have aboard."

"Who's going to launch us?"

Kowalski looked around the deck and shrugged his shoulders. "I guess I am," he said sheepishly. "But I'm sober, sir." The chief nodded at both comments, then added, "He knows more about launching procedure than I do, CAG."

"Whose bright idea was it to flip that chopper upside down with the JBD?" Jake climbed the ladder into the cockpit. The plane captain followed him up to help him strap in.

"Mine, sir," Kowalski said, looking up at Jake.

"Didn't you hear my orders on the 1-MC not to interfere with those people?"

"I didn't hear any announcement, sir," Kowalski said.

"What? I can't hear you."

"No, sir," Kowalski said, louder.

"Did you know that there was an armed nuclear weapon sitting on deck over there by the island, and the leader of that bunch had threatened to detonate it if anybody interfered with him?"

Kowalski pressed both hands against the sides of his head.

The plane captain finished strapping Jake in and went down the ladder. "I didn't hear your answer, Ski."

"No, sir. I didn't know that."

Jake motioned at the catapult captain. "Come up here." When the man's face was a foot from his, Jake said, "Do you know enough to launch these planes?"

"I've seen the shooters do it lots of times, CAG."

"You can practice on me first." Jake grabbed a handful of Kowalski's filthy T-shirt. "Son, you're a drunk. We need you sober or not at all. Promise me here and now, if you ever take another drink, you'll ask for an administrative discharge as an alcoholic."

Tears filled Kowalski's eyes. His head bobbed.

"Okay," said Jake Grafton. "Now give everybody a good shot. Take your time and be sure you know what you're doing."

"You can trust me, sir," Kowalski said and disappeared down the ladder.

28

J AKE GRAFTON eased the throttles forward to full military power and felt the nose of the fighter dip as the thrust of the engines compressed the nose wheel oleo. The Tomcat seemed to crouch, gathering strength as its two engines ripped the night apart.

"You ready back there?" he asked Toad. As usual, Jake's heart was pounding as he scanned the engine instruments.

"I'm behind you all the way, sir."

Jake glanced over at the waist catapult bubble as he flipped on the external light master switch. The bubble windows were opaque. He looked straight ahead, down the catapult track at the ink-black void.

The G pushed him back into his seat and the end of the deck hurled toward him faster and faster as the howl of the engines dropped in pitch. The deck edge flashed under the nose and the G subsided, and he released the throttles and slapped the gear handle up as he let the nose climb to its optimum, eight degrees up, attitude. Accelerating nicely . . . 180 . . . 190 . . . 200 knots, still accelerating and climbing, flaps and slats up, little wallow as they come in. . . . Passing 250 knots, he looked ahead for the lights of the KA-6 Intruder tanker, which had been the first plane off Catapult Four.

Toad was on the radio to *Gettysburg:* ". . . airborne, two miles ahead of the ship, passing two thousand and squawking . . ." Jake eased into a left turn and looked back for the next plane. God, it's dark out here! There—a mile or so behind. Back on the gauges, still climbing and turning, still accelerating—Jake breathed deeply and tried to relax as his eyes roamed across the panel, taking everything in.

The Tomcat that had launched from Catapult Four was on the inside of the turn, closing. Jake searched the night for the beaconing anticollision lights of other fighters leaving the little island of light that was the carrier. Nothing yet. Kowalski must be taking his time. That's good; better safe than sorry.

Jake eased back the throttles and leveled at 5,000 feet, still turning. The second fighter was only a hundred yards away, closing nicely. It traversed the distance and slid under Jake and stabilized on his right wing, on the outside of the turn. The tanker was on the opposite side of the ship, so Jake steepened his turn to cross the ship and rendezvous.

"Red Ace Two Zero Six, Volcano, over." "Volcano" was the radio call sign for the *Gettysburg.*

"Go ahead, Volcano," Toad replied.

"Roger. Uh, sir, we have received, uh . . ." The transmission ceased for a few seconds. "Maybe we should go secure."

"Roger."

After he turned on the scrambler, Jake glanced again at the carrier. Still no anticollision lights on deck or in the air. Come on, Ski! He turned his attention again to the little collection of lights in the great black emptiness that was the tanker.

"Red Ace," the controller aboard *Gettysburg* said when Toad had checked in again, "we have received a high-priority message from Sixth Fleet and have relayed it to Battlestar." "Battlestar" was the *United States.* "Sixth Fleet has directed that there be no planes launched to pursue the intruders unless and until authorized by the president. Battlestar suspended the launch after we relayed this message to them by flashing light. Do you wish to hold overhead until we receive presidential authorization for the mission, or do you wish to recover back aboard Battlestar?"

Jake stole a glance at his fuel gauge as he closed on the tanker on a forty-five-degree line of bearing. The totalizer had begun its relentless march toward zero when he started the engines. Fuel from the tanker would delay the inevitable, but not prevent it. "Any timetable on when you might hear from the president?" Jake asked as he matched his speed to the tanker and passed under it, surfacing on its right side.

"Wait." The controller aboard the cruiser must be questioning his superiors.

The tanker lights flashed, and Jake flashed his; now he had the lead. He could see the reflective tape on the pilot and bombar-dier-navigator's helmets whenever his own red anticollision light swept the plane. That was all. Just the outline of two helmets in the darkened cockpit. The tanker drifted aft so the pilot could look up the leading edge of Jake's left wing. Jake checked his right wing. The other Tomcat hung there motionless, suspended in this black, formless universe.

"No, sir," the controller finally said.

"Talk to you in a minute," Jake replied. He glanced at his heading indicator. Passing 210 degrees. He rolled wings level when the indicator read 180 degrees.

"Toad," Jake said over the intercom, "use your red flashlight to signal those guys to switch to two three two point six."

Tarkington did as requested while Jake dialed the radio to that frequency. "Two, you up?" Jake asked.

"Roger." This was the other fighter.

"Shotgun's with you." That was the tanker crew.

"Go secure."

The response was mike clicks.

With the scrambler engaged, Jake said, "Who's over there in the turkey?" He slowly nudged the throttles forward and lifted the nose. The needle on the altimeter began to move clockwise.

"Joe Watson and Corky Moran, CAG." The needle on the verti-cal speed indicator swung lazily up past five hundred feet a min-ute, then eight hundred, and stabilized at one thousand. It was reassuring, in a way; he could make these little needles do pre-cisely as he wished with the smallest displacement of stick or throttles. Jake added more power and tweaked the nose higher.

"Joe and Corky, huh? And you, Shotgun?"

"Belenko and Smith, sir."

"Well, this is how it is, guys. I'm going after those terrorists. Sixth Fleet ordered me not to. The president will probably approve of a pursuit, but we'll lose the chance if we wait around. Those people killed a bunch of our guys and stole two nuclear weapons. I'm going with or without you. If you want to go back, that'll be fine. If you go along, the fact that I'm the man responsible and you're just following orders may not be a big enough piece of armor plate to cover your ass. I don't have any steel underwear to give you. Think about it."

Silence. He had 90 percent RPM on both engines now and they were passing through 12,000 feet. He was wasting fuel climbing this slowly, but the tanker pilot probably had his throttles almost to the stops.

"Uh, CAG," Toad said over the intercom. "Don't I get a vote in this? I'd like to stay out of prison if at all possible. I'm pretty young, you know. Whole life before me and all that. It seems to me—"

"Shut up," Jake Grafton said. "You're flying with me."

The scrambler beeped. "What do you think they might do with those weapons, CAG?"

"They're not going to mount them on a wall somewhere as trophies."

The jets passed thorough a thin cloud layer. Above it, Jake could see the pink light of dawn to the southeast. The stars were fading rapidly. It was going to be a good day to fly.

"Red Ace Two Zero Six. This is Volcano on Guard." "Guard" was the emergency frequency, 243.0, which was constantly monitored by a separate radio receiver in each plane. "RTB. Return to base. Contact Volcano on . . ." and he named a frequency.

When that transmission ceased, the scrambler beeped in, and the voice from the other fighter said, "CAG, we hold Palermo five degrees port. What are we gonna do when we get there?"

"What about you, Belenko?"

"If you guys are going to tilt some windmills, we wanta be there to watch."

"Oh, shit," Toad sighed.

□ □ □

From his seat Colonel Qazi could see the light in the eastern sky. The airplane was heading right for the spot where the sun would shortly appear. The windows were round and small and covered with scratches which suffused the pink dawn.

El Hakim was in the after part of the cabin watching Jarvis complete the task of wiring the trigger to the bomb. In the seat facing him, the bodyguard with the Uzi kept the gun pointed at Qazi's stomach. Qazi shifted in his seat and tried to get comfortable. His wrist and head hurt from the blows of the night and his entire body ached from the exertion.

He heard someone walking this way. The dictator fell onto the seat beside the guard and leered at him.

"You know, I assume," Qazi said, "that the triggers won't work."

El Hakim's lips pulled away from his teeth, exposing them. "Oh yes. I thought you might do something along those lines, so Jarvis checked them before he left Africa. He replaced the timing devices." The dictator leaned forward. "They'll work *now.*"

Qazi looked out the window. The fiery disk of the sun had peeped over the horizon. "You tipped your hand when you subverted Ali," he said just loud enough for El Hakim to hear. "He was not a good double agent."

El Hakim sat with his hands on his knees, the knuckles whitening. The muscles in his cheeks tensed and relaxed, tensed and relaxed, rhythmically. "Another possibility to be guarded against. Another precaution to be taken." He leaned across and slapped Qazi hard. *"Look at me!"*

Qazi complied.

"You knew I might discover your sabotage of the triggers. What precaution did you take against that?"

Qazi merely looked at him.

"Answer!"

"Your only viable alternative," Qazi said slowly, calmly, "is to take these weapons back to Africa and use them as diplomatic tools. They will give you stature and respect in international councils. Your voice in the Arab world will . . . *That* is your only alternative, Excellency."

"What else did you do, Colonel? Tell me now."

"I called the Israelis and told them you were coming. You won't get within a hundred—"

El Hakim stood speechless, his mouth open. He licked his lips. It wasn't true, of course, Qazi reflected. Too risky to give an aggressive bunch like that any advance warning of his acquisition of weapons that would change the entire power structure in the Mediterranean. But El Hakim was accustomed to calculating different risks.

"You're lying," El Hakim spluttered. "You're bluffing." He tried to laugh. "It won't work with me."

"The number in Rome is 679 93 62."

El Hakim had him around the throat. He shook him like a dog shakes a snake. "Traitor! You filthy, slimy traitor!"

Qazi's cuffed hands wouldn't reach. He fought for air. He bit his tongue. The darkness closed in and his vision shrank to pinpoints. He could hear El Hakim shouting, but the words were being replaced by a roaring in his ears. Then suddenly the pressure on his neck ceased, leaving him gasping, chest heaving.

". . . too good for you. Oh, no! I will kill you slowly, make you die by inches." El Hakim stood over him, staring down. Perspiration glistened on his face. "You betrayed us. You betrayed *me*. And we *will* get through. We *will* use the weapon on the Jews." El Hakim leaned down. Saliva flecked his lips. "I have fighters coming to rendezvous. They will escort us in and we will push the weapon out the back and the parachute will open and it will detonate in an air burst a thousand meters above Tel Aviv." The perspiration was making rivulets on his face. "You will live to see it, Colonel." El Hakim struck him, then turned away toward the flight deck, breathing hard.

The three American jets came from the north, from the sea. Far below, the airmen saw the city of Palermo and they saw the thin, irregular line where the land surrendered to the sea. The land was rough, convoluted, and as the sun crept over the rim of the earth the ridges cast long shadows into dark, misty valleys.

With his throttles pulled back to max conserve, Jake remained at 25,000 feet and watched Joe Watson's plane fall away toward the city below as he listened to yet another transmission from the *Gettysburg* on Guard. The tanker was behind and to Jake's right. Both fighters had topped off just before they made landfall. In the rear cockpit Toad was scanning the sky with the radar. Nothing. At dawn on a Sunday morning in September, the sky over Sicily was empty.

"That's the seventh time they've called," Toad said, his voice revealing his irritation.

"Persistent beggars, aren't they?"

"Goddamn, CAG, Sixth Fleet! You can't give the finger to Sixth Fleet. For the love of—"

"I'm not in the mood for you today, Toad. A lot of good men died trying to stop these assholes, and you're whining. Now shut the fuck up."

The sun was a fireball just above the horizon. As his plane turned through the easterly heading Jake was blinded by the glare coming straight through his heads-up display. He squinted behind the green visor of his helmet and tried to see the instruments. They were almost indecipherable. His eyes couldn't look from brightness to darkness and accommodate anymore. It irritated him, as Toad did. So much at stake and nothing going right. What would Joe and Corky find down there? Was Qazi still there? Even if he was, where were the weapons? It was an impossible problem. He engaged the autopilot, knowing it would fly the plane more smoothly than he could and thereby save a few pints of fuel. A few gallons. He unfastened one side of his oxygen mask and swabbed his face with a gloved hand and let the mask dangle. Come on, guys. What's down there?

"There's a chopper here on the mat beside a hangar with the door closed, CAG. As near as I can tell, it looks exactly like one of those that was on the ship. No one in sight. Not a solitary soul. Nothing down here but light planes, Cessnas and Pipers. What do you think?"

Jake refastened his mask. "How many hangars?"

"Two."

"How about big trucks? Any semis parked around?"

"Empty as a politician's promise."

Had the bird flown? Jake had to make a decision and make it fast. Joe Watson was down low, burning gas at an appalling rate.

"Could they be in the hangars?"

"It's possible, I guess," Watson said, his voice dubious.

Jake cursed to himself and swung his F-14 to the south. He leveled the wings and pushed the throttles full forward as he trimmed the stick aft. "Joe, climb to about five thousand and orbit the field as long as you can. If anybody gets nervous and tries to drive off in a van or semi, or if they open a hangar and you see a big plane parked in there, shoot it up. Understand?"

"Roger."

"Watch your gas and get back to the ship. Keep your eyes peeled. Belenko, I want you to go down to Cape Passero, on the southeastern tip of the island south of Syracuse, and orbit overhead at forty grand. Wait for me there."

"Red Ace Two roger."

"Shotgun roger."

"Good luck, Joe," Jake said.

The mike clicked twice.

As they knifed upward through 30,000 feet headed southeast with the unfiltered sunlight filling the cockpit Toad murmured over the intercom. "Qazi got away, CAG, and you know it."

He did know it. Qazi had two nuclear weapons that belonged to the United States Navy and he was gone. Gone where? Tripoli or Benghazi or somewhere else? If he was on his way to Africa, he was talking to Air Traffic Control. Jake began frantically flipping through the bundles of cards on his kneeboard, looking for the Air Traffic Control sector and frequency list. Why hadn't he thought of this sooner?

He selected the frequency for the southeastern coast of Sicily and, after turning off the scrambler, dialed it in on the radio. His radio was UHF, and a transport, even a military one, would be using VHF. But the controllers normally transmitted on both VHF and UHF. Jake leveled at 40,000 feet. The throttles were in high cruise and he was clipping along at .86 Mach.

"See anything?" he growled at Toad.

"No, sir. Empty sky."

How about that frigate that went through the Strait of Messina last night? It was supposed to be off the east coast of Sicily now. Jake looked up the frequency on another kneeboard card and dialed it into the second radio. He gave them a call and got an answer. They assigned a discrete IFF code, and he squawked it. He wondered how much help he would get if Vice-Admiral Lewis was talking to them. He had to use his real call sign because the frigate could read the classified IFF code, which was specific to this aircraft. Here goes nothing. "Buckshot, we're running a little intercept exercise this morning and I wonder if you've observed any traffic out of Palermo in the last several hours headed south or southeast, over."

"Wait one."

Mount Etna was off to his left, spectacular with the sun on its flank. Normally Jake Grafton would try to make a mental note of every detail to include in his next letter to Callie, but this morning he glanced at the mountain, then ignored it.

"Red Ace, Buckshot. We can't see quite that far, but we had a North African Airways flight cross the coast southbound from Palermo about fifteen minutes ago, speed about three five zero. And we had a TWA flight cross Catania eastbound six minutes ago. He's about fifty miles east, apparently on course for Athens. Then there was a Red Cross transport eastbound past Syracuse twenty minutes ago."

"Any destinations?"

"Not specifically, but the controller asked the North African Airways flight if their trip was going to become a regular one. I gathered it was some kind of a one-time deal."

"Thanks for your help, Buckshot."

"For further assistance, give a shout. Buckshot, out."

"Just what the world needs, another clown," Toad grumped on the ICS.

With another anxious glance at the fuel readout, Jake shoved the throttles into afterburner. If Qazi was up ahead, he was going to have to catch him. He flipped the switches on the radio panel so he could monitor the Air Traffic Control frequency. Static! Someone was transmitting! He turned down the squelch and heard words in English, but they were too garbled to understand. Then the transmission ceased. Okay! Someone was on this frequency this morning. It could be anyone, but maybe, just maybe . . .

"North African Airways Three Zero Six, you are departing Italian airspace. You are cleared to leave this frequency. Good day, sir."

"I may have 'em, CAG," Toad said. "Right on the edge of the scope, heading south. We're following them. They're headed for Africa all right. Tripoli if they hold this heading."

Jake nudged the throttles deeper into afterburner. The Mach

meter indicated 1.5. He could go faster, but he was using fuel at a prodigious rate.

"He's below us, about twenty-five thousand feet or so, making three hundred fifty knots, the computer says. No, about three hundred sixty knots. Pretty slow for a jet." They crossed the coast of Sicily and headed out to sea. Malta was off to the left there, someplace.

At forty miles Jake pulled the throttles back slightly and lowered the nose. Toad turned on the Television Camera System and Jake punched up the picture on his Horizontal Situation Display. "Looks like a C-130 Hercules to me," Toad said. "Same high wing. Right speed for a turboprop."

"There aren't any Hercs going to Africa this morning," Jake said as he studied the picture. The image was still so small and it shimmered as the light was diffused by the atmosphere.

"Maybe an An-12 Cub? Didn't the Russians sell those things all over North Africa?"

"Yeah."

"What're you going to do?" Toad asked.

"Rendezvous so you can give the pilots the Hawaiian good luck sign."

"Well, we can't just shoot 'em down," Toad said acidly. "We can't just blast 'em out of the sky."

At ten miles Toad said, "Looks like this guy has a gun turret or something in the tail. That's no Herc." It's no airliner, either, Jake thought as he looked through the heads-up display and picked out the speck in the sky near the symbol that was the transport.

He came out of burner and let his speed drop as he approached the turboprop from the stern. There was a man in the gun turret, but the twin barrels remained pointed upward as the fighter rapidly traversed the last mile and Jake pulled the engines toward idle and cracked the speed brakes to kill his speed.

He slid up on the right side of the transport. A four-engine turboprop. An Antonov An-12 Cub, all right, with a glass chin for the navigator to peer out of. The Americans hadn't put a chin like that on a plane in forty years. This plane was painted in desert camouflage but lacked markings of any kind. That's curious, Jake thought. Not even a side number.

He let the fighter drift forward so he could see directly into the transport's cockpit. Both pilots were looking this way. He used his left hand to signal a turn to the left. Nothing. They just stared. Jake flipped the switches on the armament panel and triggered a short burst from the Vulcan 20-millimeter cannon mounted in the port side of the F-14's forward fuselage. He could feel the weapon's vibration as the tracers shot forward and disappeared from sight.

The Cub continued on its heading. Jake signaled vigorously for a left turn. Nothing. "They're a thick bunch," Toad muttered.

Jake triggered another burst. Still the plane continued on course. "What if the weapons aren't in there?" Toad demanded.

"What do you want me to do? Let him go to Africa and drop the bomb next week on New York?" Jake reduced power and let the transport pull ahead. Maybe a few rounds right over the wing would change this guy's mind.

He glanced left just in time. The twin barrels in the tail turret were swinging this way. He rammed the stick forward and orange fireballs flew across the top of the canopy. The negative G slung the two men upward as far as the slack in their harness restraints allowed. Jake dove under the transport and added power and kept the nose down.

"What do you want to do now, Tarkington, you goddamn flea on the elephant's ass. Got any ideas?" When Jake was several miles ahead of the Cub, he began a turn. "How many people have to die before you're willing to get your hands dirty?" He craned his neck to keep the transport in sight. It turned the opposite way and dove, trying to flee, a fatal mistake. Jake relaxed his turn and reset the armament switches. "No smirches on your lily-white soul. What do you think Farrell was fighting for?"

The Cub was in the forward quadrant now, several miles ahead as Jake completed the 270-degree turn. The tailgunner was blazing away but the shells were falling short. Jake put the pipper in the heads-up display on the plane, and got a rattling tone in his ears, the locked-on signal from the heat-seeking Sidewinder that had given the missile its name. He squeezed the red trigger on the stick pistol grip. A missile leaped off the rail in a blaze of fire. It tracked. Jake got another tone and squeezed the trigger again. The second missile shot after the first.

The gunner shot at the missiles. It was futile. They slammed into the engines of the Cub at two and a half times the speed of sound. Their 25-pound warheads flashed. The Cub rolled onto its right wing and began a spiral. The nose fell steeply.

Jake dipped a wing and watched the transport going down. It was going too fast. A piece of wing came off and the plane began to roll about its longitudinal axis, out of control, going down, down, down. Jake added power and eased the Tomcat into a climbing turn toward the north, still watching the falling plane far below. Then it exploded.

"I'm sorry, sir," Toad said.

Jake took off his oxygen mask and wiped his face. He felt like he was going to be sick. "I'm sorry, too," he muttered to the Gods, who were the only ones who could hear.

"Do you think they had the bombs?" Toad asked.

When Jake had his mask back on and adjusted, he said, "I doubt it." Qazi didn't seem the type to let himself be waylaid quite so easily. "Get on the radio. Find out where that frigate thinks that Red Cross plane is and ask the tanker to fly straight east at top speed. We'll rendezvous with him and get some more gas, then try to catch the east-bound jet."

"You don't think it's a Red Cross plane?"

"That has the earmarks of our colonel friend. An airline flies certain known routes every day, so you can't just pretend you are an airliner without confusing the controllers. He needed a one-time flight plan." Toad did as requested.

Or, Jake thought, Qazi could do what Jake was doing right now, which was fly around illegally without a flight plan and hope the controllers had their radars tuned to just receive transponder codes, not skin paints. But Qazi didn't run risks like that. Oh, no. He would be covered, with a perfectly legal international flight plan filed days in advance. For a one-time trip.

The Il-76 with Qazi, El Hakim, and the weapons aboard was circling, waiting. The fighters were late, Qazi heard one of the crewmen say. They had been circling for ten minutes. Out his defective window he could see only the blue of the ocean and the changing shadow of the wing as the transport flew a lazy circle.

El Hakim had never understood the importance of timing in clandestine operations, Qazi reflected. This ocean was an American lake, with missile-carrying surface combatants sprinkled at random. There was a carrier battle group off Cyprus. When the Americans sorted out the mess aboard *United States,* they were going to be in a very pugnacious mood, and Soviet-built transports wandering erratically in international airspace were going to attract unhealthy attention, especially if escorted by fighters. El Hakim's time was fast running out, and he didn't know it.

Noora and Jarvis were in the last row of seats in the module, their heads only occasionally visible. The guard with the Uzi had looked that way four or five times and was showing an increasing interest in their activities. That Noora, she could be relied upon to put her pleasure first. Qazi permitted himself a hint of a smile. He had not considered the possibility that she would be attracted to Jarvis. I am getting too old, he thought ruefully.

He sighed and watched the guard crane his neck, trying to see. The sexual curiosity of the Arab male could also be relied upon. He folded his hands across his lap and closed his eyes and tried to relax. The plane continued to circle.

The guard stood. It was too noisy to hear him, but Qazi sensed it. He opened his eyes to slits. The man was at the end of the aisle, looking aft. Then he passed behind the row of seats Qazi was in. Qazi lifted his right leg and drew the Walther PPK from his ankle holster. He thumbed the safety off. He laid it on his lap and covered it with his left hand.

Jake approached the tanker from the stern. The refueling drogue was extended. He flipped the refueling switch, and his refueling probe came out of the right side of the fuselage just under and forward of his cockpit. He added power and began closing on the tanker.

The drogue on the end of the fifty-foot hose hung down and behind the tail of the Intruder. Looking exactly like a large badminton birdie, the drogue oscillated gently in the lower edge of the tanker's slipstream. The air displaced by the nose of the Tomcat would push the drogue away if Jake closed too slowly, so he used the throttles to make his closure brisk and sure. But at this altitude, at this low indicated airspeed, only 210 knots due to the tanker's capabilities, the Tomcat was sluggish, responding sloppily to the controls. There, he snagged it. He pushed the drogue toward the tanker until the lights above the hose exit in the tanker's belly turned from amber to green. He was getting fuel.

"How much do you want, CAG?" the tanker pilot asked.

"All you can give me and still make it to Sigonella." They were flying east at 40,000 feet. The island of Sicily lay over a hundred miles behind them.

Toad was talking to the frigate on the other radio, as he had been for five minutes. Apparently he was conversing with one of the enlisted men in the watch section of the frigate's CIC, all very low-key, though with the scramblers engaged. Toad handled it well, seeking aid on an "oh, by the way" basis, a few traffic advisories for a Tomcat crew out for a spin and some practice intercepts this fine Sunday morning.

"Here's something interesting, Red Ace," the sailor on the frigate said. "The spooks say we have some MiGs airborne north of Benghazi. We picked up the radar emissions and some radio traffic." The transmission broke, then resumed, "And this is funny. There's an airplane circling about a hundred ten miles or so north of Benghazi."

"Ask him if he can pick up a squawk," Jake said to Toad, who made the transmission. He checked the fuel readout. Twelve thousand pounds aboard. The tanker's light was still green.

"Uh, it's that Red Cross flight. Pretty weird, huh? You guys may want to return to Sicily or turn northbound to avoid the MiGs, over."

"Yeah," Toad said. "Thanks a lot, Buckshot."

"That's it, CAG," the tanker crew said as the light over the hose hole turned red: 13,200 pounds of fuel. That would have to do.

"Thanks guys." Jake backed away from the drogue and watched his probe retract. He eased up onto the tanker's right side and gave the pilot a thumbs-up when the drogue was completely stowed. Then he pushed the throttles forward to the stops and flapped his hand good-bye. The tanker's right wing came up and the plane turned away to the left as it fell behind the accelerating fighter.

Jake reset the radio switches so he could transmit on the second radio. "Buckshot, Red Ace. Get your watch officer and put him on the horn."

The Tomcat was in burner, accelerating through Mach 1.4 when the watch officer came on the radio.

"Buckshot, this is Captain Jake Grafton. Please notify Sixth Fleet ASAP that Colonel Qazi and the weapons are probably in the Red Cross flight your controller has tracked. We are on course to intercept now. Got it?"

"Yessir. But what—"

"Just send the message. Red Ace out."

Someone was there. Qazi opened his eyes. It was El Hakim, livid, trembling with fury. "679 93 62. That is the telephone number of the Israeli embassy in Rome. Tripoli confirms it. That was the number! How did you know it?"

"I called it."

"Traitor!" The dictator's lips drew back in a sneer and he threw back his head, his favorite gesture. "You are *lying*. Hypocrite!"

"You have the weapons," Qazi said carefully. "Fly to Benghazi. The fighters are late. It's suicidal to continue to remain out here over the ocean with the Americans soon to be swarming and the Israelis on the alert. Madness. Go to Benghazi and announce your triumph. The Arabs will come to you like iron to a magnet."

"I am the Messenger, returned to lead my people from the godless ways, to purify them—"

A member of the flight crew stuck his head through the door. "Excellency, the fighters are joining us with their tanker. We have them in sight."

"East. *Now!*" He turned back to Qazi, nostrils flaring. "My mission has just begun. The unbelievers shall fall before our swords—"

"*Inshallah*," Qazi said softly, fiercely. "If Allah wills it." El Hakim was mad, of course. The ruler was a small, foolish, hollow man whose ambition and appetite had long ago won control of his soul. Ashes. Qazi's plan was ashes. He had wanted so much to give these people hope and a future, and yet this vainglorious petty tyrant was the man who ruled them. "If the Israelis don't shoot you down," Qazi muttered, suddenly laden with fatigue. "If the Americans don't strike you down. If Allah doesn't destroy you as an abomination."

El Hakim seized the Uzi of the bodyguard who stood on his right, but the weapon was on a strap over the man's right shoulder. The ruler pulled at it, trying to rip it from the strap.

"Excellency, *American fighters!* The ECM! *They are here!*"

The ruler struggled with the gun as the bodyguard tried to pull the strap from his shoulder so he could pass the weapon.

"No!" It was Noora. She leaned across El Hakim and grabbed for the gun. "No! We are pressurized. The *pressure*—"

Qazi was so tired. He raised the pistol from his lap and pointed it at the window beside him and pulled the trigger. The report was loud. A hole appeared in the crazed glass, then cracks as the scream of the escaping air dropped in pitch. Then the glass exploded outward.

The sun was well above the horizon now, an hour and ten minutes after launch. High above was a thin cirrus layer, but it would not soften the strength of the sun for at least an hour. The air was clear, visibility perfect, and Jake and Toad sat in the middle of it under their bubble canopy. The wings were swept full aft, sixty-eight degrees. The two men rode on the tip of this flat arrowhead.

Toad was busy with the radar and computer. He gave Jake a running commentary. "Six targets, two large and four small. . . . We can shoot anytime." They were well within range of the two Phoenix missiles slung under the belly, million-dollar super-missiles with a maximum head-on range of over a hundred miles. Yet Jake had to be sure; he would not shoot until fired upon. "I figure," Toad said, "that we have no more than another minute in burner before we have to bug out for Sigonella on a max-range profile." Jake eyed the fuel. Maybe not even that.

Forty miles out Jake pushed the throttles forward to the stops. His speed crept up to Mach 1.9. He lowered the nose and selected the two Phoenix missiles on his armament panel.

"The little guys are turning our way. Fighters, most likely. Nice rate of turn. They're accelerating toward us."

The ECM beeped. Jake eyed it. A J-band warning from straight ahead. MiG-23s? If so, they were armed with guns and short-range missiles.

He checked the TCS. Toad had it locked on a fighter; a small dot with lines for wings. A head-on picture.

"Twenty-six miles. They're over Mach 1, forming a line abreast." The Tomcat was in a slight descent, passing 32,000 feet, speed Mach 2.1. The planes were closing at over 2,000 knots, a mile every two seconds. They would come together in less than a minute.

"Where are the big planes?" Jake asked.

"Proceeding east, range fifty-four now."

"Don't lose them."

The tone from the ECM gear rose in pitch. One or more of the enemy fighters had switched to a higher pulse repetition frequency, trying to track him. These guys are gonna shoot!

"Mother of God," Toad breathed. "Fifteen miles. Phoenix is fire and forget." It would go with an active radar, illuminating its own target and steering itself to it.

The display in front of Jake had the targets numbered in the order of priority, one through four. Even as he glanced at it, Toad shouted, "*Missiles inbound.* Two."

Jake squeezed the trigger on the stick. The first Phoenix left in a blaze of fire. It would go after the target with the highest priority.

He punched the chaff button on the right throttle four times in quick succession with his left thumb and looked outside. A thin smoke trail on a downward vector slightly left marked the Phoenix' path.

The defensive countermeasures system was on automatic repeat; it should defeat the incoming missiles. He squeezed off more chaff while looking outside, trying to catch a glimpse of the oncoming machines and missiles in this age of superspeed war in the sky.

"Incoming's gonna miss us . . . Phoenix tracking . . . *Bull's-eye!*"

The large planes were shown on the display as targets five and six, now separating. Jake turned fifteen degrees left to intercept.

Out of the corner of his eye he caught a planform view of a sweptwing fighter turning hard, vapor pouring off the wingtips as the pilot pulled maximum G. Even as the sight registered on Jake's brain, he was by and gone, through the formation and hurling onward, nose still down a couple of degrees, Mach 2.2 on the airspeed indicator.

When the MiGs completed their turn they would fire more missiles, since it would be impossible to overtake him in a tail chase.

"Quick, the second Phoenix on that guy ahead turning south." There was no time to spare. The nuclear weapons had to be in one of those two airplanes, and a missile from the MiGs might come up their tailpipe any second.

"Locked on," Toad reported. "You can shoot!"

Jake squeezed off the last Phoenix. It, too, departed in a blaze of fire and was gone in a few heartbeats, accelerating to Mach 4 and climbing as it sought its target forty miles away.

"We're at bingo fuel," Toad said.

When the window blew out, Qazi was blinded by the dirt and trash that filled the air. His seat belt and handcuffs saved him. Eyes shut, he fought the hurricane that tried to rip him from the seat and hurl him bodily through the window.

And then the hurricane subsided, although the noise level remained unbelievably high. He opened his eyes and looked around. El Hakim was gone, as was the guard. Noora was lying on the floor at his feet, her head at an odd angle and her skirt up around her waist.

He became aware of a painful ache in his ears. And the plane was descending, its left wing down steeply. The wind coming in the empty window socket was very cold.

His hands were numb and blood oozed around the handcuffs where they had cut his wrists. He fumbled with the seat belt and got the buckle unfastened and used the pistol on the chain of the cuffs that held him to the arm of the seat. When he stood he swayed uncertainly, the pain in his ears still severe. He stepped carefully over Noora's naked legs.

Jarvis was still in his seat. Apparently he had had his seat belt fastened. He looked at Qazi terror-stricken as the aircraft continued its downward plunge. The pain in Qazi's ears was lessening, but he was beginning to feel light-headed. How high had the plane been?

El Hakim's second bodyguard, who had been in the rear cargo bay with the weapons, came staggering through the door. Qazi shot him. He stumbled before he reached the fallen man and had to crawl toward him. The man was still alive. Qazi shot him in the head this time and seized the Uzi.

He lay there by the body gasping. His vision was coming back. And the wing of the plane seemed to be rising. He could feel the Gs pressing him toward the floor as the pilots fought to pull out of their uncontrolled descent.

When the Gs subsided, he pulled himself erect and went forward toward the cockpit, steadying himself with the seat backs as he proceeded. Jarvis was cowering in his seat, still gasping for air.

He still had a chance. He would make the pilots fly to Benghazi. Once there he could put together a coalition of colonels to take over the government. It could be done. The professional soldiers had loathed and feared El Hakim and would not be sorry to see him gone. Nor would they spurn the opportunity to rule. Then all of this would not have been in vain.

The radar in the nose of the last Phoenix missile went active when the missile was still fifteen miles from the Il-76 at which it had been fired. This was the aerial tanker which had accompanied the MiGs from Benghazi and whose pilot had decided to return there forthwith when informed that the MiGs' electronic countermeasures equipment had detected the emissions of an F-14's radar. The Phoenix' small radar transmitted its signal and picked up the returning echo, and the computer sent digital signals to the canards, positioning them. This process was repeated several thousand times a second as the missile closed its target.

The missile smashed though the Ilyushin's fuselage just under the starboard wing root, at the point where the returning echo had been strongest, and was halfway through the port side of the fuselage when the warhead detonated. The shrapnel from the exploding 132-pound warhead severed the main spar of the port wing, among other things, and the wing immediately separated from the aircraft. The large plane began to roll violently as the nose fell through to the vertical. Then the starboard wing tore off under the tremendous stress. Seconds later the tail ripped away. Rolling slowly now and streaming fire, the remainder of the fuselage continued its four-mile plunge toward the sunlit, glistening sea.

Jake Grafton went for the remaining Il-76, now only twenty-two miles away, but low, only 8,000 feet or so. It was turning southward, toward the land. Great, he would be there that much sooner. He lowered the right wing and altered course to intercept.

He had used chaff to help the DECM foil the three missiles hurled after him by the MiG-23 Floggers behind. Not even a near miss. They were hopelessly behind now and would be out of the play if he could drop this Ilyushin on the first pass. Then he would turn north and fight his way toward Greece. He wouldn't make it, of course; he didn't have enough fuel. But he could get away from Africa and out over the main shipping lanes before he and Toad punched out. Maybe they could even find a freighter or oil tanker to eject alongside. But that was in the future. First he had to drop this transport. And fast. Only 5,000 pounds of fuel remaining. He eased the throttles back out of burner.

He would come in from the rear stern-quarter and pour shells in at the Vulcan cannon's maximum rate of fire, over a hundred shells a second. That should do it and then some. Automatically he fingered the switches and checked the display on the Air-Combat Maneuvering panel immediately under the heads-up display. Guns selected!

"More MiGs. Two. They were masked in the transport's return. Dead ahead. Now turning, one left and one right." Toad swore.

The symbols were on the scope and the heads-up display. But Jake had no more missiles. The tanker was moving from left to right, and one fighter was turning left away hard, probably intending a 270 degree turn. God, he was turning tightly; he must have the burner plugged in and the nose up, using the vertical plane. The other MiG had turned right and was already head-on to Jake. The ECM was beeping.

Jake altered course to the right to approach him head-on. Down to 1.5 Mach. He looked through the heads-up display. The symbol was on him. There. Coming faster than thought. A flash. Missile!

Chaff. The missile didn't track. Going under.

Jake put the pipper just short. He was aware of the fireballs from the MiG just as he pulled the trigger and eased the pipper up. A streak like lightning shot forward as the Vulcan cannon wound up to maximum rate-of-fire and the Tomcat vibrated. The MiG exploded. Jake jerked the stick aft as he released the trigger. He felt a thump. Something had hit the F-14.

"Where's the other guy?" he asked Toad as the Gs tore at him and he scanned the engine instruments and warning light panel. All okay.

"High. Ten o'clock." Right! Symbol on the heads-up display was there.

Jake kept the stick back and the Tomcat's nose climbing. He

smoothly advanced the throttles and the burners kicked him in the back. There, he saw the high man.

Jake was going up with the burners wide open, closing the gap on the MiG. He rolled, trying to pull his nose toward his opponent. The enemy pilot dumped his nose, twisting away, his burner lit and his energy level still high. Jake neutralized the stick and pulled the throttles aft, out of burner. He still had a speed advantage and was closing, but he was closing too fast to get the nose around. He opened the speed brakes, the big slabs that came out from the top and bottom of the fuselage between the twin vertical tails. The MiG was going out the left side. Boards in, burners lit, roll and pull hard, get that nose around. . . .

"We gotta get this guy quick, CAG," Toad prompted, straining against the G to get his words out. As if Jake needed a reminder. The fighter pilot's imperative was never more urgent—go in fast and kill fast. He was running out of gas and there were three more MiGs coming this way supersonic and the Ilyushin was escaping. This MiG pilot would win if he could just stay alive for a few more turns, a few more seconds.

Now, he was behind the MiG, in its stern quadrant. Burners full open. The MiG's nose was down, below the horizon, his tail white-hot. Oh for a Sidewinder . . . The MiG rolled hard right with G on. Jake slammed the stick over and followed, narrowing the distance, but the MiG was still above the plane of his gun. There, his left spoiler coming up and a max-rate roll left. Jake slammed the stick back left. Five Gs on, corkscrewing. The Tomcat had a better roll rate than the MiG, but the Mig pilot knew when he was going to roll.

"This guy's pretty fucking good, CAG," Toad said. "But we ain't got time to dance."

The Flogger's nose was too high, so now the MiG pilot slammed the stick forward and he snapped below the plane of Jake's gun. Too late Jake squeezed off a burst. Jake used forward stick to follow and the negative G threw him upward against his harness restraints. He was tempted to roll, but the instant he did the MiG would pull positive Gs and scissor away and the fight would be back to neutral.

He jammed the stick full left and squeezed the trigger on the stick. The Tomcat spun 180 degrees about its longitudinal axis vomiting shells, and as it completed its roll Jake neutralized the stick with the trigger still down. The MiG tried to fly through the river of lead. It exploded.

Stick back to avoid the expanding fireball. Roll toward Ilyushin, six Gs, get the nose up. Ten miles away. 2,500 pounds of fuel remaining. We can still get this guy!

The ECM was chattering. The other MiGs were coming back.

Qazi stood in the cockpit of the Ilyushin behind the pilots. He felt a great calm. They would either make it or they wouldn't. The pilots were nervous enough for everybody. They talked incessantly and craned their heads, trying to see behind them, and the copilot kept trying to bend the throttles over the forward stop. They were headed southwest, toward Benghazi.

He could hear the chatter of the MiG pilots over the loudspeaker. One lone American F-14. Qazi smiled wryly. It was probably Captain Grafton. *I should have killed him and done a better job of destruction of the planes on the flight deck of the* United States. *Ah well, it went as Allah willed it.* For all his professed piety and bombast, El Hakim had never understood that basic fact. A man must accept his fate; though he can use every ounce of brains and cunning he has in the interim, he must in the end submit.

Qazi squatted and looked aft, through the door to the passenger module and beyond. Hard to believe this flying leviathan could be torn to shreds . . .

He straightened and leaned against the bulkhead, listening. The MiGs had the American fighter on radar and were almost within range. Perhaps, just perhaps . . .

Jake put the pipper on the Il-76 and pulled the trigger. This would be a stern quartering deflection shot, from the starboard side. The gun spit a few shells, then went dead. *Fuck!* And it's not empty! Over a hundred rounds remaining on the counter. Sonofabitch has jammed!

He lifted the nose and flashed across the top of the transport.

"The gun's jammed," he told Toad. "Pull your harness as tight as you can stand it."

"What the fuck does that mean?"

"It means we're going to ram the bastard."

"Like fucking *shit* we are. I'll eject first. I'm *not*—"

"Oh yes you fucking *are,* Tarkington, you asshole. We're not blowing the canopy off until we've killed this guy. *There ain't no other way."*

Jake was craning back over his right shoulder. He popped some more chaff. He was about three miles ahead now. He lowered the right wing and racked the plane into a six-G turn.

"Jesus! You really *mean* it."

"Yep."

Toad struggled to talk above the G. "You're one crazy son of a bitch, Grafton."

Jake had his head back. The Tomcat was in a 90-degree angle-of-bank turn and the transport was straight overhead. He kept the G on. "I hope you make it, Tarkington. Just don't pull the handle until after we hit. Promise me."

"I'm behind you all the way, CAG," Toad mumbled.

They were almost through the turn. The ECM was wailing. Those MiGs were close. They'd be fools to risk a missile shot this close to the transport.

"I don't think you're cut out for this business, kid."

He rolled wings level and pulled the throttles aft to about 80 percent RPM.

Inside the Ilyushin the crew heard the roar of the fighter's engines as it shot over them and watched it depart toward their ten o'clock position. They cheered, then watched in silent horror as the fighter began a level turn toward their twelve o'clock.

Now it was coming back, head-on. The copilot was sobbing.

Qazi squatted behind the crew and looked forward through the windscreen, waiting for the fighter's cannon to erupt. The Tomcat looked like a bird of prey from this angle, closing, growing larger, its wings waggling as the pilot adjusted his course, straight for the Ilyushin's cockpit. The pilot must be Grafton. Why doesn't he shoot? Yet even as Qazi wondered, he knew. Without thinking, he seized a handhold and braced himself. His wrists were still cuffed together.

Oh, *too bad, too bad!*

At first the transport was just there, in the great empty blue sky in front of the F-14, fixed in space. Then it grew visibly larger.

And larger. Now it filled the windscreen. At the last possible instant Grafton slammed the left wing down and pulled.

The planes hit.

Jake's head slammed against the starboard side of the canopy and the Gs smashed him and threw him forward and he lost his grip on stick and throttles. Incredibly, the Gs increased. He was flung forward and sideways and upward all at the same time.

He fought for the lower ejection handle, between his legs, but he couldn't reach it. Even with his straps tight, the G had pushed him up and forward away from the seat and as the G tore at him, he couldn't reach the lower handle, which was closer than the upper handle. It *had* to be back under him. If Toad would only pull either of his ejection handles then both seats would fire. He saw red as the little veins in his eyeballs burst and he screamed through clenched teeth to stay conscious and fought with super-human strength to reach the handle between his legs with his left hand while he used his right to push himself backward toward the seat.

Then the cockpit disintegrated and he was slammed by wind-blast, as if he had been hurled into a wall, and his arms were flailing. The windblast subsided and the G was gone.

He was falling, still attached to the seat, falling, spinning slowly, unable to move. Through a reddish haze he saw the sun and the sea blink past, changing positions over and over. It seemed to go on forever, this fall through space. An awareness that the parachute had not deployed was there somewhere on the edge of his consciousness.

Falling and slowly spinning, under a brilliant sun toward the sea deep and blue, falling as the Gods fell, falling, falling.

29

FROM HIS BED Toad Tarkington could see the blue of the Mediterranean in the sun. The sea was three blocks away. The white sand beach was hidden by buildings, but he knew the sand was there, waiting. Maybe next week, after they put a walking cast on this leg. He would borrow some crutches and hobble to the beach even if it took all morning.

A breeze stirred the curtains. It was warm and comfortable. Toad put his head back on the pillow and sighed.

He was bored. Ten days had passed since an Israeli missile boat had plucked him from the sea. Two operations on his right leg ago. A lifetime ago. A former life, with its fears and terrors fading, though too slowly. It had taken two nights and a day for the boat to reach port. They had kept him sedated. The second day in the hospital, after he had fully recovered from the effects of the anesthesia of the first operation, the Naval Attaché from the U.S. embassy had spent two hours questioning him with a tape recorder running. The attaché had ordered Toad not to talk to any reporters, had given him a handful of Israeli money from his own pocket, and had shaken hands as he left. Toad had seen no one but hospital personnel since. Not a single reporter had wandered by for a snubbing. He had read his only magazine, a month-old international edition of *Time,* three times cover to cover. He picked it up and threw it across the room.

He glared at the telephone on the bedside table. It had not rung since he arrived. And why should it? He had tried to call his folks in Los Angeles, and when no one answered he remembered they were on vacation. They had probably gone to the mountains, and there was no use trying to reach them because there was no phone in the cabin and he would have to leave a message at that grocery store at the crossroads. A message like that would upset his mother—too ominous. No sense in alarming her. He was alright and would get well and a letter describing his adventures would be enough. She and Dad could read the letter when they got back to L.A. Still, it would be nice to talk to someone, to hear a voice from the real world.

Under the telephone was a telephone book. No listing for Judith Farrell. Or for J. Farrell. Or for any Farrell or Ferrell or Ferrel. Of course not, Toad, my man, that was an alias. He had searched the listings anyway. He was damned tired of lying on his back. Twice a day they sat him up, and occasionally they rolled him over for a while. He was sick of it. His ass was sore and his back was sore where the sheets chaffed him and he was sick of this whole rotten hospital gig.

When the nurse came he would see if she could get him some western novels, maybe some Louis L'Amour. Somebody in this corner of the world must read cowboy stories.

He turned as much as he could and slapped the pillows, trying to plump them. He cursed under his breath. When he got himself rearranged, a woman was standing in the doorway.

"Hello, Robert."

He gaped.

"May I come in?"

"Of course. Please." He remembered to smile. "How . . . ?"

She sat in the only chair, her hands on top of the purse in her lap, her knees together. Her hair was different, fluffier.

"I was thinking about you," he said at last. "Wondering, you know." She was even more lovely than he remembered.

"I'm sorry about Captain Grafton," she said.

Toad reached for the bed rails to steady himself. Whenever he thought about it he remembered the Gs, the violent slamming and the struggle to remain conscious as he fought to reach the ejection handle, and he remembered the terror. Holding the cold, smooth aluminum bed rails helped. The sun was still shining on the sea and the breeze was warm and soft and she was still sitting there in front of the window with the breeze stirring her hair.

"He was the best," Toad said at last, seeing the airliner fill the windscreen, feeling the gut-ripping jerk as Jake Grafton slammed the controls over and the fighter rolled and the transport's wing came straight at the cockpit in a blur, veering at the last fraction of a second to impact the fighter's left wing. Grafton had prevented the catastrophic head-on that would have instantly launched both him and Toad into eternity. Grafton had saved Toad's life.

Toad had passed out in the cockpit as the negative and longitudinal G-forces pooled blood in his brain. How many Gs had there been? It had started bad and gotten worse, as the shattered fighter wound itself into a rolling spin. When he recovered consciousness he was in the sea with his life vest inflated. Perhaps Grafton had ejected them, or the plane had broken up and his seat had fired somehow. He would never know. His life vest had inflated automatically when the CO_2 cartridges were immersed in salt water. After a struggle that threatened to drown him, he successfully got rid of the parachute and inflated the one-man life raft from the seat pan. With the last of his strength he dragged himself half into the raft. As far as he could see, in all directions, the sea was empty. He had been very sick from the motion of the raft and all the sea water he had swallowed. The Israeli missile boat picked him up in midafternoon and spent the rest of the day searching. The boat had found a few pieces of floating wreckage, but Toad was the only survivor, eyes shot with blood and face swollen and bruised black from the effect of the G, with a badly broken leg. But alive.

The white was coming back to his eyes now, and the swelling and splotches on his face were fading. Eventually his leg would heal. Maybe someday the nauseating panic when he recalled those moments would fade. What would he do with the life Jake Grafton had given him?

"There are so many questions," Toad said. "Who are you?"

She rose from the chair and faced the window. "We were after Colonel Qazi that night at the Vittorio. We didn't know what he was planning, merely that he was there. But if we had gotten him then, perhaps the . . . incident . . . aboard your ship would not have taken place. Perhaps the sailors who died would be still alive . . . Captain Grafton . . . Callie not a widow." She turned back toward him, and he saw her face again. It hadn't changed. "So I came to see you. You and Captain Grafton stopped Qazi and El Hakim. Both were aboard that Ilyushin transport you rammed. You succeeded where we failed."

"It's a funny world," Toad said softly because he couldn't think of anything else.

She opened her purse and removed a folded-up section of a newspaper. She came over to the bed and handed it to him, then retreated. He opened it. It was a three-day-old front section of the New York *Times.* There was a picture of the *United States* under a banner headline. And the navy had released a photo of Captain Grafton. He scanned the stories. One of them announced that Vice-Admiral Lewis, Commander U.S. Sixth Fleet, had been re-lieved and had submitted his retirement papers. The story con-tained a verbatim transcript of a radio conversation between Ad-miral Lewis and Captain Grafton that had been recorded by a ham radio operator in Clearwater, Florida, a retired railroad engi-neer. Toad read the story carefully.

"So that's why," Toad murmured, still reading. He finished the story and looked again at the photograph of Jake Grafton, the nose, the eyes, the unsmiling mouth, the ribbons on his chest. Toad folded the newspaper and laid it on the table beside the bed. He cleared his throat. "Thanks for bringing this."

She was seated again, on the front edge of the chair. She nod-ded and slowly scanned the room, taking in everything in turn. After another minute she stood. "I still have your letter."

He searched for something to say. "The doctors tell me my leg's going to be okay."

She took a step toward the door.

"If you ever . . . maybe we . . . At least tell me your real name. You won't even call me Toad. I won't tell anyone. I need to know."

She smiled brittlely. "Judith Farrell is dead. Now I am someone else, with a new past and a new future."

"Not your new name. Your real name."

"My new name is real. It can't be any other way." The smile was frozen.

"The name your parents gave you."

The smile disappeared and she twisted the strap of her purse. She stepped over to the bed and leaned over. "Hannah Mermelstein." Her lips brushed his cheek. "Good-bye, Robert," she whispered. He listened to the fading sound of her heels clicking in the corridor. He listened long after the sound was completely gone.

The sea was so blue, with flecks of light reflecting off the swells. He watched it through his tears.

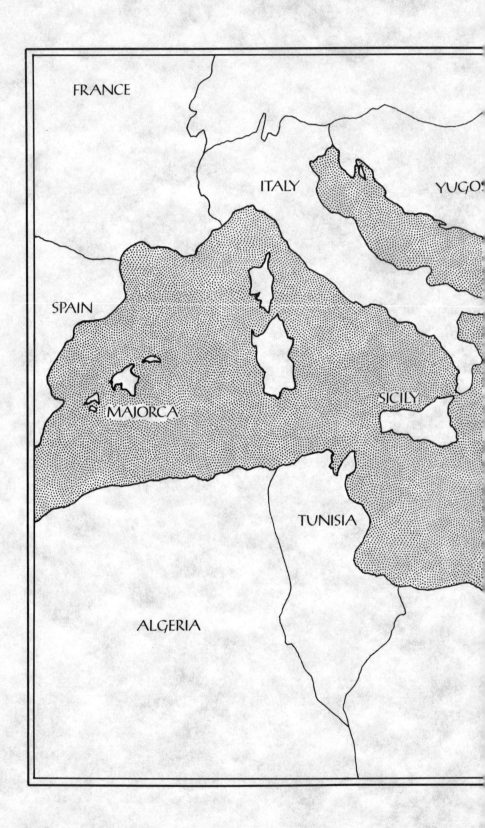